CHAPTER I

DAMNING CONFESSION

There was just so much blood. More than he could possibly survive losing. But still I was frantically pressing the palms of my paws down into the wound, with all the strength left in my body. As though it would make a difference, as though there was earnestly some chance it would staunch the life seeping out between my fingers.

It struck me then. That was his life, pooling on the deck beneath us. Ingraining itself into the wooden planks we had walked so many times together. I wondered if it would stain. Forever leave him here on this ship, where he belonged. If it hadn't been so terrible, I would have found beauty in the symbolism.

I was losing him. One damned raider with a saber had slipped past his guard, and that's all it had taken. He hadn't even been particularly skilled. I'd dispatched him in the three seconds it took for him to withdraw his blade from my Admiral's chest. And now absolutely everything he was, everything he'd ever been, was leaking out between my paws, and I couldn't stop the inevitable. Vaguely, I thought I felt the pounding footsteps of the other crew members, gathering around his fallen form and mine. The last of the raiders screamed in their jagged tongue, cut off by a dull thud, followed by the scrape of cloth and the hollow bang of a body striking the hull as it was tossed overboard.

I wish I could say time stopped in that instant, but it didn't. If anything, the seconds hastened by. My body shook. My words caught in my throat. I needed more time. I didn't know what to do, didn't know what to say. I was not prepared for this today.

Don't die. My life is just a piece of yours.

It wouldn't be until far later that I would realize why this was so much harder for me to accept than it ever had been in the past. I'd never been this close to another soldier before. I'd let our fates intertwine, slowly but surely over the four years we'd shared together. Everything I *was* right now centered around the man dying on the deck beneath me. He was taking me with him.

"Admiral—" I choked, but he silenced me, as he so often did, with a long, dark-eyed stare. There was so much red staining his white fur, and vaguely, I wondered how it had gotten there. The wound was in his chest. I didn't realize at the time how tarnished in his blood my palms had become.

"Even now, you won't... use my name?" he uttered with a long rasp, and a dying smile.

Some part of me trembled.

"...Klaus." I said, quietly. "It's just a lung wound. Bertrand pulled through a lung wound, and you're thrice the man. Dig your claws in, and hold on. The medic is coming."

He gave me that long-muzzled smile that had won me to his bed the first night, and so many since. The way his dark eyes squinted into the soft white fur along his cheeks when he smiled still made me quake, even now.

"It isn't just a lung wound." He said with a rattling rasp. Slowly, like it took near every ounce of strength he had remaining in his body; he lifted his palm to my cheek.

I could feel the paws of the deck crew around me shifting, could feel their eyes upon us. I could feel the storm approaching ... knew that over the next wave, a maelstrom brewed. I could put a stop to it. I could silence him in his last few moments of life. I could deny him the chance to say his last piece. His eyes were unfocused, and I knew his mind was spinning from blood loss. He couldn't know half the crew was here, crowded around us. Couldn't know how many ears were present. He had never touched me in public before. Neither of us would dare, and he wouldn't have now if he knew where he was. His fear of discovery was as great as mine, if not greater. He'd lived a longer life, enduring that fear.

But I couldn't say a damned thing. I could give him no peace with words. I could only accept this last gesture of affection, this last connection. The pain rose in my chest at the mere thought of pushing him away, as surely as though I'd been run through, myself. I leaned my cheek into his palm.

"Klaus..." I managed, "...thank you. For everything."

He was still smiling.

"Luther." He murmured, in what would prove to be the last breath that would ever escape his lungs. "Know that I loved you."

And then I was holding nothing. There was just the tall, statuesque form of an honored Amurescan Admiral dead on the deck of his ship. The white shepherd's body was heavy in my arms, and my knees were soaked in his blood.

And half the crew had born witness to his confession.

My breath hitched, in what would have been a laugh, if I had the stomach for it.

"You stupid, blue-blooded bastard," I hung my head over his prone form, my shoulders shaking. "You couldn't have picked a *better time* to tell me that?"

My life was over.

CHAPTER 2
HERETIC

Every day started and ended the same way, in pain.

They never used weapons, only fists, which limited them somewhat, although I'm fairly certain someone had broken my nose. Granted, I was basing that merely on the wheezing sound my breath was now filling the small cell with. I wouldn't know for sure until I felt it, but it's hard to reach around when you're manacled to the wall.

Judging by the pattern of men who came in and out for the twice daily ritual, they were trading shifts beating me. They didn't seem to need a reason anymore. They'd stopped asking questions, stopped playing at any pretense of interrogation. I think they'd finally realized there was nothing more to be had out of me, but the post had to be so damned boring that the only readily available entertainment was beating the ever living hell out of the queer. The bulldog especially seemed to relish his 'turns'.

I'd told them almost every truth I had inside me. I refused to be ashamed of a one. If they'd been questioning me about any other tryst, I would have lied like a gypsy, but I couldn't bring myself to lie about Klaus. Not to mention, it would have been a poor bluff, considering our entire fleet knew his dying words. So, I'd been an open book about my time with the fleet. My 'relationship' with Klaus, and how it had all began. Our activities while we'd been close, down to every gory detail.

Inevitably, they'd brought in a priest as soon as we'd hit the mainland. That part, I'd been through before. I knew precisely which verses to recite to convince him I'd renounced the demons inside me. That I had accepted Father's Light into my soul, and allowed him to cleanse the impurities from my body, and the illness from my mind. I had it memorized, at this point. And predictably, he'd bought it. You spout enough rhetoric at them, and I think they literally have no choice but to accept it, whether or not they really believe you. Twenty lashes, this time. That was at least twice what I'd gotten in the past. I'd assumed after that, I'd be dishonorably discharged, stripped of my coin and possessions, and put away in a work camp for ... well however long the Church decreed necessary to purge my sins *this* time. The longest I'd ever gotten in the past was six months. Then I'd skip town, hop a caravan for a few months until I got to another port, and re-enlist there. It should have gone down that way, exactly as it had every time before.

Turns out things go a whole lot worse for you when the man you're bedding is an Admiral.

We'd been in port now for ... lord it was hard to keep track. The beatings were the only way I had to tell time and if they were any indication, it had been over a month. I didn't know the guards that watched my cell anymore. My fleet might have even left by this point. I didn't know what city I was in either. They'd kept me in the brig the whole voyage home, and I'd not been conscious when they brought me in here, wherever here was.

I was skinny as a jackal, pissing blood, and I could barely stand my own reek any more. What they fed me wasn't fit for Carvecian savages, but I choked everything down, every day. I had a will to live. This had to end eventually.

Didn't it?

The bottom line was I didn't even know what they wanted any more. It had started out with questions, a lot of questions. And as I said, I'd answered them all, even when they had asked the same ones two and three times. The men they had questioning me weren't from the navy. I'm fairly certain they weren't even military. The cotton they wore was too expensive, their buttons too polished. They stunk of Pedigrees if anything, or maybe their guards. Why they wanted to know so much about me and Klaus was beyond me, but I'd told them everything they'd wanted to know, and then some. Including how righteously angry I was at the fool for ruining my life with his dying words.

Lord I hated that man. Over the last month, that hatred had sunk into every sinew of my body, until I found myself screaming at darkness and nothing all night until my throat went raw. That arrogant, selfish, pedicured piece of shit had spent every year of our shared lives together treating me like his lesser, and refusing to recognize what we had as anything other than a shameful dalliance with a midshipman ... *until* he's dying on his own bloody deck, surrounded by the crew?! I'd fought *hard* to work my way up through the ranks this time, found a ship that would have me, with a crew of fellows I was actually fond of, and...

An Admiral who had the same 'affliction' I did.

My hand clutched at a scrap of cloth I'd managed to hold onto all this time, hidden at some points beneath my shirt, or in my pocket. The guards hadn't seen any value in it, and thus hadn't deigned to steal it away from me. But it was the last tether I had to Klaus, and though a severe source of pain, I couldn't bring myself to part with it. The torn red cloth was a remnant left from his sash, a naval tradition kept to by comrades-in-arms. Were I still enlisted, I would wear it on my person at all times, as a memorial to the man I'd lost. But that would never be.

I'd found myself questioning so many things I never thought about before. Like whether I'd been transferred to his Capital Ship because he intended to bed me from the very start. Maybe he knew. I'd certainly caught a whiff of interest from him more than once, before we'd formally admitted our mutual desires to one another. Maybe everything he'd done for me, teaching me to read, to play chess, to navigate ... inevitably, the interchanged military roles we'd played, the nights I'd spent strategizing fleet movements over his charts...

Maybe it was all just for him. Just more of that selfish belief he was entitled to all things in life by his birthright, even if he had to steal them from another. He'd given all those commands, after all, while I'd stood in silence, and obeyed. Yes sir. As you say, sir. Brilliant plan, sir.

No one knew half the decisions that man had made, and more than half of his tactical brilliance, came from his midshipman. I'd call myself egotistical, but I suppose if I'd really had an ego about it, I would have spoken up, if not then, now. And I hadn't. I hadn't ever. And I never would.

Why the hell was this so confusing?!

I should have hated him outright. But my heart still seized as it had that day, every time I recalled holding his lifeless body in my hands. *Why?!*

This is usually where I started screaming.

Tonight, though, I just didn't have the energy. An ache had begun in my lungs of late, and it hurt when I swallowed. I didn't know what it was, but I was certain it wasn't good. This place was quite literally killing me. I would die here. I would die here, and it was his fault. And to add to my frustrations, I didn't even know *why*. Yes, I'd broken Cardinal Law, and yes, this time I had broken it with an Admiral. But what about that meant they starved and beat you to death in a cell? If they were going to kill me, if there was a law somewhere that decreed 'Ye who buggers nobility shall die', why weren't they just executing me?!

So instead of screaming, tonight I laughed. It came out a low whuff, and nothing more. Life wasn't just cruel. It was illogical. Nothing in a righteous world could justify doing all of this to someone, anyone, anything *alive*, just because it was made differently than every other thing like it. But the thought that people just hated what wasn't normal didn't even track. I was once told they kept black swans in the royal garden. When I asked why, my father had told me, 'because they are unusual'. Isn't that all men like Klaus and I were? Unusual?

I wasn't asking to be treasured and kept in opulence. I just didn't want to die in this cell.

A rough, metallic scraping jarred me out of my half delusional reverie, and I found myself cringing back from the sound, immediately chastising myself for the fearful response I'd had. The more I showed the guards how much their visits truly terrified me, the more of myself I'd lose to them. Dignity was all I had down here.

But still, twice in one night?

My fears were momentarily alleviated, then doubled, when I saw the silhouettes of the two guards stepping back, and another, far taller figure stepping through the doorway. The fifty pounds of metal that kept me in here clattered shut behind him, and my eyes hadn't had time to adjust. The only light in here was from the moon outside, filtering through the small, barred window, and it wasn't doing much to illuminate him. I knew at least that I didn't recognize him, and that he smelled clean. This scared me more than I cared to admit.

The only men who smelled so clean were Pedigrees, priests, or high guard. No one else could afford to bathe in clean water in the cities. This man might very well *be* my executioner.

I stared across the small room at him, as my eyes adjusted, and his features began to come into focus. There was still little I could make out, but his eyes were dark, and sharply fixed on me. Wolfhound, I was all but certain. He was tall and lean, older but not elderly. His straight-legged, shoulders-back stance suggested military. I caught a glint of something on his chest, partially obscured by his greatcoat. It was likely a sash with his insignia. Which meant he'd come here dressed down, but still needed to bandy his authority about for some reason.

His voice, deep and laced with a thick brogue, pierced the silence first.

"Your name is Luther, correct?"

"What happens if I say no?" I uttered, with a low, wheezing chuckle.

All he did was arch his eyebrow at me.

"I'm sure if you came here for me, you already know my name." I muttered.

"I want to be certain I have the right cell." He explained, matter-of-factly.

Damn. It *was* a prison. I'd been wondering that for some time. I'd been unconscious when they brought me in, though, and I hadn't ever heard any other prisoners. I'd honestly had no idea this whole while if I was in a building somewhere along the docks alone, or in an actual prison. They kept two guards permanently at my door, after all. Well, it couldn't hurt to ask.

"So I'm in a prison, then?"

The man gave me a slow nod.

"Well then I have to ask ... why keep two men on duty at my door at all times? Or is that all part of some elaborate strategy to keep morale up by giving men with very little else to do the chance to beat someone night and day?"

"I doubt very much that the chance to beat on a man improves overall morale of a force this size by much of a degree, regardless of how satisfying it might be to beat some particular men." He responded, flatly.

I had to stare at him open-mouthed. "Was that a joke?"

"I don't joke."

"Somehow, I believe you."

"I believe the reason for the devoted guard has something to do with the fact that you—" he paused, and pulled a scroll from a leather caddy hung at his hip. He unrolled it, and began scrolling down the transcript with his eyes, until he apparently found what he was looking for. "—slipped your bonds thrice in the care of your last crew, and shivved one of your crewmates with something you apparently made from a ... fish bone. And then there's the rest of your history of evading and escaping law enforcement, military sanctions, and the Church. There's your escape from the Jevine work camp, and another in Auldfuster, whereupon you escaped, were tracked as far as Lafoy, murdered two of the men sent to recapture you—"

"Those were mercenary bail officers, not military men." I insisted. "I would never slay one of my fellows."

"Except the man you shivved."

"He'll live. You can get by just fine with one eye."

"There was also the man aboard the Leviathan. He did not live."

"Is there anything written in that bloody transcript of yours that might *explain* all of these perceived crimes?!" I finally belted out. "Every mark against me in my records, *all* of it, comes down to whom I bed, and *nothing* more! I have suffered each and every time my 'affliction' has been uncovered, and after thirty years, I am bloody well sick of it! Nothing I have done is worth what I have endured! Have *you* ever spent six months in a work camp?! Spent sixteen hours a day hauling quarry rock until your paw pads chapped and bled and your throat closed up with dust?!"

"No. I cannot say that I have." He responded in that maddeningly calm voice.

"If you had, maybe you'd have fled. Don't preach at me until you've lived it." I gritted out between my teeth. "It's not as though I was a defector, or a coward in the line of fire. I'm navy through and through. Before that, I was an infantryman, from the time I was fourteen years old, until I was twenty. I have served, and fought, and followed orders. I work hard, I fall in line ... I even pray, despite the fact that my God despises me so."

That got him, for some reason. His brow knitted. “It is not for you to say how God judges you. He loves all who are faithful.”

“Then his followers have a peculiar way of showing it.”

“They only seek to cure you. A priest is for your soul what a physician is for your body.”

“Well I don’t want to be cured!” I shouted, or at least I’d meant to. I was losing my voice, and a hacking cough wracked my body. I tasted blood. It must have sounded particularly awful, because even the wolfhound went silent. I took a few moments to recover, then gathered air in my lungs, and continued speaking, far more sedately. “Every single one of those sentences was in the name of ‘cleansing my soul’ of something as natural to me as breathing, and equally as unavoidable. I’ve even had periods of my life where I swore myself to chastity, just to avoid the repercussions. It didn’t hold. Do you have a wife?” I voiced the question suddenly so as to catch him off guard, and it did. I thought for a moment I saw a pang of something emotional behind the wiry fur partially obscuring his eyes.

“I do,” he finally said.

“Do you love her?”

“I do,” he said without even a momentary pause.

“What if tomorrow, we were taken over by a neighboring nation? Say the Huudari. And their religion, whatever blasted heathen thing it is, dictated you could no longer love her? No longer lie with her at night, let alone marry her? And beyond that, you were now expected to marry a man, and make a life with him?”

“That’s ludicrous.” He shifted his shoulders. “Even the Huudari aren’t that heretical.”

“Regardless, say that’s the state of things. Imagine it. Imagine waking to that reality every day, and being punished every time you found yourself accidentally drawn towards a woman. Imagine hiding it, every second of every day, until inevitably, inexorably, you’re found out.”

“I’d imagine that would be difficult. But that is why it is an illness. It is difficult to deny how our Creator made us, when the evidence surrounds you. Procreation quite literally does not happen, between two men. What God intends for us is very obvious—"

"Would you be able to bed a man?"

He seemed less taken aback by the question than I'd hoped. "No." He responded, with no trace of doubt. "Not only do I love my wife, I would be physically incapable. I am not in any way inclined towards..."

I arched an eyebrow, and he went silent. I enjoyed that silence. I drank it up. Debating was yet another skill I'd honed during my years at Klaus's side, and I knew from my time with the platinum-furred aristocrat when I'd won by the poignant silence that always followed a point well-made.

"I see," he nodded.

"No one is going to 'cure' this." I said quietly. "After thirty years, I can safely say I am certain of that. Do you think I relish the suffering I undergo every time I'm found out? Do you think I'd willingly continue with this, if I had *any* other choice? I didn't even mean to..." I wasn't sure how to fill in the blanks about what to call my relationship with Klaus anymore, so I just paused, " ... with Klaus. It just happened. And the Admiral wasn't a man you said 'no' to, regardless of how you felt on the matter."

"So this tale about you and Admiral Richter is true?"

"Alright, enough of this," I spit over my bench, bending my sore knees out into the only reclined position I'd found I could manage here in any comfort. "What the hell is this all about? Are you some form of interrogator? Someone from the Church? You look military. Who the hell are you, and why are you here? I'm not answering any more questions until you answer some of mine."

"Apologies," he said, and I had to tilt my head. That was the only civil thing I'd heard in the last month of my life. "My name is Johannes Cuthbert. I'd offer my hand, but you're manacled."

"And I reek," I added wryly.

"That can hardly be avoided, considering your circumstances. I would hope under more favorable conditions you are more fastidious with your hygiene."

I leaned my head back against the stone, my now flea-bitten ears resting on the cool surface. One of the few comforts I'd found here. "Somehow, I think my days of 'more favorable conditions' are over." I murmured.

"Don't be so certain." The tall wolfhound stated, and I turned my gaze on him. His hand moved beneath the hem of his greatcoat, and I heard the distinctive metal symphony of a key ring being taken off his belt, before he held it into the dim light. I recognized it immediately. They used it to adjust my chains, and presumably unlock them, whenever they needed to move me ... or beat me. One brass key in particular held my gaze. He was holding it just a foot out of my reach. If I were I healthier, I'd have been devising plans in that very instant to lunge at the man, bring him down, incapacitate him and—

"I don't understand your intent here." I instead blurted out. I was too frustrated to play coy. "What is this all about? Why are you here, and why do you have those?" I knew the questions were almost idiotically simple, but damn it, I wanted them answered, and *now*.

"I take it you'd prefer not to be here?"

"That is easily the most simple-minded question I've ever been asked," I growled.

"Right, well." The keys jingled as he adjusted his cuffs at the corners, a habit I instantly knew marked him as an infantryman, or something similar, at some point in his career. It was a formality of standing at attention in winter coats. "I have been sent here from the North Country, at the behest of a man by the name of Lucius Firth Denholme." He continued. "The Denholme family, in case you are ignorant of the fact ... as I'm certain you are ... is a very powerful, very honorable and well-established bloodline to the North of Circenshire."

"Pedigrees," I sneered.

"Indeed." He narrowed his eyes at me, and for some reason, I found myself biting my tongue. The man had a way about him that was truly intimidating and lacking in false pretenses. "And right now, you may find yourself eternally grateful for that fact. Lord Denholme has sent me quite far, near three weeks travel, specifically to meet with you. To release you from confinement, and bring you before him."

I actually found myself stunned silent for a few seconds or more. I had about a dozen questions echoing in my brain at that moment, but I settled on the obvious, " ... why?"

"Much of it, I cannot speak on at present. He has authorized me only to relate to you the basic requirements he shall have of you—"

"Requirements?" I balked.

"—if you wish for him to assure your freedom, issue a pardon for your crimes, and ensure your record is expunged."

"My entire record?!" I shifted on my wooden bench. "What about my time in service? My rank!"

He narrowed his eyes at me. "I would think you would be grateful to emerge from this place alive, to start over anywhere else in the world."

"Hang that!" I growled. "I'm done starting over! I'm not a young man anymore. I've sixteen years of service under my belt, and I'd rather *die* being recognized for what I've done, even if I die here, than deny any of it happened!"

He was silent a moment. "That is admirable." He stated in a tone that suggested he was not being facetious. "But unnecessary. Your military record shall not be erased, only your arrest record. Every demerit and crime, any and all marks against you, will be gone."

"I ... what?" I almost stammered. "I don't—you're not making any sense."

"I am trying to state things as straight-forwardly as possible."

"You know what I mean!" I shifted forward as much as I could, the chains pulling taught against the wall. "Why the hell is some big-time Pedigree from the north taking an interest in me? Until this nonsense with Klaus, I didn't warrant the attention of an officer, let alone a Pedigree." I narrowed my eyes. "What could this 'Lord' of yours possibly want from me? I have nothing. I *am* nothing."

"It's precisely the intricacies of your 'relationship' ... with Klaus Richter that first caught Lord Denholme's attention." The wolfhound explained.

I leaned back. "Now you're starting to sound like the high guards that were here questioning me, a few weeks ago."

"Those were agents of my Lord, high guards of other Pedigree families in the area who share a kinship with the Denholme line. We wanted to be certain we had the right man, before my Lord sent me personally to meet with you. I am sorry if they treated you poorly."

I sighed, "Actually, all *they* did was ask me questions. Most of the damage's been done by the guards here."

"This prison is particularly notorious for the cruelty of the guard staff. I apologize for the abuse you have endured."

"It isn't your place to apologize." I found myself saying before I could really think about it. Why was I bothering excusing the damned lapdog of some Pedigree? He was probably just as much of a bastard to the lower class as every Pedigree was.

For some reason though, he didn't seem it.

"So, what exactly about Klaus and I got your Lord's trousers in a knot?" I smirked. "Your 'agents' were remarkably unspecific. They just asked about our relationship. I told them everything, even the bits that seemed to make them gag."

I swear the man rolled his eyes. "I care not for your nightly activities, nor does my Lord. And our agents were not told specifically what to ask, because my Lord wished to confirm his suspicions without prompting a false confession."

"False confession of *what*?" I sighed. "Our entire fleet already knows the most scandalous part."

"Do they?" He countered.

I was silent, the wheels in my head grinding to a sudden halt. He couldn't mean...

"My Lord knew Admiral Richter quite well. They attended

Academy together, though Klaus was easily a decade his junior. They fought together in the Tiraltic, as did I, in my youth. I even briefly served on one of his sister ships, during the Kadrush conflict."

"So the North Sea Star on your chest isn't just for show, then?" I asked, seriously.

His expression shifted from mild annoyance to offense, at that, and I could tell even beneath his wiry moustache, he was gritting his teeth. "No," he said firmly. "It is not 'for show'."

I nodded. I had no rebuke for that. The fighting in the Kadrush, the choppy, oft-frozen strait above Amuresca, had been some of the hardest-fought and most brutal naval battles our armada had seen in recent memory. Eight out of every ten men never returned home from the icy waters. The surviving raiders from the northern Kadrush peninsula were barely a remnant of the force that had once been, and even they were terrifying. The snow leopards and enormous, ashen-furred bears that lead their people were a subject of horror stories for new recruits and nightmares for all those who had actually encountered them.

"I missed the conflict by about a decade. I wish I'd had the chance to enlist then."

"No, you don't." He murmured in all seriousness, and again I found myself falling silent. "But we aren't here to discuss my military service."

"Pity, you sound like an experienced man. I'd love to share stories sometime."

"Perhaps in time, if you accept my Lord's ... very generous arrangement. I fear we will be spending more time together than either of us will care for."

"Don't sound so excited."

"I do not get excited."

"Somehow, I believe you." I reiterated my statement from earlier, with a hoarse chuckle. "All right so out with it already. What *about* your Lord and Klaus?"

"My lord knew the man well, is my point. Very well, as did I." He spoke evenly. "We knew his personality, his assets, his flaws … and his 'leadership style', if one can call it that."

"Yes, well. Perhaps cousins shouldn't marry."

"He wasn't a cunning man." The wolfhound agreed, with a sigh. "Brave, yes. Foolhardy yes, but loyal to a fault. He loved his men, and he wasn't afraid to get down in the trenches. I always respected that about him. But the man would turn a galleon into a headwind at full sail, just to watch the sails billow. What he lacked in seamanship, he made up for with even more lackluster tactical sense. He inherited his fleet purely through nepotism. And rightfully, that fleet should now be at the bottom of the sea along with every soul aboard, especially considering the incident at the Headwake."

I chuckled. "That was interesting, yes."

"My Lord and I have always wondered … how *is* it exactly that your fleet managed to sink twice your number in Cheva Runners? Details here on the mainland were sparse," he asked.

"Well," I said, leaning forward, "The Cheva Runners have a fundamental design flaw in their boarding ramps."

"The Cheva ramps are brutally efficient." The wolfhound disagreed. "Their swing-down mechanisms almost never jam, and those claws are impossible to pry loose once they've clamped down on your deck."

"They're over-specialized. They've focused so much on boarding with the ramps. They've no other way to effectively take down a vessel."

"Out-gunning them is the only way, with a Runner. Primarily due to those blasted boarding ramps. God forbid you can't sink them with the first volley." He sighed. "They're so bloody fast they are alongside you before you've a chance to reload. And once they're alongside, you're done."

"Only if they board you," I pointed out, and he tilted an ear.

"Alright, go on."

"Their ramps are forty feet long, or thereabouts. Easily enough to clear most galleons, as well as the ten foot gap in height. We'd shelled a Runner earlier that year, so we knew for sure. Plus or minus another five feet, and the ramp claws don't hit the deck, they just strike the hull. And even if they *do* get a good grip on a curved surface, which we didn't figure they would, have you ever seen a Bear climb a hull?"

"But as you said, the ramps are easily long enough to hit any galleon's deck."

"We dumped our cannons."

The wolfhound looked at me like I was insane. "You rid yourself of your guns ... your *only* means of doing sizable damage to a Runner fleet? Out-gunning them is the only way to take them down."

"There's always more than one way to win." I smiled genuinely for the first time in a while. "Klaus thought I was crazy at first, too."

Something changed in the wolfhound's expression then, and I realized I'd tipped my hand. Of all the things I'd told the high guard that questioned me, I'd never admitted to making a decision for Klaus before. It was the only thing I'd held on to. I wanted the man to retain his reputation. For what reason, I don't know. I certainly didn't owe him anything.

"Without your cannons, your ships ran higher in the water." The wolfhound murmured, in a moment of understanding. He looked impressed, which judging by his face, was not a common expression for him.

I nodded. "Yes. They didn't realize it until it was too late, of course. Their ramps hit low, they scrambled to try and board, anyway. One or two got lucky. For the most part, though, we finished off the boarding parties with crossbows and muskets, then boarded their vessels, finished them off, and shelled them."

"Admiral Richter wasn't commanding his fleet. You were." He discerned.

"In every aspect that mattered, damn it..." I hung my head. "Listen. The man's name's been drug through the mud as it is. He doesn't need this atop it all."

"Admiral Klaus Richter's death is a subject of mourning for the entire nation." The wolfhound said. "Not a dishonorable word has been spoken about him. His fleet is sworn to silence on penalty of demotion and threat of conviction for defamation of character. He was laid to rest honorably, in the Royal Cemetery, just two weeks ago. The ceremony was observed by half the Royal City."

I stomped a foot, recognition dawning on me. "*That's* what this is about, isn't it?! All of this?!" I tugged against my chains, the clang of the links against the wall echoing in the small room. "That's why I've been locked down?! To keep that bastard's secret?"

"I'm afraid so, yes." He stated, dourly. "The honor in his name, and the name of his family, is—"

"More important than a cattle dog's life," I finished for him, spitting the words out like they were venom. "Why didn't they just kill me then?!"

"Because of my Lord," he replied. "He asked that you be kept alive, until we could discern whether you were, in fact, responsible for Klaus Richter's recent naval victories. Everything the man has been doing with his fleet is so uncharacteristic, my Lord suspected he had to have a second, responsible for it all. My Lord knew of Richter's ... unusual tastes ... and when we heard he had a lover, we made the natural assumption." He put out a hand. "I know you are angry—"

"You don't know the half of it!"

"No. I'd imagine I don't. But the bottom line is this is over now. My Lord wishes to speak to you. He wishes to improve your situation in life. Vastly so."

"Let me get this straight. I get a walk, I get all the 'bad' smudged out of my record, but I retain my rank?"

"And then some," he said with what almost might have been a hint of envy.

I arched my eyebrow, "A promotion? What the hell is the catch? It has to be awful steep, for all of this."

Whatever I had expected next, it wasn't what left his mouth.

"Marriage," the man stated.

This time I laughed, sore throat be damned.

"I am being quite serious. My Lord wishes you to know upfront what will be expected of you, if you are to accept this offer. He specifically ordered that I ascertain first whether we would be wasting our time."

"I'm assuming you mean a woman?" I asked between a guffaw and a choked, final laugh. He nodded, and I had to chuckle one last time. "Alright, let me point out at least ten reasons why that won't work out—"

"It is only in name, and responsibility. We hardly expect you will make the best husband—"

"Yeah, well I'm not exactly a catch." I spit over the bench again.

"—for her." He continued with more patience than any man rightly should have. "At least as far as husbandly duties go. But you may be the best choice in all other aspects."

"And what might those aspects be?" I had to ask.

"The woman in question is Lord Denholme's only daughter ... and only living heir. His wife is now barren, and their other three children were lost in childbirth. She is his only inheritor. Do you understand the laws of inheritance?"

"Vaguely," I lied.

He sighed. "Unless Lord Denholme's wife dies before he does, and he is permitted to remarry, he will likely never have another heir. Delilah inherits everything, but being as she is a woman that inheritance passes on to whomever she marries."

"And your Lord thinks it a better idea to hand over all his holdings and fancy houses to a piece of scum like me? Somehow, I find that hard to believe."

The wolfhound narrowed his eyes. "My lord's greatest holdings are not his land. His properties are minimal, just the family grounds and one small shire."

"Oh, just that?" I laughed. "What *did* the old man sink his money into, then? Fancy spoons?"

"His fleet," he answered, the two words piercing the space between us like a saber.

And suddenly, some part of me lifted inside. Like every piece of this whole miserable puzzle had fit into place and some long-forgotten child inside of me that had always believed in who I was, and who I would someday be, had finally seen the sun rise on the horizon.

"I-I..." I fell silent.

He seized on the opportunity, and continued speaking, in a low, calm tone. "My Lord wishes to meet you. And he wishes for you to meet his daughter. We will have you taken to a physician, and your injuries treated. We will have you bathed, several times over. I'll ensure we get a good meal or two into you, and we'll have you fitted for something other than the rags on your back. You sound as though you have a cold, so if you need a week or two to recover, that will be fine."

He paused. "I must warn you. This may all sound like a blessing from God, but what my Lord will ask of you will be ... difficult."

"Marriage ... can't be worse than war." I reasoned, when I'd found my breath.

"Do not say that until you've tried it." His moustache turned up slightly in what may have been a smile, but it faded. "There is a ... complication."

"This whole thing is complicated enough as it is."

"Delilah is pregnant." The wolfhound said with a soft sigh. "She will be in her third month by the time you meet her."

"Alright." I didn't really care. "So the bitch is going to spit out a few brats in a few months."

"You will *never* refer to her as that again. In my presence or otherwise!" He barked at me, and I winced back, mostly because it was so sudden. The man hadn't raised his voice thus far. "That girl is like a daughter to me. I will not hear her spoken of in such a fashion."

"Apologies," I said as submissively as I could manage. "So I take it the father isn't fessing up?"

"We do not talk about the father of Delilah's child. If my Lord chooses to share that with you, that is his choice. But I will not speak the man's name," he all but spit. I hadn't heard such bile in the wolfhound's otherwise calm voice so far. "How it came to be does not matter. What matters is that publicly, Delilah must marry the father of her children, even if they are born out of wedlock. And my Lord will *not* be marrying her to that man."

"Well, then that means I—" I sighed, "Sorry, I'm not following."

"You will be held responsible for siring Delilah's child. Socially, you'll be regarded quite poorly for it, and outcast from most pleasant society, regarded as a scoundrel and a lothario ... etcetera."

"Oh no," I arched an eyebrow. "However will I recover?"

"Yes, well, we assumed that would not concern you. It concerns most other Pedigrees in proper society, though."

"Suppose rumors about my 'illness' somehow make their way around? Won't people start to doubt I had anything to do with siring some illegitimate child?"

"Once you marry her, the child *will* be legitimate. If not gone about in the way most would prefer. And don't concern yourself with that. We've taken careful measures to ensure all of your previous trespasses will not follow you. It's remarkably easy to erase a commoner's history."

I dropped my eyelids, giving him an annoyed stare. "Yes. Thank you."

"The timing doesn't fit either, unfortunately. You were away at sea when she conceived, but again, that is a truth easily doctored. As far as any of the other families up north will know, you were with the fleet in Circenshire while it was docked for a month in the cold season. We cannot invent a bloodline for you, so you shall remain a commoner elevated to status via marriage. All but unheard of, except when—"

"You knock boots with some Pedigree—" I paused, catching a stern glare with him, " ... lady."

"Indeed."

"Alright," I sighed, and gave one last rattling cough. "Considering my choices..." I looked back up at him. "Where do I sign?"

"There is one final thing I must ask you. And this is for my personal satisfaction." He took the few steps necessary to be right in front of me, and dropped to a knee before me, so that he was looking me in the eyes. Again, I found him silencing me with that stare, "And to satisfy my concerns for Delilah's safety."

"Alright."

"The one mark on your record that doesn't track, the one crime that does not fit amongst the others, is the murder you committed aboard the Leviathan."

I tightened my jaw at that.

"You were in no dire straits there. No work camp. No mercenaries. No cruel and unusual punishment." He stared straight through me, with those dark grey eyes. "You killed a fellow crew member during peace time. Why you weren't executed for it is a curiosity of mine, as well."

"I was keelhauled." I stated, bitterly. I swear I saw the man wince. "That was my punishment. It could well have been an execution, but I survived. They considered it punishment enough, considering the situation."

"Which was?"

I bit back my desire to tell him it was none of his damned business. I didn't like talking about this, but this man had a way of demanding answers, and we were alone, anyway. I knew he'd keep my confidence.

"He tried to violate me." I stated, quietly. The wolfhound's brow twitched at that, like I'd hit a nerve. "I'd had ... I was young, at the time. I'd been very infatuated with another man on the crew, whom

I'd shared one night with, until I discovered the following day that he'd boasted about 'making a woman' of me to half the crew, like it was some game. I found out later, it was. One of his companions, a midshipman, this enormous, nasty Bernese, tried to corner me below-decks, a few nights later. He was twice my size. He had a short sword. All I had at the time was my boot knife. I got him in the leg, while he was pinning me down. I hadn't meant to kill him, but the physician said I hit a large vein of some sort. He bled out before help got to him."

The room went silent, and I dropped my head between my knees.

"That's what happened. I don't care if you believe me or not."

He stood, slowly. Then he fingered his way through the keys on the chain, and reached behind me. I felt the second the manacles loosened, and was pulling my wrists from them almost before he'd finished turning the key.

"I believe you," he confirmed sedately, and affixed the keys back to his belt.

He stood there before me, and waited. I knew he was armed. I suppose he might have expected something, but realistically, I stood no chance against anyone in my current condition. Perhaps that's why he was so calm. Or perhaps he was just calm under fire.

Either way, I stood, and then immediately collapsed.

He looked down at me a moment. "I suppose I shouldn't be concerned with an escape attempt, then."

I coughed. "You try being off your feet for a month while someone starves and beats you. See how spry you are."

He sighed, leaned down, and much to my surprise, put his arm around my shoulders, helping me up. I steadied myself on my feet with his assistance, and glanced over at him, wryly.

"Sorry. Your clothing looked nice."

"I am burning this jacket," he muttered.

"I like you, Johannes." I smiled as we started towards the door.

"I cannot at the moment say the feeling is mutual, sir."

"If you can get past the 'sins against God' bit, I think you'll find I'm a perfectly amicable chap."

"Your sins are for God to judge, not I. It's your manner I find tiresome, sir." He stopped us at the door, and began to unlock it.

"Luther," I reiterated my name for him. "Why are you calling me 'sir'?"

"Because from this point on, Luther—" the key turned sharply in the lock, and the door began to swing open. To freedom, and God knows what else. "—I am your subordinate."

CHAPTER 3
PEDIGREE FINERY

I'd never understood the rich. Their inane customs, their frivolity, their self-destructive breeding traditions, and the way they evaluated those around them, placing importance on the most worthless aspects of people. The clothing they chose to saunter about in had always made me chuckle, too. Why would the people who owned the world *choose* to be so uncomfortable, and pay so much to be so?

For what had to be the thirtieth time today, I tugged at the hem of my waistcoat. The tailor had assured me it would soften up over time, but at the moment it was stiff and unyielding, and I didn't like how it sat right at my navel. It felt unnatural. It felt restricting.

In fact, almost everything I was wearing right now felt unnatural. I'd almost never been out of uniform for the last sixteen years of my life, and naval wear was simple, functional, and light. Even when we were in the northern seas, we just wore furs over our usual garb and wrapped our feet. The mockery they had me in now was so dandy I'd make a wharf whore look less made-up in comparison. The double-breasted waistcoat was thoroughly pointless, considering I was already wearing a shirt beneath it, and it was a warm late spring. The breeches were *far* too tight against my fur, all but hugging my legs and both buttoned *and* laced right beneath my knee, where they'd insisted I don silk spats that cost more than my yearly commission in the Navy had. Johannes had taken my boot knife, and replaced it with what I'd at first excitedly thought to be a sword, until he'd dashed my hopes by calling it a 'court blade'. What that meant, essentially, was that it had all the look of a real, honest-to-God weapon, but would likely warp if it hit anything near the density of day-old cheese. I'd never had the coin to own a blade of my own, so the thought of carrying around a piece of garbage that cost more than the real thing was particularly revolting.

There was another entirely frivolous bit of silk around my neck, stuffed down the front of my chest into the lapels of the waistcoat. I couldn't even remember what they'd called it. And if all that wasn't enough, my sheath itched from the undergarments they'd said 'it would be indecent not to wear'. I had literally *never* worn undergarments before, in my life. I honestly had thought until just yesterday that they were solely for women. Even Klaus hadn't worn these, and I'd never gotten another noble out of his clothes.

At the very least, getting fitted for those had been fun. The tailor, unfortunately for him, had been a rather attractive, blonde Afghan hound. Young, slim, and I'd *always* had a thing for blondes. I'd tried to be decent to the poor fellow, but I'd been imprisoned for almost two months and the man was putting his paws straight between my legs, presumably to measure ... something. I knew not what. In any case, despite a flag at half mast, he'd gone about the whole thing with remarkable professionalism, which really just made it even funnier. I'd kept my composure until he'd hurried out of the room, and I'd kept *my* hands to myself, but I'd been in stitches half the day thinking about it.

At the very least, the man had chosen good colors for me. Dark reds and blacks, save for the damned thing around my neck and the spats which were of course both white. The greatcoat, I had to admit, was somewhat fetching. A coat I could deal with. It was tight in the shoulders, but again, the tailor had assured me that was the style and that it would loosen up. Unfortunately, that wasn't helping me now.

"Stop panting." Johannes muttered from the seat beside me, as the carriage hit a rock and my rear bounced off the seat, landing uncomfortably on my tail.

"You have to be kidding me." I shot him a frustrated glare.

"I am not. It's considered impolite, and low-brow. It's best to start breaking the habit now."

"Look, I can do one of two things, Johannes." I growled, stabbing a finger beneath the tight coils of the insidious thing around my neck, and tugging it loose. "I can wear this nonsense and cook in it, which means I am going to pant." I was pulling at the silk with both hands now, freeing my neck from it. "Or I can die, and leave a very dapper corpse."

"Stop being so melodramatic, you'll get used to it." He responded without turning his gaze from the window and the rocky countryside rolling by.

"Not bloody likely." I muttered, before discarding the noose of fabric. "What in the hell is this thing, anyway? Does it serve *any* purpose whatsoever?"

"That is a cravat. And its purpose is to adorn your neck." He sighed, finally glancing over at me. "Will you at least make an attempt at propriety today? This whole arrangement is far from finalized, you realize. If my lord finds you unacceptable for whatever reason, everything will be called off. Nothing is promised."

"That's not true." I stretched my jaw. It was still partially healing from a minor fracture I'd sustained while imprisoned. "You still busted me out. You still got me back on my feet, got a few pounds back on my bones, and a real expensive set of clothes on my back. If your lord decides I'm dirt, at worst, I'm free. Not to mention healthy."

"In countryside you don't know. With no rank, no coin, no prospects..."

"I'm not afraid of being on the road with nothing to my name. I've slept in more meadows than beds, gone more nights hungry than full. You know, there're a lot of rodents that are real good over a fire—"

"All right, this right here?" Johannes put his hands out in front of him in an exasperated fashion. "This is precisely the sort of conversation that will ruin your chances. Think these things, if you must, but you don't need to voice *every* thought that comes to your mind. In fact, if you voiced nothing whatsoever for the rest of this trip, that would be acceptable."

"Why do you care so much whether or not I'm acceptable to your lord?" I asked, folding my arms behind my head and reclining against the hard leather seat of the carriage interior as much as I could. The whole car bounced again, and my head thudded against my palms. I really hated carriages.

"Because my lord bid me make you ready before I brought you to him and Delilah, and that's what I have tried to do. I have made every effort to clean you up, make you presentable, and teach you a bit of decorum, but you've been exceptionally stubborn."

"Bull." I snorted. "That's not what I meant, and you know it. I mean you've been really invested in my making a good impression, and the amount of effort and concern you've had over its gone *way* beyond just following your lord's orders."

"Perhaps following orders is of little importance to you, but I take the commands given by my lord very seriously."

"You got money riding on this, or something?"

He sighed, and folded his hands over a knee, leaning back in his seat. He paused just long enough before answering me that I could tell he was carefully wording what he was about to say. "Lord Denholme ... is one of the best men I have ever known. And I do not say that only because I am bound to."

"What *are* you to the old man, anyway? Some kind of personal guard? A war buddy? You can't just be high guard. You act like a Pedigree."

"I am not." He spoke evenly, in that rich brogue. That accent more than anything convinced me he was being honest about being low-born. Dogs from the islands were almost never Pedigrees. The lords that ruled over their lands were primarily from the mainland, and they didn't like to mix blood with the 'natives'.

The man was a mystery to me, though. He acted every part the role of a Pedigree. Maybe one of the poorer ones, definitely military, but it was all there. The education, the way he carried himself, the way he wore their clothing like a second skin. He was either some poor whelp scooped up into the lap of luxury by a distant relative or immaculately well-trained to give off the appearance of being so. But if that was the case, why would he have spent so much time in the military, *and* the navy? He'd let slip enough details, never telling, but confirming my suspicions through his sheer knowledge, that I knew his extensive military history was no farce. You can always smell your own.

My jaw fell open suddenly, and judging by the grim look he got, I gathered that he knew I'd put the pieces together.

"You're a Knight." I murmured, trying to keep the reverence from my voice. I'd never met one in person before. "But, I don't understand ... For one, I thought the tradition was mostly dead. And most of the ones I've heard of keep residence in the Royal Court."

"Those aren't Knights." He spoke in a low tone, which I had trouble hearing over the clatter of the carriage wheels. A fact which I suppose he was counting on, to keep our conversation from the driver. "We keep up the appearance that the tradition has faded to mere antiquated spectacle. The 'Knights' in the Royal Capital are useful for that. But it is true that the Order is a shadow of its former self now. I know only eleven others, counting the man who trained me."

I found my elbow on my knee, my knuckles resting against my teeth. I was too fascinated to care how childish I might appear in that moment. "How did you get involved with the Order?"

"Obviously, I can't fill in all the details." He reached down, adjusting his cufflinks. "Suffice to say, I was taken in young, brought up amongst the Order, and spent the better part of my life experiencing myself with the ways of warfare, both by land and sea. I met Lord Denholme when I was in the service of your Admiral Klaus. When Lucius made a request of the Order for a Knight for his family they decided my previous experience with him made me suitable for the position."

"I hear it's a lifetime commitment. Like marriage." I smirked. "Any regrets?"

"When I was chosen by the Order, I was eleven years old, and I'd lost my mother and two youngest sisters to the frost famine." He spoke on the events in that same even tone, like he wasn't relating something that had to have been horribly traumatic. I shut my jaw, letting him speak. "My eldest sister already had two pups, and I was nothing but a burden to her. She left me on a dead, rotting farm. It was God's will that the Order found me and took me in." He looked to me. "No. I have no regrets."

"Ah ... I more meant the family you eventually ended up serving..." I responded, ears tipped back.

"The Denholmes are a good family. Tragically small, but Marisa Denholme was never in the best of health, so it is unfortunately hardly surprising that she lost so many children. When I first came to serve them, Delilah was barely above my knees, and I instantly took a liking to the girl. She has a remarkably kind, if shy disposition, for a Pedigree heiress. As I was saying before, Lucius is a good man. Stern, intense, and quite strict about propriety, but I've never had a cross word from him that wasn't deserved."

"Yes, but as a Knight ... doesn't he essentially 'own' you?" I arched an eyebrow.

"You signed your life away to the Navy when you joined, as does every soldier in the military. A house servant is barely more than a fixture in a Pedigree's household. On the green islands, I would have worked another man's land." He gestured to the fields we were passing. "Just like every man who raises livestock or tills another man's land here does. My life is no less free than it would have been in any other walk of life. I'm sure you understand our destinies are all but set in stone before we so much as enter this world, owing almost entirely to our birth."

"I understand that in ways you can't even imagine," I said bitterly.

"The occasions that we have to escape our class are so rare, they verge on miracles. You have been fortunate enough to have been presented with one such opportunity. I consider being taken into the Order to have been my 'miracle'. While I'm still firmly in the servitor class, the training and the opportunities I was presented by the Order allowed for me to rise to a position of high esteem within a Pedigree family, under a man whose company and character I both respect and enjoy. I live and have been able to keep my family with means that would have otherwise been beyond me. My life has not been easy, but it has been extremely fulfilling, and because of what I've been able to do, my children will have opportunities I never had. A parent's greatest responsibility is to live well enough to improve the world for the next generation."

"All too happy to be spared that responsibility," I muttered.

"You only say that because you've never had children. Once you do—"

"Yeah, I've heard the grey muzzles talk. They 'change your life', and you can't help but fall in love with them." I rolled my eyes. "I've heard it so many, many times. I'm thoroughly convinced it's some instinctual, irrational blood-tie. The sole purpose of fatherly love is probably to ensure we don't *eat* the little bastards. Pups are infuriating."

"It goes beyond a blood connection," he insisted. "That is likely part of it though."

"Well then I've little to worry about. Someone already took care of ensuring the next generation of your lord's family—" Johannes got a supremely sour look at that, "—and provided the child, or litter, survives, the only children this Delilah of yours will have will not be mine by blood. I think that neatly severs *that* complication for me."

"Are you concerned about Delilah's offspring?" He asked with an arched eyebrow. "I didn't expect you'd even be considering them, this early on. She may miscarry, after all. They may be stillborn. Or, God forbid, the whole pregnancy may go wrong. Her mother certainly had a poor history with birthing young."

"Like I said, there's nothing to be concerned *over*." I sighed, propping a leg up over one knee, before the wolfhound curtly shoved it back over so my legs were side by side, again. He'd been doing that for nearly a week now, changing my posture whenever I did something 'crass', which was apparently *everything* I did. I glared, but continued on. "I never had any interest in being a father, and that's not exactly going to change. I won't be bedding the woman."

"That doesn't matter. Legally, her children will be yours."

"Aside the fact that I don't give a damn about the law," I arched an eyebrow and cocked a half smile. "I'm a navy man. I doubt I'll be spending much time with the little bastards."

"That is yet another term you will never again use on Delilah's children ... or any other Pedigree young, for that matter." He barely contained the whuff of indignation in his tone. It would have been funny if the man wasn't so damned intimidating.

"You're really neutering my vocabulary, you know that?"

"Be thankful that's the only thing about you I'm—"

The wheels suddenly ground to a stop, and the carriage swayed. I heard the horses tossing their reins and pawing at the dirt, and I assumed for a moment we'd just come to an intersection of roads, or a pothole. When I glanced out the window, I balked.

"That crept up on me." I admitted with a long tilt of my head upwards, following the path my eyes traced over the visage of the house sitting a few hundred yards away from us. And I didn't throw the word 'visage' around much, but this place deserved it. I'd seen estates in the cities before, but never a country mansion. The house was massive; I hesitated to even call it a 'house'. It was easily four times the size of most of the churches I'd been to when I was young.

Built entirely in stone, four towers rose at each corner, lending it the air of a fortress, if a beautiful one. Every wall had been allowed to grow over in long trellises of ivy and, closer to the earth, climbing rose bushes. The red flowers punctuated the stone and greenery like they'd been flecked there by some master painter. The house itself seemed to rise up out of the rich, rocky earth the northern country was so known for, like it had grown as naturally as the thickly gnarled, ancient oak trees that surrounded it.

The grounds were massive, and I knew I was only seeing a portion of them from the road. Of course I'd seen the manicured land the Pedigrees kept surrounding their palatial estates, but what struck me most about this place was how un-manicured it appeared. The grounds were somehow both intimidating in their wildness, yet also very clearly tamed. As if someone wanted the place shut in by nature, but wanted it very clear that the land had not beaten them. None of the trees were trimmed or uprooted to make room for vast expanses of grass, as I'd so often seen on estates. Nor was there a man-dug lake for lazy afternoons fishing out a catch which had painstakingly been forced to live in the sodden hole in the ground just the season before.

That was an aspect of Pedigree society I would never grasp. We'd destroyed any real hunting in our lands centuries ago, so that now a man couldn't take to the wilds or fish out his dinner from a stream any longer. All 'wildlife' was seeded for the pleasure of the Pedigree class. The streams were hopelessly polluted from the more industrious cities, the forests barely home to even the smallest of game any longer. The years of great stag hunts were far behind us, in this country. Now if an Amurescan canine wanted to beat his chest and feel like the predator he'd once been, he'd first have to be a Pedigree, since they were the only class allowed the permits or able to afford the expense of hunting. Or they could travel to the wilds of the new continent and hunt the game there. Either way, it was out of the question for a lowborn cur like me, but that aside, I did not understand how anyone could take joy in the thrill of killing just for the sake of it. I'd killed many times throughout my short life, and I'd never enjoyed it. These people probably didn't even eat what they caught, and fishing or shooting game that had been specifically loosed on their property for the sole purpose of being hunted struck me as ... wrong, somehow.

Either way, it was becoming very clear to me—as I stepped out and took the place in—this was not to be entirely what I expected. I'd even go so far as to say the grounds looked ... unapproachable. The road that wound through the expanse of woods before us towards the house was traversable only on foot, or by horse. I suspected they must have had another road on the other side of the house, for carriages, but this looked to be the front of the estate. Which meant—

"My Lord does not have many guests." Johannes supplied from beside me, as though he were in my thoughts. "He prefers this be a private residence only, and he values his privacy."

"No wild parties, hmm?" I smirked.

He straightened out his jacket, and then did the same for mine. "My Lord rarely holds events here. He isn't one for entertaining. When he does need to socialize, he goes out." He began shoving the collar of my waistcoat aside, and before I could make a crack about his undressing me, he was re-affixing that blasted 'cravat' into place around my neck. The thing wasn't unlike a frivolous noose. He tucked the last of it in, and sighed. "He also shares your dislike of carriages. He prefers to take to the road on horseback, generally."

I smiled. "I used to love riding my pony when I was a young shepherd, but ... isn't that a bit 'lowbrow'?"

"My lord is a military man, so he is allowed his eccentricities." Johannes walked past me towards the trail, speaking as he went, without turning. "And he does not ride a pony."

I saw what he was referring to before long, as we walked the lane towards the estate. There *was* actually an acre or so of cleared land past the thickest trees, close to what appeared to be a small natural stream, but still separated from the house by the gardens. A well-kept fence adjoined a long stable, and several of the most magnificent horses I'd ever seen peacefully wandered the grassy field. I had to stop and stare for a moment, and push back the first twinge of envy I'd felt all day. Everything this rich man owned, the house, the grounds, the many fineries ... it could all rot, as far as I was concerned. I had very little interest in the trappings of the Pedigrees. Land was only good for farming and taxing, and I had no interest in either. A house was only good for growing old and dying in, and I doubted very strongly I'd ever live long enough to die of old age. And fineries weren't good for anything.

But a horse was one expense I'd always dreamed of somehow affording for myself. I'd ridden my father's pony from a young age, but it was an old weathered creature, and though I'd oft ridden her in the meadows pretending I was atop a charger, she was far from the real thing.

My love for the sea had eventually eclipsed a young, foolish desire to be a cavalryman, but even a navy man spent a sizable amount of time at port or in their homeland. Having any one of the magnificent beasts that wandered this man's picturesque paddock meant unbridled freedom. And if things here went south, freedom would become a very valuable thing, very quickly.

I walked, and plotted, casting my eyes only once more to the pasture to select which one I'd steal, if the time came. The dappled mare looked promising.

It took me a moment to realize Cuthbert was looking my way. When I finally turned, afraid I'd been caught in my moment of scheming. I was surprised to see the corners of his mouth turned up in what might have been a smile.

"Fond of horses, are you?" He asked knowingly.

"Oh ah, yes." I unashamedly admitted.

"That's unusual for a navy man. Can you ride?"

"Like I said, I learned when I was young." I turned my eyes back to the estate. "So the old man has all this, *and* a fleet?"

"This is actually a very modest estate." He responded, ignoring my scoff. "The Denholmes once owned a far more significant part of the countryside around these parts. Lucius's father sold it all, when the family came on hard times a generation back. He put what was left after the family had repaid their debts into something he considered lasting ... the *Cerberus*, and her sister ships."

I found myself grinning almost despite myself. "The *Cerberus*? That's a hell of a name for a war vessel. Most fleet ships seem to have been named after poncy ideals, nowadays. Like the '*Independence*', or the '*Reliant*'. Hell, Klaus's vessel was named '*Winnipeg*'. Why, I never knew."

"It was his mother's family's estate. He spent much of the more pleasant years of his youth there."

I frowned somewhat at that, not out of displeasure at the discovery of my previous lover's past, but some strange sense of betrayal that this wolfhound knew intimate details of his life he'd never seen fit to tell me. "He never told me that."

"Klaus Richter kept much about himself close to the chest. I never even knew of his deviancy until my lord told me of it, a month ago."

I stopped in my tracks, and flattened my ears back against my skull. He stopped after a few more paces, turning and looking back at me, arching an eyebrow. "Is everything alright?" he inquired.

"No." I stated, curling a lip. "Listen. We are about twenty paces from your lord's estate, so I am only going to say this once more, and if you can't grasp it this time, I'm leaving. I'm willing to do all this ridiculous nonsense you've asked of me, and I'm glad for the opportunity, but I am *not* letting you call me a deviant once more to my face." He opened his muzzle, but I cut him off. "You can believe whatever you want, and let the Church doctrines color how you feel about me, if that's how you like to form your opinions on people. You can even hate me because of it, if you've got to. But I am *not* doing all of this, and letting you and your people insult me to my face, like it's some kind of joke. I'd rather be hated than a laughing-stock, or an embarrassment!"

"Please, lower your voice—" he began

"No." I bit back a growl. "I bed men, alright? I'm guessing everyone's going to know that. You, your lord, and his little daughter, and that's fine. I'm even fine doing this sham of a marriage, knowing the girl's probably going to hate me and be disgusted by me. I'm pretty sure it'll be the first and foremost thing you all judge me for, every other bit of my person aside. I'm used to that. But I'm not going to stand by and be casually mocked as if I haven't ears. I have my pride. And I happen to think there's nothing wrong with me, regardless of what your gospel says. God wouldn't make someone wrong just for the hell of it. And if he did, he's a bastard, and I don't want in his kingdom." The words felt good, and so did the hackles rising against the stiff collar of my waistcoat.

Unfortunately, it was at that moment that I realized Cuthbert's stunned and concerned expression was not focused on me, but rather, over my shoulder.

"Well." A deep, thoughtful voice spoke from behind me. "I'll give you this, soldier. You are certainly ... spirited."

CHAPTER 4

LUCIUS AND DELILAH DENHOLME

The man who stood before me had barely two or three inches on me and stood with a cane, heavily favoring his left leg, which brought us about level. Despite this, I had the overwhelming feeling I was being looked down upon. I leveled my stare, unwilling to give ground, even in my posture. I'd stared down many a Pedigree in my life, and I wasn't going to let this man think he could intimidate me from our very first meeting.

To be honest, I was surprised. The way Johannes spoke about the old man in such reverence, I'd expected one of the Pedigree lines from the Royal Court, some tall, statuesque giant like a Mastiff, or a fine-featured Dane. Of all the possibilities I'd considered, a spaniel was not amongst them.

But, there he was. I wouldn't say the man was diminutive. He had a sturdy, stocky frame, and despite his obvious handicap he looked as though he kept in fighting trim, or as close as a man of his age could. He wore the garments of his class in a far more dignified fashion than I did, and like Johannes he wore a saber ... and his was not for show. His expression was severe, his dark eyes assessing me in a way I could feel boring straight to my bones. One of his ears was ragged, and I thought I saw the hint of a continuing scar along his neckline, but he wore one of those 'cravats' as well, which covered most of it.

His fur was well-groomed, also unlike me. Although Johannes's groomer had *tried* to tame my coarse coat God bless him. His coloration looked to have been white and liver with ticking along his face, although a sizable amount of grey had since grown in. He was probably fairly attractive in his time, if you went in for spaniels. He had that bearing every Pedigree had, like they knew the world answered to them. Unlike many of the others I'd met, though, there was no false pleasantry in his expression. The way he looked at me was probably precisely as judgmental and unpleasant as he actually felt towards me.

To be fair, I'd just gone on a tirade about my sexual preferences ... loudly ... in his garden. I could taste my foot.

I took a moment to remind myself that I didn't care, and steeled myself. If this was going to go badly, best that it does so at the start. I was fit and healthy, and even without a real weapon, I liked my chances against the old man. Johannes would probably be much more of a threat...

"I've seen that look in a man's eye before when he was on his way to the gallows, plotting escape." The old spaniel cocked an eyebrow at me. I quirked a jowl to the side, annoyed that he'd read me so easily. "Calm down, boy. I didn't have you cleaned up and brought all this way just to kill you. They could have managed that just fine where you came from."

I forced a wry grin. "I've had a bad month. I'm a little ... defensive."

"At ease," the lord murmured, in the dismissive tone of a man who'd given such an order many times in his life. He closed the distance between us in no great hurry, and stopped a foot or so from me. His eyes continued to sweep my figure, sizing up ... what, I wasn't sure. And for some reason, that irritated me. Like if I came up lacking for some reason, I wouldn't even know why.

"Like what you see, old man?" I questioned, keeping none of the sarcasm from my tone. I could practically hear Cuthbert's palm hitting his forehead, as all of our careful preparation over the last few weeks shattered before his eyes.

I'd warned him this wouldn't work. I couldn't pass for anything other than what I was, and I didn't much care to play at his farce for the rest of my life, anyway.

"No." The spaniel replied bluntly. "But I am also hardly surprised. I didn't expect to be impressed."

I gave a whuff. "Pardon me for falling short."

"I didn't say you'd fallen short, either." He knitted his brow. "You are just exactly what I expected." He turned his gaze from me suddenly, and began speaking to Cuthbert. "They said a cattle dog ... I'd hoped he'd have some trace of an obvious bloodline somewhere. It's going to be difficult to pass this off as anything but a scandal."

"I'm afraid so, sir." Johannes sighed.

"Hey now!" I barked. "I *have* a bloodline. Heelers are well-regarded in the Dales! My father and mother both were from good families."

"Poor families," he stated, without any trace of pity. At least there was that. "And I doubt you have papers."

"No one but Pedigrees keep papers." I growled. "And that's beside the point. I'm not some mongrel!"

"No, you are not. At least there's that." He glanced back at Johannes. "A Heeler..." he seemed to give that some thought for a few moments, before nodding, "I suppose we can make it work. He'll barely pass at Court, and it might be difficult to explain the pups, but—"

"It's hardly unheard of for a Pedigree line to take prominence in children in cases of mixed breeding," Johannes supplied.

"Wasn't the breeding 'mixed' anyway?" I asked what I thought was an innocent question, before both of the two canines' heads snapped to regard me, and leveled equally cold stares at me. I put my paws up, tipping my ears back. "I just mean ... the father—"

"The ... father..." Lord Lucius curled his lip in a manner strikingly similar to Cuthbert's thorny reaction every time the subject of this woman's lover was brought up, "Lord Irving ... is of the spaniel bloodline, as well. He has a tricolor coat, which I suspect will show in her pups, but the man is certainly no ... Heeler."

"Hold on." I shook my head. "Listen, you'll have to excuse the language here, but I can't think of a fancier way to put this, at the moment."

I saw Johannes start to put a hand up as though to stop me from speaking, but I think he gave up before he really tried. He'd learned by now that trying to keep my mouth shut was a futile effort.

"Your girl knocked boots with another Pedigree, and you're marrying her off to scum like me, instead of the rightful father?" I watched as the man took a moment to digest that, and simply nodded, which led me to ask the obvious question.

"*Why*?"

"The reasons shouldn't matter to you. I am dissatisfied with the thought of Lord Irving as the heir to my family fortune, or the keeper of my fleet."

"And the keeper of your daughter," I finished for him, although to be honest, a few moments after I'd said it, I wasn't certain it *was* a consideration for him. He regarded it with barely a nod, like it was an afterthought.

Perhaps this was why Johannes was so protective of the girl. The Pedigree class was *not* known for their kindly treatment of the fairer sex.

"Look." I sighed, trying to level with the man. "I'm just saying, if the girl had an affair with another Pedigree, why not just let the two of them marry, and be done with it? Sounds like this lord's even from the right 'stock'."

"You're arguing for me to offer all I have to another man, instead of yourself?" The spaniel tilted his head, regarding me with that maddeningly calm expression. "That seems ... not to be in your best interest, young man. I'm offering you a small kingdom, compared to what you come from."

"Think about how crazy that sounds for a second." I said, dropping my hands. "Look, this ... whole thing ... would be a hell of a windfall for me, yes. But it's insane. You don't know me. Your daughter doesn't know me."

"We can rectify that, momentarily."

"I don't like the idea of separating two lovers, alright?!" I bit out. "I don't know what your issue with this man is, but if he and your daughter—"

"Lord Irving ... is *not* in love with my daughter." The lord's voice broke just a bit, for the first time, belaying what might have almost been a growl under the words. I fell silent. "And she is most certainly not in love with him. There is no affair. There is no relationship. There is *nothing*. Lord Irving's *only* interest in my family is my fleet, and what remains of my properties. I will never give that man permission to wed my daughter, regardless of how many bastards of his she has in her womb." He snarled the next word. "Never. And I will *not* speak on this matter any longer. That man is not mentioned in this house, to me, and most certainly *never* to my daughter. Is that understood? What transpired before you were brought here is of no bearing on your future with this family."

I had no response to the spaniel's sudden tirade and he must have taken my silence as acceptance, because he relaxed his shoulders slightly after a few quiet moments had passed, and continued.

"At the very least, I ... appreciate that you are taking my daughter's feelings into consideration. It shows some moral character, and that is in short supply in today's world."

"*Someone* ought to take your daughter's feelings into consideration." I murmured, crossing my arms over my chest.

"Oh?" He looked down his muzzle at me. "I suppose you find my orchestrating my daughter's future distasteful? Don't think yourself so morally superior. You do not understand the complex nature of Pedigree society, and how truly difficult it is to balance ensuring your family's future with the desire to not see your daughter's fragile heart broken in the process. I care very much for my daughter, and I am the only living family member she has with the knowledge and wherewithal to make the right decisions for her. A Pedigree woman cannot by law choose her own mate, she can only seek the favor of one, and hope her family approves. My daughter no longer has that option. Any allegiance with another family now would be rejected in a few months' time, when the man in question discovered her 'condition'. Our choices for her at this point are limited, and believe me when I say you *are* the last option we considered."

"I don't understand why I'm an option at *all*." I said, exasperated. "We've barely met, and it's already becoming apparent that you aren't fond of me. I'm sure your daughter won't be, either. I am never going to integrate well into you blue-bloods, you've said so yourself. Everyone amongst your circle of ... society ... is going to despise me just as much as you do."

"Yes, I believe you're right. I instructed Cuthbert to make that clear to you before you came here. We assumed a man such as you would be accustomed to being hated. I didn't believe it would be a problem." I gave him an angry glare at that, but he only shrugged. "It is the truth, is it not? Your disciplinary file was extensive, even amongst alpha dog navy men I've seen before. But then, when a man's got a secret like yours, I suppose a lot of violent overcompensation is all but inevitable."

"Over the last few minutes, you've called me low-bred, ignorant, and violent." I felt my hackles rising. "How in the hell can you stand there and say all these things about me, and ask me to marry your *daughter* in the same breath?"

He leveled a long stare at me, and spoke quietly, "Because Klaus trusted you."

I don't know how, or why, but for the first time in almost two months, hearing my lover's name fell on me softly, instead of pounding into my chest like a heart attack. Ever since the noble had died in my arms, there'd been a slowly building weight inside me, like the blood in my veins was freezing. Even breathing became difficult, when I thought of him. It felt like ... when I'd fallen into the glacial waters in the North Country, and swallowed nearly a gallon of the icy seawater before I was pulled to safety by my crewmates. I'd honestly thought for a few seconds there that my lungs would freeze, my heart would stop, and I'd die with a block of ice lodged in my chest.

But for the first time since it had happened, now, of all times, hearing this man talk about Klaus in a voice that somehow echoed the same sharp pain ... I felt less alone in my grief. And more importantly, I felt as though it might be *alright* to grieve for him. If a man this important, this strong, this powerful, could have that much pain in his voice when he spoke of his friend; perhaps I wasn't as weak as I thought.

It was so damned freeing.

Unfortunately, that meant I was free to feel all the sadness I'd been holding back for so long. All the pain I'd been too humiliated to feel. I needed to grieve his death.

But this wasn't the most ideal time.

Almost miraculously, despite the fact that I was certain the nobleman saw my paws shaking, and the fierceness with which I was holding back the water in my eyes and belting my mouth shut, he spared my pride by turning around.

Or maybe he was sparing his own.

"Come ... sit with me in the garden. I need to rest my leg." He murmured. "Let's talk as men, as equals. No more of this pointless dominance play between classes. We're both soldiers. We're both men of the world. That is what matters."

A few minutes later I found myself in the garden, seated beside the nobleman, and staring into a small pond fed by one of the gargoyles from high overhead on the house parapets. Some kind of brightly-colored fish was swimming beneath the lily pads. It was a deceptively serene setting, considering the conversation at hand.

"Lung wound, hmm?" Lucius mused, somberly. "I always told

Klaus he needed to guard his chest better. He was reckless in all things, though. I did not expect he would die in his bed. The fact that he made it to forty-four is nothing short of a miracle."

"He was forty-six." I said softly. "We celebrated his birth date with some good whiskey, a month before he died."

He turned to regard me, tipping an ear. "Forty-six, was it? I'd forgotten. Or he lied to me about his age. That certainly wouldn't surprise me. Klaus didn't have a very good relationship with honesty."

"Or he lied to me." I sighed, my eyes falling back to the peaceful pond, and its lone, multicolored occupant.

"It's possible the man forgot his own age, honestly." Lucius chuckled. "I doubt he would have lied one way or the other by two years ... it would hardly make a difference."

"I don't know." I muttered. "Sometimes I think he lied or obfuscated the truth just for the sake of it. When you really get right down to it, I know so little about him ... and we spent four years together."

I felt a paw on my shoulder, and looked up in mild surprise. It was rare that any man who knew of my 'secret' deigned to touch me. Even Johannes seemed physically uncomfortable around me, and on the few occasions we had made contact, it was because he'd been hauling my ass around, or correcting my posture or clothing.

In any case, I'd certainly not expected any physical gestures of comfort from him, let alone this lord I'd been growling at just ten minutes earlier.

"Try not to reflect on your doubts." He spoke in a calm voice, which I was beginning to find less irritating every moment. I'd thought his tone to be some haughty, aristocratic inflection, but the more I listened to him, the more I felt his honesty in every word. I was beginning to suspect the man simply didn't care what he said, and had the station in life to allow him that right. I'd probably be pretty damned relaxed if I knew no one could reprimand me for saying what I felt.

"Klaus is passed, now, and so is whatever the two of you had." He said evenly, without that vague disgust I was so used to hearing whenever Johannes spoke to me about the white shepherd's 'relationship' with me. "Honor the dead, honor his memory, and focus on what good came of your time together. Klaus had many flaws, but one thing he excelled at was finding pleasure in life, wherever his life took him. I'm certain he'd want you to do the same."

"I have to ask..." I said carefully, not wanting to ruin the upswing of our conversation, but maddening curiosity had finally gotten the better of me. "You were clearly close with Klaus. Johannes says your fleets sailed together for some time, and that you knew him in the Academy. And, if you'll pardon my saying so, you clearly know he and I were lovers, but..." I paused, my tongue dry. "You haven't a hint of the derision or disgust I hear so evidently in Cuthbert's tone, every time the subject arises. Were you—"

He laughed, suddenly, which startled me more than it should have. But I'd been bracing for an angry retort of some sort, so I suppose a laugh wasn't as bad.

"No." He put out a hand, waving it in the air between shoulder-shaking chuckles. "Let me ... just ... de-rail that before you go any further with it. I assure you, Klaus and I did not harbor the same ... connection ... you and he did. Ours was purely a platonic, brotherly relationship. We earnestly *were* just schoolmates, and then comrades-in-arms." He sighed, nostalgically. "I have been, and shall always be, quite the skirt-chaser, actually ... bit of a bad habit, for a man of my station."

"Sir..." Johannes warned from his position tucked aside one of the ivy trellises nearby. I'd honestly forgotten he was there. I also noted, with some amusement, that he was using a strikingly similar tone with the spaniel as I'd heard him use on *me* many times over the last few weeks, when I had said or done something inappropriate.

Lucius only waved him off, though. "Oh, give it a rest, old chap. We know enough of the boy's secrets to hang him thrice over. I highly doubt he'll go about running his mouth that I'm a cad. Besides, half of Court knows it by now."

I smirked to myself. If this man valued propriety, as Johannes had said, he clearly let the leash go slack every now and then.

"Klaus was, too, you know." He sighed, crossing his arms over his waistcoat. "It took me a few years to realize he wasn't bringing any of his girls back to the dorms. I really should have caught on sooner. I think half the reason the man wanted to go to sea so badly, and eventually ended up spending every waking hour he *could* on the Winnipeg, out at sea, was to avoid suspicion on land. A man his age really should have married long ago. But when you're at sea..."

"Nothing matters but the boat and the water." I said quietly.

Lucius nodded, "Everything else is ultimately meaningless, when you're at sea. Class, money, family, connections, breeding ... when you're plugging a cannon shot that can sink your boat and every soul aboard, it all breaks down, and you realize how little it all means. All that matters is the boat, and the water ... and keeping the one atop the other.

"I had ... issues, with Klaus's lifestyle, when I first discovered it. It more mystified me than enraged me, honestly. I couldn't see why anyone would choose it." His muzzle twitched uncomfortably, "It was only after I visited with his family one winter, and watched his own mother humiliate him in front of a prospective bride and half his extended family, that I realized ... it wasn't a choice. No one would subject themselves to so much pain if they had any choice in the matter."

"No one understands that." I spoke solemnly.

"I'd imagine it must have been even worse for you than Klaus, without the protection of money, and a powerful family."

"That wasn't my first stay behind bars ... or my first lashing."

"You're fortunate to be alive." He sighed. "Some of the hard-liners in the Church believe there's no redeeming a sexual deviant."

I bit my tongue, but I still saw Cuthbert's hand hover over his sword hilt.

"I really," I grated out, "don't like ... being called that."

"Apologies," he lifted an eyebrow. "What shall I call it, then? I've learned no other term for someone who flouts society's norms."

"It doesn't matter if the definition fits. It isn't 'deviant' for us." I glared. "That's just the problem. It *is* the norm for us ... being like *you* would be unnatural. Calling us that says we aren't normal."

"You aren't," he rebuffed.

"Whom I bed doesn't change anything else *about* me." I said, annoyed. "It doesn't affect anyone, except the people I bed. The only reason it's been *bad* for me is because of other people who are against it."

"Again, you have my apologies for offending you." The man answered in that calm tone, which was once again beginning to irritate me. I got frustrated with men that were hard to rile. I'd become accustomed over the years to settling most disputes with a fight, but he just refused to take my bait.

"If you honestly want to know," I sighed, "the vernacular amongst the few of us that haven't been snuffed out is 'gay'."

"That so?" He sniffed, apparently oblivious to how close that had just come to a brawl. "Well, whatever terminology you prefer. As I said, to a navy man, such things are meaningless. You spend enough time at sea and you gain that mindset on land as well. And I have spent nearly half my life at sea. I care not whom you bed."

I leaned back against the stone bench. "Shouldn't you, though? I mean, for the marriage, for your daughter's sake."

"Son," he flitted his eyes up towards the sky, the sunlight catching in them and reducing his irises to pinpricks, "if anything, your 'preferences' were a mark in your favor. It's rare that a father has a chance to see his daughter married to a man whom he knows will never abuse her in obscene ways."

I laughed, despite myself. "Father in Heaven ... you make even married, straight sex sound so ... dirty."

"My daughter has a gentle disposition." He said quietly. "Earnestly too, many Pedigree women play at the docility and reserve expected of their station, but Delilah is truly a soft-hearted girl. I have worried my entire life over the day I would need to pass her into the hands of another man. She is so placating, I feared the abuses a marriage might bring upon her ... both emotional and intimate." He turned his eyes back on me, at that moment.

"If you never touch her, over the whole course of your marriage, I will be very content."

"But—" I began.

"I don't care if this pregnancy bears no healthy heirs." He shook his head. "I don't care if my family line dies *here*, with her. Don't feel you need to bed her, even if we lose these pups."

"Good." I sighed. "Because, in all honesty, I don't think I can."

"That gives me great comfort." He stood, pushing himself up by his cane. He turned and looked down at me. "Delilah deserves to be happy, and provided this all goes through well, I believe she will be. She'll have the burden of marriage lifted from her shoulders. She will, God-willing, have children to raise and never again have to risk pregnancy. And I will have an able and intelligent steward for my fleet who will rarely be home to inconvenience her. In a way, it's the perfect marriage."

"In that it isn't a marriage." I remarked, with a roll of my eyes.

"I know it might be hard for you to accept this, but I really *do* have my daughter's best interests at heart, in all of this." He let out a breath. "Ever since ... I became aware of her 'condition', I have been in a mad scramble to save her honor, and ensure she is not cast out from all polite society for the rest of her years. I am doing this *for* my daughter. Were I a callous man, I would simply cast her aside, and disinherit her and her children. I cannot bring myself to do that, and I am unwilling to marry her to the father of the children, so the only other option left available to us is to marry her to another. Someone so desperate, they would accept a woman carrying another man's pups, and would be willing to fess to siring them and accept the dishonor that came with that."

He looked my way. "No nobleman worth his salt would accept my terms. My only other option is a merchant hungry for my title, and I will *not* entrust my fleet to someone likely to sell it off, and invest in … olive oil." I whuffed a laugh, and he continued. "I began looking for a navy man, someone lacking in station, but with great potential. I didn't anticipate the criminal element, I'll admit—"

"But it does give you something to hold over my head, for the rest of my life." I muttered.

He tipped his cane to me. "There's that sharp mind of yours, again. You see how well this works out, for both of us. Regardless of whom I chose to wed my daughter, they would also by right inherit my fleet. That is how the law works. Finding someone suitable for being caretaker to both was quite the struggle."

"About the fleet—" I began.

"My flagship is the *Cerberus*." He said, beginning to walk further into the garden. I stood and followed. "She has three sister-ships, and four very able Captains, men I served with during my time in the Navy … before this." He tapped his own leg with his cane.

"Who Captains the *Cerberus*?" I queried.

"That would be me." Johannes's deep voice from behind me made my hackles rise in surprise. For such a huge dog, he could really creep up on you.

"Ah. Sorry to be … replacing you, old boy." I suddenly understood some of his annoyance from earlier. But I honestly didn't expect that. It was almost unheard of for a lord to appoint a low-born man to a Command rank, let alone as a Captain of one of his vessels.

Then again, this was the same man who was offering his *daughter* to someone like me. And the fleet that came with her…

"That's quite the ego, there. You think I'll just appoint you right-off?" Lucius chuckled at me.

"Well, I—"

"I need to see your skills for myself, first, young man." The spaniel smiled. "All we have is your word that it was the mind in that thick skull of yours making Klaus's command decisions for him over the last four years…"

"Well it certainly wasn't *him*." I groused.

"No, I'd imagine not." He chuckled again. "You know, Johannes and I were getting reports in from Naval Headquarters for the last few years, puzzling over the sudden upswing of that man's career. I guessed there had to be someone else behind it all. Klaus has always functioned far better as an inspiring leader with a thinker somewhere in the ranks, making his calls for him. You were actually not the first."

"He mentioned a fox he used to travel with..."

"See, now? The man didn't keep everything from you." He paused for a moment, sniffing the wind. For what, I knew not. "In any case, I'd be a fool to appoint you right off the bat. There will be a substantial probationary period where you serve as Cuthbert's First Mate. Even if you do eventually prove yourself as able a tactician and sailor as we suspect, I intend to keep Johannes about to keep your baser instincts in check, and assure my fleet is not being commanded by a madman. Before *any* of that, though, I'd like to get to know you better. We have roughly five weeks before it's the point of no return, with Delilah. I have one other option put aside for her, if either she or I find you unsatisfactory. But I'll admit I find the man too ambitious for my liking. I've no doubt he'll treat my daughter amicably, and that he will keep the fleet in the family, but I don't always like the way he Captains his own ship, and I don't like how quickly he agreed to the arrangement."

"One of the Captains in your fleet?" I guessed.

He glanced briefly at me, and then flicked his eyes back to the trail. "Yes. Very good, how did you know?"

"Men I've fought beside are the only ones I'd trust with sensitive information like that." I replied. "Besides, he can't be nobility, or he'd turn the idea down flat, like you said. Which means he's lower born. You mentioned he Captained a ship, he must be one of your Captains. You'd never tell anyone about your daughter's situation if you didn't think you had something to hold over their head to keep them from ruining her reputation. A man like that won't get a position in any other fleet than yours, and he won't risk losing his boat, so you knew you could trust him."

“Alright, stop.” He sighed. “I can see already I’m going to have a difficult time keeping things from you.”

“I’m sorry.” I shrugged. “I didn’t mean to pry. It doesn’t matter to me who the other man is. He won’t command your fleet like I will. You won’t choose him.”

“I see poverty has not kept you modest.” He paused near one of the rose trellises, looking down the lane. I found my attention diverted to a bird bath, where a particularly fat sparrow was hopping about. My stomach rumbled. I barely heard the man continuing. “Arrogance will make you few friends, lad.”

“It’s not arrogance if it’s true...” I muttered, my eyes still pinned on that bird. I realized, of course, that it would be extremely crass to pounce on a songbird in the estate garden of the man whose daughter I was potentially marrying, but my instincts and my stomach were trying to convince me otherwise. Sparrows were good eating.

I was very absorbed in my fixation with the fat bird, so that when I felt Johannes’s firm hand plant on my shoulder and yank me into a more upright stance, I shot him an annoyed glare without realizing suddenly that every other set of eyes in the garden was looking elsewhere.

“Papa?” A quiet, feminine voice queried from far to my left, and my ears snapped to the side, my head soon following. The young woman standing beside one of the white rose trellises took a timid step back as my eyes came to bear on her, and I honestly thought for a moment that she might bolt. Her stance reminded me of a spring doe, caught in the moment between noticing a predator, and flight.

The resemblance to her father was uncanny, so I knew immediately this had to be the lord’s daughter. The liver-colored fur patterning around her eyes and the freckled spotting along her white cheeks and muzzle were lighter and spaced farther apart, and she lacked the hardness in her wide brown eyes, but their features were unmistakable. The fur on her ears was grown out longer, and fell in curls on either side of her cheeks, and she was noticeably shorter than her father. She had the bearing of so many Pedigree women I'd seen before ... meek, submissive, and small, wearing a long white gown with lace along the seams, lending her an almost doll-like appearance ... just the way their men preferred them.

She was petite, but not thin, and I thought I saw the hint of a poke in her belly. But then, she'd be more than three months along by now, so that was hardly surprising, especially if she was carrying a litter rather than just a single pup. She seemed to wilt under my gaze, crossing her arms shyly over her midsection and stumbling over a breath that might have been a word, if she'd been determined enough to get it out.

I swallowed, hard. In less than twenty seconds, I was beginning to see exactly what Lucius had meant, when he'd been speaking about his daughter. This girl was not what I'd expected. She had no false bearing, no scent of deceit on her. All I smelled on her was fear.

All of my encounters with Pedigree women throughout my lifetime had been with the gold-digging, conniving few who deigned to stalk military men when they felt like slumming it. The way Klaus spoke about the women at court, they were all liars, each of them putting up the farce of gentility and delicate feminine grace, when in actuality all they ever really wanted was to get their hands in your inheritance and spit out a few pups they could abandon to be raised by the servant staff.

Klaus ... hadn't had the best relationship with his mother...

I'll admit, I was probably a bit sexist, myself. I'd never known my mother, and I hadn't had reason to associate with women much throughout my life. I had a tendency to color all my beliefs about the fairer sex on what little I'd heard, and everything I'd heard about women came primarily from sailors, so...

But this girl was terrified. If she was a conniving witch, she was also a *damn* good actress. I couldn't see how someone like this had gotten herself involved in an affair, to begin with ... let alone gotten herself knocked up.

"Luther." Lucius's voice split the silence. "This is Delilah, my daughter. Delilah," the woman turned just slightly to regard her father, but her eyes skipped back to me a few times, as though to assure herself I wasn't planning on pouncing her like the sparrow, "this is the navy man from Klaus Richter's fleet I spoke with you about."

I cleared my throat, quietly. "Afternoon, lady," I was struggling to remember all the things Johannes had tried to cram into my skull over the last few weeks, and drawing a blank. For some reason, I felt as though this little creature deserved to be treated decently.

"H-hello," She managed, quietly. And then she curtseyed, the graceful hem of her dress just barely brushing the paving stones of the garden path. I stood there like a fool, trying to remember exactly what it was I was supposed to do now. Johannes had gone over all the nonsense about decorum again and again, and I was starting to wish I'd listened.

My mind went instead to one of the books I'd learned on, when Klaus had been teaching me to read. He had a large collection of what amounted to 'romance novels' in his cabin, which we'd delight ourselves with on quiet nights by reading aloud, swapping out all the female roles with svelte male foxes, or harem boys from the Huudari lands.

So, I steeled myself like I had many a time before when a battle was before me, and approached the young woman. I felt both of the other men's' eyes upon me, and the girl's far meeker gaze having trouble meeting mine. I stepped to within a few feet of her, and put my palm out. She blinked, as if momentarily unsure if she should reciprocate, but she must have felt it would be rude not to because a few seconds later, her far smaller paw settled gently into mine.

I dropped to one knee, and as gingerly as I could manage, kissed the girl's hand. I closed my eyes at that moment, so I'm not sure exactly what sort of reaction that evoked from the young spaniel woman, but her hand trembled somewhat.

And when I stood, I caught out of the corner of my eye that Cuthbert seemed relaxed, and Lucius was even vaguely smiling. Either what I'd just done was antiquated and laughable, or it was acceptable. Either way, it was a small victory. The girl was looking up at me, wide-eyed, and she was still holding my paw, which I took as a good sign.

"I think perhaps Johannes and I should depart for a bit." Lucius said, clearing his throat, "So that you two might become better acquainted."

She turned quickly to her father at that, and a little of that fear returned. "Papa, I-I-"

"Don't worry, Delilah." Cuthbert nodded at her. "We'll be just along the trail. If you need us, for any reason, just call out for either of us." He shot a hard look at me at that, and for the girl's sake, I gave the appearance of being suitably intimidated. It wasn't hard, honestly. I thoroughly believed the wolfhound *would* kill me, if I harmed this girl.

That seemed to set her at ease, and she looked down for a moment, and then gave a small nod. The two men turned and started off down the lane, leaving us in relative privacy. She was still holding my hand, so I made it obvious that I was releasing it, with a gentle pat. She jumped a bit at that, but quieted after I released it.

How could *anyone* hurt this girl?

I extended an arm to her, a gesture I'd actually remembered from one of Johannes's talks. She tentatively reached one paw up and took me gently by the crook of my arm, and we began to walk.

"Your name is ... Luther?" she asked quietly, surprising me by being the first to speak.

"It is." I nodded, looking down at her, "Delilah, right? Beautiful name, reminds me of a flower, for some reason."

"Your name is quite fine, too." She replied, pur

mentary, I'm sure.

I shrugged. "I was named after my grandfat

silence for a while after that, passing another o

this one with three fish in it. And about a thous

I sighed, wondering what the hell Johannes and his lord expected me to say to this woman.

"Ah ... I think your surname is ... Denholme, Johannes said."

She nodded. "You haven't a surname?"

"My family were herders," I replied. "If you're not a Pedigree, and you don't really have a craft, most people just sort of refer to you by the area you're from."

"For someone not of noble birth," she began, and I wondered if I'd been wrong about the girl's humble mannerisms, "you ... wear our garments very well."

That caught me off-guard. Either she was struggling to find things to be polite about, or that was an honest admission that she found me attractive.

"Uh not really, honestly," I glanced down at myself. "The tailor had a lot of trouble fitting me, and I can't say wearing all of this comes naturally to me."

"You are..." she was clearly struggling to find a polite way to phrase something, " ... more lean than most Pedigree men. The tailor was probably more accustomed to wider waistlines."

"Well, I've always had trouble maintaining any real bulk. We don't eat as well as you elites do. And they weren't exactly feeding me well..." I paused, realizing belatedly that it might not be in my best interests to admit to the skittish young woman that I'd just gotten out of prison, " ... where I came from."

"I-I don't mind any of that." She said quietly. "Your appearance ... matters very little to me."

"Well, you brought it up." I pointed out, hiding a slight smirk.

She looked down, abashedly. "Well, I—"

"It's alright, lady. I know I'm hardly a dashing p
like quite the stray compared to the sort of men y
to."

"No, No—" she began, but I just started chuc

"It's alright." I smiled down at her. "Ever
standards, you know. I prefer the roguish sorts

noblemen usually just make me roll my eyes. I don't expect that I'll ever 'fit in' with your society, and that's alright by me. I'd rather be who I am."

"Well," she glanced quickly up at me, then back down to her feet, "now that you mention it..."

I arched an eyebrow.

"Your ... ah ... your cravat is on inside-out."

"Shit," I muttered, stopping in my tracks and glancing down at the thing. I gave a long, frustrated sigh, and dug my fingers beneath the neckline, trying to pull it out of the complicated knot Johannes had tied it in. I would never have noticed it, but the girl was right ... the side with the stitching was facing up. It made sense, Johannes probably had little experience putting someone *else's* clothing on, and he'd probably done it the same way he did his own.

It took me a few moments of struggling in vain with the thing to realize that the young woman beside me was giggling. I looked her way, helplessly. She covered her muzzle with one small paw, trying to cover her mirth, but I could still see it in her eyes.

"H-hold on," She said, in between soft laughs. She reached up, and disentangled my hand from the knotted fabric, then slipped her own paws to my neckline and began undoing the adornment. I sighed, and stood still while she fixed the thing.

Her muzzle was very close to mine in the few moments it took her. Her nose was pink and brown spotted, and I noted to myself that she seemed to be blushing. These girls ... they hardly ever came within a foot of men until the night of their marriage.

Still, she was smiling ... and for some reason, I was happy for that. I'd been thinking on what sort of harpy I'd have to be wedded to for the sake of this fleet ever since Johannes had told me about it, and I hadn't ever considered what the woman would have to endure, being married to *me*. I was no better than the Pedigrees who used their women like possessions or bargaining chips for politics and ncial gain.

lly didn't want to hurt this girl. I hoped silently that she already knew about my 'condition', as her father and Johannes put it. The only thing worse than a false marriage to a woman who loathed me, would be a marriage to a woman who earnestly cared for me and couldn't understand why I didn't return her feelings.

"That was almost too painless." Johannes remarked, frowning at the newly-acquainted couple standing near one of the garden terraces.

"My girl rarely warms up to anyone so quickly." Lucius agreed, leaning on his cane. "But ... why tempt fate? If they like one another then all the better."

"You've spoken to your daughter about *why* he was cast out of the Navy, yes?" The wolfhound questioned, quietly.

"I've related the specifics in their entirety. I intend to keep nothing from her, where her prospective husband is concerned." The spaniel murmured. "To be honest with you, though it *was* at first difficult to explain, the thought of having a man at her side with no interest in women whatsoever seemed if anything to ease her fears."

"It eases mine, as well." Johannes narrowed his eyes, and dropped his hand to ghost over the hilt of his sword. "I wasn't there for her, when she needed me most. I will not let another man harm her, ever again."

"Nothing can be done about that, Johannes." Lucius spoke resentfully, but wearily. "We must focus on the future, now ... not the past." He lifted his head, and looked out over the garden, settling his gaze again on the cattle dog speaking quietly with his daughter. They were both smiling, now.

"It's sad ... isn't it, old boy?" The lord murmured.

"What's that, sir?"

"That I trust my own daughter with a sexual deviant we dredged out of prison more than I would with one of my own fellows."

Cuthbert followed his lord's gaze to the two young people in the garden, shielding his eyes with one palm against the fading sunlight.

"I trust no one, sir."

CHAPTER 5
SIRE

"Because I don't want you there," Lucius's uneven footsteps and the answering clunk of his cane thudded down the wooden floor of the hallway, as though punctuating his annoyed declaration.

"I *live* here. I will literally have to go four halls over to avoid the gathering." I argued, following in his wake, my arms spread.

"That's fine. Young men like you can stand the exercise just fine." He grumbled, reaching to his waistline to retrieve something from in his pocket, likely the key to his study. That was confirmed a moment later when he produced said key.

I sighed. "You can't just avoid this conversation by creeping off into your study. Let's talk about this—"

"That is what we have been doing, and I believe I gave you my answer." He pushed the old brass key into the lock on the big, mahogany doors.

I arched my shoulders against the two stiff collars of my dress shirt and waistcoat, and belted, "If you honestly want me to lead these people someday, I am going to have to *meet* them at some point ... *Dad*."

That got his attention. The grinding of the key in the lock halted and he turned to glare at me. "You know how much I loathe it when you call me that."

"Yeah, well you'd best get used to it." I gave a derisive smirk. "In less than a month, it'll be legal, and then you can't stop me."

"I can stop the whole affair, if I want to," he threatened, turning and settling both hands heavily on the handle of his cane. "In fact, I can send you back to the stocks. And if you don't stop pestering me about this, I might consider it."

"With Delilah a few weeks away from popping?" I snuffed. "Let's play chicken. I'll bet I win."

He arched an eyebrow, and I smiled in triumph, which only earned a more irritated look from the old man. "The time isn't right." He insisted, stubbornly. "We should at least wait until you're officially married, and we need to wait until after Delilah's given birth and recovered, for that."

"That still doesn't make any sense to me." I muttered, leaning back against one of the massive old wooden frames hanging in the hallway. The painting in it was of some long-forgotten shipyard. "If you're so worried about how all of this looks, why are we waiting until *after* the pups are born?"

"Because," he explained, for about the thousandth time, "it's not the timing that really matters. It is how the whole affair appears, and how it makes our family appear. A successful breeding in a family of prominence is always looked on well, regardless of how it came about. What's important is that we show we are not ashamed of the child. Rushing her to the altar when she's thick with pups is crass, frantic ... indicative of panic. There is no need to rush. The birth, the wedding, it must all look as though we intended it, no matter the timing. It would be a scandal if you didn't *marry* her after siring her pups, of course, but—"

"Not my pups." I reminded him, with a hand up. He could play at this ruse all he wanted, but I'd be damned if he expected me to honestly accept the responsibility for the litter. I took too much shit around here for everything else, I wasn't about to go accepting blame for some other man's mistake.

Besides ... I hated pups.

"Regardless." He narrowed his eyes at me. "To the world, they will be. They will also be yours by *law*, once you marry her. Do not forget that. Whether or not you maintain this callous and disconnected once they are born, which, speaking as a father, I believe you will have trouble doing—"

"Prepare to be disappointed." I muttered.

"For this family, and for my daughter, having healthy children will be a blessing. And the physician seems to think the pregnancy is coming along well, so it is highly possible at this point that she will." He loosened his grip on his cane some, and sighed. "However it came about ... it is good for us. Breeding is paramount, amongst Pedigree society, even if your children aren't of the finest bloodline. Anyone with a decent grasp on math would easily have known my daughter was pregnant before marriage, even if we'd wed you to her the day you arrived, so there was no point in trying to fool anyone. I wanted to ensure you were right for her, first, and the two of you seem to have gotten on very well, over the last few months. I am also far more confident in your skills as a tactician, after having personally assessed them—"

"How much longer are you going to 'strategize' before we finish that match, anyway, old man? Board's been set up in the game room for over a day now. I'm pretty sure that rook isn't going to move itself." I smirked.

"I'm still thinking!" He quirked a jowl in annoyance, "We'll get back to it when I have the time—"

"And have found some clever ploy to get out of that check? Give it up. Let's just start a new game."

"That's your problem, Luther." He turned, and finally opened the door into his study, stepping inside. "You're on to the next thing before you've seen the previous thing through."

"Only when I've already won."

"You're not even married to my daughter yet, and you want to meet the Captains ... of a fleet you won't even command for another several years. *If* your tutelage under Johannes goes well," He headed into the musky study. I followed him into the large, darkened room. It was easily bigger than the house I'd grown up in, but for some reason it still managed to feel cramped. The curtains were always drawn. The floor was a darker wood than most of the rest of the house, and the light seemed to sink into every surface like water into porous wood, giving the whole place the feel of a cave lit by torchlight. The walls were covered in weaponry, flags, and trophies from what must have been a *very* extensive naval career. Nothing valuable, really ... probably all just keepsakes from the lands he'd visited. I found the place fascinating. It might have stunk of cigar smoke and old leather, but I had to marvel at the sheer diversity of the things he'd gathered, and the stories each must have entailed.

"You need to look before you leap, Luther." Lucius murmured, heading over to one of the racks along the walls, and running a palm along the wooden dowels propping up several sheathed sabers. "For someone with so much to fear from the world you choose to surround yourself with, you are startlingly reckless."

"I didn't choose the world." I said, distractedly, my eyes moving over the many oddities hanging on his walls, or resting on wooden shelves. "And if I had, I wouldn't have made it so that everyone in it hates me so much."

"But you chose the Navy. You chose to maroon yourself at sea for months at a time, with only your fellows, in close quarters ... where secrets are all but impossible to keep for long. You chose to remain in Amuresca, despite your disagreements with the Church—"

"I joined the navy *to* travel." I pointed out.

"Then why not just hop ship somewhere in Mataa, where they sell men on the corner of every street, and don't give a damn who beds whom?"

"I don't use prostitutes." I growled, distastefully. "I know it's an old naval past-time, but it's really not my thing. I enjoy my health too much. Besides, it isn't just about the sex—"

"Then you could have settled somewhere with someone whose company you enjoyed." He countered, and it was beginning to irk me how much he was starting to remind me of my own common sense, when it dared rear its head. "Somewhere quiet, somewhere you wouldn't have been bothered. You could have taken up herding again, lived an average life, and rarely risked discovery."

"Maybe I don't think I should *have* to live in hiding." I stayed in the argument, but felt myself drawn towards a peculiarly terrifying ... thing ... hanging against the wood-paneled wall, in front of a torn foreign banner of some sort. The banner pictured something vaguely reptilian? I wasn't sure. It was dyed into exotic leather I couldn't even identify. The object hung above it looked to all appearances to be a ... skull, of some sort. Some kind of beast, the likes of which I had never seen before, its brow tapered up into two long horns, with several shorter ones crowning its brow, small eye sockets, but massive sunken pits between the eyes and the long muzzle. Its jaw brimmed with razor sharp teeth. Not just canines. *Every* single tooth was sharp.

"My point is, young man ... you're careless, and foolhardy. You have a brilliant mind, I'll grant you, but perhaps *because* you're so sharp, you tend to act on the fly. It might work out well for you in combat, but it translates poorly into social situations. The people amongst my circle are already predisposed to think poorly of you, considering the story they've been told about your ... relations with my daughter."

I smirked. "Yeah, it *was* quite the sultry affair ... that never existed." I had to admit, I'd enjoyed playing the role of the strutting lowborn scoundrel who'd romanced the impressionable young daughter of a nobleman, perhaps too much.

"Your behavior at the few events I've dared bring you to over the last few months has been reprehensible." He glared. "I am *trying* to retain some dignity throughout these events. For myself, my family, and my daughter, and so far you have not proven to me that 'dignity' exists in your vocabulary."

"You're ... exaggerating—" I stammered.

"There was the incident with the Baroness—"

"Everyone in that room was thinking it. I tried to be subtle. I told a joke."

"About flatulence," he glared.

"She got the point." I crossed my arms over my chest. "Besides, if you're going to be belting them out, you may as well laugh about it."

"Fine, but you didn't need to press the issue." He glowered. "She insisted it wasn't her."

"Denial just makes it funnier."

"And then there was the ball at the Glausschtens'..."

I laughed, at the mere memory. "Did you honestly expect me to keep a straight face, listening to that man rant about tax levies? He was so *angry*."

"I fail to see why that's amusing."

"He was a dachshund!" I exclaimed. "It was *adorable*."

"Hans Glausschten is one of the wealthiest landowners in the entire north country—"

"His feet," I sputtered, between laughs, "dangled off ... the ... chair..." I made a little kicking motion with two of my fingers.

"This is, of course, all *nothing* in comparison to the incident with Lord Ethridge's son." He got a particularly sour look at that, and I shut my muzzle, clearing my throat.

"Look ... anyone who wears britches that tight *wants* you to look." I insisted, memories of the far-too-pretty golden retriever filtering through my mind.

"It's *your* neck on the line if you're found out again!" He barked. "I won't protect you again!"

I shrugged, helplessly. "I ... have a serious weakness for blondes..." His brow only furrowed deeper at that, and I exhaled. "And besides, I have tried to play the lady's man, too, and you didn't approve of *that*, either."

"Perhaps if you had been more subtle about it! Commenting on a young lady's *bust line* isn't acceptable at a dinner party!"

"I thought that's what straight men talked about to break the ice."

"To her father?!"

"I didn't *know* it was her father, at the time." I rolled my eyes. "How many shepherds are there at any one dinner party? Honestly."

"You're impossible! I swear. I cannot bring you *anywhere*." The spaniel angrily pulled a drawer from his desk out until it clacked against its hinges. He began rifling through it before producing a cigar, and then stood and headed over to the book stand, where he lit it on a tapered candle. "You've done little but expose yourself to ridicule, ever since I dared take you to any of our social gatherings. Give me one good reason why I should allow you to meet with the people I'm having over tonight."

"Because I didn't *want* to go to your galas or balls, those people were worlds apart from me. The men you're having over tonight are all soldiers. I *want* to meet them." I sighed. "And besides, what does it matter if I made a bad impression on a few nobles? You've said yourself; those people already loathe me strictly based on my birth. I could tell the second I spoke to a one of them. Did you really expect me to stand there quietly and be mocked, and be on my best behavior? If they're going to treat me like dirt, I may as well be who I am. And that's what I am, dirt."

"You're not dirt, Luther." The old man let out a breath, the cigar smoke lifting around him like fog from a harbor. He looked through it, at me. "You're a brilliant young lad with a lot of unrealized potential, a stubborn, stalwart constitution, and ... I am beginning to suspect, a good heart. Despite all of your attempts to obfuscate the fact, the care you've shown my daughter throughout the last few months has been ... extraordinary."

He put his cigar down in the marble ash tray on his desk, staring at nothing on his desk for a few seconds, before looking up at me. "For that, you have my gratitude. Neither I nor Delilah's mother has been able to bring her any peace, since this whole situation arose. How you do it, I'm not certain, but..."

I glanced back at the open doorway, and the thin strip of light leading back out into the hallway. "She's not doing too great today, actually. She says she hasn't been feeling well."

"She is in her last few weeks. It's always a difficult time. I only hope it ends more favorably for her than it has so many times for her mother." The old man's eyes clenched as he relived what must have been a painful memory.

I only nodded at that. Lucius's wife was almost a non-person around here. I'd seen her once or twice, but she was a ghost. She was utterly out of touch with the world, and only vaguely drifted through moments of lucidity. She spent most of her time in her bedroom. I barely knew her, and I suspected her own family barely knew her, anymore. Apparently she'd had a string of miscarriages following Delilah's birth, and at some point a birth had gone horribly wrong, and she'd been barren ever since. I wasn't really certain on the details, if her mental state was somehow connected to her issues with childbirth, or if the old woman had just slipped away over the years for any other number of reasons, but it was a sad state of affairs. I spoke with Delilah about it, from time to time.

We talked a lot, actually. Apparently the physician felt she needed to be shut into her room more often than not, to ensure the pregnancy went well. Often, I'd go weeks without seeing her. But during the times I was permitted to spend time with her, we would walk the garden, or sit in the library, and just ... talk. Most of the time, she didn't even require we talk back and forth, which suited me just fine. The girl wasn't actually as quiet as her father made her out to be ... or as timid. She was remarkably open, if you just sat and listened, and let her work up to it on her own.

I honestly couldn't understand why so many men claimed women were so difficult, or hard to understand. The girl seemed perfectly rational, and clear about her feelings, to me. And I'd been braced for the worst. I'd heard pregnant women were especially manic. Her father and Cuthbert both often spoke to me in confounded astonishment that I'd 'broken through' to the young girl, a task they apparently saw as mountainously hard. It really hadn't been all that difficult.

I just ... listened.

Lucius sat, and stretched his leg out with a wince I'd seen from many a man who'd taken a grievous injury in the line of duty. I often wondered about that wound. How bad it was, beneath his clothing, beneath his skin ... and how he'd gotten it.

"I suppose," he said, breaking my reverie, "I ought to show you some consideration, at least, for the efforts you've put into the one area of this whole farce that really matters."

"Sir?"

"Your relationship with my daughter," He leaned back in his chair. "You may be a complete scoundrel at court, and a holy terror on the chess board, but you've been treating Delilah well. And whether or not your care for her is genuine ... my girl has seemed far less unhappy, of late." He sighed. "I suppose that is worth letting you off your leash for *one* night."

I tried not to wag my tail. Finally! I hadn't been away from the sea this long since my teenage years. The least I could do was fraternize with a few real soldiers and mariners, for once, instead of these prancing Pedigrees and their sycophants.

"You won't regret it, sir." I smiled. "I promise you, I blend in far better with my own."

"These aren't midshipman. They aren't 'your' own." Lucius lowered his brow. "This is an Officer's Ball. I don't host many events here, but I hold this gathering every year. It's a shame it fell when it did this year. I'd hoped Delilah would have had her pups by the time it came around, but the weather being what it is, we had to schedule it now. The Northern ports are going to freeze up soon."

"I hope some of the men are from the Tiraltic." I mused. "I've been itching to hear about how they're faring against the Selthsan Privateers this season."

"Poorly, from what I hear." Lucius grumbled. "Admiral Cross is the only man with any gumption out in the South Sea, and his boats are woefully outgunned and outnumbered. He can't cover enough of the trade routes. There are a dozen young bucks with better galleons, of course ... getting fat and pissing their careers away in the Shanivaar. They're all cowards. They won't go into open water. They just hug the coastlines in Huudari-protected waters, and claim they just can't *find* the Privateers."

I smiled, letting the man grumble in his low, gravelly tone until he finished his cigar, some ten minutes later. I always enjoyed listening to Lucius talk about the Navy, both past and present. He was a font of knowledge, and there was always a new story to be heard, a new land I'd never even heard of, that he somehow knew like the back of his paw.

Speaking of which...

"Sir?" I spoke in a moment of silence, not wanting to interrupt him.

"Hrm?" He snuffed out the stub of his cigar, looking up.

I turned, my eyes once again inexorably drawn to the torn, foreign banner on the wall. Lucius had a number of wild game from many different lands mounted on his walls, but for some reason, the dark, empty eye sockets of the skull that rested above the banner were boring into me with a great sense of foreboding. It was primal ... and strangely terrifying.

And I wasn't an easily frightened man.

Lucius seemed to know. His tone fell to an almost inaudible level, as he spoke.

"Cathazra," he rumbled quietly.

I looked back over at him, oddly concerned about taking my eyes off the skull. "I—what?"

"I should burn the damned thing." He murmured darkly. "I don't even know why I've kept it all these years ... or why I brought it back, to begin with. But I felt as though ... after everything we went through, I needed to remind myself every day why I left, and perhaps to prevent myself from ever returning."

"You've lost me, sir." I admitted.

"That is one of their war banners." He pointed to the scaly hide, with the reptilian symbol emblazoned upon it, "The... creatures ... from the Dark Continent."

My eyes widened. "You've been to the Dark Continent?!"

He cast his eyes down a moment. "Almost seven years ago. I was with one of the first landing forces that lay claim to the northern mountain forests. We named the Colony 'Serwich'. Humble place ... mostly logging, and a bit of fishing to keep the workers fed. It's since grown ... I believe there are between two and three thousand souls living there, now."

"I've heard only rumors about the Dark Continent." I admitted. "And most of it, I'm really not certain whether or not I can believe. The goods that come back are real, but—"

"The whole place is real." Lucius ground his teeth. "And they are just as ferocious and terrible as the rumors say, if not worse. Take every horror any sailor has told you, and magnify it several times. The insects carry plagues the likes of which no physician has ever seen. Men die spitting up their innards, with boils on their skin and maggots in their wounds. Any injury in the wild is immediately infested or swarmed on ... the vermin there are ravenous. The forests will devour you whole, even the earth can drag a man beneath it where the mud is thick. There was a mountain range ... we never knew how far it was, no one dared venture that deep into the forests ... but one morning, the whole of the world shook, and we woke to see plumes of hellish smoke belching into the sky from its peak. Our priest said beyond that peak was the mouth of Hell. I believed him."

I tipped my ears back. " ... and people *live* in this place? There are natives?"

"Not people, son." He squeezed at his aching knee, eyes unfocused. "Beasts, Demons." He pointed again at the banner, or perhaps above it. "That there ... is one of their skulls, the Cathazra. The men called those 'Dragons'. They're usually the leaders."

I grimaced. "You took one of their skulls?"

"They're barely above animals, less so, at times. Animals rarely eat their own dead."

"They're cannibals?" I leaned back away from the thing, a little more. Every second, it was beginning to bother me more and more. I shuddered to think what it must have looked like when it was alive. The skull was massive.

He nodded, and took a hold of his cane, slowly pushing himself up into a standing position. "They're not what I'd call 'civilized' ... we tried at negotiations for a while, but ... it went nowhere. Eventually we just approached it like we would exterminating any predator threatening a town. It should have been easy ... there weren't many of them, their weaponry is to say the least archaic..." He got that distant look again, and I couldn't even imagine what he must have been remembering. " ... but they knew the land. They can blend right into the forests, and they always spring from ambush. You see the drakes circling first, in the skies. Then the legless ones come up from the water or the brush ... and the Dragons followed. If it's a particularly bad day, you stumble on a Basilisk, and you'd better hope your men can run."

"What the hell is a Basilisk?" I arched an eyebrow.

He looked my way, and then ran a paw over his knee again, slowly.

"Pray you never find out."

I was getting the feeling the old man badly wanted off the topic at hand, so I cleared my throat, and gave him an out. "So, how long 'til the party? I should probably get ready."

He waved a paw. "They should begin arriving within the hour, and don't worry ... your attire is fine as it is. This isn't like the balls I've taken you to. A few of the men will be Pedigrees, but all are military or navy. That's what matters. Just be on your best behavior. Please." He looked meaningfully at me at that. "Remember that above all, these men may someday be under your command. This is your very first impression. I am trusting you, Luther. Don't let me down."

"Yes, sir." I nodded.

"Good." He headed back over to his desk, and began sifting through some of the mail there, pulling out a pewter letter opener from a drawer. He was midway through opening one of the envelopes when he looked back up at me. "And get out of my study." He groused, as though it were obvious.

"Oh! Right..." I did as the man bade, and headed out. As fascinating as I found the place, I knew better than to bother the old mariner for long when he retreated there. It was something of a sanctuary for him. Not even Cuthbert bothered him much when he was in here.

"Luther." The sudden, deep voice nearly made me leap out of my skin, when I turned the corner of the hallway, and nearly bumped right into the devil in question.

"Good *God*, man." I clamped a hand over my heart, willing it to slow its pace. "How the hell do you do that? No one your size should be so stealthy."

He quirked an eyebrow, "Apologies Sir."

"Just ... Luther, please—" I insisted for about the ten thousandth time.

"However you please, Sir Luther." He folded his arms at the small of his back, and I let out a long breath. Over the last few months, I'd somehow fallen into the same category for the wolfhound as the old man apparently did, because he was treating me the same. Practice, I suppose, for when he served under me in the future, but for the moment, it didn't feel natural.

"What is it, Johannes?" I asked, fussing with the hem of my waistcoat, settling the easily-creased fabric.

"Miss Delilah has been asking for you."

"Oh." I ran a paw up through my neck scruff, scratching at where the collar of the offending garment I was wearing rubbed into my skin. I could not *wait* until I got back in naval wear. As it was, I'd taken to sleeping nude ever since I got here. Firstly because there was absolutely *nothing* these people wore that was even remotely comfortable enough to sleep in and that was counting their sleep shirts. But secondly, because there was some sort of man servant they had waiting on me here, some old Dane mix who was delightfully frumpy and easily offended, and I loved watching him get mad every day when he insisted on changing my sheets because I'd 'been indecent' in them.

I wondered often if the man would have a heart attack were I to honestly 'be indecent' in them for real, one of these nights.

"Is she in her bed?" I questioned.

"No. She has decided to take a turn about the house. The doctor said the walking is beneficial for her." He looked over his shoulder, at the staircase nearby. "She's in the east wing, near the Giuseppe painting."

I gave him a blank look, and he sighed, "The one of the two white horses."

"Oh!" I patted him on the shoulder, and strode past. "You could've just said that, old boy."

"I was mistakenly hoping you had acquired some culture, sir." I heard him say to my retreating figure, and I just smiled. Johannes was alright. Truth be told, I'd spent more time with him than my soon-to-be bride, but then Johannes wasn't pregnant. He had been briefing me on Lucius's fleet and on the men captaining the *Cerberus's* sister ships. I'd also discovered he had a decent hand at fencing, and we had a daily ritual in the practice hall, and then the archery range out back. My skills with a longbow were lacking, but I managed alright with a crossbow. I usually beat him with the sword, but Johannes was a crack shot. I'd never been much for projectile weapons. I'd suspected since I was very young that my vision wasn't excellent ... I had trouble focusing on objects at a distance. I found if I shut my left eye, it improved, but Johannes insisted I keep both open.

Still, provided we kept to activities we both enjoyed, I'd found him fairly amicable. I could certainly see myself being very comfortable with him at sea. He was dependable and calm, and despite his fierce religious beliefs, he did the world the favor of keeping them to himself. He didn't even seem to take much offense to my 'condition', anymore. On the few occasions it came up, and I asked him how it was he kept company with a 'sinner', he'd only said that it was God's place to judge, not his. If all the men in the Church were like him, I probably wouldn't have had such a bad relationship with it.

I saw Delilah as I rounded the corner into the east wing. The long hallway was primarily an art gallery, with windows overlooking the back lawn, which was pierced down the center by a long gravel road. I'd discovered soon after taking up residence here that the back of the house was where primary access to the manor for most of the non-family members was. The road there was traversable by carriage, unlike the front path.

Delilah was standing near one of the large windows, staring through the frosting panes. It was an unusually cold autumn this year. The leaves had barely begun to turn, and we'd already had our first frost. Delilah's eyes seemed fixed on the goings-on around the carriage road. I could hear the first of the evening's guests arriving. Horses, carriages, muffled voices ... Delilah was looking down on it all, her muzzle pursed, fingers knitted in front of her large belly in an uncomfortable jumble. She was scratching her small, blunt claws over the back of one hand in a way I'd often noticed she did when she was lamenting something, or just generally unhappy.

"You'll be able to join your father and the family again soon." I spoke quietly, trying not to startle her. I hadn't meant to creep up on her, but she was so focused, she probably hadn't heard me approach. She jumped a little bit, then calmed when she saw it was me.

She gave a weak smile at me, and then looked out the windows again. "I know." She mumbled. "I just ... feel almost like I'm ... imprisoned by this. I-I know it's for my health, but..." She went silent for a few moments, and I stepped in beside her, looking down at the assortment of carriages, with their various passengers disembarking.

"Luther, I'm scared." She spoke softly, but I could hear the tremble in her voice.

"I know." I said as comfortingly as I could.

"There's this inevitable ... event ... coming upon me." She ran her paw down along her swollen belly. "And I feel like ... I have no choice in the matter. I have no say. This is going to happen and ... When it does, I-I may die." She swallowed. "Or ... they may die..." Her brown eyes fell to her midsection. "And I can't do anything. I can't really prepare for it. I can't practice, so I'll be better at it, when the time comes. I can't affect the outcome of this in any way."

"It's alright to be scared, Delilah." I tried to give her the most assuring tone I could. But in reality, I felt helpless to comfort the poor girl. Everything she was saying was entirely true, and it was something we'd spoken on more than once, already. Giving birth was a terrifying thing, and I couldn't even imagine what it must be like to be in her position. I don't think any man ever could.

"I feel helpless." She spoke with her head down, the long trellises of fur along her ears covering half of her face. "As though I ... never ... asked ... for any of this. And now it's happening, and I have no choice in how or when it happens, either. I'm not ready."

"Do you wish you'd never conceived?" I asked, honestly not sure what her answer would be.

So when she responded "Yes." In utter certainty, I was surprised. I knew the young woman was uncertain, uncomfortable, even unhappy, much of the time, but...

"It's not that I didn't want to have children, someday." She murmured. "I have always wanted to do my duty, and be a good mother. I don't even mind the physical symptoms so much ... they are not as bad as what I had heard. I just didn't want to have children—"

"So young?" I supplied.

She looked up at me. "In this way," she finished, looking into my eyes.

I made my best attempt at self-deprecation, since that always seemed to cheer her up. "I know I'm a scruffy lout, but am I really all *that* bad?"

She smiled almost despite herself. "It's not you, Luther. You know that."

"The father, then?" I asked, and she stiffened. I slipped a hand down, and took hers, immediately regretting bringing that up. She froze up every time I did, I don't know why I'd thought it would be different this time. That was one subject she'd never opened up to me about, not once in the last few months we'd been speaking. "It's alright." I assured her.

Her hand was shaking in mine. I squeezed it softly, and that seemed to help some.

"I can't tell you I understand, Delilah." I spoke. "I don't think any man could, honestly. But I know what it feels like to be helpless against something you cannot control. And how destructive it can be to spend your days cursing the way things are. Some things in life, we can't change. You can dash yourself against the rocks all you like, but in the end, all you'll really do is waste your time, and bloody your nose. Some things just are what they are, and regardless of how they came to be, we need to accept that they're a part of us, and learn how to live with them."

I looked down at her. "I don't know how these pups came to be, but they're a part of you now. I have every faith in you to bring them into the world. When the time comes, I know you'll tough it out, and do what needs to be done to get through it. And whether or not you have a healthy litter afterwards, you'll be stronger for it. You'll be a good mother someday. You're kind, canny ... and stronger than you think."

I saw her eyes glistening somewhat, and had to turn away. The girl wasn't exactly an emotional basket case, but I couldn't deal with female crying. It made me uncomfortable.

She only sniffed once, though ... reserved in all ways. Then she whispered a quiet, "Thank you, Luther."

I only gave her a nod, and another squeeze of her hand.

"You don't know how envious I am of you men, sometimes." She admitted, with a weak smile. "I'd rather ... write, or hunt, or work a trade, or even go to war than go through childbirth, any day."

"Mnh," I had to agree with that. "Our lives would both be drastically improved if you were a man."

She elbowed me in the ribs at that, and I clutched at my midsection in mock pain, while she smiled, mirthfully. She began to say something else, but interrupted herself with a sudden, "Oh!" clutching at her belly.

I gave her a nervous look. The litter wasn't due for weeks. "Are you alright?" I asked, worriedly.

"I-I'm fine. They do this sometimes..." She rubbed her tummy slowly, and swayed a little, as though already trying to rock the restless little buggers to sleep.

"Not even born, and they're already holy terrors." I muttered. "I live in fear of the day they start walking."

She gave me a contemplative look momentarily, and I felt a strange pang of fear that she was about to involve me in this whole 'pup situation' more than I honestly wanted to be. My instincts proved to be on the money.

"Luther?" She reached over and took my hand again. "Would you like to feel them? They're moving about."

"No, no." I slipped my hand out of hers, trying to be as inoffensive as possible. "That's quite alright. I ... ah—I really shouldn't. I'm ... not supposed to touch you, before the wedding. Johannes says even the hand-holding is technically off-limits, and I'm already fulfilling my rebellious streak there."

She knitted her brow at me in a startling similar fashion to her father. "Luther. You aren't even going to be touching me *after* the wedding."

"Exactly," I nodded.

"So what does it matter?" She countered. "I know *you* won't be inappropriate with me. Besides, I'm fully clothed. I'm actually wearing *two* slips ... the physician insisted I keep warm."

"Then I'll hardly feel anything, anyway. I really need to be getting downstairs—" I started to take my leave, and the little woman gave a frustrated sigh, and just reached over and took hold of my wrist, tugging my hand over onto her belly, and pressing it down against the soft fabric of her dress. I was so shocked by her boldness. I wasn't even able to yank my paw away before I made contact.

And before I could, it was too late.

I was aware of movement the moment my paw touched her, and then I was transfixed. The thin fabric of her garments did little to mask the sensation. I could feel them, two small, living things, shifting around as though already eager to see more of the world than just the safety of their mother's womb. I'm not sure why, but somehow that moment brought the whole thing into the realm of reality, for me. Previously, the fact that Delilah was pregnant had really just been more of a ... concept. For the first time, I was coming to grips with the gravity of what she'd been trying to explain to me.

And I was still an outsider. I couldn't even imagine how heavy this must have been for her.

"That's—"

"Incredible, isn't it?" She said with the slightest hint of a smile. It was an expression tempered with a lot of pain, and difficulty, but it warmed me to see her happy at all. She moved her paw over mine, and for a moment, the four of us were connected. I can't explain it ... these little creatures were always inside of her, and I'd taken her hand and been close beside her many times over the last few months, but I had *never* felt like this before.

It didn't matter whether we shared a bed. I had to take care of this woman, and her children. They needed me.

The little pups twitched beneath my paw, and it took me a moment to realize Delilah had stiffened, too. I glanced to her features, and found them suddenly, shockingly terrified ... her gaze riveted out the window, down towards the men collecting at the back gate.

Faster than I could so much as get a word out to ask her if she was alright, she bolted from my hold, and fled down the hallway. I was too confused to stop her.

She hurriedly pulled open the door to her room, and while I was calling out her name, slammed the door behind her. The whole thing happened so quickly, I wasn't sure what I should do ... or what exactly had just happened.

Perhaps she was ill? She'd had bouts of sickness ever since the pregnancy had progressed.

I began to head for her room, worriedly, before a voice caught my attention from the stairs.

"Luther!" Cuthbert called from down the old wooden staircase. I saw just his head and shoulders, as he came up just far enough to see me. "Come. The guests are arriving. Lucius wants you in the great room to greet them all."

"I ... need to check on Delilah..." I insisted, torn.

He took the last few long strides up the staircase, and headed towards me. "What's wrong?" He asked immediately.

"I honestly have no idea." I said, exasperated. "She just ... ran for her room, and I'm worried she's not feeling well, or—"

"I'll see to her. Go." He put a paw on my shoulder, and walked past me. "Lucius is expecting you." He called over his shoulder, heading for her room.

I gave one last hesitant look at the doorway, then turned and started heading downstairs. I wondered the whole way if I'd made the right choice. But, I'd fought hard to go to this event, and unfortunately, I honestly didn't have the time right now to sit with my future wife. Later, I promised myself. Whatever it was, it was going to have to wait.

CHAPTER 6
SOME MEN JUST NEED KILLING

I headed downstairs, immediately greeted by the sight of half a dozen fully uniformed men heading towards the great room, with more filing in behind. They were a mixed lot ... I stood and watched the crowd coming in through the back doors of the mansion for a good minute or so, trying to get a feel for what to expect. Some of them were clearly Pedigrees. You could see it not only in the insignia and the uniforms they wore to distinguish them as Officers, but in their bearing, and breeding. I'd served under many Pedigree Officers, Captains and Admirals over my career, of course, but I'd never seen so much brass in one place. It was admittedly a little intimidating.

Amongst them, though, were a decent amount of what must have been First Mates, lower-class Officers and perhaps some as simple as trusted fellows. I saw quite a few men amongst the lot who looked more like the type of boys I used to serve with, and most of them weren't even uniformed.

Well, Lucius *had* always seemed the type to me that kept company with men based more on merit than breeding, especially where navy men and military men were concerned. I watched a little while longer from my inconspicuous spot in the darkness beside one of the staircase entranceways, until I was sufficiently certain my confidence was where it needed to be. These weren't like the Pedigrees at the balls, and galas. These were my kind of men. I was on equal footing with them.

And some day, as Lucius had said, I might command them, which meant I needed to make the best possible first impression. Not too humble, not too arrogant. Strong and sure of myself, but not overbearing.

I steeled myself.

I began to step out into the hall, adjusting my cufflinks as I did ... and then I heard the pounding of footsteps on the stairs behind me, and Johannes was suddenly pushing past me, hurrying into the crowded hall beyond. Something in his eyes stopped me in my tracks. The man was harried, and turning his muzzle sharply around the room, as though on the trail of something, or someone.

And he looked ... angry.

I saw the moment he fixed his eyes on his prey, and followed his line of sight to a stocky tricolor spaniel. The tall wolfhound shoved his way through the crowd towards the Pedigree, who spotted him about four or five seconds before Johannes made it to him ... and I swear the spaniel smirked.

And then Johannes was on him, shoving a hand against the other man's shoulder and pushing him backwards into one of the doors to the servant hallways. They shared a few words I couldn't hear, and then Johannes pushed open the door, and bulled the man inside. The whole thing happened quickly and it looked as though the wolfhound had been *trying* to be discreet about it, but there was no masking the antagonism there. Several of the guests noticed, murmurs sifting up from the crowd.

What in the hell...?

The pieces fell together all at once, and my eyes widened. That had to be him. This Lord Irving Lucius had spoken of.

The sire of Delilah's pups.

I clenched my fist. In the room beyond me, I knew Lucius was waiting, expecting me. There were a few dozen men here that might someday put their lives in my hands. But I was tired of everything in this family being drawn behind a veil. Before I took up a rank in the Denholmes' fleet, I needed to understand the family I was going to be a part of it. I deserved to. I couldn't stand being in the dark anymore. I couldn't shake the feeling that something about all of this was terribly wrong ... that Delilah's happiness, and perhaps even her life, were being toyed with, and I was playing some unwitting role in all of it.

If they wouldn't tell me what sort of a relationship she'd had with this man, I was going to find out on my own. They had *made* me a part of all of this. It was time I got the full story.

I ducked back into the dining room, and made my way for the servants' entrance, where they brought the food up from the kitchen. I'd gotten to know the servants' hallways fairly well since I'd moved in here on account of getting to know the servants themselves better. I related far better with them than I did almost anyone else around this place. Besides, the cook— an old calico woman with a waistline I couldn't wrap my arms around—was exceptionally good at her craft and often snuck me scraps in between meals.

I fell back on my guerilla training as I slunk through the dimly candlelit passageways, stepping on the pads of my feet and lifting my claws with considerable strain, so they didn't sound on the wooden floorboards. The servants' hallways were only meant for the staff here to move from place to place unseen when they were carrying about their mundane, everyday tasks. The walls were poorly painted, flimsy, and hardly soundproof, but the muted noises from the party in the main room helped cover my footfalls. I crept around what I knew to be the staircase entranceway, towards the crawlspace that separated the great room from the back landing where all the guests had been coming in. The servants rarely went here, but it would get me close to the great room's access hallway and the lamp closet, which is where Johannes had dragged that man towards.

I stopped when I heard the distinctive brogue of Cuthbert's voice, answered a moment later by another. The man's voice was considerably calmer than I expected it to be. It stunk of self-satisfaction, even from a distance. I even thought I heard him chuckling.

I leaned against the wall of the crawl space, pressing my ear to the thin wood. As soon as I did, the conversation became far more clear, although it was obvious I'd come in halfway through something key.

"—invitation was made to the entire Brackenwall Fleet. If your Lord meant to exclude me, perhaps he should have annotated as such." The spaniel spoke.

There was a sudden shudder of the wall, and my ears rang as someone was shoved, hard, into the shelves I knew lined the interior of the lamp closet. I heard a shattering noise, the scuffle of claws on hardwood, and then another shudder.

"It should be *clear* to you that you are not *welcome* in this house!" Cuthbert's snarl was evident in his voice, and it sent a chill down my spine. I knew without a doubt that he was the one pinning that noble up against the shelves inside the closet right now. I had *never* heard him this angry, before.

"Rightfully, I should be living in this house." The spaniel's voice replied, some hint of his calm gone, likely because there was a very strong, very intimidating, wolfhound pinning him against the wall. Probably painfully so.

I smirked. Atta boy, Johannes.

"Rightfully, you should be at the *gallows*!" Johannes bellowed, not bothering to check his voice as much as he probably should have, considering the crowded house just beyond these walls. The man was losing his restraint.

What the hell was this all about? I was honestly considering stepping away from the wall. I'd heard arguments like these before, and they usually ended at sword point. And if he ran him through, I was on the other side of the thin plaster.

"Now, that would require a crime." That man's voice was starting to slither through my head in uncomfortable ways. Something about the way he spoke just set my fur on end, and I didn't know why. "The only crime perpetrated here was against *my* honor ... and you have your whoring heiress to blame for that."

Oh God. Cold sunk into my bones. This man was no lover of Delilah's. Up until now, I'd been wondering at the girl's wisdom, at throwing herself on someone this arrogant. I hadn't even considered...

"If you," I heard the restraint slipping from Johannes's tone, word by word, "so much as speak ... one more ... slight against that girl—"

"Accusations are an ugly thing." There was a growl in the spaniel's tone, "And dreadfully unfair, when you get right down to it. It all comes down to belief, and who warrants more of it, from a Judge. Whom do you think they will believe, your island filth?" The wall creaked, as the spaniel's girth pushed back into it. His voice grew tighter, and it occurred to me now that Johannes must have had a paw clamped partially over his throat. "Your unmarried, pregnant, heiress who lied about her condition for months? Or an honored captain in the King's Armada?"

"You are going to die by this family's hands, Irving." Johannes's voice was low, barely above a harsh whisper. "That is inevitable, the only question is when."

I felt the wall suddenly bow back to its former position, and heard the distinctive, sharp sounds of Johannes's claws as he stepped back.

I thought I heard the spaniel cough. "Go ahead." He spat. "See what happens when you blink first. Not a soul will believe her. *You* barely believe her."

"I believe her." Cuthbert spoke, quietly. Or maybe it was just because he was farther away now.

The spaniel laughed. "And yet you had to dredge up some waste of life from the regulars, as her 'stud'? If you thought anyone else would believe a woman, you'd have been out about it. But you didn't.

You got yourself a different man to blame, and new lies to tell. Where did you even find someone so self-loathing and desperate, to fess to another man's spawn? You stink of desperation. This whole house does. And for what? How much better off is she now, 'Knight'?"

"As long as she is safe from you, she is better off."

"I would have given your family what it so *dearly* lacks!" The spaniel raised his voice, that growl still simmering under every word. "*Honor*! *A bloodline*! Perhaps even instill some sense of obedience and respect for the greater gender into that *harpy* of a woman!" His voice fell in tone at that, but was no less threatening. "But, do as you please. Go to the authorities. See whose words they value. Even if they gave her *any* credence, I can bear the shame of an illegitimate heir. Can your family? Can she?"

I heard Johannes turn, and his voice faded, as his footsteps retreated.

"If they knew," his voice echoed quietly, as he left the man behind in the lamp closet, "that you had tried to force your way into this family ... you would be executed."

What the spaniel did after that, I do not know. Because I had fled from the crawlspace, my desire for silence lost. My feet pounded down the empty, cramped corridors, until I sprung from the dining room servants' exit, colliding into a crowd of newly arrived guests, shoving past them roughly with little care anymore for who they were, or what impression I was making upon them.

I don't think I'd ever run that fast up those stairs. Delilah's room seemed miles away. I tore down the hallway of the east wing, Cuthbert's words echoing in my mind.

'Force your way into this family'? He couldn't mean...

My gut began to ache, and by the time my footpads were skidding against the ancient floorboards in front of Delilah's doors, there was a sickening coil of revulsion and dread building inside me, fearing what my fiancé would tell me.

In the recesses of my mind, I already knew. But I wanted to hear it from her.

I slammed my fist repeatedly on the door, calling out her name at the top of my lungs. I realized I must have sounded terrifying to the already distressed woman, but I wasn't going to let her shut me out. Not anymore.

"*Delilah*!" I cried out once more, before there was an answer. Not in the form of a voice, but in the click of the door unlocking. I pushed inside, slamming the heavy wooden door behind me as soon as I was behind it.

The young girl was standing just a few feet away from me, tearstained and frightened. I realized with a pang of guilt that I was at least partially responsible for some of that fear.

I tried to settle my hackles, and lowered my lips back over my teeth again, putting out a paw for her, tentatively.

"Delilah, I-I ... I'm sorry. I didn't mean to be so loud ... and I'm not angry at you." I promised quietly, coaxing her to me with a gentle beckoning gesture of my paw. She stood just a few feet from me, frozen in place. She looked to me, her freckled muzzle quivering. It was all there. It had always been there. In the way she shied from me, from any man, in our anger. In the way she always seemed poised to run, like she had been hurt before.

In that instant, I knew my fears were correct. And she saw that I knew. Before I could say a word, she rushed to me, and threw herself into my arms.

I wrapped her up immediately in a tight embrace, moving one paw through the fur along the back of her neck, the other around her waist. Her shaking turned to sobbing almost immediately, and this time I didn't care. She was clinging to me like I was driftwood in a maelstrom. I could feel this horrible, wracking pain every time she sobbed, and I was becoming confused as to whether it was hers or mine.

The only thing beginning to eclipse the grief inside me was the anger.

I steadied my voice as much as I could, only for her sake. "How did it happen?" I spoke quietly into her ear, trying not to make the question a demand.

"H-he came ... Lord Irving ... he came to father's Officers' Balls, every year. I-I never even ... knew him well." Her tears were sinking into the collar of my coat. "Father said ... his family had a ... fleet ... in the southern seas, but ... they lost most of their ships in a b-bad ... storm."

I swallowed. An entire fleet? That was a hell of a tragedy, but the storms in the South Seas were notoriously bad.

"Lord Irving ... Jeremiah," she all but whispered the man's name, like a curse, " ... he was supposed to inherit it. But then, they lost the fleet. Ever since then, he wanted ... to combine our families. I-I barely knew his name, but, last year..." she turned her eyes down to the floor, the wide, brown orbs lost in a memory. " ... h-he asked me ... into the garden, and he ... p-proposed ... to me."

She turned her face up suddenly to look at mine, eyes wide. "I didn't even turn him down!" She insisted, desperately. "I-I only ... said that I did not know him well, that I would have to think on it. Talk to my father." Her eyes fixed on the floor, and she went utterly silent for a few seconds. At length, she continued, in a timid, frightened tone, "He told me ... there was nothing to think on. That we were intended for one another by God and that we would make ... pure ... children..." Her whole body shuddered, "...and that we were ... already as good as ... wed."

I didn't want to hear any more. I could feel my pulse thudding in my ears. I could smell her fear. Every fiber of my body was screaming at me like it did before we boarded an enemy vessel. I wanted blood.

Somehow, I stayed there, holding her. It took everything I had.

Any man who could hurt this gentle, kind, tiny little creature in my arms was a monster. And that monster was downstairs, right now.

"We were in the garden." She repeated quietly, her gaze lost and unfocused. "I know ... he could smell ... that I was in heat..."

I shut my eyes.

"Maybe ... he planned it that night ... because he knew." She murmured, sadly. "He told me he would make me his wife. And then..." her voice fell off, at that point, like the words were there, but she hadn't the breath for them. I wish I could have said something to comfort her. Anything, but I was too angry to speak.

She cast her eyes aside. "I kept it all inside me ... for as long as I could. I didn't want to disgrace my father ... my family ... myself." Her voice broke on the last word. "I tried to stop him, but he was ... so ... strong..."

I had to pull away from her at that point, because I was earnestly afraid of myself, and my rage. I stalked a few paces from her, my mind a wild tangle, my body numb. I had been in the military. I had been in the navy. I'd been to war. I'd lost friends, lovers, and seen my share of despicable acts perpetrated on both.

But right now, the images stirring in my mind disturbed me on a level I couldn't even comprehend. You hear about these things happening. You hear about it all the time. Everyone agrees that it's despicable ... it's terrible. But I ... knew ... this girl. To think that a man would abuse her was ... literally inconceivable. I could not come to grips with the thought of it.

Or what should be done about it.

No.

I set my brow at that. No, that was the simplest answer, in all of this. Nothing else made sense right now. But what needed to be done was very, very clear.

"Luther—" Delilah began, putting a hand out for mine. I left her reaching for me, strode out, pulling open the brass-hinged doors with enough force to bang them into the perfectly papered walls of Delilah's room.

I heard her call out my name frantically once more, and turned my ears from the sound, lest it shake my resolve. The door slammed behind me. I would apologize to her when this was all done.

I was nearly at the stairs before I saw Cuthbert. The damned man was everywhere in this house today *except* the one place he *should* have been.

He cut me off, putting his broad, gloved paws out to stop me by the shoulders, and I shoved past him. "Get out of my way." I gave him one warning growl, one. That's all he got, and that was a courtesy.

"Luther, stop." He grabbed me forcefully by the shoulder this time, and I spun and shoved him off of me. Much to my shock, he actually fell back into the wall, thudding into and rattling a large wooden frame.

I stood there, ears tipped back, the barest hint of my teeth showing. I hadn't realized I was that strong these days. Johannes was a big man, if lean. But that hadn't taken as much as I'd thought. I saw the realization in his eyes, too. I wasn't the scrawny little peasant he'd dug out of a prison. It's amazing what five months of good food and exercise can put in your body.

In the navy I'd been in a fight every other day, either for entertainment, or just to establish the pecking order. The whole while I'd been here in this prim, proper place, I'd had no need. But now that familiar rush was surging through me, and for once, I had a damned good reason. I lunged slightly at Johannes with one foot, challenging him. He didn't flinch, but nor did he move.

"Luther." He spoke evenly. "This isn't necessary. I am not your enemy. Calm yourself."

"*Calm*?!" I snarled. "That's what's important, isn't it?! You're all so damned obsessed with propriety, so fixated on 'civility'. Everyone's so goddamn *calm*; you all sat back and *let* a man violate Delilah!"

I thought for a moment he almost looked hurt, at that. His grey eyes fell to the carpeted floor, lost. "I failed to protect her." He spoke, voice laden with guilt.

"*Do* something about it, then!" I howled, in righteous indignation, "How long have you known about this?!"

"Since we discovered her ... condition," He admitted, ruefully.

"She tried to hide it for as long as she could, but ... the maids knew something was wrong. She admitted everything to us when her father and I questioned her about it."

"Her *father* knows?!" I swung my arms out to my sides, only to keep them from striking the wolfhound. "How could the both of you know about this, and do *nothing*?!"

"Don't belittle the pain and the tribulation this has caused all of us!" Johannes bit back. "Ever since we knew of it, it has been a *daily* struggle trying to keep this family, this house, and that girl from falling apart! The misery it has cost us is immeasurable..."

"My heart bleeds for you and the old man." I curled a lip, derisively. "It must have been awful difficult sitting on this, doing *nothing*, while that girl *suffered*."

"You have no idea how difficult!" He shoved himself off the wall, and came at me, stopping but a few inches from my face. "Do you not think I am as *outraged* as you are?! Don't presume you understand my pain! You have known that girl for five months ... I have known her since she was a *child*! She is as close to me as one of my own daughters!"

I lowered my snarl slightly at that ... but more than at his words, at the tremble in his voice. It reminded me of the way he'd spoken to the spaniel, in the lamp closet. Restraint, pulled taut to its breaking point. Decades of discipline were on the verge of cracking.

"Outrage is easy!" He shook. "Anger is easy! And trust me, I've *plenty* of it! Do you have any idea how often I lie awake at night, contemplating breaking my oaths to Kingdom and Lord, to the Knight's Code, to every law in this land, just to see justice done to that man?!"

"I don't understand how the law could protect a man like that!" I gestured frantically down the stairs. "How is he free?! Why can the law and the Church convict a man like *me*, for having *consensual* relations with other men, but they can't convict a *rapist*?!"

"This isn't about you." He growled. "And don't make it so."

"No. It's about my daughter."

I heard the voice seconds before my head turned to regard where it had come from. The third footstep, the clack of a cane alongside his two heavy footfalls, confirmed it was Lucius before I'd even looked. I turned an angry expression on the Lord, withholding none of the venom I'd shown Cuthbert.

"I'm the only man here who gives a damn about your daughter." I lowered my brow over my golden eyes.

"You're an ignorant, arrogant child, Luther," Lucius quirked a jowl. "You barely know my daughter ... you aren't even a part of this family, yet. So do not pretend you have any idea what is best for her welfare."

"I'm sorry, sir." Cuthbert murmured from where he stood. "I didn't intend for him to hear—"

"It's fine Johannes," Lucius gave a long, tired sigh, and then a rumbling growl. "I honestly never expected that bastard would be so bold as to show himself at this house, again. He seemed in one piece, so I congratulate you on your restraint. I'd only barely noticed his presence when our young friend here nearly knocked over Captain Shaw on his way up the stairs. I don't know what happened between you and Lord Irving, Johannes, but our cattle dog here was playing spy, in the servants' hallways ... so it can hardly be helped."

Cuthbert looked back at me at that, his ears perking. He looked annoyed ... perhaps because I'd caught him in his moment of anger with Irving in the lamp closet.

"It doesn't matter how I knew!" I belted. "It's unbelievable that you kept it from me to begin with! How the hell can letting that man walk around unpunished for his crimes be what's best for your daughter's welfare?!" I pinned my eyes straight on the old lord's, my tone desperate. "He *raped* your little girl!"

The old spaniel's eyes closed, and the hallway went deathly silent, my words echoing through the walls. The silence, if anything, made it very clear to me how far our voices carried. I shut my muzzle.

"Say it louder." Lucius said at length, opening two sad brown orbs. "So everyone downstairs can hear you. Better yet ... scream it, so my daughter a few rooms down can hear you, again. It's not as though she isn't already reminded of it each and every day, with that man's children growing inside of her."

I bit my tongue. God, Delilah. I had honestly forgotten we were but thirty feet from her door. I couldn't imagine what a state she must have been in, right now.

"I know the anger you are feeling right now, Luther." Lucius said, the weariness in his tone evident in every word, "But ever since Irving ... violated my family..." The pure hatred in his voice was palpable. "My daughter was put in a desperate, terrible situation, with very few options laid before her. We have chosen the most difficult for ourselves, because it is what is best for *her*. There isn't a day my self-restraint is not tested. Believe me. I know this may be hard for you to understand now, but the best chance Delilah has for a good future is if that man is *never* tried for his crime. This whole travesty needs to remain as it is now, out of the public eye, as though it never happened."

"That's an insult on her honor, and yours!" I thrashed my tail.

"Hang *my* honor!" Lucius barked. "I don't give a damn! It is precisely my daughter's honor I am concerned over! I know you're lower-class, but you have to have some idea how this would play out, if we brought it to the law. It's her word against his. He claims she was willing."

"I haven't known your daughter half a year, and I know that's a lie!"

"It doesn't matter." Lucius stated. "The bottom line is, Luther ... she is a woman." He let that hang poignantly in the air for a moment or more, and I swallowed back the reality. Throughout my whole life, I'd had even less occasion to become acquainted with females than most mariners. I had never really had any grasp of how helpless they must have felt, until now, cursed by a random chance at birth. It was no wonder Delilah and I got on so well. Fighting the insurmountable wall of sex, and sexual identity ... we were more kindred spirits than I realized.

Only I'd been able to raise my fist to defend myself. This girl was literally barred from even speaking against the wrongs done to her.

I lowered my brow, paws collapsing into tight fists at either side of my body. It might have been a sexist thing to say in and of itself, but I wanted to fight that girl's battle for her. Maybe afterwards, we could work on her own ability to defend herself, from now on.

"I don't care." I stated, bluntly. "This will not stand. I won't let it."

Lucius arched an eyebrow, warily. "What exactly do you intend to do, Luther? Because I warn you, if you threaten the reputation of my little girl, I will send you back where you came from, no questions asked. I have taken great pains to keep *myself* from making any foolish mistakes that would risk all of this coming out into the open. And Irving may not let on as much, but he has a vested interest in keeping it that way, as well."

"You could fight him in court. You have money and influence."

"So does his family. More so, in both areas," Lucius admitted with what sounded like shame. "The Irving's would crush this family if they thought we threatened their treasured son in any way. They may have lost their fleet, but they are still a wealthy, influential, connected family, and that boy is their prized progenitor. They will not let his name be slandered. They have high hopes for marriage, for him."

"Then tell the Church!" I insisted. "All their fire and brimstone has to be good for *something*! I didn't pay much attention as a child, but I know rape is a sin!"

"A primary sin," Cuthbert's voice was low, and threatening. "Unforgivable. It is a violation of the body, in the holiest act of union. The greatest gift God bestowed upon us ... the ability to breed. To create life anew," He turned his dark grey eyes to the both of us, his arms crossed over his chest like a guardian statue. "The penalty is execution, by hanging."

"The Church will disgrace my daughter, as well as Irving." Lucius growled. I thought I heard a hint of the hatred in his tone I often felt, when I spoke of our country's great religion. I wouldn't blame the man. "Her children will be declared bastards ... no better than mixed breeds of the lowest rung. They will be born of sin, and she will be stained by it. I have spoken to her of this option. She does not want it. Not for her own sake ... but for theirs. The children will be rejected from all good society for the rest of their lives. They will be untouchable." His knuckles tensed over his cane handle, his eyes falling to the floor. " ... should ... her children not survive the pregnancy ... we have both decided this is an acceptable option. Delilah is willing to bear the shame. She just does not want her children to bear it, as well."

I grit my teeth. None of this was an acceptable option, so far as I was concerned. Delilah didn't deserve to be punished again. Nor did her children, nor did this family.

"He can't fight your family, or cause you any more pain, if he's dead." I finally uttered.

The way the two men slowly turned to regard me, I knew this was something they had both already considered. Lucius even exhaled slowly, although it was Cuthbert who was the first to speak.

"Murder is not an acceptable option. And it's a foolish one." He spoke quietly.

"But you've considered it." I leveled a gaze across the hallway at him. He looked away, which was uncommon for Johannes in any situation.

"He is too well-protected for a common thug." Lucius stated, matter-of-factly. "And anything more planned-out would raise suspicion with the law that a family of means was involved. The incident between Lord Irving and my daughter might not be known, but the fact that he and his family have been fixated on acquiring my fleet is well talked-about in our circles, and a subject of some scandal. By now, everyone knows at the very least that his proposal was rejected, and there is much speculation as to why. The waters between our families are ... tense. I am the first man the authorities would look to, if he were to meet an unfortunate end."

"There *is* another option." Cuthbert grated out, and I could tell it was a subject he'd been leaning on for some time with the old man.

"That is *not* an option, Johannes." Lucius stated firmly. "Disregarding the fact that you have a family that needs you in their lives very badly," I saw the wolfhound's jowls twitch at the old man's cogent point, "you must have a legitimate grievance to issue a duel. And save the subject we are *trying* to keep out of the public light, neither you nor I have any other quarrel with Jeremiah Irving."

"Duel?" I questioned sharply.

"A formal duel between two Lords is a legal, recognized manner of settling disputes—" Cuthbert began, but Lucius cut him off with a snarl.

"Do *not* put this in his head, Johannes!" He warned. "This is precisely the sort of thing that young, *stupid* men lose their lives to—"

"Isn't that the damned point?!" I pressed. "If there's a legal way to kill that bastard, why haven't you taken it?!"

"Because—" Cuthbert started, and was again interrupted by Lucius.

"Because Johannes has seven children at home, a wife he loves dearly, and *no* call to issue a duel against a man who is both wholly unconnected with him, and outside his sphere of society!" Lucius bellowed. "And neither do you, young man!" He stabbed a finger in my direction. "I don't even want to hear this *spoken* of again, do you understand me?! The best thing either of you can do for my daughter right now, if you *truly* care about her, is to stay by her side! She needs a living guardian, a living father, and a living husband! Making a corpse of yourself will only cause her *more* grief!"

"I don't know, Johannes ... I would've liked your chances." I muttered.

"Thank you." He glanced over at me, his expression still looking defeated. "But, Lord Denholme is correct. I have no standing, technically ... and no connection with Irving. I could not justify it, as much as I've fantasized about the possibility."

"Also seven children," I murmured, then stopped myself and looked up at him, arching an eyebrow. "Honestly Johannes. Really? Seven?"

He only barely hid a smile, "And two more on the way. My wife is beautiful."

"She must be."

"Are either of you listening to me?!" Lucius stomped his cane in frustration. I glanced back at him.

"How exactly are one of these duels issued?" I asked.

"I am not educating you *any* further!"

"Fine," I reached down to my neckline, undid my cravat, and then ran my hands down my waistcoat, undoing the buttons until I had sizably more freedom of motion in my chest and arms. I stretched my shoulder out with a few rolls as I pushed past Lucius, and headed towards the stairs. "I'll figure it out on my own."

"*Luther*!" He roared, and I heard his objections amongst some very colorful language I honestly hadn't known the old man was capable of, all the way down. I heard him following me, but I had two working legs and youth on my side, a very unfair advantage.

Cuthbert *did* catch up with me, but only right before I'd made it down the stairs.

"You've never even met Irving, Luther." He insisted, following at my heels as I began navigating my way through what had become a very crowded hallway, towards the great room. A lot of people were looking my way, likely because my formal wear was partially undone, and I was being none-too-polite in pushing my way through the crowd. I honestly didn't give a damn about what these people thought any more. That could all wait. My eyes were scanning the room for the big spaniel. Cuthbert was still talking.

"You don't even know him." He insisted. "You have *no* call to issue a duel against him. You need a grievance against the man."

"Then I'll make one." I split from the stunned wolfhound, as I finally found my target. The stocky, tricolor dog was standing near a large group of well-dressed ponces. He was big, for a spaniel. Five or six inches on me, at least, and probably about a hundred pounds. The good life had certainly been treating him well. He was supposedly navy, but in the clothing these people wore, it was hard to tell how much of him was firm. I rolled up my sleeve.

Well, I'd never had a problem picking a fight with bigger dogs, before.

Some of his friends saw me approaching before he did. He finished off the wine in a glass he was holding in his left hand, before slowing turning to regard me.

Too slowly.

His broad, thick muzzle, when turned in profile, was almost too perfect a target. I nailed him dead-on in one blow, my knuckles resounding with the familiar pain of landing a punch partially on the unforgiving surface of someone's cheekbone. I got a very satisfying crunch from his jaw as a tooth cracked, and I sealed my canines together in a grin as he spun into the table behind him. He tumbled partially over the edge and ripped down the tablecloth and several sets of silverware and plates as he clutched at it frantically, to keep himself moderately upright. He looked stunned and disoriented for a full ten or fifteen seconds, and I heard chairs tipping over and the rapid succession of footfalls as the crowd parted around us. And then he was just staring at me, gape-jawed in shock.

"Get up, soldier." I nodded my chin at him. "I won't hit you again while you're down."

He finally bared his teeth at me, the left side of his jowls beginning to bleed. He shoved himself upright, knocking over the chair in front of him and sending it spinning across the floor a few feet. So there *was* some power, there.

"What the hell is in your mind, madman?!" He demanded, around what had to be a swelling cheek. "Who *are* you?!"

"Luther." I shook out my hand, cracking my knuckles. I was getting out-of-practice at this.

" ... who?" He looked at me confused.

"Just Luther is fine." I said. The room had gone very silent, save low murmurs. Somewhere, I was all but certain Cuthbert was watching ... but he had yet to intervene. Everyone was giving us a wide berth.

"What the hell is the meaning of this?!" He howled.

"I heard you had designs on my girl." I raised my voice, so all could hear if they chose to. I began to shove off my jacket. "I wanted to lay down the law with you ... make it clear who's ground you're treading on."

He lifted his lip in a mixture of derision and confusion, for only a few seconds more. Then his eyes widened just slightly, before realization dawned on him. "You're the scum that old fool's heiress is marrying."

"Scum?" I tossed my jacket over a nearby chair. "Now that sounded like an insult on my person, sir."

He sneered. "The 'insult' is that you're even permitted on Pedigree grounds, mongrel. But then, with you marrying into the line, I suppose we can't call the Denholme line Pedigree any longer, can we?" His eyes fixed over my shoulder, and I just knew that Lucius had stepped into the room that moment, by the angry grin that crept over the spaniel's features. "Shame, they used to have so much promise."

"Yeah, the way I hear it, you've still got your sights fixed on my woman's inheritance." I challenged him, in the most low-class drawl I could dredge up from many a night spent at dockside boarding houses. "Back off!" I barked. "She's marrying *me*. Those're *my* pups in her belly!"

He smiled in a way that made me feel sick inside. "Are you sure?" He rumbled.

I arched an eyebrow, feigning ignorance. "What do you mean?"

He held the stare a moment longer, and then began to cross the table length separating us, stepping over the scattered remnants of the table's contents. For a moment, I was honestly concerned he might out his sins against the poor girl, just to spite me.

But I was a good judge of people, and I'd never lost a game of chicken. He chose the coward's way out.

"Only that if the heiress of the Denholme was base enough to bend for the likes of you, that she might have done so with half the docks." He chuckled.

"*Irving*!" Lucius bellowed from across the room. "I will *not* tolerate such crass, baseless insults against my family, in my *own* house! Leave *now*!"

Irving leveled a finger across the room at the old man, shouting back. "You invited this low-class, worthless *scum* into your house, Lucius! You have shamed yourself and your entire family by associating with such *refuse*, and allowing him to breed your little harlot! You will never—"

I cut him off, swinging a paw up to clamp him by the wrist, and yanking it backwards to the small of his back, before kicking him in the back of the knees. The heavy dog crumpled like a sack of flour, not expecting to suddenly lose his balance, and I vaguely thought I saw one of his knees slam down onto a fork. He cried out in surprise and I released him. I could have had him in a pin in seconds, if I'd wanted.

This was going to be easier than I'd thought.

"You know what, Irving?" I stepped around him, stalking over a serving tray and its scattered contents. "I am starting to feel disinclined towards you. I really dislike the insults, both to myself, and my wife to be. I'd go so far as to say I have a legitimate grievance with you. One I might want to see settled."

"You *attacked* me!" He spat blood.

"A good brawl's how we scummy lower-classers settle our differences." I shrugged. "You went and made it personal."

"And what the hell do you think you're going to do about it?" He snarled, pushing himself back up onto his feet, warily. I think he'd gathered by now that he wasn't a match for me in a fight. He might have had some strength on me ... although I'd have to get hit by him to be certain of that ... but he was just too damned slow.

"How about a duel?" I smirked down at him. What was left of his superior expression disappeared entirely at that.

As did all conversation in the room. I hadn't even realized how many people had been murmuring quietly until that moment, because it went dead silent.

"You *are* mad." He gave a very forced, nervous smile.

I shrugged. "Some would say. But it's still a legitimate challenge. What say you?"

"A duel is to the *death*, you simpleton!"

"I'm aware." I narrowed my eyes.

Again, silence consumed the room.

"What say you, Irving?" Cuthbert spoke from somewhere behind me, his deep, heavy voice commanding all in the room to ask the very same question in their minds. For a brief flicker of a moment, I thought I saw fear on the spaniel's face. Every eye in the room was fixed on him. He had no escape, save obvious public cowardice. I knew many a man who would gladly take that to avoid death. But this was a Pedigree.

"Fine," he bore his canines at me. "I accept. Choose your time of death, lowborn."

"One day from now ought to be fine. Right here, in the garden." I smirked.

"Good. They can bury you where you fall, and fertilize the roses." He sneered. "As defendant in this challenge, the choice of weapon is mine."

Like I gave a damn what I killed him with. The man was a sack of shit. I had almost two decades of real combat experience behind me. I'd kill him with a spoon, if I had to.

"Fine," I shrugged. "Name your weapon."

He grinned darkly, "Flintlock pistols."

I tried not to show my surprise. From behind me, I heard Cuthbert give a long, exasperated sigh, and I quirked my head, arching an eyebrow. "You want to fight to the death with ... guns?"

"I doubt you've your own, so I will provide a matched set." The man straightened his waistcoat out over his midsection, and smoothed out his lapels. He still had wine and some kind of egg custard on him, so it did little to alleviate the problem, but I honestly couldn't find the humor in it, at the moment.

Guns?

"I'll see you on the morrow then." The spaniel snuffed once more at me, and ran the back of his paw along his jawline, wiping away a thin trail of blood. "At sunset," the crowd parted around him as he headed out, all but ignoring Lucius on his way out the door. "Prepare yourself."

And then he was gone. The room remained silent. And I scratched at my scalp, introspectively. Cuthbert stepped up to my side and lowered his head, so he could drop his voice and I'd still hear him.

"If you had listened to me, I would have warned you about the rights of the defendant ... and the likelihood that he would *not* choose a melee weapon."

"Well," I scratched somewhat nervously at my neck scruff, "firing a pistol can't ... be *terribly* different than firing a crossbow."

"Ensuring a flintlock fires at all is a trained skill, and even then, it is less accurate at ten feet than a crossbow at fifty." He clasped a hand on my shoulder. "All of this, of course, is a moot point ... because you are piss-poor with *any* ranged weapon."

"I assumed a 'duel' would involve swords." I muttered.

"Next time you're going to put your life on the line, Luther ... consult with me over your decision, and I'll tell you if you're being a jackass."

"Noted."

CHAPTER 7
DEATH

"How could you do something so foolish?!"

The angry shriek in her tone was as shocking as glacial water, and cut straight to my bones in almost the same way as the chill of the northern seas did. I stared at her helplessly in surprise for a few moments, stumbling over what I was going to say in response. This was not what I had expected to hear from her, at all.

"Delilah, I-I-" I began.

"You *know* how much pain that man has already caused me!" She threw her arms down by her sides, shaking, tears streaming down her already tear-stained cheeks. "How could you do this?! How could you *give* him the chance to take *more* away from this family?!"

Her condition alone all but demanded a response, but for some reason, I was having trouble digging up the many, what I considered righteous, reasons for my challenging the spaniel lord to a duel. I licked the inside of my muzzle dryly and began with, "The pain he's caused you is precisely *why* I felt I had to do this, to take back your honor—"

"Don't you *dare* say that, Luther!" Her voice broke on my name.

"Don't you dare pretend this was for me! My honor can't be won back through causing a man's *death*! It is *mine* to reclaim! And I will do that with time, grace, and the will to live my life, raise my family and be happy, *despite* him! Putting him in the ground doesn't change what happened to me!"

"But," I stammered, "You were in so much pain, and grief ... I thought—"

"If you'd been thinking of me, Luther, you would have *asked* me what I wanted." She stated, quaking. Her fragility was lost in this rare moment of anger, but her pain was evident. And this time, I was the cause. It was even harder to stomach, seeing the bulge in her belly, and knowing I'd brought this all on a pregnant woman. The moment was almost surreal. Just minutes ago, I'd been all fire and righteous indignation. I'd been proud of myself for defending this woman.

I hadn't even considered whether or not she wanted to be defended. In fact, I'd done what I'd done despite the warnings and wishes of her father and Cuthbert. Who, it turned out, actually did know her better than I did. Sometimes, my arrogance stood out in such stark contrast, even I realized how much of a jackass I was.

Cuthbert stepped up behind the young woman and took her by the shoulders, steadying her. "Please try to quiet yourself, Delilah." He pleaded. "This can't be good for you in your condition."

She turned herself in his arms, and buried her muzzle against his chest, sobbing softly. He kept a paw on her shoulder comfortingly, and looked over the top of the short woman's head to me. His look alone was condemning.

Lucius spoke from behind me, after an uncomfortably long silence had settled in the room. It was for the best, since I could think of nothing more to say.

"Regardless of our young man here going off half-cocked ... it is done now." He said resolutely. "All we can do at this point is prepare. And we have very little time to do so. Irving has already called a Judge. The date is set."

I looked up at that. "A judge?"

"These matches are very formal." Lucius explained. "They have to be, considering they are practically legally sanctioned murder."

Delilah shuddered in Cuthbert's arms at that, and I winced. She turned, fixing her bloodshot eyes on me. There was more fear than anger in them, now.

"You're going to win. Right, Luther?" She demanded, quietly. "You're a soldier. You can beat him, right?"

"Yes." I said as firmly as I could, trying to assure her. "I've been a soldier since I was barely a man. Before, in fact ... I lied about my age and enlisted in a militia when I was fourteen. That man's a pompous, overstuffed bully, with no real combat experience. All he has on me is size." I tried to give her my cockiest smile. "I laid him out quite handily in the living room, actually."

Her expression shifted to something closer to hopeful at that, and with perhaps an inkling of satisfaction, "Really? Right in the living room?"

I smirked, but our brief moment of positive thinking was interrupted by Lucius, who as usual had to subvert the mood with cold reality.

"None of that matters if you're dueling with flintlocks."

Delilah immediately looked worried again, "Flintlocks?"

Cuthbert stepped away from her at that, and she looked after him, then to me, knitting her hands together. "I-I don't ... what's wrong? A flintlock is a ... gun ... right? Luther, you can use a gun, can't you?"

"I learned how to fire rifles when I was infantry, and I'm well studied with crossbows ... it isn't much different." I promised her. "He doesn't stand a chance."

She seemed uncertain, so I stepped up to her, and put my paws out to take hers. I was not rebuffed. She was still shaking. I rubbed my thumbs up the center of her palms over her paw pads, in the way I knew comforted her when we spoke on difficult things.

"Delilah," I began, wetting my tongue as I spoke, "listen to me."

She looked up, and I locked my gaze with hers so she knew I was speaking earnestly to her. "I am going to win tomorrow. But..." her ears tipped back at that, and I squeezed her hands. "Should the worst happen, by some chance, I want you to know that none of this was in any way your doing. I chose to do this, because that man offended every sensibility inside me. I loathe men like that. I grew up poor. My mother died in the months following my birth, because she couldn't afford to see a physician after she gave birth to me, and she just ... grew weaker, and weaker, and died. Most of the time, my father and I didn't even have meat to eat. The herd we tended wasn't ours ... and even when we were starving, we couldn't risk slaughtering a one, or the Lord who owned our land would come down on us like a hammer."

I felt a heavy silence settle in the room, and saw my fiancé's muzzle quivering. I had never spoken to any of these people about my upbringing. It was an awkward topic, considering the Denholmes were Pedigrees, and even Cuthbert had spent the better portion of his life well-off. The subject of money was just not something I thought we could ever come to an equal understanding on, being who we were, and the gap between us. I knew in the back of their minds, they all knew how I'd grown up ... but I don't think any of them truly understood.

"I've been a poor, skinny ... mongrel, my entire life. Until I met all of you," I spoke, quietly. "And until I met all of you, I had a lot of hatred inside me for Pedigrees, and the rich, in general. It's taken months of living with your family, speaking to and learning from your father and basking in your kindness, for me to really come to accept that you're all ... people, not much unlike me. That you all have your own troubles, and pain."

She cast her eyes aside at that, and I stroked the back of her hand again.

"But that man ... is *everything* I loathe in the world. He is what I always pictured the Pedigree class to be, arrogant, cruel, and entitled. Even casting aside what he did to you, and your family," I reached down and brushed a thumb over the soft fur of her chin, "I am doing this because I wish to. Because I am a selfish, angry, person who didn't consider your feelings in this matter, at all. I just wanted to strike back at the sort of person whose lifestyle assured my family's poverty throughout my youth."

Her eyes flicked back up to mine, and I stroked her cheek. "So regardless of what happens ... please know it had nothing to do with you. And please continue to be strong, and reclaim your honor on your own terms."

She sniffed, quietly, her long lashes dropping over her eyes. "You're a good liar, Luther," she murmured, "but I'll always know you did this for me." She pressed her muzzle into my paw, closing her eyes. "Please just win. Please..."

I tried to force a wry smile. "At worst, you're spared marrying a scruffy lout like me."

She opened her eyes slowly, and looked up at me shyly, "Luther, why are you so certain I don't want to marry you?"

"Well," I gave an uneasy huff, "it's a bit of a ... farce. This whole thing, wouldn't you prefer a real marriage? To someone who could honestly be a decent husband do you?"

"What makes you think you wouldn't make me happy as a husband?" She asked quietly. Before I could respond with the obvious, she replied preemptively, "Because we won't bed one another?"

I shifted a bit uncomfortably, but wasn't sure how to respond. Yes? This wasn't something we'd ever discussed, but she ... knew. She knew about my relationship with Klaus. She knew why I'd been in prison. She wasn't ignorant of what our marriage would ultimately be. Still, the subject of the marriage bed was one we'd never spoken on. It seemed a moot point, and honestly, I didn't want to offend the woman's sensibilities. The whole thing was incredibly awkward.

Especially with her father in the room.

"Luther, I don't care." She stated, looking up at me openly. And I could tell she meant it. "I've known what I was agreeing to the whole while, and it never concerned me then, either. All I was concerned with was whether or not you were a decent man." Her gaze dropped to my chest, and the one hand that was still in mine gripped it as tightly as she was able. "And you ... are."

My mouth was dry again, and I couldn't seem to wet it, this time. I had no response for this. I was caught flat-footed. Delilah and I got on fairly well, but I'd always imagined given any alternative, she wouldn't want me. Or at the very least that she'd be indifferent.

"I want to be your wife." She said, meekly. "I know if you were my husband ... you would make me happy. I do not care if we never share a bed. You do not need to bed someone to love them..."

I stood there in dumbstruck silence. Everything she was saying registered, and I knew she deserved a response. I just wasn't sure what to say. This woman was pouring her heart out to me, likely because she thought it possible I would be dead in a day. And for the first time, that was beginning to seem like a possibility to me, as well. I'd stared death down the barrel of a cannon or a sword so many times, it was easy to brush it off.

But there was honestly a very good chance that tomorrow, I would no longer exist. Everything, this whole world, everything that made up my consciousness, could be ended with one small lead ball piercing my heart. Whatever misery I'd endured up until this point, any pain or pleasure that was yet to come would cease to be. And where I'd go after that, I had no idea. I'd always found it hard to believe in what the men of the Church said, about the ladder of the afterlife, and how we rose towards heaven with each birth and death. If transcendence was truly earned through living at our given station in life, and following the tenets so we would be born higher in the next, consecutively for countless lives and deaths, until we hit the pinnacle of divine breed ... I was at the bottom of the ladder, currently. I had a long way to go.

And if they were wrong, there was nothing but death beyond, just blackness, earth, and worms. All I had was today, this life, and this one chance.

And right now ... this woman. I hadn't realized how much her happiness hinged on me. The idea of being someone's husband seemed like such a sham, I hadn't even thought it might really mean something to the unfortunate girl involved. I might not have ever considered a woman as a partner in life, but I didn't want to cause pain to her, either. And I did like her. She was intelligent, caring, and a genuinely good person, in a horrible situation. Even if we were never lovers, she needed me.

And in many ways, I needed her. Whatever this was, romantic or not, friendship or something more, perhaps some strange undefined mixture of the two, I did care for the girl. And the thought of leaving her alone in the world, after she'd lost so much of her innocence already, was particularly painful.

She was still looking up at me, helpless and lost. And it was no wonder. She'd just opened her heart to me, and I had given her no response. What she must have been thinking...

I wasn't good at expressing myself through words. I never had been. Action was my strong suit. So that's what I fell back on.

I shifted the paw on her cheek to more firmly cup her jawline, and leaned down to kiss her. I saw her eyes widen at the last moment, but she didn't resist. If anything, I felt her go somewhat limp beneath me, and even if I had no particular carnal interest in a woman, the alpha ego in the back of my mind got a real kick of satisfaction out of that. It had been years since I'd made someone submit with one kiss. Apparently, I hadn't lost my skills.

I lingered longer than I probably should have, to ensure I had made my point. Let no one say I didn't put my all into everything. I was expecting a heel to the back or some kind of grapple hold at any moment, via her father or Cuthbert, but oddly the attack never came.

Instead, the old spaniel spoke up from behind me. "If you're going to kiss my daughter like that, son," he state gruffly, "you need to marry her."

I separated from a now very flush, very hazy-eyed young lady, and turned to regard him, "Provided I survive tomorrow, sir, that's my plan."

"Wrong again, lad." He turned, and retrieved his cane from the end table he'd left it standing against.

Cuthbert only nodded, as though he knew his lord's thoughts, somehow. The way the two communicated without words sometimes was almost eerie. "Shall I perform the service then, sir?"

I arched an eyebrow. "Excuse me?"

Lucius turned and pointed his cane at the both of us. "I had the timing on this very well worked-out, until you pulled this stunt. There was absolutely no rush to marry you two until after the children were born. Now you've gone and ruined that."

"I've done everything you told me to." I insisted. "I took the rap for the pups. I've been your public scapegoat. At worst now, if I die tomorrow, you can pass if off as ... the father of her children meeting an unfortunate end. She can't be blamed for that."

"Why do you constantly believe you know what's best to be done in situations you flagrantly don't understand?" The lord snorted, dismissively. "If you had done everything I *told* you to, you would not have charged downstairs and challenged that man to a duel! If you die tomorrow, Delilah's children are bastards! There was no rush to marry you when I was certain you would be *alive* for the marriage, you fool. The marriage legitimizes the pups, regardless of when they are born. If you *die* before you're married..."

I gave a mortified grimace. "Ah..." I glanced back at Delilah, who was staring down at the carpet, fingers knitted over her swollen belly, nervously. "Well," I cleared my throat, "I suppose this whole ... duel thing was ... a bit of a bad idea."

"You think so?" Lucius virtually spat the words, in angry sarcasm. "Get changed into something *not* covered in Lord Irving's blood and half the dessert cart, please. You are marrying my daughter *tonight*."

"But, how—" I stammered.

"Johannes is a Knight." Lucius sighed, glaring at me even as he turned to start out of the room, "The Knights are a Holy Order. He's ordained."

. . .

The garden was dark, the air damp and cold. I stood on the stone walkway, under a trellis draped in dying rose vines. It was going to be a drab, colorless autumn, too early for the leaves to start turning, but too cold for them to survive. Everything was just dying, and falling off the branch.

I stood staring at the cold pond, and the prone, still bodies of the fish sitting in the leafy matter along the bottom, readying themselves for an early winter. Some of them would probably die, too.

I might die tomorrow. And in half an hour, I was getting married.

I heard Johannes's footsteps, recognized them as his because of the lack of a cane. I stood where I was, letting him approach me.

"Are you ready?" He asked quietly.

"I am." I responded, without turning to face him.

There was just enough silence that I knew he was carefully measuring what he was going to say. Johannes wasn't a dim man, but he also wasn't terribly quick-witted. He tended to take his time in conversations, especially when he was about to say something difficult, for him.

"Luther ... no one is forcing you to do this." He said, "None of this. The duel, the marriage ... you are a free man. I've seen you look to the horse paddock before. I know the look of a man who intends to flee. I've seen enough men go AWOL. I want you to know ... we will not keep you here. If you wish to leave—"

"I'm not running away." I sighed, finally glancing back at him. "You mistake me. I'm not scared of that man. I'm not even frightened of death. If I've any concern, it's that it's no longer only my life on the line when I do things like this. I hate entanglements like this, for exactly this reason. I'd prefer that when I risk my life, it's only *my* life I need worry about. This is too complicated."

"You can't be alone forever, Luther." He spoke in that maddeningly even tone. "Besides which ... I assumed your lone wolf lifestyle was not by choice. You rant and bark in righteous indignation about how you aren't permitted to love as you see fit. What is all that anger for? I assumed you wouldn't be so angry at the social morays that disallow you to be close to a person of your choosing, unless ... you were lonely."

I went quiet at that. I didn't want to admit to myself how right he was.

"Do you not wish to marry, because you don't want that tether to another person?" He questioned. "Because if so, I believe you are too late. You can lie to that young woman all you wish, but I firmly believe what she believes. You did this for her. Class disputes aside. You care about her. And while I'm certain it's not what you want," I snorted at that, but he continued, "I think it's important that you understand, you are not weaker for doing this."

I looked his way at that, curious what he meant.

"By marrying a woman, you aren't letting go of who you are." He stated, leveling his gaze at me. "You aren't letting the Church, society, and every force that has ever demonized what you are, win. You aren't doing this to be what they want you to be. You aren't doing this in some quest to be right in the eyes of God, or to impress your peers ... or even to simply be 'normal'." He looked up at the walls of the large stone house, towards a distant lit window. "You are doing this for one young, desperate girl who needs you. Marriage is a duty for all men. It can be a duty one enjoys, or not, but regardless it is ultimately done for the sake of a woman. To give them the promise and security to raise a family, and be cared for ... in a world where they are often not permitted to care for themselves."

I wrinkled my nose up at his words, hating the way they bounced around in my brain.

"It may not be right, but it is the truth." He looked back down at me, the moonlight reflecting in his grey eyes. "I love my wife. I enjoy being married to her. But I married her because she needed a man to promise her he would be there for her if we were to start a family together. Whatever happiness a man finds in marriage, it is secondary to his wife's happiness. In every other aspect of life, they must respect us ... but in love and marriage, we are their servants."

"This sort of talk reeks of the same kind of Church doctrine that demands I be lashed and tortured until I spit demons out every orifice, just because I fell in love with a man." I bristled. "Women are only helpless and dependent on men because we've *made* them so. Delilah is a strong, intelligent girl. She knows four languages. She knows history. She's even well studied in seafaring, and naval warfare, thanks to her father. But she'll never walk the decks of her family's *own* ships, because she's a woman and some ancient superstition about keeping a woman aboard a naval vessel. It's not right."

"No, it isn't." He conceded. "But it is the world we live in. A day may come where this will all change. Where men like you can love as they wish and Delilah could be an Admiral and inherit her family's fleet. But that is not today. You can only fight so many battles, Luther." He narrowed his eyes. "Sometimes, life is a triage. You need to choose the ones most important, and win those."

I found my eyes drawn up to the window. I wasn't even certain if it was Delilah's, but somewhere inside, she was waiting for me.

I sighed, my ears dropping back. "I haven't even got a ring for her." I murmured.

"Lucius has had a ring ready for your ceremony for months now."

"Fine, but ... it's not from *me*." I insisted. "I have nothing. I am offering her ... nothing. "

"You are offering her yourself."

"That's not exactly much of a gift." I snorted.

"Isn't it?" He quirked an ear. "This is a sacrifice for you. You must know she realizes that. That's why she was so hesitant to tell you what she did today."

"Maybe she just didn't realize she liked me until she realized I might die." I remarked, dryly.

"She did." He spoke with such certainty I knew there had to be more to it. I looked to him. He smiled, just a bit. "You think you're the only one she speaks to in confidence?"

He turned, and put a hand on my shoulder as he strode past. "Delilah likes flowers." He said. "She's never been one for jewelry."

I glanced around in the nearly dead garden. "I-I can't even bring her that. Everything's dead."

He only pointed skyward, as he headed back towards the house. "The climbing roses are more resistant to the cold."

"They're also nowhere near the ground!" I exclaimed, exasperated. But he was gone by the time the words left my mouth, and then I was alone in the dark garden again. I gave a long, ragged sigh. Then I tilted my head upwards slowly, my eyes travelling the expansive stone walls of the manor, until they settled on some of the few surviving white roses, high along the walls of the East Wing's second floor.

I glared at the distant thorny blooms, and rolled up my sleeves.

"What in the hell happened to *that* vest?!" Lucius demanded, as I strode into the now empty great room of his manor, a hand clutched behind the small of my back.

I glanced down at the grey vest I'd donned just an hour before, after Lucius had told me to change. It was now smeared down the front with a heavy coat of dust and green, likely from the moss growing along the manor walls. And I'd apparently snapped loose a button or two. Even Cuthbert was giving me an odd expression, yet with an underlying tiredness to it ... like I'd gone and frustrated him again.

"What's the look for, old chap?" I smirked. "You gave me the idea."

"Where in the hell have you been?!" Lucius interrupted, his tone more than irritated. "You were supposed to be *here*, half an hour ago, marrying my daughter!"

Delilah looked up at me, expectantly and worried. I did my best to give her a comforting, confident smile.

"I was just retrieving something." I hand-waved the old man, "For my fiancé."

"Your lip is bleeding." Delilah suddenly noticed, concerned.

"Oh..." I paused, "Right. There were thorns, and well, it was difficult to climb with one hand holding something, so I held them in my teeth—"

"What, for God's sake?!" Lucius growled, losing his patience.

"Pardon me for attempting to build up suspense." I sighed. "I don't have much to work with, here ... I wanted to at least be dashing about it."

I produced the single rose I'd managed to snag from behind my back, at that. It wasn't on a straight stem, and it wasn't even particularly large or picturesque ... the vine I'd ripped from the wall still had thorns on it, in fact. But I plucked it off the curling green stem so Delilah didn't have to risk the thorns, and reached tentatively over to her. She stared up at me, mouth just slightly open, as I gently tucked it behind the brown curls of fur along one of her ears.

" ... but ... all the flowers in the garden are dead." She murmured, confused.

"It's one of the climbing roses, from along the East Wing's tower wall." I smiled, triumphantly.

"H-how on earth—"

"It wasn't much worse than climbing rigging." I explained with a shrug, not wanting her to know it had in fact been *far* more difficult than that. "I only lost my footing once ... that's, uh ... how I ended up skidding against the wall and ruining my vest."

Lucius just put a hand to his brow, and Cuthbert narrowed his eyes at me. "Luther," he sighed, "for God's sake ... how can a man as intelligent as you be so incredibly stupid?"

"Wh—" I stammered, "you were the one who—"

"I meant for you to go *inside*, climb the stairs to the second story of the East Wing, and find one of the rooms where the roses grew near the *windows*." He whuffed in frustration.

"Oh." I said after a moment. "I ... didn't think of that. I went with the obvious solution."

"Honestly." Johannes closed his eyes and pinched his brow. "Only *you* would think risking your life climbing a slick stone wall for a flower was the obvious solution."

"Hey now," I insisted, "you really can't argue with results—"

I was interrupted by a petite, heavily pregnant spaniel woman throwing her arms around me, and trying very amateurishly to kiss me. I just smirked down at her, wrapped an arm around her waist, and showed her how it was done until she was weak in the legs.

Vaguely, I heard her father clearing his throat, and speaking irately.

"Are we bothering with this marriage, then? Or do you both just enjoy trampling common decency and propriety with these nauseating displays of pre-marital intimacy?"

Cuthbert performed the ceremony that night. Afterwards, Church tradition apparently dictated we share a bed for the night. Neither she nor I were particularly opposed to this, and apparently by this point even Lucius had no concerns over what I'd do to his daughter, because he only threatened my life once before he closed the door behind us.

It wasn't even as awkward as I imagined it would be. Delilah was exhausted. Her servants helped her dress into her sleeping gown before I entered the room and exited once she was settled into bed, leaving me alone with her. She was almost asleep when I settled down next to her, sitting on the edge of the bed.

I reached over and took her hand. She looked up at me, glassy-eyed, and I gave a quiet sigh.

"Please don't cry." I begged, in a low whisper.

"Will you be alive when I wake up?" She asked.

I swallowed. "The duel isn't until sunset. So ... yes."

"Will you be alive when I wake the day following?" She squeezed my hand.

"I ... will do everything in my power to be so." I promised, unable to lie to the woman in that moment.

"I believe in you, Luther." She said quietly. "You can do anything."

I leaned down, and nuzzled her brow. I lingered there a moment, before whispering, "Get some sleep."

She seemed to want to stay awake with me, but her physical condition would not allow it. She was asleep in minutes.

I didn't sleep all night. I sat at her side, staring out the window, and thinking on the day that had passed ... and the life behind it.

If I died tomorrow, would I have any regrets? Almost certainly, but what man could say he had no regrets, when he died?

But would they outweigh the life I'd lived? Had I experienced enough, in the thirty years I'd walked the earth, to say I felt content? I wasn't certain. Maybe every man felt this way when he had a long while to contemplate his death. Every time I'd faced death in the past, it had been a sudden thing. And then when it hadn't come, it was easily dismissed. This was the first time in my life I had the time to really consider it as something that could, and was likely to happen.

I was a miserable shot with a rifle, a miserable shot with a crossbow, and I had never so much as picked up a flintlock in my life. They were weapons for the rich. What the hell had I been thinking, accepting this?

There was a tremble in my chest, like I'd false-started a race and been disqualified. Like none of this was supposed to happen. My finish line was much farther off. I was certain of that. I wasn't supposed to die tomorrow. There was more for me, something in the future that would complete my life, for better or for worse.

I glanced down at the woman sleeping beside me. Maybe it was her. Maybe it was a distant battlefield. Maybe it was another soul, waiting for me. As much as I'd loved Klaus ... and I could say that to myself now, I *had* loved the man ... what we'd had was fated to failure from the start. We found each other out of a mutual need for companionship which rare others could provide, but being with someone simply because there were no other like-minded men around was a poor reason to share your life with someone.

Maybe my future *was* this woman. The idea of a chaste love had never even truly occurred to me, but Delilah's statement was beginning to put me to shame. Why did sex *have* to be part of the equation?

Cuthbert's words haunted me, as well. Giving in, that *is* what this felt like. I was doing everything society and the Church wanted me to do, by marrying a woman, and living a lie. And it *did* feel like defeat. It did feel like I was giving up who I was.

But life is about compromises. Maybe this *is* what I was meant for. Maybe I just needed to swallow my pride, and give some thought to another's welfare above my own. Delilah needed me. I was putting my life on the line for her tomorrow. Perhaps I did love her.

Maybe it was just fear making me feel as though I was meant for more. Or wishful thinking.

At thirty, I was a wreck of a man, both physically and emotionally. What miserable soul would want a man like me?

"Explain it to me once more." I sighed, staring down the sights of the heavy firearm.

"Half-cock the hammer." Cuthbert dictated patiently, and again took the pistol from me, and pulled the hammer back with his thumb to the half-cocked position. "Some hammers require a decent amount of force to cock or half-cock. This gun is old, so ... apply a decent amount of pressure."

I nodded, watching. He took out the powder, and poured it carefully down the barrel. "Watch me." He instructed, strictly. "We haven't any powder charges, so you're going to have to measure by hand. If Irving brings charges, use them ... but he may not. Use precisely this much. Do you need me to show you again?"

"Probably," I admitted. "But let's just fire this thing once."

"Take one of the lead balls." He pointed to the table we'd moved outside. The air was still cold, the sky overcast and dark. It was early morning. "Wrap it in one of those bits of paper." He instructed. "In fact, I'd prep a few before the duel, and keep them on hand."

"Why are we using paper?" I questioned, but did as he said.

"When you ram the bullet down the barrel, the paper will provide a good fit between it and the gunpowder. That's very important." He pulled the ramrod from the long barrel, and loaded the lead ball down, pounding it in, then straightening the flintlock and tipping just a bit more powder into the pan. "Make sure your powder and your pan is dry." He glanced upwards at the overcast sky. "Anything at all ... a stray droplet of dew from a tree, a raindrop, and you're done. Understand?"

"Bad day for this, then," I muttered.

"If we're lucky, you'll both be unable to fire, and they'll call off the duel." He said without missing a beat, and then clicked something on the gun. "That's the frizzen." He explained, and slowly raised the gun towards the tree line. "That's what your flint is going to strike to ignite your powder. Fully cock the hammer," he did so, holding the long-barreled pistol at eye level with one hand, "and fire."

He pulled the trigger, and the cracking boom of the pistol rang through the clearing. A shower of sparks shot up from the fired weapon for a split second, and a cloud of thick white smoke hung in the air. The noise made my ears ring, and shook me in my bones. I'd never been fond of guns. Not even canons. There was something so impersonal about gunpowder, in general.

Cuthbert let his steady arm drop slowly, and placed the weapon back on the table, carefully. He seemed coldly indifferent to the act of firing the weapon, and for a moment, I envied the access he's had to arms training. I'd been trained in very few weapons. Only those fit for low-class militia and navy men. There was no point in training a poor man in a weapon he'd never be able to afford, after all. And they didn't waste good weapons on grunt troops.

Cuthbert wasn't as specialized in some weapons as I was, save his dead-on accuracy with a crossbow, but he knew how to use dozens more. I had a day to learn from him. It wasn't nearly enough, for a weapon this complicated, with so many things that could go wrong.

A sword didn't stop working when it got wet, and it didn't have so many blasted moving parts. This thing could arbitrarily just ... stop working, and I would die before I'd even had a chance to fight back. That thought alone was infuriating.

"Luther." Cuthbert broke my reverie. "Stop glaring at the gun, and show me you can fire it."

"Right," I murmured, picking the weapon up. Out of the corner of my eye, I saw a window open on the second floor of the house, and a silhouette standing in stark contrast against candlelight, in the dim grey of the early morning. I didn't even have to look closely to know it was Delilah. The gunshot must have woken her up.

I narrowed my eyes, and went for my powder.

"What are you forgetting?" Cuthbert asked me, strictly.

I thought back hard on the lesson from a few moments ago, and then nodded. "Right ... cock the hammer."

"Half cock it." He showed me again, pressing his thumb on mine to show me how. "This part ought to be easy for you, Luther ... you're prone to going off half-cocked often enough."

I gave a smirk, flashing canines. "Thanks. I'll remember that."

Irving arrived with this 'Judge' almost precisely an hour before sunset. I'd spent most of the day firing that blasted weapon, with a sizable amount of failed firings, and the weather was only getting worse as it got later.

The most troubling part, though, was how long it took to reload the weapon. Cuthbert had tried working with me on my speed, but every time I tried to reload it quickly I'd pour too little or too much powder, not pack it tightly enough, or it wouldn't light because I'd been careless with the powder in the pan. It took ages to load the damned thing and my accuracy was beyond bad. I had enough trouble hitting my targets with a crossbow, and they fired where you *wanted* them to.

My only hope was that Irving would miss too, and it would take him just as long to reload. Cuthbert had merely been quiet, when I'd voiced that hope.

At five o'clock or so, two hours before the intended duel, the wolfhound had told me there wasn't much more to be gained from practice for me and that my time might be better spent having dinner with my wife. I took that as a bad sign.

We'd done our best not to let on about our concerns over dinner with the family. Truthfully, I hadn't much in the way of an appetite, but I picked at the meal and held my wife's hand the whole while. If I was frightened, she was terrified. She was shaking the entire hour. I didn't know what to do for her.

When I strode out onto the lawn to meet Irving and the tall, stern greyhound he'd brought with him, it was almost a relief. The spaniel looked as much the pompous bastard as he'd been the night before, although I noted with some satisfaction that his cheek was swollen.

The greyhound with him was dressed in robes that almost marked him as part of the clergy, but the colors were wrong. Church men wore nothing but black. These were grey, and a bit more formal. Government man, I imagined. Perhaps an actual Judge from the local court system, I wasn't sure exactly what sort of people oversaw these things.

It hardly mattered. I stood waiting for them in the yard, Cuthbert at my side. Lucius was several paces behind us, and with him was Delilah. I'd fought her as hard on the matter as I felt I was entitled to, but she'd absolutely insisted on bearing witness to the damned duel. She'd claimed something about it being her right, as my wife. I suspected that legally, she was right, but I wish to God the woman had just listened to me. This wasn't anything she needed to see, regardless of how it ended.

As it was, Irving noticed her almost immediately, and the slim smile of satisfaction he gave upon seeing her bulging belly made me nauseous and angry all at once. The nausea I could live without, but the anger, I was glad for. I felt my hackles rising, and did nothing to quell the rage building inside me.

"Delilah, darling," Irving spread his arms, as he climbed the hill towards us. I saw her recoil at his words, shifting closer to her father. He put an arm around her protectively, and I swear I thought I heard him crack the handle of his cane in a tightening fist. Irving only chuckled. "Don't you look pretty, all swollen up. Looks like a litter, eh? Two? Three?"

"Shut your mouth, scum." The words came from Lucius just a second before I was about to say something even less polite. The man's teeth were pressing together so tightly, I could hear them grinding from here.

"And kindly take your eyes off my wife." I commanded, dropping my ears and flashing him a snarl of my own.

He only arched an eyebrow at that. "Oh?" He paused and then chuckled. "I see. Married her last night, did you? What, did the islander there perform the ceremony for you?" He gestured to Cuthbert, and chuckled again, before his smile disappeared into a bitter frown. "Disgraceful." He literally spat, at that, "Your whole house, your name, your fleet, Denholme ... all of it. You're a disgrace. And your daughter's a disgrace now, too. You can have her. I've no further interest in that filthy whore."

"Say that again, Irving!" I roared across the otherwise silent hilltop at him. "Give me an excuse! I'll kill you, duel or no! They can drag me off to hang! I would die a happy man knowing I took you with me!"

He gave a derisive laugh, which I suspect covered an air of nervousness. So the man *was* afraid.

Good.

"Where the hell did you dig this dreg up, Denholme?" He gestured at me. "He's—"

"Are you going to keep talking, or are we going to get on with this?!" I demanded. "Your fear is showing, Irving!"

He glared at me, then crisply turned and snapped at the greyhound beside him, who calmly strode to the center of the grassy hill. Irving followed him. I noticed for the first time that he was carrying a black leather case. I headed towards the two men. When I reached them, the Judge stepped between the two of us and opened the leather case. Inside were two pistols unlike Cuthbert's personal pistol. These were new, well-polished, and a matched set.

And something else was wrong.

I stared down at the unfamiliar weapons, confused. Finally, I looked up at Irving, who was barely covering a smug expression. I glared, and angrily exclaimed, "These aren't flintlocks, you bastard!"

"What?" I heard both Cuthbert and Lucius intone in unison, from behind me. Moments later, Cuthbert was striding up the hill to join us, and when he reached the gathering, he looked down into the case.

"Percussion pistols?" he took hold of one of the weapons and lifted it, inspecting it. At length, he stared down the barrel at Irving, and grated out, "These were not the agreed-upon weapons for this duel."

"I said dueling pistols, did I not?" Irving lifted an eyebrow.

"You—" I began, but was cut off by Cuthbert, who was managing to keep a civil tone, despite the situation.

"You specifically stated flintlock pistols. I was present in the room when you said it."

"Did I?" Irving smirked as well as he could with his swollen jaw. "I'm sorry, I'd entirely forgotten. I suffered a rather bad blow to the *head* that night, you see." He curled a lip at me.

"These are incredibly rare firearms." Cuthbert growled. "Why would you specifically bring these over flintlock pistols? Flintlocks are the standard."

"And horribly inefficient in damp weather," Irving looked skyward. "It's been threatening rain all day. I had these weapons, and they are far more accurate and not nearly so inconvenienced by weather. They were the logical choice."

"Then you should have stated they were your choice yesterday!" Cuthbert raised his voice, for the first time. Irving's attitude was even getting to him.

"What difference would it have made if I had?" Irving narrowed his eyes, knowingly. "Would you have had one in your worn-down old manor to train the boy on, in a day's time?"

"This *is* grounds for annulling the duel." The Judge finally spoke up, and I noted that he bore a hint of annoyance at the situation, too. Well, at least he wasn't in Irving's pocket.

"That's what we'll be doing." Cuthbert ground out angrily.

"Have it your way." Irving snorted. "This whole thing was ridiculous from the outset. Besides..." he looked past me for some reason, and it took me a moment to realize he was looking at Delilah again. "There's nothing worth fighting over, anymore."

He began to head back down the hill, at that.

"The duel is on." I snapped.

Irving stopped in mid-stride. "Excuse me?" He said with what I was certain was a nervous pause, this time.

"You heard me." I snarled. "I issued this duel ... I say whether it's on or not. And it's on. I accept your terms."

Irving looked at me disbelievingly for a time, until the Judge interrupted the silence on the hilltop. "Very well," He spoke evenly. "Terms have been accepted by both parties. This duel will commence in five minutes." He looked between the both of us. It satisfied me some to see the worry evident on Irving's features.

"Ready yourselves." The judge said, before offering the case again.

I took one of the pistols. After the few moments it took him to realize he had no other way out, Irving took the other. And then I turned to join Cuthbert, and headed down the hill with him. He was oddly silent.

"I was expecting a lot more screaming from you," I admitted, "Something with the word 'fool' thrown in a few dozen times."

"I understand why you're doing this." He stated simply, if grimly. "I only wish I was in your place." He glanced down at me. "I am also assuming you have a plan."

"Coming up with one as I go..." I murmured. When we reached the bottom of the hill, I looked the gun over. It was nothing like the flintlock, at least not on any of the parts that mattered for loading. Cuthbert gave it a long look, as well ... before turning to Lucius.

"Sir, can you—"

"Give it here." The old man reached a paw out, and took both the pistol, and the small bag they'd given us with its bullets, powder, and some kind of cap, which he began carefully applying over the end of a metal nipple on the hammer. I watched, mystified ... and so did Cuthbert.

"Good God." I glanced at him. "Even you don't know how to fire this thing?"

"They're a Carvecian design ... and an extremely new one, at that." Cuthbert sighed. "I've heard of them, even seen them fired once or twice ... there's talk they're the new revolution in firearms, but I've never fired one myself."

"I find it hard to believe the Carvecians have revolutionized *anything*." I snorted.

"Say what you will about Colonists," Lucius interrupted, half-cocking back the hammer on the gun, "they know their guns. Here," he handed me the gun, and I took it gingerly. "Watch the cap, make sure it doesn't fall off. There's no pressure against it at the moment."

"Why not just fully cock the hammer, then?"

"These models will fire if you strike the hammer even accidentally." He explained. "Keep it half-cocked and level until you're ready to fire, and then make sure you cock it before you pull the trigger. You'll only have the one shot, Luther." He warned, quietly. "Once the duel begins, I cannot load it for you again. I hope you know what you're doing."

"I'm going to kill that man." I stated resolutely, "One way or another." I turned to look up at the hill, where Irving was beginning to walk towards the Judge again. I turned back to Lucius. "Thank you for loading this for me. But if all goes well, even the one shot I have won't matter."

"Excuse me?" Lucius blinked.

"Luther?" I heard Delilah's quiet, terrified voice, and saw her timidly approaching me from the tree she'd been standing near. I closed the distance between us, and wrapped an arm around her waist, kissing her brow, softly. She looked up at me, and then down at the paw I wasn't holding the pistol with. She took it, and placed it over her belly.

I could feel the restless little creatures inside her again, and I smiled, despite myself.

"We're all scared." She said, her eyes watering just a little, but stopping short of tears. She was being so strong.

"I'll see you when this is over." I promised her, and the little ones beneath my paw.

The Judge was sounding down the last thirty seconds we had to prepare, so with more difficulty than I'd ever thought I would have, I pulled myself away from my wife and headed up the hill. Every step sped my heartbeat, and the pistol in my paw felt like it was beginning to burn.

"Rules of the Duel are as follows!" The Judge began, as I stepped onto the level ground at the top of the hill and stared across the yellowing grass at my opponent. The sun was dropping below the horizon, casting his figure in stark silhouette.

"Opponents must fire simultaneously on the first shot, at the count of ten!" The Judge continued. "Opponents must fire their weapons from twenty paces apart! Opponents may not employ any other form of weapon but the chosen weapon! If ye are both prepared, say aye."

"Aye," I spoke first. Irving followed a moment later, and I liked to imagine I heard a tremble in his voice.

The Judge began to count down. As he did, Cuthbert's words from earlier in the day rang out in my mind. Stand facing your opponent with your side to them. It provides a slimmer target, and protects your heart. Irving was facing me. It would probably increase his aim, but I suppose in his case, he couldn't provide a slimmer target no matter how he stood.

My aim hardly mattered, so I did as Cuthbert had said, and stood with my pistol arm out, my body turned to the side. And I braced myself, and tried to aim, anyway.

"*Nine ... Ten*!" The judge's final words rung out across the clearing, and I heard the crack of Irving's gun moments before I pulled my own trigger.

All but instantly, my world exploded in pain, and I staggered back from the streak of fire that had pounded its way through the side of my shoulder, into my chest. My vision went white for a second or more, and I felt the stinging heaviness in my limbs and the spiraling darkness in my brain that signaled I was about to pass out.

I fought it. I fought it with everything I had, shaking myself violently to stave it off. Not now. *Not yet.*

I had never felt pain like this before. My body was on *fire*, and something was very, very wrong with my arm. It hung limp at the shoulder like a rag doll. I could also tell I was bleeding ... a lot. I was wounded, possibly mortally. I could feel the blood spilling down my arm, coating my paw. And I could hear Delilah screaming my name.

The fact that I had remained standing seemed to be taking Irving by surprise, although to be entirely honest, my vision was beginning to blur, so it was hard to entirely make him out. I knew at least that I had not hit him. Not surprising.

This next part would have been easier if the bastard hadn't hit me on the first shot.

"Judge!" I rasped, closing one eye to try and get some focus back to my vision. "I can't ... fire ... from less than twenty paces ... right?!" I demanded, sucking in a few short pants between the flashes of pain.

“That’s ... correct,” He answered, clearly not so blasé about this practice that he couldn’t still be bothered by a man covered in blood and likely dying.

“I can’t *fire* from less than twenty paces?!” I demanded once more. “And ... I have to ... use this weapon ... to kill him?”

“Yes. Correct.” He replied, in a clipped tone, clearly confused as to why I was asking him questions when the other man was likely reloading.

I snarled, and leaned down to pick up the pistol with my remaining good hand. And I bolted as fast as my legs could carry me across the space between myself and Irving. As I got closer, my blurred vision improved enough that I caught him at the tail end of loading his weapon. He looked up in shock as he realized I was just a few feet from him, and raised the pistol to fire.

But this time, he was panicked, and he’d forgotten to entirely cock the hammer. He tried to fire, and failed, and I was on him.

The first pistol whip I leveled at him caught him right across the jaw I’d damaged the day before, and this time, I heard more than his teeth crack. He toppled over, crashing to the ground, clutching at his face and giving an agonized scream. I dropped to my knees over him, straddling his prone body and flipping the pistol in my hand to grip it by the barrel. It was still hot and it seared into my paw pads, but I didn’t care.

I brought the heavy butt of the weapon down on his skull, with every ounce of strength I had in my body. His head shuddered with the blow, and he bucked beneath me, wailing and shoving frantically at me. But I dug my knees down into his shoulders, kept him pinned, and wound back my uninjured arm to strike him across the skull once more.

This time, the gun came back bloody, and his screaming turned to a terrified, piteous gurgle. His face was chopped meat ... I hardly knew what I was hitting anymore. But I brought the gun down again, and again, and again ... endlessly. Until all I could smell, hear and see was blood, and screaming.

I'm not even sure how long it took me to realize Irving had gone limp, and the screaming was my own.

Cuthbert and Lucius joined the unnerved greyhound at the hilltop, the three men looking on the scene of carnage playing out before them with mixed expressions. The Judge spoke, at length, although there was a tremble in his voice.

"I-I am not certain this is ... entirely within the spirit of the rules, for this tradition..."

"If you'd like to explain that to him, you can be my guest." Lucius regarded the judge without turning his eyes away from the scene. The greyhound was silent another long moment, before clearing his throat.

"I suppose, considering the discrepancy with the guns ... I am willing to provide your man a little leeway."

"Good call." Cuthbert muttered, before being the first to approach the bloody cattle dog. He'd gone silent finally, hunkered over the dead spaniel lord ... whose face would at this point be unrecognizable even to his closest family when his body was inevitably returned to them.

"Luther."

I heard my name, distantly. Or maybe ... perhaps ... close. It was so hard to tell. Everything echoed and shimmered like I was hearing and seeing it through water. White spots had begun to punctuate my vision, blanking out entire features in the wolfhound's face. I stared up at him, trying to remember if I knew him.

He put a hand on my shoulder, then leaned down and moved the other beneath my good arm, pulling me up from locked knees and doing a sizable amount of the work in standing for me. He grunted as he nearly carried me down the hill. For some reason, I was reminded of a man who'd helped me from a cell, not so long ago.

" ... Johannes?" I stumbled, trying to blink back the fog from my eyes.

"Stay with me, Luther. Please. Your wife—"

He stopped speaking and walking at that, and I felt him go stiff.

Out of the corner of my vision, I thought I saw Lucius drop his cane on his way down the hill, and break into a run. I wondered vaguely what in the hell could possibly make the old codger run on that lame leg of his...

...and then I saw the woman, crumpled against the tree she'd been standing near. A pained whine left her, so I knew she must have been conscious, but she had collapsed on the ground and was curled up, moaning. Her father fell to her side as soon as he got to her, trying to gather the young woman up into his arms. As he did, I saw the stains on her dress.

My world snapped back into focus all at once, like my heart had restarted. I struggled against Johannes, but even if my mind was trying desperately to obey me, my legs were still failing.

"Please ... I need to be with her!" I begged.

"You need to see a physician. *Now,*" Johannes put his entire back into it and began dragging me across the yard, towards the house.

"She's going into labor!" I cried out.

"I'm aware." He grit out, half carrying me as my vision once more began to blacken.

"It's too ... soon..." I moaned, breathlessly.

"I know." He murmured worriedly.

CHAPTER 8

LIFE

Broad, calloused paw pads moved over the dense, sharp scruff along the back of my neck, making my skin prickle. I kept my eyes closed and stretched my body out over top the warm, soft fur of my bed partner. It had taken me some time to grow accustomed to the way his body could swallow mine, and while beneath it I still felt overpowered and unnerved, atop it he made for the most comfortable mattress. Even if he'd taken to the Pedigree lifestyle like a duck to the desert, he'd not skimped on taking care of himself, and his beautiful white fur was always a pleasure to feel against my own coarse, freckled hide.

I buried my nose against his chest, inhaling slowly. He smelled like rope fibers, wood, and the pine soap he always insisted upon having on hand. If his scent were the only one I smelled for the rest of my life, I thought, I'd be content.

"Luther." His chest rumbled beneath me, and I kept my eyes closed. He didn't need to know I was awake. Not yet.

His paw settled on my shoulder and oddly, he shook me. I gave an irate noise and burrowed further down into his fur, trying to make it obvious that I was not yet ready to rise. Admiral or no, he wasn't getting me up until I was ready.

"Luther." He spoke more sternly, and the inflection of his voice sounded odd. Too low, and with something akin to an accent on the last syllable of my name, "You need to wake up." He spoke in that strangely deep voice, again. Klaus had some bass in his voice, but not like this.

I finally opened my eyes and tipped my head to the side just enough that I could look into those dark black eyes. Grey stared back at me, and everything about his features was wrong. My vision began to blur.

"Klaus ... ?" I blinked, dizzily.

"Luther," he responded, his brows knitted. "Please wake. Your wife is dying."

I rolled over onto my back, sucking in a gasp and groaning. The world spun and burned up into white spots, then abruptly snapped back into focus. I felt like I was staring straight into the sun, as the intensity of the light in the room momentarily blinded me.

"Draw the shades." I heard that voice say again, and I fisted a hand in the sheets, my body tensing and twisting in ways I knew I wasn't commanding it to. My nerves felt on fire and my muscles wouldn't obey me. Everything from the waist up on my left side was in knots and I couldn't move my arm, but the rest of my body was moving against my will, jumping against the sheets I was entangled in. I'd never felt something so physically terrifying, and beyond my control.

"I told you we shouldn't have woken him this soon." Another voice said hurriedly, before I felt two hands pinning me down by the chest on either side, holding me down as the last of the spasms finally began to die off. I panted and twisted my head around frantically, trying to make sense of everything around me, and why my body felt as though I'd been slain and brought back to life.

Where was Klaus? Who were—

The other man, a wolfhound, came into my field of vision. He belonged to one of the sets of paws holding me down. A name pounded at the back of my brain. Johannes.

It all came rushing back at once. The duel. I'd been shot. I'd killed that bastard. I'd been taken off by Johannes, as—

"Delilah..." I croaked, finding my throat caked with something coppery and dry.

The wolfhound looked relieved at that and slowly let up the pressure on my chest. I saw another man, a black lab in a bloodstained vest and gloves, looking down on me as well. He still looked concerned. He turned to regard Johannes, speaking quietly. "You really must be extremely careful not to excite him, or he may seize again and tear the stitches, or worse. It would have been safer to keep him unconscious ... he'll be in a lot of pain..."

"He would have wanted me to wake him." Johannes insisted, somberly, and then looked down on me. "Luther. Are you with me, sir?"

"Where ... is ... Delilah?" I asked, feeling cracks along my jowls, like I'd bitten at myself.

"I'm afraid she is not doing well, sir." The wolfhound responded. I had quite literally never seen the man so disheveled. His vest was unbuttoned, for God's sake. His eyes were red, as though he hadn't been sleeping, and his fur was limp and uncombed. "I thought it prudent you be awoken ... in case you wished to see her once more."

I tried to push myself up to a sitting position, but using my shoulder in *any* way at the moment was not happening. A bolt of pain hit me the second I put any weight on my nearly limp left arm, and I cried out and fell back the few inches I'd managed.

"H-how long ... have I ... been out?" I grated out between grit teeth, closing my eyes as my body screamed at me, trying to avoid slipping back into that nameless, confused state from before.

"Over twenty hours now." Johannes informed me.

"Twenty ... hours?" I opened my eyes, staring at the ceiling. Delilah had been ... in labor ... for twenty hours? "What is happening to her?" I demanded, although my voice lacked any real strength, try as I might.

"Delilah delivered a healthy pup twelve hours ago, sir." He told me. "You have a son."

I stared at the ceiling, trying to wrap my head around that. It wasn't my son. It was Irving's son. The man I'd just killed. I'd known that would be the case for months now. But something about the words still floored me. What had a merely been a concept before now was a ... person. A living, breathing creature, and as far as he would ever know, I *was* his father.

But if that was the case, then why—

"The second child is breeched." Johannes answered my unspoken question. "They have been trying, without success, to turn it for nearly half a day now. Delilah is growing weaker. It cannot go on much longer..."

My eyes widened at the very real sadness in his tone. He meant every word he said. Johannes earnestly believed that Delilah was dying. And that man was not one to give up easily.

I knew nothing about birth, except that it very often killed the mother, the child, or both, either before or after the actual delivery. I didn't know why, or how. But Delilah wasn't going to face this alone. Regardless of the outcome, I needed to be there with her.

"Johannes." I took as much air into my lungs as I could, trying to breathe past the pain. "Please take me to her."

"Please, sir." The lab leaned into my field of vision. "I only just finished extracting a ball of lead from your shoulder not ... four hours ago. You've lost an immense amount of blood, and your body has been in and out of shock all day. I've drained the worst of the fluids from you, but now your body needs to recover—"

"Take me to my wife!" I demanded as loudly as I could, but it came out hoarse and weak.

The both of them were silent, and the lab looked away from me, running a gloved hand up over the crown of his head. At length, it was Johannes who spoke.

"I'll help you walk, sir."

They'd sequestered me in one of the servants' rooms downstairs, likely because it had been the closest to the door. The journey up the stairs was excruciatingly painful, not only because my legs would barely obey me, but because every step shook my torso and sent a bolt of pain through the hole in my shoulder. I vaguely heard the physician following us, informing me of my injuries, and begging again that I return to rest. I had a broken collarbone, a possible infection, and massive blood loss.

None of it mattered. Delilah could be dead by the time I made it upstairs. One foot after another. Three steps left...

I heard a door close as we reached the top of the stairs. Lucius stepped out into the hallway, as disheveled as Johannes, if not more so. His expression only made me heighten my pace.

He noticed us when we were a door down, and tipped his ears up, striding the last few paces towards us with a minor hint of relief in his features. "Luther!" He exclaimed, his voice hoarse and worn. He put a hand out, placing it on my good shoulder. The fact that I was entirely shirtless didn't seem to matter to the man so hung up on propriety, at the moment.

"Good God man ... you shouldn't be walking." He gave me a long look, and then sighed. "But it's good to see you up, regardless. You had us very worried for a while there, while the surgeon was working on you. I thought I'd be losing my son-in-law for certain."

"He *still* should not be moving!" The physician insisted, irritably. "If he seizes standing, he'll do even more damage to himself."

I barely heard the conversation that followed. My eyes fell to Lucius's beltline, and an object of immediate interest to me. I pulled past Johannes's grip on my shoulder to grab at the flask, easily pulling it away from the spaniel lord, before he'd even realized what I was going for.

"I ... ah," Lucius paused. "You could have just asked, man." He gave a narrowed glare at the physician, as I pulled the cap off with my teeth, and drank. "I told you to get him some whiskey as soon as he woke. The man's in pain, for God's sake!"

"He *certainly* shouldn't be drinking!" The physician groaned.

"You scholars think you know everything. Navy medicine always suited me just fine." Lucius growled. "Man knows what he needs ... let him be."

I finished off what was left in the flask which unfortunately wasn't that much. Lucius had clearly been going pretty hard on it. I could smell it on him, and it only made me more in fear for Delilah's life.

"Delilah—" I started, as Lucius took the flask back from me, and Cuthbert helped me up by the shoulder again, steadying my legs. Damn this blood loss ... I felt like I was moving through water, and my vision wouldn't clear. The pain was starting to fade beneath the welcoming haze of the alcohol burning its way down my throat, though, and that was a relief.

"They are attempting to turn the child again. I was asked to leave ... it's a delicate procedure." Lucius said, his eyes sparing a fleeting glance back towards the doorway. "Delilah is..." he took a moment to steady his voice, " ... very tired. She hasn't much strength left in her. This will likely be the last attempt they make."

"What happens if this try fails, as well?" Cuthbert asked, and there was an actual tremble in his voice. I couldn't see his face over my shoulder, but there was a weakness in his tone I'd rarely if ever heard before.

Lucius was silent for some time.

"If the pup is left as it is, both the mother and the child will die." He finally murmured. "That is what the physician says. The midwife has explained this to Delilah..." He was again silent for far too long, and I stomped a foot, weakly.

"Tell me what's happening to my wife, damn it!" I demanded.

Lucius turned to regard me, specifically. "She wants them to cut the child out of her."

I felt Johannes's chest fall behind me, like some invisible weight had slammed into him. "What are her chances of surviving—"

"She will not." Lucius stated, quietly.

The silence that fell over the hallway was smothering. I shook where I stood, and I wasn't certain anymore if it was from blood loss. I felt Johannes's presence behind me, and his arm around me felt more like comfort than physical support. His physical proximity was all I had holding me up in the world, but it struck me that it went deeper than that.

For that moment, due chiefly to my injuries, the straight-laced man was embracing me, and no one could fault us or shame us for it.

The silence was punctuated by the one and only person that mattered in that moment, Delilah. She was screaming. It would honestly have been more encouraging if she'd screamed louder, but the noise we heard was more a piteous, whimpering moan. It tore at my insides.

I pulled at Cuthbert, and stumbled towards the door. Lucius wrenched my hand away from the doorknob, trying to block me, and I found much to my dismay that he was. I was too weak to overpower the older dog.

"I know what you're feeling!" He insisted, desperately. "But the physician must be allowed to work. He insisted they needed to work on her—"

We were both shocked when the door suddenly opened inwards, sending much of my weight falling forward. I felt Cuthbert grab at me in the last moment, keeping me standing. An alarmed young rat in a stained maid's outfit stood at the open doorway, looking between us all. I could hear Delilah more clearly now, crying.

"The ... physician wanted me to relay the situation to you, sir." She said to Lucius over my shoulder.

"What's going on?!" Lucius shoved the door entirely open, and stepped in past me. "I thought turning the child wasn't supposed to hurt her..."

"No, sir," the rat shook her head. "Only ... the turning was successful, this time."

I felt the air shift in the room, saw both Lucius and Cuthbert's expressions grow hopeful, but the rat was still wiping her hands worriedly on her smock and she still seemed scared.

"She is in labor again." She spoke, looking over her shoulder once, then back to us. Beyond her, all I could see was the curtained-off-area where Delilah and the physician and midwife must have been. Men weren't permitted to bear witness to a woman giving birth.

I turned back to the rat. "Then what's wrong?" I pressed.

"She is very weak, sir." The rat dropped her brown eyes to the floor. "It's still very possible she will not be able to deliver the pup ... and very likely the pup was ... damaged."

I pushed past the woman at that. I heard her protests, and Lucius yelling my name at me, but it didn't register. I shoved aside the curtains, and staggered towards the sound of my wife.

The scent of blood hit me first, the smell of hers mixing with my own. The poor, small woman was tangled in bloodstained blankets on her bed, an older vulpine woman wetting a bloodstained rag in a bowl of warm water. The sheets were pushed up around Delilah's legs, and a hound with his stained shirtsleeves pushed up around his biceps had his hands beneath them, gaze fixed there until I stumbled into the scene. At which point they were both, of course, looking to me. Delilah barely looked conscious ... I wasn't certain if she even realized I was there. I'd never seen a woman ... or any person ... in such obvious pain, before. It made my stomach churn.

The Vulpine woman squeezed out the rag in her bloody hands, her muzzle twitching in concern. "And wot might you be doin' 'ere?" She questioned, before standing, tiredly.

"I'm guessing the husband." The man, likely the physician, murmured. He'd fixed his gaze back on Delilah. "Bryce was treating him."

"Oy!" The Vulpine woman smacked me in the abdomen with

the bloody cloth, and I stared at her, gape-jawed at her audacity. She didn't seem deterred, she got right up into my face before yelling, "Ye couldn't'a thought offa bettah' time t'go gettin' in a fight?!" She wiped the cloth over her arms, cleaning them, before muttering " ... men..." and wandering back over to the other side of the bed.

" ... Luther?" I heard Delilah's voice, finally. It was weak and quiet, but it was the greatest relief I'd had since I'd woken up. I stumbled over towards her, and kneeled beside the bed, reaching my good hand out to brush my paw pads lightly over her cheek. She looked so tired...

I was rewarded with a pained, exhausted smile when she saw me. Her normally bright, round chocolate eyes were mere slits, reddened and dull. I brushed my thumb gently over one of her soft brown ears, and she closed her eyes a moment. What began as a wince suddenly increased to a whine, and she tensed.

"You're going to have to try harder, dear." The physician murmured. "We aren't making any progress."

"Ain't you Pedigrees got somethin' against seeing a woman like this?" The midwife muttered in that same annoyed tone.

"Let him stay." The physician said. "He can't do any harm." The speckled old hound looked back up at me. "If you can, sir ... impress upon her that she *must* push, with whatever strength she has left. Even if the child is dead, we need to remove it, and I'd really rather not use the clamps in the case the pup is still alive. But... I will have to, if this goes on much longer..."

"Luther..." Delilah moaned, and I felt her hand reaching for mine. I shifted my paw to hold hers, and gave it a tight squeeze, looking down into her eyes.

"I know you're tired, Delilah." I spoke quietly, but furtively. "But ... the hardest part is over. The doctors have done their job. This child depends on you, now. Only you have the strength, and the ability, to do this."

She looked up at me, desperately. I laced my fingers through hers, and leaned down, pressing my muzzle against her soft cheek, and whispering.

"Fight, you need to fight." I closed my eyes, as a wave of weakness hit me, and I pushed it back. "Please." I begged. "I love you."

She whimpered and I squeezed her hand, tighter. "Don't leave me alone with our children ... they need you." I murmured. "I need you."

She tensed suddenly, and screamed. I held her hand, but was powerless to do anything more. I'd never felt so helpless in my entire life.

This repeated more times than I could count, and her screaming grew more intense, tears leaking endlessly down her cheeks. My own injury screamed at me and I felt as though my pain paled in comparison, but there was a kinship there that I'd felt before, with men in the navy. Being in pain together had always felt less hopeless, somehow ... like you were all but certain to survive and endure, because another soul was joining you in the agony.

At length, I heard what I suspect everyone around Delilah, and everyone waiting in the doorway, had been hoping and praying for, the low, unmistakable whimpering of a puppy.

Delilah's head fell, breath escaping her lungs in a gasp. I leaned over her, heedless of my shoulder, and pressed my forehead to hers, brushing my hand through the soft, curling fur along her ears.

" ... good girl," I whispered. All I got from her was a soft whimper. I stroked her cheek, gently.

"Alright, now ye gotta git out." The vulpine rapped me on the shoulder ... thankfully my good one, but none-too-gently, all the same. In the time it took me to stand, shakily, she'd managed to make it over to me, and shove me away from the bed. "Git now, I said!" She snapped.

My eyes met Delilah's once more before I was pushed past the curtain.

The waiting felt like an eternity. The physician treating me had gone inside to tend to Delilah and the pups, but that had been ... it felt like *hours* ago, and we three men had been marooned outside the door once more.

Lucius had at the very least summoned a servant to bring more whiskey. And it was testament to how bad things were that even Johannes took a swig or two. I swear, Lucius finished half the flask ... and he was *still* wearing a path in the carpet from pacing. The rhythmic sound of footfalls punctuated by cane tap was the only noise in the hallway.

When the door finally opened, I was dismayed to see it was the vulpine midwife who opened it. She immediately crinkled up her greying muzzle at us.

"Smells like a damned brewery out 'ere. Ye all sober 'nuff?"

"We're fine." Lucius growled, impatiently. "What about my daughter, and my grandchildren?!"

She gave him a sour look. "All livin'. The lady's gotta be on bed rest for a few months, but she oughta' get on fine once she's got 'er strength back."

The tension finally began to flood out of the air at that, and I saw Lucius and Cuthbert's shoulders visibly unwind. The vulpine woman stepped forward, and put a hand out in Lucius's direction. "You wanna see th'pups ... y'lose the poison." He blinked at her, confused, and after a moment she sighed, and just took the flask out of his hand.

By that point, I'd crept past her into the room. I heard her grumbling something about navy men being slovenly drunks, but my attention was pulled immediately towards one corner of the room as soon as I entered. The rat, a maid I now had enough lucidity to remember was named Adele, and one of Delilah's personal servants, was standing over a bundled mess of blankets in a long basket resting near the foot of the bed. Delilah looked to be asleep ... I could see her breathing, thank God ... and the physician was cleaning some rags in a bloody water bin.

There was whining coming from the basket.

Adele looked up in time to see me slowly making my way across the room. She smiled wearily at me ... she'd probably been up for over a day now, so I hardly blamed her. "Would you like to see them, sir?" She asked, keeping her voice low.

I took the last few steps to the bedside, peering down hesitantly into the basket. All I could make out at first were two bundles, and two very small, fuzzy noses just barely peeking out from beneath the blankets. I gingerly reached down to shift the small blue blanket aside with one claw.

No battle, no enemy, no challenge in warfare could prepare me for that moment. Every personal strife I'd endured, defeated and riled against paled in comparison to the immense weight of responsibility and fulfillment that suddenly fell upon me, all at once.

The pups were ... absolutely perfect. They didn't appear damaged, in any way. They seemed small to me, but admittedly, I didn't know pups well ... Their fur was fine and thin, their ears and paws impossibly small, their eyes closed. They were white and liver-colored, like their mother ... speckled and spotty along their tiny muzzles and paws, just like her.

They were alive. And they were my responsibility now. I'd quite literally taken their real father away from them. These were my children ... no matter how they'd come into the world.

"A little girl and a boy," Adele said with a smile. "They look so much like their mother..."

I heard the distinctive tap of Lucius's cane, but I couldn't avert my eyes from the pups. I felt him leaning over my shoulder, though.

"Thank God for that." He murmured.

Johannes was at my other side a few seconds later, and we all stood in silence, and looked down at the little whimpering balls of fur. I was frozen in place. I didn't know what to do, or say, or—

"Sir?" Adele's voice caught my attention, and I saw her leaning in from the corner of my eye. "Would you like to hold them?"

"I-" I stammered, "I-I only have ... the one arm..."

"They don't weigh much, sir." Adele smiled. "But I'll help you, if you'd like."

She reached down, and lifted one of the pups ... it looked like the little girl, wrapping her up in another small blanket as she did. I extended my right paw before I knew what I was doing, and she slowly, gingerly settled the pup down into my hold. I held the babe above me for just a moment, watching as her small paw clutched blindly at me.

"Lean her against your chest." Adele offered. I heeded her words and did so, settling the little creature against my good shoulder. There, she proceeded to nestle into the scruff along my neck, burying her nose in my fur and whimpering.

" ... oh, hell." I murmured, defeated.

"I warned you." Lucius arched an eyebrow, barely covering a slight smirk.

"Don't take it as a weakness, sir." Cuthbert spoke from the other end of the bed, his grey eyes assessing the scene. It was always hard to tell, with the moustache of fur along his jowls, but I could tell just from the angle of his eyes that he was smiling. "We can be men of the world and warriors all, and still be fathers. Just try not to let her wrap you around her finger, or you're truly lost."

"I resent that statement." Lucius scoffed.

"Has Delilah named her?" I questioned quietly, letting the little pup nestle firmly into my neck scruff. My head was swimming, trying to tackle the sudden influx of complex emotions this was all stirring up inside me. I was overwhelmed. I wasn't ready for this ... I wasn't going to be worth a damn as a father...

"Brook, after her grandmother," Lucius stated. "At least, that's what she told me when we spoke on it a few months ago. If she had a daughter, or two daughters, she wanted to name at least one after her grandmother. She left naming any sons to me..." He paused. "Although to be honest with you, I have no male relatives I particularly care for, or think well of ... so I haven't any thoughts on what to name the boy..." He sighed. "I'm not going to be one of those simple-minded fools who names his children or grandchildren after himself. Those poor boys always end up being called 'Junior' for the rest of their lives and that seems emasculating."

I almost laughed at his statement, and looked down from the little girl in my arm to the small male pup curled up in the basket, whimpering for his sister.

"I..." I began, but let the words fall off. The name rising to the top of my mind wasn't appropriate, and I knew it. I couldn't help that it was the first that came to me, but it wasn't right to utter it.

"Luther." I heard Lucius speak, after a moment. "It's alright. He is your son. You have the right to name him as you see fit."

"I don't think—" I began.

"He was a good friend of the family." Lucius stated, and put his paw on my shoulder. "That's all the boy need ever know, if he asks. I know his death pains you ... it pains me, too." He admitted, quietly. "I'd be honored ... and I know he would."

I looked down on the little pup curled up in the blankets.

"Welcome to the world, Klaus." I murmured.

CHAPTER 9

TO HONOR AND BE FAITHFUL

"Your capitalized L's still lack a proper flourish." Cuthbert murmured, his eyes scanning the paper before him. The light filtered through the lettering from the window behind him, illuminating the many scribbled ink blots I'd covered my mistakes with. My fingers felt sticky from handling the quill inexpertly for the last several hours, and I couldn't wait to get the hell out of here and wash them.

"I got the rest of it right." I stabbed a finger in his direction, "This time."

"I see some improvement, yes." He set the paper down, glancing across the desk at me. His eyes fell to the third person in the room, curled up and resting over my chest and part of my shoulder. The little pup shifted in his sleep.

"Your strokes would probably improve if you shifted him to your right shoulder." Cuthbert pointed out, with a raised brow.

I glanced down, and then reshuffled Klaus further up onto my shoulder. He stirred, but didn't wake. "Klaus is helping me strengthen my arm. If I can't handle a quill with a couple pounds of pressure, I damn sure can't handle a sword." I smiled down at the sleeping pup, who seemed oblivious to my training regiments.

"It's only been three months, sir." Cuthbert sighed, leaning back in his chair. "Allow yourself more time to heal before you start testing the muscle."

"Got to work it while it's healing," I murmured, distracted. It was hard not to look at Klaus when he yawned. "It'll be all that much sooner I can get back on active duty."

"Honestly sir, your skill with a sword is not what you need to exercise if you want Lucius to let you anywhere near the fleet this year."

"I've been essentially a civilian for almost a year now." I muttered. "It's starting to wear on me. I've not been away from the sea so long since I was eighteen. I'm getting landsick, unpracticed, and soft."

"No one with your regimen could get soft." Cuthbert said, exasperated. "If you'd listen to the physician and stop straining yourself, you might actually heal faster—"

"I can't practice my penmanship and my court manners all day, every damned day!" I gave an irritated whuff, shoving the pile of poorly-scribed papers off the desk. The quill clattered to the ground with them and before I knew what I was doing I was standing, staring down at Cuthbert. "I'm a soldier, dammit! Not some fat, docile peacock!"

Klaus began to whine, and I winced. Cuthbert gave me that long, disapproving look he was so very good at and I fell silent and tipped my ears back.

"Calm down, Luther." He spoke evenly.

I sighed, trying to work out the frustration of the last few months with that one long breath. It barely made a dent. I had no idea what had gotten into me of late, but it was getting worse every day. Some great, gnawing frustration was eating at my insides, compelling me to wanderlust on the grounds and increasingly more violent interactions with Johannes during sparring practice. I'd caught the man in the hand the other day. Even with a practice blade, the blow had still been hard enough to dislocate his wrist, and I'd been mortified ever since. His hand was still wrapped. I gave it a long look, guilt eating at me.

What the hell was wrong with me?

"I'm sorry." I whispered, and rubbed Klaus's back gently, trying to coax him back to sleep. Luckily, it didn't take much. The little boy was the easiest child, I swear. It seemed like all he did was sleep and eat. Compared to his far more rambunctious sister, he was a peaceful, quiet little thing.

Wasn't taking much after his namesake...

"Yes, well ... in any case, I think we're done for the day." Cuthbert stood, and headed over to the discarded pile of papers, collecting them. He moved across the room towards the fireplace afterwards, and tossed them in. "Your penmanship is improving, but you're still quite far off from being able to write your own communications for the fleet."

"Can't I just let a scribe handle that?" I sighed.

"Not in the case of confidential documents or secret correspondence within the fleet. We can't risk more eyes on it than are necessary, and you may not always have me present to scribe your letters for you." Johannes headed for the door, and I followed. "Besides ... the written language is one of the greatest inventions of civilization. You are a Pedigree now ... it is expected this is an art form you will master."

"I only learned to read and write two years ago." I sighed, stepping out into the hallway and heading down the hallway with the tall wolfhound.

"I did say I was impressed by your progress, didn't I?" Johannes said.

"Thank you."

"I understand this has all been difficult for you, sir—"

"Luther." I stopped in my tracks, looking back at him. "Just ...

Luther. Please. This 'sir' business sets me ill at ease. You're a friend, Johannes ... not a subordinate."

"I find its better that I get into the habit now." He said. "With the children born and your marriage technically on the books, the time is rapidly coming nigh that we return to the *Cerberus* and her sister ships. They'll be returning to port once the northern seas thaw. You'll be meeting your fellow Officers and the Captains of the fleet for the first time, and taking up a temporary post as Captain of the *Cerberus* herself."

My head always spun when we spoke about the fleet I'd be inheriting. It was hard to connect an idea like that to reality, despite all I'd been through since I'd come here. I would be a Captain and then an Admiral eventually. They were *my* ships, my men, and my crew.

Four Pedigree Captains, under my command.

It made my claws tap against the ground, my fur bristling in excited anticipation. Never in my life had I dreamed I'd be so fortunate ... so astoundingly lucky. It seemed like it couldn't be real. When I'd first come here it had been a distant, ludicrous concept. Something I honestly never thought would come to pass. I'd assumed by now I'd be long gone from this house, chased off by the family I'd come to love, or hated and mistrusted so greatly, they'd no longer want me.

Now I was finding myself in quite the opposite situation. I wanted to return to the sea more than anything, but the idea of leaving this place was actually painful to think about.

I looked down at the weight on my shoulder, and gave a long sigh.

The last few months *had* softened me, in a very real way. Not physically, but ... for my children, for my wife ... even for Johannes, and my father-in-law ... I'd let myself get swallowed by a life I'd once sneered at. It had happened gradually at first, and then became punctuated with gut-wrenching realizations. Responsibility to the woman I'd married, to fatherhood and friendship.

It was enough to make a man embarrassed. I'd dismissed

connections like these throughout my whole life, because of what they did to men. I'd dismissed men who fought for their families as fools. I'd needed no motivation to go into battle. I fought for myself.

But there was no escaping it anymore. I was just as weakened by this life as any other man. And I'd let it happen. I'd welcomed it. Despite every reservation I'd ever had, I was an emotional man at my core. What made me the aggressive firebrand I was so proud to be also meant I was far more vulnerable to the more tender emotions in life, and these people stirred them up inside me plenty.

The last time I'd felt this way about anyone, it had been Klaus. It was love and I knew it. I'd said it outright to Delilah, although she'd been so out of her senses in pain at the time, she couldn't have remembered it. Thank God for small miracles.

The last time anyone had told me they loved me it had at once ruined and changed my life in one breath. If it hadn't been for Klaus's dying confession, I wouldn't have been tortured and nearly killed in the depths of that God-forsaken prison. But Lucius also would never have come to know of me, and none of this could have happened.

Emotions like this turned your life upside-down ... and at the moment, I was strangely content with my life. I had a promising career ahead of me, all the wealth I could ever need, and several people I trusted with my secrets had just as many reasons to keep mine as I did theirs.

For once, I had no interest in shaking up my life ... only exploring the next chapter. The last thing I needed to do was complicate things. I cared about my wife, even if we were never going to have a particularly intimate physical connection. Even if I could never really be a husband to her, she seemed to accept that I cared about her. I had two beautiful children, a father-in-law who could talk seafaring late into the night with me, and a good friend I was beginning to think might be able to get over his religious beliefs long enough to respect me as I did him.

Still, for some reason, I was restless. I'd convinced myself, night after night that the strange frustration I'd been battling was due to my absence from the navy for so long. That all but had to be it. Because the alternative wasn't something I was willing to explore.

I was a married man, and I was a man with self-control. I'd made peace, the day Delilah had given birth, that this would be my life from this point on. I was *not* going to ruin all of this. Not this time.

"Have you been well, sir?" Johannes's voice broke my reverie, and I perked my ears, but averted my eyes.

"Fine," I responded. "The wound's healing well. You know that ... you check up with the physician constantly—"

"I meant personally, sir." He stopped near the top of the staircase, preparing to head down. I was going on further to Delilah's room, so I stopped, but didn't turn around. "You've seemed ... out-of-spirits, of late. Is there something wrong?" He asked knowingly

Again, I didn't turn. I didn't because I knew if I did I'd see his injured hand and feel compelled to be honest with him. And I didn't know what to say, so honesty right now would probably be whatever raw thing came to my mind. And right now that would just be more venting. I hated what this was doing to me ... it was turning me snappy and aggressive at the people I cared most about, just because they were *there*. I'd even been short with Delilah the other day when she'd asked me the very same question Johannes was now asking, although I'd stopped short of yelling at her.

"Just ... landsick," I said with a sigh, finally.

Johannes seemed to accept that. "I understand, sir. Lucius is away on business at present, but rest assured, once he gets back we'll be making plans for a trip to port. Even before the thaw. Lucius wants to meet with some suppliers, and he intends to bring you. At the very least, you'll smell the sea air soon enough." I heard the creak of his footfalls heading downstairs at that, and I stood there looking out the frost-caked window at the snowy forest outside the windows as he retreated downstairs to his quarters.

Johannes took his role as the family 'knight' extremely seriously, in that I'd rarely ever seen him leave the family house. I know his family lived a few lanes down, I'd even been to his humble house once or twice to visit with them ... and his wife *was* in fact particularly beautiful, but his children drove me insane. It's not that they were poorly-behaved, but that there were just so *many* of them, and they loved to ask questions. It made me happy Delilah would only ever have the two. Brook was looking to be extremely active, but neither of them had been difficult, per se.

Then again, the servants handled all the muck and muck of caring for them, so ... I suppose I was spoiled. I'm sure if I'd had to change and feed Brook and Klaus, I'd be much less enamored with fatherhood.

But Johannes spent more time with this family than his own. Apparently that wasn't uncommon, even amongst normal house servants, but it made me wonder how I'd fare being away at sea, possibly for years at a time, and leaving my pups and Delilah to live and grow without me...

As if on cue, Klaus began to whimper again, and I rubbed his back. "Hungry?" I queried down at the little boy. He pawed at my shoulder, wriggling in my arms, and I nodded. "Let's get you back to your mother, and your nurse."

"Are you feeling any better today, Luther?" Delilah asked softly, and I closed my eyes, pinching a few fingers over my brow.

"I'm fine." I sighed. "I was fine yesterday. I'm just still recovering."

"I'm sorry." She murmured, pulling her legs up to her chin under the covers, and laying her head atop them. "I suppose there isn't much for me to do cooped up in here but worry, I don't mean to bother."

"It's alright." I said in a softer tone, and reached over to rub her knee. She smiled, and nuzzled into my paw ... and I couldn't help but smile back.

"I ain't never seen a married couple so in love." The middle-aged nursemaid in the corner of the room crooned, rocking Brook in her arms. The bloodhound was probably one of the sweetest, most good-natured women I'd ever met, save Delilah ... but she still got on my nerves, at times. She was always around, now that the children had been born. Rare were the moments I used to have, where I could be truly alone with Delilah, which was ironic when you really sat down and thought about it. I was her husband now.

But she was still recovering from giving birth, and despite my earliest certainty that these people were all worrisome, paranoid Pedigree hangers-on who didn't understand how strong Delilah was, I'd since come to realize ... she honestly *needed* this bed rest. Physically, Delilah had recovered fairly quickly after the birth, but she'd gone through a strange, terrifying period of bleak, dull depression in the months following the twins' birth. I didn't understand it, but apparently Lucius and the physicians had been prepared. When I'd asked him, at length, he'd admitted that Delilah's mother suffered the same affliction following every birth and miscarriage. He was convinced it was what had made her mad, eventually.

Delilah, by the grace of God, had recovered. She'd been far better specifically over the last few weeks, and was finally able to enjoy her children. I could tell already that she was going to be a wonderful mother.

Unfortunately, the fact that she was on bed rest meant that without fail, she always had a maid or a nurse present. We weren't even permitted to sleep in the same room ... although apparently even after her bed rest was over, it was considered 'crass' if we shared the same room every night. It was assumed if we did, I was ... using it for what the marriage bed was intended ... every night I took her to it. And apparently 'relations' that frequent were a subject of scandal.

Or something.

I swear nothing about Pedigree society made sense. They had all the money and privileges in the world, but they wore the most uncomfortable clothing imaginable, locked themselves in their houses for ludicrous stretches of time, and restricted how much they were allowed to rut. This house had twenty four rooms, and the 'marriage bed' was located in a different wing than each of our individual bedrooms ... thus literally making it *inconvenient* to rut, even if we wanted to.

Why would any sane person live this way?!

Delilah and I had never been intimate, obviously ... and likely never would, so none of this truly mattered. But we'd shared the same bedroom on the night of our marriage, and I honestly wasn't opposed to the idea. In fact, I wish I could share the same room as my children. But a married couple sharing the same room while their children were present was *unheard* of. Lucius had literally used that word.

I was annoyed at my inability to be close to my family, in a farce marriage. I couldn't imagine how frustrating it must have been for most of these men.

It was just another batch of kindling to dump onto the flames. I swear, I felt like something was coiling inside me, like I was winding back my sword arm, and someone or *something* was going to get in the way of me eventually, and then—

The snap of paper caught my attention, and I saw Delilah gingerly working a letter opener under the seam of a wax-sealed envelope, opening it up and beginning to read. I looked at it, curiously.

"Is that from Lucius?"

She looked my way, and then smiled. "No, but ... it is from one of his messengers. A man arrived early this morning with it, and a few things my father sent home from his trip to the city."

"Oh?" I wasn't honestly interested in whatever goods Lucius had sent home from the Capital, but I was curious for any news of when he'd arrive home again. Honestly, I missed the old codger. Johannes was good company, but I'd grown strangely fond of watching Lucius chew on his cigars and swear during our chess matches, or taking walks with him through the grounds whenever he needed to 'work his knee', as he called it. The old man had grown on me, and I'd found a kinship with him I couldn't quite describe ... but I knew it was something I'd never had.

"Still no word of when he'll be coming home. He actually sent this messenger a few weeks ago, to pick up something from the Port of Gibraldt, and bring it back to the house for him..." She paused, and then blinked, having to re-read something.

"What?" I asked, curiously.

"A ... horse," She tipped her head, and then looked up at me. "He bought a horse."

I'd spent quite a lot of time out in the stables over the last few months, burning time and getting back into the swing of riding ... and Lucius had over a dozen to choose from, enough that I shouldn't have bored of riding. But for some reason, perhaps because life here had become sorely uneventful and dull of late, the thought of a new horse had me taking long, hurried strides across the grounds. The manor's immaculate stables loomed before me before long, and I was soon beating a hasty path through the center aisle, seeking a new face.

I didn't have far to go. The new beast stood out, it would have stood out from a mile away. Most of the horses Lucius kept were long-legged, elegant thoroughbreds and quarter horses. The animal an unfamiliar stable-hand was attempting to ease into a stall at the end of the barn was shorter and stockier, just slightly larger than a pony, but powerful and muscled.

And by the look of it, the beast was wild. I hurried my way towards the unfortunate man trying to hang tight to the lead and avoid its rearing hooves, and took hold of the bridle, easing the bit back to gain control of the mare's head. The man was panicking, which was only riling her further...

"Calm down." I said to him, putting both my hands into holding the mare still. "You're only frightening her more. She's come a long way ... it's natural she'd be skittish."

"I know." The man, a slightly potbellied mouse, insisted. "I'm the one who had to drag this beast across five counties. She bit my own horse more times than I could count..."

I smirked, reaching over and stroking the mare's nose, lightly. She kept her ears pinned back, showing me no signs of complacency, "Headstrong girl, hmm?"

"She's supposed to be broken." The mouse cursed, and shoved the lead at me. I took it, not releasing the hold I had on her bridle just yet. "Damned Carvecian animal!"

I looked back at the mare. "She's from the Colonies?"

"Everything from that blasted continent is wild." The mouse sneered. "But the lord insisted he wanted one of these creatures. Said they've got a good gait for his long rides ... breeder called it the 'single-foot'. I don't know about that ... all she wants to do for me is rear and kick."

"She's beautiful." I remarked, looking the horse over. I was struck for the first time by her unusual coloration. Her body was a deep, rich chocolate color, but her mane and tail were pale, almost cream-colored, and she had a blaze of white down her entire head and nose.

"All she's good for." The mouse muttered, and leaned down to pick up his pack. "The breeder called them 'Specters' ... apparently that's what they've taken to calling 'em on the continent, b'cause of th'way they look in the dark with that white mane an' tail. Like a damned ghost," he sighed, hefting his pack over his shoulder. "Well, lord's orders were to deliver her into one of his stalls, and feed 'er. Think you can handle that?"

I nodded, and dug into my pocket for a crown, flicking it his way. He caught it with a gap-toothed smile. "Thank ye, lord. You're most gracious."

I spent the better part of the next hour getting the mare accustomed to her stall, which was easily done once I brought out some oats, then currying out her coat and mane. Whether from the road or the trip across the sea, she was in bad need of grooming. Her hooves looked like they could use some work, too. We'd have to call a farrier.

I found a strange sort of peace in the work ... it reminded me of taking care of the pony we'd had when I was young. And this mare calmed down plenty once she had some food and water ... and perhaps a calmer hand. That's not to say she wasn't a difficult animal ... she stomped at me every now and then, kept her ears firmly back the whole while I was in the stall with her, and I wouldn't dare get near her rear hooves, but ... we could work on that.

She reminded me of a cattle horse in a lot of ways ... at least in build. And while I saw why the idea of an ambling gate appealed to someone like Lucius, who did a lot of long rides, I found myself secretly hoping he found the mare too difficult to handle and needed someone to work her for him...

It was starting to get later in the day. The air had grown cold, but my winter coat had come in just fine and I'd always been thick-furred, so I didn't mind. The last thing I expected to hear was a carriage coming down the lane. The only company we ever had that came via carriage were some of Delilah's friends from court, and they'd have no reason to come out this late.

I put down the curry comb, stepped carefully out of the stable and closed the gate behind me, then headed towards the barn door, so I could catch sight of who'd pulled up.

I recognized the carriage immediately, because it belonged to the family ... as did the two horses that pulled it. The driver was already opening the door when I'd made it outside, and I felt an earnest smile come over my face when I saw Lucius step out. Just like him not to warn us. He'd probably hoped to surprise Delilah.

The happiness became mild confusion, when I realized he wasn't alone. It was almost unheard of for Lucius to bring company by, personally. As it was, he hated visitors.

What's more, though they were at a distance from where I stood, I could clearly tell the man with him was vulpine. There was no mistaking that tail. He was dressed in garb that looked vaguely northern, but definitely city wear. He was a slight fellow and probably young ... maybe my age. Other than that, I couldn't make out much about him.

Before I could think much more on the oddity, Lucius was staring my way. He'd clearly noticed me. Hardly surprising, the man could smell an eagle on the wind. I stepped out of the barn, wiping my hands on a rag, and knowing I was in no condition to meet one of Lucius's high-brow friends. My vest was open, the shirt I wore beneath it was covered in barn dust, and I was fairly certain there was hay stuck in my fur. I brushed a hand over the back of my neck, trying to shake anything out.

Regardless of all this, he immediately began crossing the yard towards me, his friend following in tow. The way the fox carefully picked his footing through the melted patches of snow confirmed he was from the city. He even had a sort of gentility to his gait, his tail bobbing with each careful step.

I kept my eyes on Lucius. Now was most certainly a *bad* time to let my eyes wander.

"Luther!" He greeted me warmly, and went so far as to clap a hand on my shoulder, which I knew to be an extremely close gesture, for Lucius. "You look years better than you were when I left. I've heard you've been mending well ... Delilah's kept me updated via letter. Unwrapped you, have they?"

I nodded. "Last week. The surface damage is all but entirely healed over. It's mostly stiff, at this point."

The fox made it to us at that point and waited patiently behind the spaniel lord, his gold-eyed gaze taking in his surroundings. Now that he was closer, I noticed that his fur was unusually pale, for a red fox ... like burnished gold, with a deeper rust color where his kin usually had black fur, so definitely northern. He was very slim, not terribly tall, and wore heavy gold earrings that dangled from each delicate ear, accenting his already intense, fine features. His muzzle and as far down his throat as I could see were snow white, and he clearly kept meticulous care of himself. His coat was immaculate, and swept back along his cheekbones.

I'd thought I was doing a decent job not staring, but apparently, I was lying to myself ... because he caught me, and stared straight into my eyes.

And then he smiled.

Lucius had been talking, but I'd honestly completely lost track of what he'd been saying. What's more, he seemed to realize, because when I only nodded dumbly to what he'd said he arched an eyebrow and glanced behind him.

"Ah ... apologies, I haven't introduced you two." He stepped aside, and gestured from the fox to me, "Mikhail, my son-in-law."

"Luther." I managed.

"Mikhail Vyacheslav." He smiled.

"Ah..." I paused. "Pleasure, Mikhail."

"Likewise," That smile didn't fade. There was something about a fox smiling that always set my body on edge. Like somewhere, there was a fire or some other mischief, and only they knew about it. There was always something hidden in their eyes, something they knew that you didn't. Normally I pushed the feeling off as my mind feeding into stereotypes, but this one ... this Mikhail ... the feeling was almost overwhelming. It was like he was hiding a knife, either real or metaphorical, behind his back.

I had to admit, it wasn't altogether unpleasant. I liked men who kept me on my toes, kept me guessing. I'd always found it more exciting. Foxes had always gotten me riled up, in all the right ways. It didn't hurt that this one was tremendously attractive on top of that.

"So..." I paused, " ... are you here for ... business, or for a social call, sir?"

Lucius arched an eyebrow at me, clearly confused that I'd suddenly remembered my court manners, for about the first time ever.

"Social." The fox reached up and pulled his fur-lined cape tighter over his slim shoulders. "Lucius and I have known each other for many years, but this is the first time I've ever visited his grounds. I'd imagine they're even more beautiful in the summer ... but I must admit, Lucius, you were right ... this place has many handsome sights to take in."

I swallowed.

"Mikhail works in the Capital, with some associates of mine." Lucius explained, and I tried to focus more on the old man while he spoke, but it was *really* damned hard with that fox continuing to look at me that way.

What the hell was he about? Why wouldn't he just go back to staring at trees?!

"He'll be staying for the remainder of the winter ... poor man needed to get out of that noisy hellhole for a spell, eh?" Lucius chuckled, and stepped past me into the barn. "Now, with introductions out of the way ... where's my bloody horse?"

Oh God no. This man ... was going to be staying at the house ... at the house I was living in ... For the next *two months*?

How the hell could Lucius do this to me?

"You're a Heeler, are you not?" the fox questioned, snapping me back into reality and forcing me to realize Lucius had left me alone with him.

"I ... yes," I confirmed. "I'm surprised you know the line."

"I grew up in a very small northern province called Vezysnaya." The fox leaned back on one of the supports near the door to the barn, brushing a few stray snowflakes from his cloak. It had begun to snow again. "Herding was the chief trade for most farmers, since the ground is difficult to work. They'd bring herds down from the mountains each winter, heading south. I saw many Heelers, they were good, hard-working families."

I took the compliment with a nod. "Have to work to eat."

"Hard-workers, good people ... but not Pedigrees," The fox said with a smile.

"No." I muttered, and I didn't bother keeping the irate tone from my voice. I'm certain the fox was rich, judging by the way he was dressed and the fact that he kept in the same circles as Lucius, somehow. But still ... he was a fox. Vulpines were no higher in society than wolves, so far as the Church was concerned. They were considered part of canine society chiefly due to their similarity in appearance, but little else. They couldn't even interbreed with us like wolves could. From what little I'd gathered from the few days I'd paid attention at Church, vulpines were considered to be what happened when a canine soul fell so far, they could never be redeemed. They were excluded from giving birth to higher souls, from breeding towards the divine, because of some grave misdeed in one of their previous lives. Their only hope for elevating themselves in God's eyes was to live an entirely pious life in service to the Church, and hope to be reborn canine again.

To be fair, I didn't exactly follow all of the Church's rhetoric. The idea of breeding towards divine perfection to reach some nameless heaven in my final life didn't ... really sound like something to aim for, even if I wasn't already so 'cursed' that it was out of reach. If we truly were reborn over and over again in different rungs of society, until we lived piously enough to be born Pedigree, I'd rather wallow in sin forever, and be born again and again, and live it up. Heaven could have its Pedigrees. If they were the only ones there, I wouldn't exactly fit in.

The point was, rich or not, this Mikhail had no right to look down on me for being common-born. I didn't care if he accused me of being poor ... it was technically true, until I inherited Lucius's fortune, but he had no ground to stand on if he took issue with my breeding.

"That's incredible." He smiled, and then leaned in closer, dropping his voice. "You must tell me how you managed something so clever! Did you con your way into the family ... woo the daughter somehow? Or is it Lucius you have at your mercy, with some kind of dark secret held over the old dog's head?" His eyes almost twinkled at that. "I'm sure there's a terribly scandalous, engaging story here ... and I would die to hear it..."

I blinked. "I ... barely know you." I said at length. "You expect me to start dispensing family secrets, just like that?"

"Oh ... this must be interesting." He smirked. "I smell loyalty."

I lowered my brow, "Who exactly do you think you—"

He waved a hand, chuckling. "Please, take no offense. I'm just toying with you. Consider it professional curiosity. I work with a lot of people like Lucius, and working within the Pedigree circles when you aren't one yourself is an endless struggle. Whenever I meet someone who has managed to penetrate their pretentious defenses so thoroughly, I'm always curious what their secrets are."

"If you want secrets to not pissing them off, avoiding calling them 'pretentious' is a good start." I said. "Especially since Lucius is barely fifty feet away, and he has excellent hearing..."

"Oh, Lucius is one of the rare good ones." Mikhail looked in the old man's direction. "Always courteous, always prompt on payment in business dealings, and a decent fellow to boot."

"What is it you do, anyway?" I had to ask. I was assuming a merchant of some sort ... a lot of merchant families came down to the Capital from the north, and built trade empires with northern goods.

He glanced back at me, pausing for just a moment, before responding, "I'm an aspiring thespian. I work in the arts ... mainly acting, and singing. A bit of dancing, when a role calls for it ... but I'll admit, it's not my strong suit."

"You're an actor?" I quirked an eyebrow. I actually don't think I had met an actor in my entire life before now. And I'd known men that sang, but ... the sort of songs they sung were always more yelled off-key while drunk, and involved women in heat.

"Aspiring," he smiled. "We'll say aspiring. I haven't really had that ... life-changing role, yet. But someday."

"I didn't realize Lucius had much of an interest in the arts." I muttered. I suppose there was a lot I still didn't know about the old man. "Well ... he is still a Pedigree, after all." I shrugged. "I'm sure he has a lot of expensive interests I'm not aware of."

"Many." The fox smiled again. I heard Lucius cursing, distantly, deeper in the barn. I suspect the mare had bitten him. Inwardly, I smiled.

That horse was mine. I'd known it when I *saw* her.

"So, Luther..." the fox leaned back languidly against the wooden post, his tail flicking about in ways that couldn't fail to catch my attention. "What are your interests?"

"My..." I paused, and gave him a long look. That tone in his voice had sounded dangerously close to flirting.

Or had it? Damn this man. Everything about the way he spoke, moved, expressed himself ... even the way he was just *leaning* there, looked like flirtation, to me. Or maybe that's just what my mind wanted to believe.

Or maybe he was just a fox.

I just didn't know. And his expression wasn't giving me much. It was still that low, simmering smile, hiding all the knowledge in the world behind those two big golden eyes, giving me *nothing*. No hint of what was in his mind, no inkling as to what he wanted.

"My interests..." I said carefully, " ... are in people who say what they mean."

Now it was my turn to catch him off-guard. "Excuse me?" He queried.

"You heard me." I muttered. "I barely know you, but you've already started snooping around about very personal details of this family. Let me make this entirely clear ... this is *my* family, as far as I'm concerned. If you're hoping to dig at me for information, just because I'm the new man here, prepare to be disappointed. I know you're Lucius' friend, and since we'll be sharing the same house for some time, I'd prefer to be cordial, so ... let me just make this clear. I prefer people who are forward about what they say and do, and honest about their intentions. Keep that in mind, and we'll get along fine."

He gave a slow smile. "I believe I understand you, sir. Please forgive my earlier behavior ... Lucius told me a bit about you, but I wasn't certain precisely how you prefer things. Thank you for being so blunt and informative."

"No problem." I relaxed a bit, at that. If the man was just toying with me because he had been uncomfortable with me, that was fine. I'd had the same issues with Pedigrees, before I'd been elevated. Being amongst the upper class when you weren't a part of their world had made me damned near violent, on many occasions ... I could see how it could make someone who played roles for a living act coy and pleasing, even if it was to another man.

"I earnestly am curious what your interests are, though." The fox piped up, before I began to head back inside.

I paused. "Oh ... well ... I'm ... a navy man. Generally, obviously not at this moment, but soon I'll be returning to sea." I stepped back inside, and he followed me in. "I'm fond of riding," I continued, "the occasional chess match, swimming, traveling ... swordplay."

"Oh, fencing!" The fox seemed to light up at that. "I've learned a little. Enough to muddle my way through a few parts at least..."

I gave a grim smile. "I wouldn't call what I do 'fencing', exactly."

"Have you ever killed a man?" The fox asked with a morbidly excited smile.

"Ah ... yes." I answered after a moment, somewhat uncomfortably. It wasn't something I liked to boast about, "More than once."

"How many?" He pressed.

I sighed, reaching up to deposit the curry comb on a nail near the supply rack in one of the dusty back rooms we kept all the tack and feed in. The fox followed me in.

"Directly in combat, one-on-one," I responded at length, "seventeen. With projectile weapons and ship-to-ship gun, I'm not certain."

He must have understood then that I didn't like speaking about the topic, because he went quiet at that. I kept my head cast down, setting the new mare's bridle carefully over an empty post, and running the leather straps through my hands, smoothing out the creases, trying not to remember every detail of every single death I'd caused over the years ... which of course meant I did exactly that. A heavy silence settled over the small, dusty supply room, and for a moment I felt as though the wooden planks beneath my feet were those of the *Winnipeg* ... coated in the spilt blood of the raiders ... and Klaus...

I could almost feel it beneath my paw pads, sticking to them, making the deck tacky.

The warmth of two hands moving up along my back to stroke softly over my shoulders gave me perhaps the most sudden moment of simultaneous comfort and panic I had ever known. I all but leapt away from it, as dearly as I wanted to remain, and grabbed at the offending wrists, clamping my hands around the fox's thin arms and shoving him back against the wall with startling ease. He went completely limp and pliant beneath my hold, tucked his ears and tail back, and looked up at me with the first real expression of surprise I'd seen from him yet. I held him there for a few moments of silence, save my own startled panting ... trying not to focus on how *right* he felt, pinned beneath me, completely submitting to my sudden, aggressive gesture.

"What the hell was that?" I demanded.

"I-I'm sorry," he half-whispered. "I-I just ... I could tell ... I had upset you, and ... I just ... wanted to comfort you..." He swallowed, and then repeated, "I'm sorry."

"No, I meant, what was—" I began, but I heard Lucius calling for me. I glanced out the open doorway, and then back to the fox, who looked up at me, worriedly. I even thought I saw a hint of fear there.

"I didn't mean to startle you." He said quietly. "Perhaps we should ... continue this conversation another time? Later?"

"Perhaps we should." I agreed, glancing out the door, then back to him. I wanted to say more ... *anything* more, to confirm or deny what had just happened ... but Lucius was calling for me again. I released the fox and stepped back. He stayed pressed against the wall, and I was momentarily mortified that I'd nearly hurt such a defenseless, delicate person.

"I'm sorry, as well." I said, and straightened out my vest some. "Reflexes ... when you spend as much time in the military and the navy as I have ... you ... get a hair trigger..."

He nodded, and relaxed some, slipping away from the wall and closing his cloak up, visibly wrapping his arms around himself, beneath it. "I understand." He murmured.

I headed for the door, and headed back out into the barn ... the incident in the supply closet running again and again through my brain, replaying out every minute detail, trying to make sense of it...

By dinner time, I was only more confused. Confused, paranoid, worried for my family, worried for myself...

I could brush off the way he leaned on the stable beam with his hip cocked out at the perfect angle to display his figure, the way he smiled at me like a lover who'd known me for years, the way he spoke to me like his words were silk and he wanted to wrap me in them ... all of those could be monstrous exaggerations of what was actually there, perpetuated by my wild imagination.

But men didn't touch each other like that. Not Pedigrees, not peasants, not even foxes. Men didn't caress one another's shoulders, thread their fingers up through your neck scruff and lightly rub at the nape of your neck with their thumbs...

Not unless those two men were intimate. In the sense I *wasn't* with my wife. I had only *ever* been touched in such a way by men I was bedding, by my lovers.

My romantic experiences over the years weren't terribly vast, I'll admit. I'd had five, almost six lovers, over the course of my life ... and most of those had been desperate, fleeting acquaintances. So I couldn't really say I was well versed in how two men would ... court...

But what had happened in the supply closet ... I couldn't imagine what else it could be. This couldn't be my imagination anymore.

If it was right, what the hell did it mean? What the hell did I do?

I glanced over my uneaten food across the table at the young fox, who looked even more brilliant in candlelight, the soft flickering light catching in the shifting gold of his fur. Around us, the family ate and chatted, Delilah happily speaking with her father, having come down from her room finally to join us all at the table. She'd been overjoyed ever since she'd seen her father again, and he seemed both relieved and content that she was well again. Johannes sat nearer to the end of the table, looking over the newcomer only sparingly. I'd honestly expected him to be more watchful with the man, as protective as he was over the family, but if anything he seemed to be avoiding eye contact with the fox, like he made him uncomfortable.

All were oblivious to my inner struggle. And that was for the best, because I was a maelstrom inside.

This man, Mikhail, had already blatantly displayed that he was willing to dig around for dirt, and suspected I'd done the same to gain my position here ... which meant he'd probably done the same many times in his life. What the hell was he? Was he even truly Lucius's friend? I couldn't imagine Lucius trusting a creature like this. He was a canny old dog, and he had to know the boy played games with people like him. Had the fox really fooled him, convinced him he was only a friend of the family, rather than some gold-digging, sly con-man?

But if the fox was truly here to dig up dirt on the Denholme family, why would he be so blatant as to *tell* me so? Did he think I was like him? Some kind of con man who'd wormed my way in? Would a con man make an assumption like that off the bat?

He'd certainly found me out. That was one of the few things I was positive of. Maybe I'd just been too obvious. Maybe the way I gawked had betrayed me ... maybe he knew the signs. Whatever the case, he knew my secret. And that could mean a number of things, none of which ended well.

Maybe he'd found just the secret he was looking for. My secret alone, if made public, would destroy my marriage, destroy Delilah's claims to legitimacy for her pups, and destroy Lucius's reputation. If he'd come here to find something to hold over the Denholme family's head, to pinch them for money, or whatever he wanted ... he had it. And it was my fault.

Maybe that's all he'd been doing in the stables, testing the waters, seeing if he was right.

Or maybe I was being paranoid. Maybe all of *this* was my wild imagination. Maybe the fox was just ... like me.

Maybe Lucius knew that.

Maybe, in a moment of senility, the old dog had thought bringing home a young, attractive man who shared my 'condition' would be good for me ... that we'd bond, talk about our problems ... become friends.

I was dreaming, I knew. But even though that was the best case scenario in all of this, it was still a bloody stupid idea. I was earnestly trying to take my vows to his daughter seriously. This was a temptation I did *not* need.

It didn't matter. That was so implausible it almost made me laugh aloud. Lucius knew the boy through business, and that was all. The old spaniel didn't associate with people unless he absolutely *had* to, and he certainly didn't invite just anyone to his house, let alone to stay for several months. Mikhail must have been the rich son of some merchant or trade baron Lucius did business with, in which case, if he wanted anything from the family it was probably power, or prestige, not money. Maybe he was a merchant who supplied the fleet, and Mikhail was hoping to blackmail Lucius for better rates, or exclusivity. The fox was hiding something from me ... I was certain of it. I wasn't always the best judge of character, but I *knew* a man with a secret. I saw one in the mirror every day.

Either way, I wasn't going to wait to find out.

After dinner, the family generally went to the sitting room for a while, but I asked to be excused early, complaining that my wound was acting up. Lucius only hand waved me, nodding. Cuthbert, strangely, said nothing, he only excused himself without another word as though something was bothering him as well. Delilah was the only one to notice something was off about me, and followed me out into the hallway. Try as I might, I couldn't turn my back on the young woman. She deserved my attention.

"Luther?" She stepped up to me, and took one of my hands, looking up at me with those big, round, brown eyes. "I ... won't ask if you're alright."

"Delilah, it's—"

"I just wanted you to know it's going to be alright." She said, quietly. "It's alright, Luther. You don't need to be so worried all the time. No matter your concerns, no matter your troubles ... I will always be here for you. Whatever comes to pass," she gave a soft, if slightly forced smile. "It's alright."

I felt my body unwind just slightly, from her mere words. There was something so infinitely comforting in hearing the vague words of comfort from her. This woman didn't know what troubled me, and she'd probably never fully understand some of the struggles I dealt with, but she still wanted to help me. She still wanted me to know she was there for me. It was one of the kindest gestures I'd ever received, completely unconditional acceptance.

"I love you." She smiled genuinely at that, and leaned up to kiss me, softly. "And I know you love me. I heard you..."

"You remembered that?" I sighed, mortified.

"I will always remember it." She looked down at the tiled floor, then back up to me. "And ... I want you always know ... how much it means to me. I know ... what sacrifices you had to make ... for me..."

"Delilah, it's not—"

"I understand things better than you all give me credit for." She said quietly. "I understand how difficult this has been for you." She paused. "Luther..." she began, as though she were carefully choosing her words, " ... I just want you to be content. Happy, fulfilled. Please do not ever see me as an impediment."

"Delilah, you will never impede my happiness." I promised,

leaning down and kissing her back. I wrapped my arms around her and held her for a time.

It was she who pulled away, eventually. “I’m actually very tired.” She admitted. “I’m going to turn in early. Have a good night, Luther.”

“Goodnight, Delilah.” I murmured. She slipped away from me, and began to slowly head up the stairs. I watched her until she disappeared into the hallway of the east wing, and gave a long, ragged sigh.

That had been oddly-timed. Everything about today had been odd. It felt like a conspiracy ... everyone was acting strangely, save Lucius...

I heard Mikhail’s light footfalls in the hallway, smelled the distinctive, sandalwood scent on his fur, and turned in time to see him stop in his tracks, pinned under my gaze.

“Are you going to follow me all the way out to the stables?” I questioned. “Because that’s where I’m going.”

“If ... that’s what you’d like.” He answered, carefully.

I sighed, best to get this over with sooner than later.

“Alright,” I murmured.

The scent of hay calmed my nerves ... bringing up quiet memories of my youth, of the time I’d spent alone with the herd, and the peace I’d had then that I’d since never relived. Before I’d known what love was, and that my type of love was wrong. Before my father had started beating me, before I’d known violence at all. Life had been so much simpler then.

The mare ... I’d been considering just calling her ‘Specter’, after what the mouse had called her breed, ate from my hand, her nose brushing over my paw pads and helping calm me further still. I’d told the stable hands not to handle her feeding from this point on ... I wanted to be the one she came to expect, to rely upon. I’d be coming by at least twice a day from now on to tend to her, to lunge her, feed her, and groom her. I was going to make this horse mine. I didn't believe much in fate, but sometimes you just feel something is meant to be.

Mikhail sat on a beam nearby, one leg propped up. He balanced with no sign of difficulty on the thin plank of wood, staring out a nearby window into the cold, clear, starlit sky. The moon was full tonight ... I didn't even need to look outside to know it. I could feel it in my bones ... in the feral recesses of my mind.

We'd said nothing so far ... he'd let me go about taking care of Specter, the two of us sharing a few quiet moments in the flickering lantern light, contrasting against the blue-lit reflections from the snow and ice which filtered through the many small stable windows.

I was pouring fresh water over the stable door into her pail when I heard the crunch of paws on the straw-lined floor, and heard him approaching me from behind.

"I'm behind you." He warned me quietly, this time ... and I only nodded.

And then those warm, gentle paws were on me again ... this time running slowly down my back, along my shoulders, and down my spine. I was wearing only my undershirt, and I could feel every one of his claws. I shuddered, but I didn't push him away this time.

When his paws reached my hips, they circled slowly around my waist, his fingertips brushing over my hip bones and running gently back and forth there, along my waistline. When he was not further rebuked, or whenever I suppose he felt comfortable enough to do so ... I felt his weight lean against my back entirely, and his slender muzzle pressed gently into the fur along the nape of my neck.

I gave a staggered sigh, trying to steady my breathing so I didn't pant. The barn was only ten or twenty degrees warmer than it was outside, but for some reason, I was burning. Anywhere his fur touched mine was lighting a fire like flint to tinder.

"Why are you doing this?" I had to ask, despite every instinct inside me not to question him ... not to do *anything* that might put a stop to this.

This was a horrible, terrible mistake. I shouldn't—*couldn't* be doing this. Everything was on the line. Absolutely everything, everything I'd sworn I wouldn't risk losing this time.

"I thought this was why we came out here..." He whispered against my ear, his whiskers brushing over my fur and making my whole body shudder.

This man was rendering me weak in the knees with the slightest of touches. I couldn't help but feel he had to know what he was doing ... that he had some malicious intent, that any moment now, he was going to bury a stiletto between my ribs...

I hadn't realized my hips were craning against his softly stroking paws until they crept along my waistline and deftly undid a button. The pressure it released was ... extremely welcome ... but it signaled a very definitive change in the atmosphere between us.

He was entirely right. This *was* why we'd come out here. I could lie to myself all I wanted, but it wasn't accomplishing anything. This was the point of no return ... right here. I could be a good man, make the right decision for once in my life. Or I could go on being the same irresponsible, immoral bastard I'd always been...

I probably shouldn't have hung on the edge of that decision so long, because Mikhail wasn't stopping. Before I'd settled on a choice, his paw had slipped past the hem of my pants and he was rubbing the soft paw pads of his hand over my sheath, and my peeking tip, while his other hand slipped up between my legs to cup, and caress.

And at that point, I ceased being able to make complicated decisions anymore.

I turned and took him by the shoulder and the wrist, and quickly wrested control over the situation, pushing him up against a stall door. Some part of me hoped I'd get that same alarmed, momentarily frightened expression from him again. I was not disappointed.

I think he intended to say something, but I didn't let him, because moments after I had him against the stall I'd pressed my muzzle into his, keeping none of the frustration or need from the kiss. He went breathless and powerless beneath me, and at length, he moaned softly into my muzzle. Relief washed through my body like monsoon waters.

This was how to vent.

I made a better bastard than a good man, anyway...

I only broke the kiss off eventually because we both needed to breathe, but I took it as a good indication that my skills were still intact when the fox tried to chase my mouth with his. I finally did what I'd wanted to do since he arrived and put my hands on him, pushing beneath his cloak to run my thick paw pads down his lithe, slim waist, wrapping my hands around either hip. I stroked his far smaller body, feeling his back arch against the wall towards me, and wondering blissfully what he'd look like when I got him out of the bulky northern clothing. I pictured him stretched out languidly beneath me, with that soft, pale tail brushing over my body...

His paw had moved back down my body, undoing every button on my shirt as it went, until he could put both of his paws through my fur, stroking them slowly down my chest.

God, he was going to undress me right here.

"I don't..." I gave a soft 'nnffhh' as his muzzle pressed gently into the hollow of my throat, and I felt his tongue, then his teeth, licking and nipping their way teasingly down my chest.

"Here?" I barely managed, still unable to stop touching him.

"You seem to like it here." He smiled slyly up at me, his tail tossing about behind him.

I did, honestly. And it was about as far from the house as we could get ... I still couldn't help but cast a look to the barn doors every now and then, in fear a stable-hand or ... anyone ... who might walk in on us, but...

This was about as safe as we were going to get.

I yanked his shirt free from where it was tucked into his pants, and he smirked, leaning up to kiss me again. I found his muzzle just as eager as mine, and before long, we'd both trespassed one another's canines to take our first taste of each other. I suspect I tasted like bourbon ... it was practically all I'd had for dinner ... but somehow, despite the fact that dinner had been barely an hour ago, and we'd had no dessert I'd seen, he tasted like peppermint. It was intoxicating.

Everything about Mikhail smelled, tasted, and felt amazing. It was like he had been made for me and every one of my senses. He even created the most alluring soft whines as my hands crept up his figure slowly, taking his shirt with them. When I reached his shoulders, I pushed it and the cloak he wore up over his head at once. He shucked them both off, hurriedly, the heavy gold earrings he wore tossing back with the motion. On an impulse, I leaned in close to press my body against his, and nuzzled into the soft, white fur along his neck and clavicle, inhaling his scent and beginning to nip my way up along the hollow of his throat. My efforts were rewarded with another of those low whines, sending a bolt of need which shot straight down between my legs and pushed me from my sheath even further. There was so much heat between us, the chill night air was little deterrent.

I shouldered off my shirt in its entirety, and kissed him deeply once or twice more. His paws found purchase on me wherever they pleased, but now with my chest bare, he was running them far more hungrily over my figure.

"The fact that a man like you has to wear clothing is a sin." He murmured, one of his paws slipping up my abdomen as the other crept lower towards my growing length and settled those warm, soft paw pads around me. He stroked me gently, but completely ... the perfect motions of his paw suggesting he had an unusual amount of experience with this...

I was swiftly growing to full mast beneath his expert ministrations, and *all* I wanted at that moment was to flip him over, tear him free from his britches, and push up beneath that soft gold tail. But, even if desperation and need were driving me to violate my family's trust in me and cheat on my wife ... there was one thing I simply wouldn't do, no matter how badly I wanted to ... or rather, one thing I wouldn't do this *without*...

"Do you have anything at all?" I asked hopefully ... my hand brushing over the infinitely soft fur along his ears. "Anything to ease..."

He paused at that, and I knew instantly what the answer was by the expression of dismay that passed over his features.

"Not here." He admitted. "It's ... with my things..." his ears drooped, " ... in the house. I'm sorry."

I slipped my hands down along his slim, soft figure, and my hands stalled at his hipline for a moment or two ... before I unhooked his belt, and began to pull it off of him. He let me, the jerking motions I used to rid him of the hindrance tugging him closer against my body, where he chose to remain once I was done. I could see for a fact that he was not unaffected by our encounter, even with his britches still on, and I took the opportunity to press my palm up between his slim legs, and squeeze at him firmly ... not hard enough to hurt, but enough that he was reminded who was in control here.

" ... wh-at do you want me to—" he began, but at that point I took hold of his hips again, and lifted him nearly effortlessly to sit on the same beam he'd been perched on, before. Then I unbuttoned his pants, and let him fall free, taking in the sight hungrily from where I stood.

He was about proportionate to his body size, and that was to say not very, but he was nearly fully erect, and that's what mattered. Thanks to Klaus and a lifetime spent in the navy, I had quite a lot of experience at this, but I hated when it took too long. I hoped silently that he wasn't long-winded.

I wrapped a paw around him, and stroked him firmly, showing him a bit of my own technique. No reason to get up close and personal until he was entirely ready ... that could get frustrating. Luckily, he earnestly must have been in need himself because he was ready in my paw in very little time. I leaned forward to kiss him once more and he gave me a taste of that wonderful muzzle of his again, before I slowly pulled away, and took a knee.

This act in and of itself had been a peace treaty between myself and Klaus on many occasions, since neither of us exactly enjoyed submitting to the other, but pleasing another man with your muzzle was arguably not submission. After all, you had a certain amount of power over the man you were working on, and there had to be a measure of trust between the both of you. It had probably saved my relationship with the white shepherd from escalating into full-fledged warfare in the bedroom, on more than one occasion.

And thanks to the many, *many* times we'd clashed on the subject, I was very practiced.

I lathed his tip with my broad tongue at first ... back and forth, gently, then with slight circular motions. His whines were coming closer together at that, and I tasted precum, so I took him fully into my muzzle. I could feel his tail thrashing where it hung over the beam, the soft fur brushing repeatedly over my chest and shoulders. It was *highly* distracting, so I deftly caught it in one hand and wrapped it loosely around my shoulders, where it twitched, but mostly stayed put.

My free hand slipped up to cup and squeeze beneath his burgeoning knot. I found I had no trouble taking him in his entirety ... an issue I *had* had with Klaus ... so I pressed my muzzle flat to his soft fur on each down stroke, and curled my tongue around him inside my mouth.

I'm not sure how long I kept things up, but when I felt the telling spasms in his legs and tail, I pulled up just enough to suckle shallowly at his tip, increasing my pace ... and was very swiftly rewarded for my efforts soon afterwards.

I certainly hope none of the stable-hands were near the barn that night, because they would have heard him. He was *not* shy about being vocal, and while it was certainly an ego boost, it was a little unnerving to hear how much it echoed in the vast stable house.

He tasted wholly different than a canine, but I didn't find it unpleasant, exactly ... just different. I pulled back and spit it in my palm, leaving him panting and clinging to the beam for life. I was still hard as a rock, and no less impatient, so I gave him one firm command of "Get down, and face the wall."

"I honestly don't know if I'll stay standing." He admitted, as he weakly lowered himself off the beam, and shucked off his britches in their entirety.

"Then get on your knees." I stated, stroking my slickened hand over my length. It wasn't perfect, but it was better than nothing.

He did as I said, slipping to his knees in the hay, in the flickering lantern light of the dark barn. And for a moment, I had everything lain out before me that I'd wanted from this. His slim, golden-furred body was beneath me, prone and stretched out for my eyes to drink in, and my body to anticipate. His tail danced against my legs, tempting me towards him. And as I began to move over him, he turned to look over his shoulder, catching me with those gold eyes, and that smile...

A year of frustration and need crested at once, and I pushed up beneath his tail with a low, aching groan. I pinned my arms on either side of him, pressing up slowly, until I was sheathed to the hilt. The way he moaned made a shiver pass up my spine, but the way he tensed around me made *me* moan.

I was rolling my hips into his in slow, shallow thrusts at first ... measuring my strokes, in hopes this would last longer. But I was raw with need, and considering how much self-control I'd let slip by already tonight, here seemed a pointless place to hold back. So what began as an easy, deliberate pace gradually crested towards what this truly was ... an out-and-out rut.

He moaned and whimpered for me, and I watched his sleek-furred back arch on my deepest thrusts, his tail tossed back against my chest, his foot paws curling. He eventually began to move his hips back against mine, but I couldn't take him fast enough ... I took hold of his thin hips with both paws and began to pull his body into my thrusts.

He tensed every time I struck him deep, in one particular spot ... and I committed it to memory, for the next time ... but at the moment, I was losing control, fast, feeling everything I'd held back for months building inside me ... and the way his body was tensing around mine on each and every thrust wasn't helping...

I growled and pulled him into me one last, final time ... and took him the very last degree, past my knot, burying myself entirely in him as I spilled.

Waves of relief, bliss, and exhaustion hit me all at once. Mikhail moaned softly beneath me, his dark red paws clutching at the hay-strewn ground, body pressed down into the cold wooden planks. Fleetingly, I realized how glad I was he'd taken his britches off, entirely. Whenever I inevitably was able to pull from him, he was going to be a mess.

Lucius's stables were the cleanest I'd ever seen, but we were both going to be picking hay out of our fur for weeks, after this, and I was certain we'd need multiple baths just to get the dust out...

Lucius's stable.

Oh ... shit.

As it so often did immediately following a mind-blowing, incredible rut reality began to sink in.

Right, my life was over.

The people in my life ... Lucius, Delilah, Cuthbert ... they didn't deserve this betrayal, but at the very least, they deserved my honesty. Besides which, Mikhail was an amazing lay, but I didn't trust him for a second to keep his mouth shut about this. Whatever his ulterior motives were ... and I was finding I cared less by the second ... my family deserved to know before the rest of the world did.

I just had to find the right time.

Despite the calamity about to befall me when my trespasses came to light, that night, I slept like a rock. It was probably the first time I'd slept so well in ... Well, since I'd been here. In fact, I slept through half of the next day, waking only when there was a knock at my door.

I came out of a dead sleep in a panic, only to terrify the maid who'd entered with toast and tea.

"I-I'm sorry, sir!" She yelped, setting her tray down before she dropped it. "I assumed you'd be awake by now..."

I looked at her, blearily, sitting in an awkward, tangled slump amidst sheets I'd mostly tossed off over the course of the night. I was coming out of a dead sleep, so it took me a few moments to realize the little basset hound woman was gawking at me, somewhat.

I muttered something unintelligible, and went to get up, but at that point she hurriedly peeled off towards the door, excusing herself.

It took me fully two minutes to realize I was naked.

I got through breakfast without too much incident ... rang a different maid to draw me a bath, and washed off most of the grime from the night before.

I went out to check on Specter, and feed her. The barn was empty that morning, save the horses ... but I was never going to see the place the same way again. It stirred memories and parts of my anatomy even now.

I headed upstairs to see Klaus and Brook, and found them with Delilah. We sat together, and I held my children awhile, Delilah all the while blissfully unaware that anything was wrong.

I got through almost the entire day without incident, actually.

But then, around six ... one of the servants found me in the parlor, while I was reading and informed me that Lucius needed to speak to me.

I don't know how I knew, but I just knew. The damned fox had been missing all day. I hadn't seen hide nor hair of him since our fling in the stables last night, which I'd left very abruptly, so he wouldn't follow me. I figured if I got out before he was dressed, there was no way he'd be able to tail me to my room. It seemed to have worked.

But as I headed down the hallway, past the large, old paintings of ships and shipyards towards Lucius's office, I just knew. He'd gone to

Lucius. I don't know why, or what he'd asked for, but I knew he'd done it. He was probably already in a carriage, beating a hasty retreat off the grounds, with whatever prize he'd claimed.

I opened the door to Lucius's office, and stepped solemnly inside. The scent of cigar smoke and brandy hit me, as well as the usual scents associated with the old, amazing room. Lucius was where he always was, seated at his desk, cane propped up next to him. He seemed to be reading one of his old books, although he looked up when I entered.

And strangely, he didn't look as though he was planning to immediately flay my flesh from my bones.

"Ah, Luther," he licked a finger, and turned one of the old pages, looking back down at the book. "Please, come in."

I did ... hesitantly. But, I reminded myself as I took each step towards the chair he always kept on the other side of the desk ... I was a man. I needed to face up to the things I'd done with dignity. I sat, and waited.

"I spoke with Mikhail earlier today." He began, and I braced myself. "He seemed ... concerned ... about something that occurred last night."

I was silent.

"He was polite enough to spare me the details," he cleared his throat, and closed his book, putting his reading glasses down, "but ... he did tell me you left him without a word, and in quite a hurry ... in a state of disarray . As though there had been a problem. He was very concerned he'd done something wrong."

"I..." I tried to come up with a response, but I honestly wasn't sure what the old man was trying to say. What had Mikhail told him, exactly? Had the fox actually kept what happened to himself? It sounded, perhaps, like Lucius knew, but ... he was being evasive...

Now even Lucius was acting insane. I didn't understand *what* was going on. What had happened to my life over the last two days?

Lucius sighed. "Listen ... Luther. I know any previous experiences you may have had with men like Mikhail may have been ... different

... but you need to treat these people with a little respect, regardless of your personal feelings. Especially since Mikhail was intended to remain with us for the next two months. I'd hoped you'd make him feel welcome." He reached over to his ash tray and picked up his half-finished cigar, taking a drag, and giving a long sigh. "Now, I *know* you're a good man ... so what's wrong with treating him with a little decency? Is he not to your liking?"

"What ... the *hell* ... are you talking about?!" I finally bit out. "Please, sir ... I'm begging you. Speak plainly. What exactly did Mikhail talk to you about?"

He must have sensed the desperation in my tone, because Lucius immediately looked far more worried, and concerned. "Luther, are you well?"

"I'm well!" I said, exasperated. "I'm *really* bloody well, for the first time in almost a year. Everything in my life, at this current moment, is *wonderful*." Lucius looked alarmed at my tone, but I continued. "I just want to know if tomorrow, I have to move out, or run for my life!"

"Why on earth would you have to do that?" The old man balked.

I put my hands to my forehead, leaning my elbows on my knees. I'd failed to be a good man, last night. This was literally my last chance.

"Because," I grit out, after a long pause, my heart thudding in my chest, "I ... slept with him."

I didn't have the nerve to look back up at him after that. There was a silence ... that strangely, didn't last as long as I'd expected.

"Good. Then I'm getting my money's worth, after all."

My head shot up at that, just in time to see him taking a long, calm drag of his cigar.

"*Excuse me*?!" I almost bit my tongue.

"What, did you think he worked for free?" Lucius chuckled around his cigar, and then patted out a few ashes in his tray. "I'm sure you fancy yourself quite the stud, but..."

"Mikhail is a *prostitute*?!" I stood from my chair, and heard it clatter to the floor behind me.

"Of course he is." Lucius stated, lifting an eyebrow. "How many young, effeminate, ludicrously attractive male foxes do you think I know?"

"Why did you bring a *whore* to the estate?!" I demanded, hoarsely.

Lucius gave me the sort of look that suggested he was becoming uncomfortable with the direction the conversation was going in, finally. "Do I ... really need to answer that?" He sighed, and began to pour himself more brandy, like he suspected he'd need it.

"*Some* kind of indication at the outset would have been beneficial!"

He shrugged. "You seemed to have figured it out ... so what's wrong?" He lifted his sifter to his muzzle and took a slow, long drink. "Don't tell me you're one of those men who are overly picky. I have absolutely no inkling of what men prefer in other men, but you seemed to have it out for blondes, and Mikhail was fairly close."

"How do you even *know* a male prostitute?!" I asked, desperately confused.

"Ah ... well, it's not ... what you think." He insisted, although I'd *never* seen the old dog so uncomfortable in my life. If I wasn't so angry, it would have been worth all of this. "I was being honest with you, when I introduced the two of you." He continued. "Mikhail *is* a friend of the family, in a way. I've known him for almost eight years now, through ... mutual acquaintances ... that I have... entered into business arrangements with."

It took a moment for that to sink in, but when it did, I slumped back into my chair, putting my head in one of my hands.

"Oh, God," I muttered, my voice partially muffled by my hand.

"Now, there's no need to sound so humiliated." Lucius scoffed. "There's no need for us to be ... speaking about this at all, honestly ... and I'd rather we didn't."

"Not speaking about this is what led me to *fuck* a prostitute without *knowing* it!" I belted out, angrily.

"For God's sake Luther, keep your voice down!" Lucius growled with more authority. "The whole house will hear you!"

"What the hell is the point in keeping it hidden anymore?!" I spread my arms. "God, Johannes knew ... he knew the whole damned time, didn't he?!"

"Yes ... I'd know that sour look of his anywhere." Lucius admitted with a grimace. "Never gets any easier. It's like having a priest in the house, I swear. Never outright condemns, but damn if he can't make you feel it."

"Delilah ... Delilah knew too, didn't she?!" My memory flashed back to the night before, and the odd conversation we'd had ... how she'd all but released me to go ... do as I pleased. God, did she even mean any of it? Or had she merely said all those things because she knew it was inevitable? What kind of pain must it have caused her to sit at *dinner* with the man?!

Everything made sense now. The coy way he smiled at me, every movement he took so deliberately, like he was on display. The suddenness with which things had commenced between us and the repeated changes in personality he'd had, to suit whatever was pleasing to me at the time ... even the most minor things, I should have noticed. How immaculate he was about his upkeep, the peppermint on his breath, even the fact that he'd *alluded* to having some kind of lubricant back with his belongings...

The man was a *whore*, and I hadn't seen it. I was a damned fool. Everything made sense.

Except one thing.

"Why didn't you tell me?!" I demanded again, "Why didn't *he*?!"

"Luther, every person of note in this house knew what that man was." Lucius stated. "I suspect even some of the servants do. I assumed you would, as well! It was obvious!" He sighed, and leaned back in his chair. "It's considered incredibly ... crass ... to outright *say* what the nature of your transaction with these people is. Amongst our circles, they aren't whores, or prostitutes ... they aren't some gutter trash you pick up on a wharf and toss a penny at for a rut in an alleyway. Mikhail is a courtesan."

"What the hell is the difference?!"

He narrowed his eyes at me. "The difference is they're clean, healthy, and discreet. They work out of houses, they take extended leaves with clients, they attend events at court ... some men even keep one at their side for decades, or buy a house for them, provide for them ... see that they're comfortable and taken care of."

"They're still selling their bodies." I snarled.

"So is every man who takes a commission in the army, or the navy." Lucius's tone suddenly got angry, and I found myself taken aback by it. I'd apparently struck a nerve, finally ... because he was no longer amused. "When you put your life on the line for God and country, it's your body you risk. I fail to see why what these people do is any more sinful or wrong than warfare, and *you* of all people should not be making value judgments about what lovers others choose to take!"

I found myself cowed and fell silent, averting my gaze to my lap. Lucius let his words sink deep, before he put out his cigar and looked out the nearby window.

"I'm sorry that you were taken by surprise. I hadn't meant for that. I had no intention of fooling you into this ... I earnestly just thought you'd realize. If I'd known, I would have introduced him as a courtesan, and when that continued to confuse you, I'd have used the vernacular you're more familiar with. In *front* of the poor boy, if need be. Because I would rather humiliate him than you, but I thought we could avoid all of that. It didn't occur to me that you weren't aware of courtesans, and that was a rich man's presumption. I often forget the discrepancy between our classes, because I can speak to you as an equal..."

"It was a mistake," he sighed. "And I'm sorry."

I slowly spread my hands, eyes still on the ground.

"I just..." I paused, "I don't understand ... why..."

"Honestly?" Lucius finished off his drink, and leaned back in his chair. "Because you've been an insufferable asshole, of late, and from one insufferable asshole to another ... I know the signs when a man's just got an itch he can't scratch."

I put a hand to my brow. "I don't know if I can handle hearing this conversation from you." I muttered.

"And why not? If you're going to call me 'Dad' whenever you want to piss me off, I'm damn well going to lecture you like one whenever I think you need it." He retorted. "Luther ... we're men. And you and I are very ... similar men, in some ways. There are men in the world like Johannes, who can live a monk-like existence, married to the same woman for eighteen years, spending most of their time away from her, and get by just fine. And then there are men who can't.

Now, it's not as though we're going to die, without passion in our lives." He scoffed. "It's not a matter of self-control, or weakness of character. We'd survive. But we'd be some real miserable bastards. And despite what the Church might tell you, there's no damned reason to torture yourself with an avoidable situation."

"What about your wife?" I pressed.

"My wife has been certifiably committable for over a decade, son." He spoke in a low tone. "The only reason she lives here still is that I've a staff of four to tend to her every need, and keep her sedated. My poor, beautiful Marisa..." he murmured, quietly. "She hadn't a chance from birth. Five generations of madness Luther, five. Every single woman ... they suffer increasing levels of melancholy and dementia, following every child they bring into the world..." His jowls twitched, and his expression was hard to pin. "I don't understand why God feels my wife must suffer, for bringing life into the world. The Church says it's a woman's place, but ... yet..."

He looked up at me, finally. "Marisa lived in agony long before she went completely mad ... her depression grew worse every year, and after Delilah ... it never left. She has been lost to me for far longer than she was officially declared insane. I went three years without bedding her at a stretch, for fear she'd become pregnant, again. She was never made barren." He admitted, quietly. "I just ... didn't want to do it to her anymore."

"That's when you began seeing..."

"Yes." He admitted, with no trace of shame in his voice. "And I refuse to feel as though I have committed a sin. I pay the women well, I treat them well, with dignity and respect ... and I feel I've been a better man to my family, because I am not forcing myself to live in celibacy and discomfort. Is that so wrong?"

" ... I'm sorry, sir." I said after a time. "I've been ... a continuing ass..."

"Happens to the best of us," he finally smiled. "Now, then ... with that settled, I suppose I'll send Mikhail home. No reason to keep him here and make everyone uncomfortable." He stood, and grabbed at his cane, pushing himself up and moving out from behind the desk, heading for his strongbox.

"Sir?" I caught his attention as he was fishing out a stack of crowns.

"Hmm?"

"Do ... you trust him?" I asked, carefully.

"I wouldn't have brought him to live in my home if I didn't."

"Why do you trust him?" I continued. I needed an answer to this...

He took a moment, and then responded, "Mikhail is the son of one of the most senior women who run the house I frequent. I specifically prefer their house, because it is run by people in the trade, and they are very invested in keeping up the best possible reputation. And that means discretion, and sealed lips ... lest they lose their customers' faith ... and money. I have known Mikhail since he was fourteen, and I know his mother ... exceedingly well. I would not have trusted your secret to just anyone. And I would suggest you do the same."

He strode over towards me, and set the wrapped stack of crowns on the desk.

"This is the remainder of Mikhail's pay for his intended two-month stay. I leave it to you whether or not he remains here, but ... do see that he is paid in full, regardless." He leaned back on his desk. "So ... what do you intend to do?" He regarded me from where I stood.

I remained in my chair, my arms hanging from the elbows on my knees, eyes still cast down.

"I need to talk to my wife." I said at length.

"You didn't know?"

I bit my lip, irritably. Damn it. Even she'd known. And this was a girl who, I was fairly convinced was so sheltered, still didn't truly know all the ins and outs of how babies were made. Despite having had two of her own.

"I-I'm sorry." She stammered, rubbing the sleep out of her eyes. I'd woken her from a mid-afternoon nap. "I don't ... mean to tease you." She reached over and stroked my arm. "I'd just thought ... it was obvious."

"I don't know a thing about this 'courtesan' trade." I muttered. "And all of the ... people of that persuasion whom I've run across in the Navy ... most certainly did *not* look like Mikhail. Not to mention, I've never ... availed myself of their services. Not even the peasant variety."

"I can't say I understand it, myself." Delilah admitted, shyly. "It seems a wholly unpleasant thing to pay for. But I suppose for a man, it isn't."

"Your experience was poor, Delilah." I stroked her hand. "But ... intimacy can be ... a very enjoyable experience, for men *and* women. Someday, you'll know what it's truly like."

"No, I won't." She said, quietly.

Her statement hit my brain like an ice pick. In three simple, modest words, she'd just told me she took our marriage oaths more seriously than I had, or ever would. I had no response. What could I tell her? That she should go out and hire a whore of her own, just because I'd done it, and was considering doing it again? That it would balance the scales, somehow? Alleviate *my* guilt.

Once again, my wife ended my inner turmoil by, in her serene, humble way ... being a better person than I would ever be.

"Luther, please stop torturing yourself over this." She said softly, slipping her paw over mine, and threading her small, soft fingers through my own. "How can I convince you that I meant what I said? I want you to be happy ... the way you make me happy. You already treat me with decency, value what I have to say ... and you're becoming a wonderful father. That's ... all I wanted in a husband. I don't ... need you, intimately..." she insisted quietly.

"That's only because someone abused you terribly, and stained that part of your life." I murmured.

"Luther, you're doing that thing where ... you think you know something about me better than I do." She chided me, with a soft smile.

I looked up at her, and she reached over to me, to stroke my cheek. "I have ... female friends, you know." She said quietly. "Most of them are married. And most of them don't enjoy intimacy with their husbands, either..."

"That's just because you Pedigree do it wrong." I scoffed. "I'm convinced all those frumpy sorts at court would do it through a hole in the sheets, if they didn't think it'd ruin the linens."

"Some of them do." She said with a slight smirk.

I put a hand to my brow. "What is wrong with this country?" I wondered, aloud.

I heard her giggle, and despite the situation, I had to laugh, too. I chuckled lowly for a while ... at my life ... at the last two days ... at the thought of two old Pedigrees humping through a hole in a comforter...

Sex was unbelievably ridiculous, at its core. How is it I'd been going to war and dealing with Privateers and Raiders since I was a teenager, but *this* was the single defining issue that had caused most of the pain in my life?

"Luther, just ... enjoy your fox." She said, between giggles, quieting herself with a hand over her muzzle. "I swear to you ... I don't mind."

I sighed, and stood, straightening my coat and feeling the weight of the crowns in my pocket. I began to head for the door, but a few final, quiet words from my wife caught my attention.

" ... although I wouldn't mind ... seeing you two ... perhaps ... together ... at some point..."

I had to turn, and arch an eyebrow.

"Doing what, dare I ask?" I queried.

She just kept her eyes on what she was crocheting; smiling to herself in the most sheepish, girlish way I think I'd ever seen. "I'm sure I don't know." She said at length. "But you are both very attractive ... I'm sure it's a sight I would not soon forget."

"Delilah," I opened the door to the hallway, "You truly are your father's daughter."

I found Mikhail in the room Lucius had made ready for him the night before, and I found that much to my chagrin, he was almost afraid to open the door for me. I set him at ease enough to allow me inside, after apologizing for being a tremendous ass the night before, and telling him we needed to have a long talk...

"I know my behavior must have seemed ... odd." I said with a long sigh, after about ten minutes of talking with him. "I hope, in retrospect, you understand why and will forgive me. I didn't mean to treat you so abominably I just didn't understand the situation, and was understandably ... confused, and, protective of my secret and my family's secrets. I'm sure from your perspective it must have been terribly confusing, as well."

He just sat on his bed, legs crossed, staring at me. When he finally spoke, it was following a long, relieved breath, and an exclamation.

"Oh thank *God*!" He ran a hand over his brow. "To be completely honest with you, I thought you were some violent, crazy trick who was *really* into playing head-games. I was half expecting you to pull a knife on me the whole time."

CHAPTER 10
THE FLEET

The icy wind hit my cheeks and froze the ocean spray on my eyelashes. My vision was staggered by the overwhelming desire to continuously blink, and I put my paw up to shield my face somewhat from the onslaught. The surf was doing it's very best to overturn our small skiff, as we pulled into the Port of Cheron. The weather this time of year was notoriously bad in the northern ports, and it didn't seem to be making any considerations for our visit today. The salt water stung my nose and eyes, the cold winds off the sea were merciless, and the combination of the two was a recipe for sheer misery.

God, I'd missed this.

"And just what's got *you* smiling like a dumb hound?" Lucius growled, planting a paw firmly against the side of the skiff to keep his balance as we pulled onshore.

"I haven't seen the sea in over a year!" I exclaimed loudly, over the roaring surf. "It feels like coming home."

"I would call this—" Lucius began, but then the boat shook and we came to a complete halt. We were all pitched forward a foot or so when it struck the bank. Cuthbert and I caught our balance well enough, but the old man had lost a lot of strength in his bad leg, and I put out a hand to catch him. He gave me an annoyed look and pushed my paw off his shoulder. "I'm not a damned invalid." He grumbled, shoving himself up with his cane.

We all stepped out onto the shore. The Port of Cheron was barely a port at all ... more an accident of geography that happened to be a safe place to dock ships. It was perfect, if you didn't care about things like comfort, civilization, or warmth. There were the docks, and the uneven shanty town of plank buildings that had sprung up around it, connected over the rocky coastline by a series of equally uneven, wooden walkways. Most of that was masked at present by the fog rolling in off the harbor, but I'd stopped here once before when I was aboard the Winnipeg, so I knew what to expect. Then there was a small collection of rustic trade shops further back into the forest, but most of them were furriers or game butchers. You couldn't really live in Cheron. You could barely dock there, really, unless you already had a lot of supplies on hand.

But apparently, Cheron had been the dock the *Cerberus* fleet had been closest to along our route up north, and Lucius had sent word to meet them here. They were en route to the Port of Rhinemouth, where they would be resupplying for the season. We'd just come from there, and I'd spent a maddening week toiling around town, following at Lucius's heels while he walked me through the drudgery of learning each and every single supplier he sourced for his fleet. I knew it was probably extremely important, and I had done as well as I could to pay attention to it all, but it was just *so much math*.

Academics had never been my strong suit. I'd only ever gone to school when I was at Church, as a very young child, and I'd stopped going once I was old enough to work with my father. I'd learned enough with Klaus and with some quick tutelage from Cuthbert, that I could understand the supply sheets and the way they kept track of their inventory. I understood how important it was to the upkeep of the fleet, but it still made my head spin.

More than that though, being so close to port, but unable to actually go out to sea had been immensely frustrating. The happiest moment of this entire trip had been when we found out the roads were washed out ahead of us and we'd had to take a skiff from a nearby landing to make it to Cheron. It wasn't much of a boat, but getting on the water at *all* had eased my heart in places I hadn't known I was aching.

My feet hit the cold, wet sand, I felt the surf wash up between my toes, and I took a long breath of pine, smoke, and sea foam. This place may have been a hell-hole to dock a fleet at, but I wouldn't mind spending a few days here. The pure wildness of the area washed through my nostrils and sent a shiver up my spine, like I'd set foot in a foreign land. So much of Amuresca was developed, the land stripped for cities, farming, or livestock, the rivers awash with runoff from civilization's less attractive byproducts. When I was twenty-four, I'd spent eight months in Carvecia while we were hunting a particularly elusive fleet of Privateers. Their land had reminded me of this place, wild, untouched, and dangerous. The jungles of Mataa often felt the same. It's like we'd tamed the world, and stolen all its majesty ... except in rare places like these.

Lucius was cursing about something or other, likely the fact that he was having difficulty finding purchase on the wet sand with a cane and a bum leg. But he again pushed Cuthbert off when he attempted to offer him a hand so really he had no one to blame but himself.

I smiled, ruefully. The old man had his pride. He wasn't even particularly ancient, he was just getting through life with a difficult injury. It made me wonder what a firebrand he must have been before he'd gone lame.

"Hang this festering port." He snarled, stalking over towards the loose planks resting in the sand that almost made up a walkway towards the actual 'town'. And I used the term loosely. "As I was attempting to say on the boat ... if rotting wooden buildings, constant grey skies and no bloody *women* for fifty miles is what you call home—"

"Think about whom you're talking to, sir." Cuthbert muttered, passing us both on his way up the rocky embankment, checking his pistol as he went. Why he'd come armed to this meeting, I wasn't sure, but he'd assured me he never went to the fleet without a firearm on him at all times.

It made me all the more eager to meet the Captains.

Lucius grunted. "I suppose the Navy's quite the heavenly place for someone of your ... predilection."

"I don't mind women." I shrugged, holding back to walk at Lucius's side. "But for the most part, I do agree that they don't belong on ships, thought strictly for their own safety. It's a superstition I wouldn't mind seeing broken every now and then, but ... but wait, why aren't there women in town? This is a small town, but..."

"The only souls living in Cheron are seasonal trappers, and they don't generally keep a permanent residence. The rest are monks." Lucius spoke as we walked, the fog rolling in off the harbor still masking much of the port and the small town beyond. He glanced at me. "And that's not an analogy ... they're quite literally monks. Whole town was founded by them. They've got a temple up further on the mountain, and they run everything in town."

It had been cold all day, but for some reason, it was only now that I noticed it. I shuddered slightly, looking up into the misty pine forests. "Monks?" I murmured.

"Men of God," Cuthbert said, his voice resounding with a twinge of respect. "The most selfless of holy men ... the Neutren."

I winced, knowing full well what he meant.

"They've cut themselves off from the cycle of breeding and rebirth, to pay penance for their sins." Cuthbert finally seemed content that his gun was dry, and placed it back in its holster. "It's a noble sacrifice, and the only option available to most of them, save prison."

"Mn-hnh." I ground my teeth a bit. "Well I hope God's grateful they cut their boys off for him. It seems a bit harsh for 'penance'."

"They're all heretics." Cuthbert said, and I kept my eyes on the port I knew was there, beyond the fog. "Murderers, rapists, traitors—"

"Deviants?" I supplied, glaring at him.

He paused on the walkway, looking right back at me. "Perhaps," he merely responded, after a few moments of silence.

I didn't like this. A jagged, confrontational kind of silence had grown between Cuthbert and I over the last month, and it couldn't be worse-timed. I'd be meeting the Captains of the fleet today, and a month from now when the fleet was resupplied, taking my position under Cuthbert's wing for a trial period, for potentially many years, until Lucius felt I was ready to make major decisions for his ships. Cuthbert and I had grown so close over the last year despite our many differences, and I'd thought this was all actually going to work out well. Now it seemed, we were right back to where we began a year ago with him judging me. Except now I knew that he knew what kind of man I was, and he was *still* judging me, and so it bothered me more.

I knew where it all stemmed from, of course. It was the fact that Mikhail had been staying at the house. I'd caught Johannes looking extremely displeased during the few moments he'd seen the young fox and I together, and we'd been very considerate not to share our exploits with anyone else in the house, so it's not as though he'd caught us doing anything scandalous.

Had he only become so understanding before because he hadn't actually been physically faced with what he considered to be my 'sins'? Was he re-thinking his respect for me now that it had become a reality he had to contend with in his life?

"There's my old girl." Lucius interrupted my increasingly angrier train of thought, and I looked up to see what he was speaking of. Hadn't he said there weren't any—

My breath caught in my throat, as the masts poked through the fog, and the misty shroud began to roll back and reveal the beauty we'd all come here for.

And they *were* beautiful.

The sails were drawn up, so the line of bare masts arranged in the small harbor resembled a forest sprouting from the sea, gently swaying like reeds in the wind. I saw the distinctive sweeping beaks proudly jutting from the waters, the lateen mizzenmasts and the elegant curvature of the four galleons' hulls. These had to be them, the Denholme fleet.

My fleet.

The crimson red of the Amurescan flags, battering back and forth like birds in a storm, counted the ships at four, just as Lucius had said. They must have been the only ships in port, or at the very least, the only ones on their scale.

They were absolutely breathtaking. I stood there beside Lucius for what felt like an eternity, looking down into the bay. I'm not certain how long I was staring, but eventually, I noticed that the old man was smiling at me. I could see the pride in his eyes.

"What do you think of my ladies?" He asked, in a low voice.

" ... I can't believe this is actually happening." I uttered, at length.

Lucius only laughed, and clapped me on the back. "Come on then, boy ... let's have a closer look, shall we? The men will be hunkering down for the night, but the brass ought to be waiting for us at the inn." He strode past me, up the steps towards the shanty town and I swear he was limping less.

I felt a similar energy rising inside me, and followed his swift lead. I heard Cuthbert shout from behind us, in a warning tone, "Sir! Steady your pace. These walkways are wet, I'd hate for you to take a fall."

"Oh for Gods' sake, Johannes, stop treating me like an old man." Lucius grumbled.

"Begging your pardon sir, but you *are* approaching your fifty-third year, and I'm only looking out for y—"

"The day I can't handle some wet steps, Johannes, take me out back and shoot me." Lucius barked out a laugh, and continued on. "Getting old is for the weak."

One of the buildings in the distance was lit far more brightly than the others, and seemed to be the largest structure. As we grew closer, I noticed a worn wooden sign creaking at its post, painted at some point long ago with a crudely-drawn tankard. At least I think that's what it was intended to be. It had been awhile since I'd been to Cheron, but I believe I'd been here, before. Something about the old, salt-stained wooden structure felt familiar.

And it seemed to be our destination. The loose wooden boards of a morosely creaking walkway led onto the precarious, rocky cliff-side the structure was nestled into, with more of the same inadequate wooden walkways and staircases heading further down towards the docks below.

A wave of deja vu struck me, and I momentarily stopped in place, gripping the frayed rope railing nearby. Something about all of this...

"Luther!" Lucius called back at me. "Don't tell me you've got vertigo, boy. You climbed my damned house."

"I'm fine." I said insistently, and pushed myself down the last of the walkway. What the hell *had* that been about? Some kind of memory associated with this place ... and a lurching feeling, like my senses were warning me of something. It was the same way I felt every time I could smell a storm coming.

Fear, don't sail here.

I blinked, walking across the muddy stone towards the inn. Why here? Why now? I couldn't remember anything particularly bad having happened in Cheron, and I hadn't been here that long ago. It had been two ... three years ago perhaps? And Klaus and I had spent most of it drunk, rutting in his quarters on the Winnipeg. We'd only been here two days, to wait out a storm.

Cuthbert opened the door and a blast of welcome, warm air and the mixed scents of alcohol, tobacco, cooking meat and the musk of many men hit me all at once. The distinctive scent of this place struck a chord with that same nameless, fearful memory, and it was beginning to frustrate me that I couldn't pin down what it was. Had it happened here? I know we'd been to an inn ... was this the only inn in town?

God damn it, why had I gotten so drunk? My stay here was a blur.

As we stepped inside, I noted Lucius had been right about the sort of men who frequented this port. The menagerie near the bar was a loose mixture of low-bred, wild creatures. A lot were wolves, which made sense. The few tribes that still kept within our borders stayed mostly in the northern provinces. The distinctive pale, rosette-lined sweeping tail alone marked a fur-cloaked patron at the bar as one of the snow cats from the mountains. A thick-chested badger was having a raucous conversation with a dark silver-furred fox with all the earmarks of a local road warden ... I even saw the lumbering figure of a bear somewhere distantly at one of the tables, with a small group of mixed canines.

The place was busy, but I was already picking out crewmen. Even in port, they kept their red sashes ever-present. It was a point of pride within the navy, a superstition for many, and a very real source of protection when you were in strange ports. A sign to any and all that we stood unified, and if you had the nerve to harm one of us ... the whole of us would come down on you.

I'd known men who'd been beat on by their *own* crew for not wearing their sash. It may have been a small thing, but most mariners took it seriously. The sea was a lonely place to be, and by traversing its waters to all corners of the world, we marooned ourselves away from the country that birthed and protected us. The Navy was essential to securing the prosperity and the pride of the country, but it was in many ways a sacrifice to be a part of the force that threw itself into the great unknown. We were the outstretched arms of our nation, capturing spoils and warding off attacks.

But we were also the most vulnerable of any soldiers, at the mercy of the seas, the policies of foreign nations and cut off from most information or contact with the motherland. An entire fleet could be lost, and the Crown might never discover why.

It was that isolation, ironically, that created such unity amongst fleets. When you were at sea, politics, coin and class just ... mattered less. Men depended on one another for survival, and who you were outside your tasks aboard your ship had little meaning or value. Merit mattered, in the navy. The fact that I was where I was now was proof of that.

There were barriers, of course. I'd been absurdly fortunate. Money and class still mattered in many regards ... but at sea, all could be trespassed, if you really had the nerve for it.

All of this was what had attracted me to the navy to begin with. I'd learned from a young age that I hadn't the patience to be a shepherd like my father, that I'd never fit into lower-class society so long as I didn't do the things expected of me ... namely marry, have children, and be miserable for as many years as I could eke out a meager existence. But necessity had compelled me to learn how to defend myself over my youth into my teenage years ... necessity being the constant beatings from my father. The day I realized I'd grown good enough to really scare my old man was the day I first considered joining the army. And that very same day, I'd left home, and he hadn't been able to stop me. I hadn't seen him since, but I suppose I should have been grateful to him. He taught me that if you get hit, you've got to hit back harder. It's the only thing that works.

I was good at killing people. It seemed to be what I was put on earth to do. But I'd never been content in the militia. It was a job and it kept me fed, but it kept me confined to the same social restrictions I'd had tending goats and sheep, or any other trade.

The sea was freedom, at its purest. It physically separated me from my homeland, and took me away from everything there that had ever caused me pain. Some of the same laws followed, but in general, the sea was its own jurisdiction. And provided you were tough, reliable, and mean, even a man like me could get by. Until the incident with Klaus, I had. I'd had a few tight scrapes, but I'd always slipped free of them and just ... moved on to a different port. That was another wonderful thing about the navy ... you were never in the same place long. It was easy to keep people at arms' length.

I'd always known my future was at sea. It called to me over the tides, like a distant, exotic voice beckoning. And soon, I'd be returning. After all the trials and tribulations, I was facing my destiny ... with a fleet at my back. This was my calling in life, and it had *finally* been answered. In ways I had never imagined possible.

My thoughts were back on the ships not a few hundred meters away, so I'd phased out much of what Lucius and Cuthbert had been discussing. I wasn't even certain if they were talking to me. I followed their line of sight, though ... across the crowded room full of tables and hunkered furriers and trappers ... towards another group, gathered at the farthest table in the room. They were easy to pick out, now that I'd noticed them. They all wore the deep, expensively-dyed blue coats of Officers, but the gold trim and buttons signified far more.

Those were the Captains we'd come here to see. The four Captains of Lucius's fleet. In the dingy atmosphere and amongst the motley assortment of dirty patrons, they stood apart. A fact I suspect wasn't accidental. They could have chosen to dress down while in a port like this ... Klaus often had.

Could be they were a bunch of arrogant twats. Could also be they wanted us to be able to find them. I'd have to assess that for myself once I got to know them better.

"The two thin fellows there are Captain Addison, and Captain Singh." Lucius kept his voice low as we looked across the smoky dining area, indicating a slim, sharp-faced silver greyhound who had to be close to Cuthbert's age. The other was a younger, lanky, mantle-colored Dane. Lucius had of course briefed me a bit about his fleet Captains over the last few months, but I'd honestly forgotten their breeds by this point, so the reminder was welcome. I'd always been terrible at associating a man by breed ... it seemed a poor thing to base an impression on, especially before I'd even met them. When Lucius had told me about these men, it was the first thing he'd mentioned, and I honestly couldn't have given a rat's ass.

These were Pedigrees, though. It would matter to them.

"And the massive fellow?" I asked quietly. I may not have known every bloodline out there, but I knew a damned Mastiff when I saw one. They were amongst the highest echelon breeds ... the King himself was a Mastiff, as was the entire Royal family. The imposing man across the room was a monstrous, black-furred behemoth, even for their breed. He wore half of his coat over one shoulder, and I could see the signs of a recent injury ... bandages wrapped tightly around his arm. Even still, he looked like he could rip me in half. He caught my eye as I looked in their direction, and I fought the urge to tuck my tail. I didn't need to let these bastards know they intimidated me. I was determined to go into this with my head held high.

"Shaw." Lucius said, nodding to the man from across the room. The large fellow gave me a long even stare before turning his gaze to Lucius, and nodding back. Then he said something to his fellows that I couldn't catch over the din in the room, and suddenly ... they were all looking our way.

"Cornelius Shaw." Lucius straightened his cane, and started picking his way through the tables, still speaking lowly to me as we went. "He is the only Captain remaining in my fleet from my time spent as Admiral. He was with me in the jungles of the Dark Continent. You'll never find a tougher, more reliable man ... and he runs his ship like a bloody Huudari taskmaster. But you might be hard-pressed to win his favor, son. Cornelius is a Duke by birthright ... he and I always had disagreements over how he regards lower-class rank elevation. He nearly left the fleet when I took on Reynolds."

"That leaves the sheep dog." I eyed the young Collie, skeptically. He *had* to be younger than me ... and Collies were not a well-respected breed, none of us herders or cattle dogs were.

Lucius almost laughed. "Don't ... call him that. He hates that." He chuckled. "Finnegan Reynolds. Call him Finn, he won't mind. He's a good lad. He *is* Pedigree by birth ... on paper. But families like his..." he sighed, " ... men like Cornelius don't like the idea of new bloodlines, in this day and age."

"Collies are hardly a 'new' bloodline." I rolled my eyes. "They've been working the country next to families like mine for centuries."

"The Pedigree lines were established over many centuries,"

Lucius sighed, "and the ruling lines don't like the idea of amending the list to include more and more breeds. Many of the ruling lines don't even regard families like the Reynolds as Pedigree, even if they have managed to make themselves so on paper."

"Oh yeah?" I smirked. "How'd they go and do that?"

"Money," he replied. "The Crown's been exhausting its treasury trying to colonize that damned fetid pit of a continent down south. Pedigree is for sale, these days."

"Mnh," I tried to keep from smiling further. "I can see how that might piss off someone raised to think they were better than the rest of the world."

Lucius cleared his throat. "My family is Pedigree, Luther..."

I patted him on the shoulder. "It's alright, dad. I've forgiven you."

He shoved my hand off his shoulder, and glared at me, as we approached the table. "You *will* be obedient tonight, Luther. I swear to God, if you give even one obstinate word to these men, I will hand you to Shaw to break in half, and then hang from the mizzenmast. You are *not* these men's superior officer ... in fact, at the moment, you hold no rank whatsoever. You will *earn* that rank. Nothing is being handed to you here. Is that understood?"

I tipped my ears back, catching the very real seriousness in his tone. And I nodded, giving a firm, "Yes, sir."

"Lord Denholme." The Mastiff addressed us, in a voice befitting his frame. "We are honored by your visit."

Lucius stopped before the table, perching both thick paws on the handle of his cane, and gave a fierce smile. "It's been too long, gentlemen. Nearly a year now, I believe ... I hope you'll forgive my visits dropping off. We've been a bit busy on the home front."

"Clearly," the greyhound curled a lip, his pale grey eyes assessing me.

"Singh," The mastiff turned his dark gaze on the greyhound, lowering his heavy-lidded eyes at the man. "Stand at attention in the presence of your Admiral ... or I'll lift you by the collar."

The greyhound sniffed, and brushed a hand over his head,

smoothing back the already sleek fur over his crown, then straightened his shoulders, and went so far as to salute. The other three men weren't long following. The Mastiff's demeanor seemed genuine, but I could smell the derision on the greyhound, and the Dane seemed almost half-hearted, his eyes clearly more focused on the scrolls laid out in front of them all on the long wooden table. The Collie ... this Finnegan fellow ... was actually looking almost entirely at me at this point. And I swore there was the hint of a smile there.

Or that could have just been the general Collie face. It was so hard to tell, with sheep dogs. They tended to bubble over with energy and vigor ... and this man seemed no exception. I could see him shifting in his chair, tail occasionally twitching. The battle to not wag in social situations was a lifelong fight, for some of us. I understood his pain.

"At ease," Lucius chuckled. "There's really no need, Cornelius ... especially considering your—" he paused. "Good God man ... what happened to your hand?"

The Mastiff glanced almost dismissively down at his wrapped stump. "Frostbite," he responded. "The North Sea claims what it will. It's not my sword arm. I'm fine."

Lucius sighed. "Only you would insist you're fine while missing an appendage, Shaw." He shook his head. "In any case ... I haven't been your active Admiral for many, many years now. These men should be saluting you, as my interim."

"Your Knight was our interim, sir." Shaw turned to Johannes, who I'd almost forgotten was with us. He was leaning against the wall nearby, watching the scene unfold in his usual stoic silence. "I will not deign to aspire to a rank I was never awarded."

I searched for any sign of accusation in his voice, but oddly, I found none. He didn't even sound aggressive when he spoke about Cuthbert's previous role as Admiral of the fleet ... and considering what Lucius had told me about the man, that struck me as odd. Johannes may have been a Knight, but he was born just as lowly as I was. How had *he* won this man's respect?

I filed it away as something I'd have to talk to Cuthbert about at some point in the future. If the fool would ever talk to me again, that is.

"So ... shall we be saluting the goat herder, next?" The distinctive, aristocratic voice of the greyhound cut through the moment. "Considering this ... pup ... is to be inheriting your position, Lucius. Perhaps we should bow, in fact. I'd hate to offend."

"Singh," The mastiff warned, in a low growl.

"What?" The silver-furred pedigree scoffed. "There's no point in avoiding the issue. Let's have our say, before any more false pleasantries are exchanged. You're both as outraged as I am, and I believe in keeping an open dialogue."

"Honestly, I take no issue with—" the Collie began.

"Shut your maw, Reynolds." The greyhound bristled.

"Gentlemen!" Lucius's voice rose over the clamor of the entire room, for a moment, silencing more than just the men at our table. He waited for the Captains to turn their attention entirely back on him. He tapped his cane, and then began to walk around the table, crossing by Singh as he went, and keeping his eyes on the greyhound. I noticed the obstinate pedigree's ears wilt, as he did.

"I believe I must first apologize for having so little involvement with the fleet, over the last several years." He began. "Most of you have never served directly under me, save by correspondence, and I know that leaves much to be desired for leadership. You were all fortunate enough," he emphasized 'fortunate', "to serve under my second for most of those years, however ... and if he did not make one point *overwhelmingly* clear about this fleet ... allow me to do so now."

He turned his gaze back on the four men, and growled out the next few words.

"Those ships in the harbor ... are *my boats*. They were built with my family's fortune, and I put them to task over the course of the first twenty adult years of my life, sinking Privateers and smugglers whose careers ended before most of you were even born. I captured a

Colony with those boats, I saw men die for, and on those boats, and I've weathered more storms inside those hulls than most of you will in your lifetime."

He pointed out one of the darkened windows. "It is *my* family's Coat of Arms on those sails. The next time you believe you've a better idea how this fleet is to be run, you would do well to remember that." He turned his gaze specifically to Singh at that. "I picked most of you based on ability, not family standing, breeding, or personality ... and you should be damn glad for the last, or you would still be land-bound, growing fat in your manors. If *any* of you think you can find a better Command position on another man's ship, I invite you to leave. Your replacement will be grateful for the opportunity. This fleet has a peerless reputation and proud standing in His Majesty's Court ... I know twenty lads who will *whine* far less and would take the offer the moment it was given."

The table was deathly silent for a long while following that. I stood where I was, awkwardly. I hadn't even been introduced yet, and already, things had come to a head. In some ways, it was a relief. I hadn't even had the chance to ruin these men's opinions of me. They already hated me. For once, Lucius couldn't exactly blame it on me.

"Sir," the greyhound broke the silence, with a long, exasperated sigh. "We aren't challenging your command. I just ... feel we deserve to have some questions answered, here. "

"Such as?" Lucius replied, unflinching.

Singh *did* flinch. "Well, I ... understand the boy—"

"His name is Luther." Lucius interrupted him. "Although it might be more appropriate to call him by my surname, now ... as that will be his title with the men."

The greyhound gave a barely-masked look of incredulity. "He didn't even have his own?" He let out a low, decidedly disgusted breath.

"No. And I consider it an honor for my son-in-law to inherit the Denholme name." Lucius stated, matter-of-factly. "My line would have ended with my daughter, had she married a titled man. It really worked out well for me in the end."

The statement was spoken with bitter irony, but Lucius was so damned serious when he said everything, I had to bite back a laugh. The Collie didn't bother covering his, which earned him another irate look from Singh.

"Yes, about that." Singh said. "I realize this young ... man ... has recently married into your family, sir. I wish to know the circumstances. I believe we're entitled to know them, being as these ... nuptials ... will inevitably affect all of our fates. How is it a man who hasn't even an Officer's rank was considered for such a ... union ... with your great family?"

He actually turned to address me at that, and I didn't avert my gaze when he did. Unlike the mastiff, this man was failing in every regard to intimidate me ... as much as he was trying. I'd served under, ignored, and cursed out pedigree officers just like him too many times in the past to count. I could smell his uneasiness and hear his claws shifting against the wooden floorboards. He might have been full of contempt, but he had no nerve. This was a man with a lot of entitlement, and no guts to back it up. The sort of man whose crew ran amok behind his back, and got a lot of laughs at his expense, and I'm sure he knew it.

That was one of the things Klaus had told me that had always stuck in my head, because it was one of the few things he *did* do exceptionally well, as a Fleet Admiral. A leader has to have confidence, even when he's uncertain ... or his crew will know it. And that's a vicious cycle. The less in-control you are of your men, the more they doubted your competence ... and the less control you can exert over them. And so on.

Singh struck me as the sort of man who'd been battling that his entire career. I'd seen many, many other Officers like him. He probably never should have gone into the navy, but I suspected he had some kind of skill for it, or Lucius never would have taken him on.

It wasn't all about skill. It was skill, and force of personality that commanded men. You needed charisma, and Singh had none.

Oh ... this man and I were *not* going to get along.

"I understand your concerns, Singh," Lucius responded, breaking me out of my reverie, "but I assure you ... I choose *every* man fulfilling a Command position within my fleet by merit. The fact that Luther has become my son-in-law is happy coincidence, but little else. And he will *not* be assuming control over the fleet until either I am deceased, or Cuthbert abdicates the position. He will be serving as First Mate on the *Cerberus*, with Shaw remaining as Captain, and Johannes retaking fleet admiral rank."

"I have trouble shaking the feeling that his sudden ... ascension in ranks has more to do with his association with your daughter than his previous naval career." Singh said.

"You're close to the line, Singh." Shaw growled.

" ... can't help feeling he crossed that line when he called the man a goat herder," the Collie muttered, his muzzle half-covered by an ale mug. "If you want my opinion."

"No one gives a damn about your opinion, Reynolds." The Dane spoke up, for the first time. "You're just relieved not to be the lowest man on the totem pole, anymore."

There was a moment of silence around the table, before the Collie tilted his head at the tall, gangly dog, and quirked an eyebrow. "And that is?"

The Dane seemed annoyed, but he wasn't getting anything but confused looks from around the table. I blinked. Even Lucius ... did none of these men honestly know what a 'totem pole' was?

The Dane gave a long sigh. "It's a carved ... log. A tribal symbol, the native Carvecians use them to denote their—"

"Ouuu, Carvecian tribal references," the Collie chuckled. "You've really got your game on, eh sage? It's not every night I warrant the strange foreign insults."

"Both of you, *enough*," Lucius slammed his cane down, and the bickering immediately stopped, although Singh still looked irate. Lucius looked to him first. "Singh ... I will say this only once. My family matters are *not* this fleet's business. They are not your business. You have no right to intrude upon my family's privacy, and you *will* take me at my word when I say ... the decisions I have made for this fleet were painstakingly made, for the *good* of this fleet. You will have many years to assess for yourself whether or not my daughter's choice in husband will make for an adequate Commanding Officer, but I assure you ... if he is not ... he will *never* inherit my ships. Not even when I leave this world." He paused to emphasize that ... both to them, and to me, I'd imagine. "I have left that sole power, in my will, to Johannes Cuthbert."

All eyes turned on the wolfhound standing, still silent, against the nearby wall. He looked back on them all impassively. The same coldness was directed my way, and I again felt a wash of resentment. What the hell had I done to deserve that look?

"He is to be Warden of this fleet both while at sea, and in the event of my death." Lucius stated. "Should my son-in-law fall short of all of your expectations over the next few years ... he will inherit nothing but my crumbling old manor." His brown eyes met mine, and I straightened my shoulders on instinct. Lucius was the sort of man that commanded authority, no matter the situation, but I'd never seen him commanding men before. It made me again wish I'd known him when he was younger.

"Luther. Introduce yourself. And explain to these men why you will *not* be disappointing them ... or me."

I kept myself from visibly swallowing, despite the fact that my throat was dry and I felt like I hadn't spoken in years.

"I believe you gentlemen know my name by this point." I began. "I am the son of a man named William, from Evelshire." I didn't bother mentioning my 'breed', because I didn't want to invite the opinion that I gave a damn, "I have been serving on the navy rosters for twelve years now. And I would rather not speak on my prowess, sirs ... if that's quite alright. I think it would be arrogant to assume I'm not going to disappoint you all. That is always a possibility, and speaking on my skills is an empty boast until I prove them on the water. I can only swear that I will give my all to the fleet, I will serve with honor, and that the idea of disappointing Lucius frightens me to the very core of my being ... so if I fail spectacularly in my duties aboard your ship, Sir Shaw ... you need not pitch me overboard. I will be doing so myself, to avoid facing my father-in-law's wrath."

The stunned silence I got from Singh filled me with a certain sense of satisfaction, and both the Dane and the collie were giving me incredulous looks, but it was the Mastiff's reaction that shocked me the most.

He gave a rumbling chuckle, which rose to full-throated laughter after a few moments. It was strangely terrifying.

"Lucius," he glanced down over the folds his laughter was causing in his jowls at the far shorter spaniel, "it's uncanny. Are you sure he isn't your *actual* son?"

"That would make his marriage to my daughter fairly blasphemous." Lucius pointed out.

"Indeed." The big dog's chuckles finally died off. "Alright, young man," He addressed me for the first time since I arrived, " I can't say I approve of this situation, and I suspect, as Singh has so ineloquently been trying to imply for the last ten minutes, that you conned your way into a place in society you have *no* place in. But if Johannes is to play watchdog over you for a time, that's his burden ... not ours. The day it becomes our problem, I will determine then how I feel about the matter. Until then ... stay out of our way." He looked to Johannes, and gave the slightest of bows in his direction. "It will be an honor to serve under you again, Sir Cuthbert."

I let out a long breath, biting back my frustration. What on *earth* had Johannes done to win these men over? Even Singh hadn't voiced a single complaint about Cuthbert being reappointed.

Lucius and Shaw had begun talking, and I was very clearly no longer the focus of the conversation, but my eyes were drawn to the table. Likely what *should* have been the subject of conversation this whole time, I had overlooked it entirely. Splayed out across the wooden surface were parchments with long written passages, foreign locations and names, even loose scribbling of what had to be trade routes and cartographers' notes. Each had a different stamped seal, partially covered in the cracked, red wax seal of the crown's royal messengers. I wasn't sure what I was looking at, but I started reading the heading on one of the scrolls, curiously.

I was midway through a passage about some small settlement named 'Serwich', when the fur on the scruff of my neck stood up, and I had the unmistakable sensation of knowing there were eyes on me. I turned, peering into the crowd.

I didn't have far to look. I'd been so distracted with the mess this meeting had become I'd neglected to even notice our nearest table neighbors. And I should have. There were three of them, hunkered over bowls of cheap gruel, with small cups of pale, weak tea. They all wore the thick, rough brown robes—tied at the waist with dingy white rope—of monks. Neutren.

And one of them was outright staring at me. He turned almost the instant I looked back on him, but I felt a heavy weight settle in my stomach the moment I saw his face. The tired eyes of the black lab were far too old for someone his age, and his entire stance was, like many Neutren, cowed and pitiful ... but it was the discolored patch of fur on his chin, likely the result of a burn in his past, that made my heart skip.

It finally came back to me ... in an incomplete jumble. Flashes, a vague memory of waking the following morning, thinking I'd dreamt it ... I'd put it out of my mind then, never to think on it again.

Until now. That man was real. He was not a dream. He was real, he had really been here many years ago...

And he had seen Klaus and I together.

We'd both been drunk. We'd left the inn ... barely made it twenty paces away, along the cliff face, laughing raucously about something together. Klaus's broad shoulders shook, and I remembered ... loving the way he smiled, at that moment. His grins always split his face, running up into his long white cheeks. And I just ... wanted to kiss him.

And I had. And we'd stood there in the rain, him pushing me back against the protruding roots of one of the cliff side trees far above us, and holding me there.

Neither of us had noticed the monk in time. And when we'd finally seen him ... Klaus had only shouted a threat at him, until he'd fled into the night. We'd gone back to the ship after that and made love. Forgotten...

Until now. Oh God, he recognized me. After all this time, the bastard recognized me. He'd probably never forgotten me.

It's not every day you see a man kissing a Fleet Admiral.

I was frozen in place. I didn't know what to do. I couldn't possibly beat a retreat from this place, now ... not now. Not the first night I was meeting these men. What excuse could I possibly make?

The monk seemed determined to ignore me, now. I stared a hole in his back, but he didn't turn to meet my gaze again. Maybe he was trying to forget me, too. Maybe he wanted as little to do with me as I did with him.

My luck had never been that good.

"Do they make you uncomfortable, too?" A voice said from off to my left, and I almost jumped. I turned to see the collie addressing me, looking in the direction of the monks, as well.

"A little." I understated.

"Mnh," The collie agreed, finishing off his ale with one last swallow. "Makes me shudder just thinking' about it. I don't know about you, but my devotion to God is from the waist up, anything below that's pure sinning territory."

"Agreed," I muttered. The man didn't know how right he was.

The sheep dog fixed his bright blue gaze on mine, and some part of my brain clicked on, and forced me to assess the rest of him, for the first time. Not bad ... a bit heavy for my tastes, but somehow, the thicker build seemed to fit him. I'd never really found black and white coats attractive, for whatever reason. They were just so ... domesticated.

It was probably for the best that I didn't find any of these men overwhelmingly attractive, honestly. That would make working with them exceedingly complicated.

"So ... I'd imagine as far as first impressions go, we must seem an awfully dysfunctional bunch." The collie smiled.

"That's putting it mildly." I said, trying to put the monk from my mind, for now. Short of going over there and asking him if he remembered watching me be intimate with my now-deceased lover, I didn't know what I *could* do about him. I just had to let this play its course.

"It's not as bad as it seems." The collie sighed. "We all have our own little nook, y'see. We fit together well enough in the big picture. Lucius picks his men so our skills complement each other. We don't really *need* to get on well in our personal lives ... we spend most of our time on different ships. It's an odd dynamic, but it works. And all the bickerin' sure does make shore leave interesting."

"I'd imagine so." I pulled up a chair, sitting beside the man, while Lucius continued his conversation with Shaw. I watched them for a time, the collie following my gaze.

"Shaw's the disciplinarian. Keeps the men in line ... keeps Singh in line."

"What about Addison?" I queried, eyeing the Dane. He seemed to be inspecting one of the scrolls on the table, closely. "He hasn't spoken up much, but he seems to concur with Singh."

The collie rolled his eyes, and pounded his mug on the table, gesturing to one of the servers for a refill. "Addison concurs with whoever's shouting loud enough. The man's a glorified bookkeeper. If you need an expert on foreign policy, or what the weather patterns in the ... Purungi peninsulas are going to be like in March, he's your man, but he has less say in the fleet than I do. We needed at least one Captain in our fleet able to handle diplomacy without needing to draw steel, though, so..."

"I'm getting the idea." I replied.

He nodded. "He'd be a better man if he didn't latch onto Singh so often. But apparently their families know each other, so..."

"You're being very candid. Thank you." I said earnestly. I was learning more about these men in two minutes than Lucius had told me in nearly a year and I believed every word the collie was saying. He had a very easy way of speaking, like everything rolled off his shoulders.

All in all, he just seemed a pleasant fellow. I suspect he probably dealt with his fellow Captains' derision on a regular basis, and he clearly hadn't let it bother him. I'd have to try and model my behavior off of his, somewhat. It seemed to be working for him.

Still...

"Can I ask you something ... ah ... Finnegan?" I queried, not sure if I should be on a first-name basis with him yet, but remembering what Lucius had said earlier.

"Finn's just fine." He smiled, affirming what Lucius had said.

"How is it ... you're here?" I asked, trying not to make the words sound offensive, but not sure how else to phrase them. He laughed, and I found myself apologizing. "I don't mean to be insulting—"

"No, it's quite alright." He said. "It's an obvious question. I stick out like a sore thumb, I know. If even ... and you'll excuse me on this ... if even someone low-born can pick that out, it must be more obvious than I thought."

I gave an uneasy shrug. "Well, beyond the issue of breeding ... Lucius has spoken on Shaw and Singh's capabilities in naval warfare, when we went over some of the raids you've intercepted over the last few years. I know Shaw's an old war buddy of Lucius ... and Singh, I can only assume, must have some indispensable traits, or Lucius would have gotten rid of him by now."

Finnegan leaned back in his chair, the legs creaking. "Singh is ... unfortunately ... one of the better minds out there, when it comes to naval tactics. His head's like a damned library, I swear ... he must have spent his entire childhood studying historic naval battles, because he can cite the dates and men to almost every strategy he's employed. He takes an obnoxious amount of pride in it."

"That doesn't sound particularly ... creative." I snorted. "How do you adapt to a scenario that's never *been* in the history books?"

He shrugged. "You might be right. But Shaw apparently holds his knowledge in high esteem, because he defers to him on most major decisions. The big man's never been much of a thinker."

"So where do you fit in?" I had to ask.

His response was a smile that showed off his canines. "Artillery," he stated, with more than a hint of excitement in his voice, like a man who really loved his work. "If you need something shot, I'm your man. Your father-in-law there went digging through the Engineering Academies a few years ago, when it became woefully obvious his guns were in horrible disrepair. I was first mate on a powder ship, at the time ... fresh out of the Academy, and looking to get my feet wet somewhere. I guess the idea of re-outfitting a 124-gun fleet frightened off most of the others out there, but I was happy to take it on. Almost every demi-culverin needed work. I installed the broad side of the *Cerberus* with demi-cannons ... it became a year-long affair. He offered me a position on afterwards, and I've been serving since. After Captain Tannis retired last year, Lucius offered command of the *Fenrir* to me, and I'd have been a fool to turn him down."

I was still hung on what he'd said a few sentences previous.

"The *Cerberus* has demi-cannons?" I repeated, gape-jawed.

He gave a fierce smirk. "Yes. Yes she does."

"I need to get on this ship..." I whispered.

He laughed again. "You will, soon enough. I hope you enjoy my handiwork."

"I suspect I will." I leaned back in my chair, as one of the servers came and dropped off a fresh mug of ale in front of Finnegan. He licked his chops, and fished a few coins out of his pocket. "Thank you, Finn." I said, as the server headed off. "Honestly ... I'm very glad my father-in-law took you on. For purely selfish reasons." I admitted.

"It's a relief to know I'll have someone in the command ranks I can speak to on the level who doesn't loathe me."

"You've a chance of winning their trust eventually." He said, as he began to sip at his beverage again. "Your watchdog there did, somehow. Although I'll admit, I wasn't about when he first took up the old man's role, so I'm not sure how that all played out. But he's got Shaw's respect, which means the impossible *is* possible, right?"

"I seem to have your trust already." I noted. "You've been extremely frank with me."

"Well ... I have an unfair advantage." He said elusively, downing another long drink of his brew.

I gave him a long look, trying to discern what he meant by that. "I'm ... not following." I admitted, at length, scrunching up my brow.

"I know you earned your way into Lucius's family, Luther." He said, matter-of-factly. "I know you didn't steal his little girl away ... that the marriage was a result of whatever deeds you must have done that impressed Lucius. And I know those deeds must have been great in his estimation, because he pulled you out of a very dark place to put you where you are now. Lucius is the sort of person who values men based on what they're made of, not who made them. So I'm certain if he chose you, you must have been the better man for the role."

I balked, some of that fear returning from earlier, except this time all at once. How in the hell could he possibly ... ?

'Better man'? The way he was phrasing what he was saying...

My ears snapped up, and I glanced down the table at Lucius, who was too occupied in his argument with Shaw to take note of anything else. The Dane was still reading over one of the scrolls, and Singh was listening in on Shaw and Lucius's argument, probably wondering which way he should lean, when the time came.

I dropped my voice, turning my attention back on Finn. "You're the other man." I stated; certain of it now. "Aren't you?"

He winked at me, then glanced around the table, and continued. "Lucius spoke to me last year, shortly after he'd given command of the *Fenrir* to me. He offered the very same deal to me I'd imagine he offered to you ... but he told me point-blank I was one of two men he was considering ... and that he'd be meeting with you shortly."

"How much did he tell you?" I demanded, in a harsh whisper.

He arched an eyebrow. " ... about you? Very little. I caught on over time that you were somewhere ... ah ... shall we say ... under lock and key. That they'd sent men out to question you, and that his Knight would be 'retrieving' you shortly. Honestly, I thought at that point I was a shoe-in." He shrugged. "Goes to show, you can never guess which way the wind will blow."

"What about Delilah?" I asked, fearful for my wife's secrets.

His expression darkened at that. It didn't suit him, and I could tell he'd suddenly become uncomfortable. " ... he told me why such a rash course of action was necessary, and ... time-sensitive. I determined the rest on my own. I'd met his daughter several times, over the years. I knew she wasn't capable of acting so disgracefully. When I confronted him to tell me the truth, he did." He was silent a few moments. "It didn't change anything. I would have married the sweet thing, if you hadn't come sweeping in like you did."

" 'Sweeping in'?" I queried, dumbfounded.

"Lucius and I met several times during your stay at the manor." He explained. "I suppose he was still very uncertain of you, and he wanted to keep me on hand, in case things ... fell through. But I knew by the fifth month that I'd been bested. The old man had a real grudging admiration for you that got less and less grudging, as time went on." He chuckled. "I even stopped to see Delilah every now and then, when I was at the manor. I'm not certain what you did, but ... I have never seen that girl so happy ... and in such a terrible situation, too." He smiled. "I think the right man won."

I had no reply for the collie. I just sat there, trying to process what he'd said. All those months ... I had known Lucius had another man in mind, but I hadn't known he was making visits to the house. I suppose I could see why Lucius would keep it from me, but...

His last words were ringing in my head, reverberating like a church bell. The right man. This man honestly held no grudge over losing a marriage into a wealthy family, marrying a beautiful woman he was fond of, who was presumably fond of him, if Lucius had even considered him worthy of her, and from inheriting the fleet ... which he was already a part of.

This was the right man. This easygoing, kind-hearted, genuine man, who was already a part of the Denholme fleet, already a part of Delilah's life far before I came along ... who would have been a *real* husband to her, and treated her well ... given her children that were *his*, and loved her in all the ways socially acceptable men did.

What the hell had Lucius been thinking?

"I'm sorry ... did I lay that on you too fast?" The collie asked, looking concerned. "I supposed I should've waited until our second or third meeting for the 'rivals for the same girl' speech, eh?"

"Don't you feel like you were the better choice?" I asked.

He tipped his head slightly, quirking one ear. "I trust Lucius." He said, and raised his glass. "And you should, too. Don't go doubting it now. It's a bit late, aye?" He chuckled. "And don't worry. I'm more'n content with how things worked out. Admiral's a lot of responsibility, and I'm probably going to be fat and useless far before the old man ever kicks the bucket, anyway. My plan is to retire when I hit 40, come hell or high water. Lucius wanted someone with a lot more passion, I think. I'm on the sea because that's where the biggest guns are. If boats could fly, I'd be in the clouds. Lucius said you're one of those men that gets landsick ... and a man with a real love for the water is who should be leadin' this fleet. I'm just along for the ride."

"You would have been better for Delilah..." I stated quietly.

"Ah ... you're one of those men whose got confidence for everything but women, aren't you?" He chuckled. "Listen..." he leaned in close, "between you and me, I laid down a sweet little thing in Gilasch a few years back, and judgin' by her letters, I've got a bastard comin' for my fortune once he's got the will to find me. We've all got our dirty laundry ... men are mortal, an' we make mistakes. Your woman'll forgive you, whatever trespasses got you in hot water when Lucius found you ... she clearly still took a shine to you then, and she'll love you through the rest, too. That's the wonderful thing about women. They bring out the best in us, and forgive the worst in us." He laughed. "Buck up. I'm sure there's no more deserving man for the lass." He gave me a few hearty claps on the shoulder.

His words sat inside me like a stone, and reminded me of each and every single one of my failings. The Church, the military, and the law itself had failed to make me feel guilt over the choices I'd made in my life, and the choices that had been made *for* me ... but being married was beginning to do the trick. I physically couldn't be the man Delilah deserved. And a better candidate was sitting right across from me, blissfully unaware that the man who'd been chosen over him to marry the woman he'd had his eye on ... couldn't even consummate the union.

It reminded me to look to the table behind us, where the monks had been quietly eating their dinner, searching for the black lab with the discolored fur from my dreams.

They were gone.

CHAPTER 11
FAMILY BONDS

"Luther!"

The voice of my wife carried across the lawn. It was coming from somewhere beyond the tree line of the cobbled roadway leading towards the manor. I turned my nose to the wind, alarmed that I'd missed the scent of her, when she was so close. I'd been preoccupied with thoughts of our trip to Cheron the whole way home...

I gave Specter a light kick with my heels, and she accelerated to a canter, pushing me past Lucius and Cuthbert on their geldings. I loved the way the mare felt beneath me, her gate smooth, but firm. It had taken some months, but we'd eventually come to an understanding with one another and Lucius had inevitably yielded the horse to me. She would have been too much for a man with a lame leg to handle, anyway ... it had all worked out for the best. She would always have that wild spark the Carvecian horses seemed prone to, but her temper suited me just fine. 'A difficult horse for a difficult man', Lucius had said.

It had been two weeks travel from Cheron and unlike the journey there, we'd made few stops on the way home. I'd been stubborn enough to insist I made the daily trips by horse, because I was intent on entirely breaking Specter in before I went out to sea for the next eight months, but by this point I was regretting that decision. My lower back and thighs ached and even with the smooth pace Specter set, my rear was faring no better.

The stay in Cheron had been brief, but eventful. Regretfully, I hadn't spent as much of it on the ships as I'd wished to ... and the only time I'd spent at sea outside the shallows had been on the skiff. I'd gotten a good feel for the *Cerberus*, at least. She was every bit the beauty inside as out, and her sister ships were no disappointment, either.

Unfortunately though, really getting to know the ships and settle in just wasn't possible. They were only moored in Cheron for two days following our arrival, and then they had to head to Rhinemouth to resupply for the coming year ... and we'd had to head home. Lucius's knee was giving him trouble—travelling so much in the chill of the early spring air—and apparently there were some very important correspondences the old man had to make before he sent his fleet off for the coming season. I suspect they had something to do with the profuse amount of paperwork the Captains had been quarreling over with him in Cheron.

I'd tried picking his brain about it the whole way home, but he'd seemed to have a lot on his mind. From what little he had said on the matter, it involved where the fleet would be commissioned this upcoming year, but he apparently didn't want to say much more until he'd made a few decisions. He'd been reading over the documents the whole way home. Whatever it was, it seemed to be tying him in knots.

This was the part of Fleet command I wasn't looking forward to. Once I was out on the water, I had no issue making calls. I'd done it for Klaus many, many times in the past. But politics and paperwork were far from my areas of expertise, and I knew if I ever came to a point in my life where I was faced with these sorts of decisions, I'd probably have just as much, if not more trouble than the old man seemed to be having. I didn't envy him.

I'd had a small taste of what lay ahead of me, and I was impatient to return. That being said ... I was glad to be coming back to the manor. The realization that I was longing for the place had hit me a few days ago, and I'd been floored. I think I was honestly starting to view these grounds as my home. And that wasn't just strange for me. It was unheard of. I couldn't even remember being so attached to one place in my *childhood*, and I'd certainly never longed for any kind of 'home' in my adult life.

Maybe I was just getting old, but the idea of having a safe place like this to lie my head, and let my sails unfurl ... a place where everyone knew who I was, and the outside world left me the hell alone ... it was something I couldn't even find at sea. I'd spent so much of my life hiding, I hadn't realized how paranoid and frightened it had made me.

But even the servants here left me alone, and left me to my own devices. Lucius had a discreet staff who were used to keeping secrets. Mikhail had been residing at the manor for several months now, and no one had even batted an eye, even though I was certain most of them knew who and what he was. There weren't many staff at the Denholme manor ... a little less than a dozen, from what I knew. But it really shouldn't have surprised me that Lucius had a discreet staff. Delilah had been hiding a pregnancy for most of the months before we were married.

Speak of the devil...

Delilah was bounding down the uneven path towards us, muddying her petticoat edges in the occasional puddle from last night's storm. Despite my sore ... everything ... I had to smile. I'd never felt what it was like to have someone happy to see me, to welcome me anywhere. Not before this place. Not before this family.

My family...

I tightened up on the reins and brought Specter to a stop, swinging a leg over and dismounting in one motion. My feet struck the muddy, cobbled road only seconds before my wife crashed into my arms, and I had to chuckle.

"We were barely gone a month, love." I brushed my free hand over her head and down one long, soft ear, the other still holding Specter's reins. "How well will you fare when we actually go to sea?"

"I don't want to think about it." She murmured against my still rain-soaked collar, holding tight to me despite my damp, road-worn clothing. "Besides," she looked up at me, brown eyes half-lidded with her smile, "you *all* went. Usually at least father stays home."

I smiled down at her, and leaned in to kiss her, gently. She never refused me. Although when she pulled back, she reached up and brushed back some of the ragged, un-brushed fur along my cheeks, looking concerned. " ... you look exhausted." She said quietly. "I hope you don't take ill. You weren't riding in the rain, were you?"

"Not through the worst of it." I assured her. "But we left from Gilven without the carriage. It would have been a day-longer trip, if we'd relied on that blasted thing ... and we all concurred we'd rather go mounted. We overnighted at the road station in Debonshire though, so don't worry. We missed most of the storm. We just got drizzled on a bit this morning."

She stroked my cheek, her expression still seeming concerned. A flash of gold and orange caught my attention at that moment, though ... following far less hurriedly along the road, towards us. He was wearing his fur cape, as he generally did, tail bobbing carefully above the ground so as not to soil the pale fur, and he was picking his way through the puddles, unlike my wife.

I narrowed my eyes. What in the hell was he holding ... ?

I sighed, as the little bundle shifted, and poked its nose out. And I arched an eyebrow at my wife. "Delilah," I said with a sigh, "why does Mikhail have Klaus?"

"Oh," she glanced over her shoulder, " ... we were walking the grounds ... and then I saw you all coming down the road..."

I gently separated myself from her and strode past her towards the slender young fox holding my child. He had that ever-present smile of his, and I had to remind myself in that moment that Lucius and Cuthbert were not twenty feet behind me, lest I greet him the same way I had my wife...

I chose to focus on the pair's poor judgment instead, putting on my 'irate' face. "Mikhail," I said with a sigh, "please explain to me why my son is out in this weather. He's not even a one-year-old, and I'd like him to make it to adulthood, if at all possible."

The fox only patted the little babe's back and nosed the pup, who at this point was squirming around excitedly. He was wrapped in a blanket, at least ... *and* under Mikhail's fur cloak. He was probably warmer than all of us, but I still couldn't shake the urge that I needed to whisk him away inside as fast as possible. It was cold outside. Moderately. Sort of cold.

He was a baby. He didn't need to be in any kind of cold weather, regardless how minor. He was *my* baby.

"I was just accompanying Delilah." Mikhail insisted, doing his best act of flattening his ears and acting contrite, looking up his dainty nose at me with those big ... stupid fox eyes.

Damn him.

I sighed, and turned back to address my wife. "What were you thinking?" I asked. "This is no kind of weather for a babe to be out in. What if it had started raining again?"

"We would have gone back inside." Delilah responded from where she was beside her father's horse. The man couldn't dismount until we got back to the house, but that hadn't stopped him from embracing the young girl with one arm. She looked back at me, and crossed her petite arms over her chest. "Stop being so over-protective, Luther. The twins need some fresh air every now and then, they've been cooped up all winter. I needed some fresh air. And I didn't go alone ... I brought Mikhail."

"Ya ... never fear." He smiled. "I was playing the role of fearless protector, while you were out."

Cuthbert's heavy shire mix moved past us, the man not bothering to stop, or even so much as look our way as he headed on down the lane towards the manor. I felt the cold shoulder from where I was, though. I watched him depart for a few moments, my heart sinking just a bit further.

He hadn't even greeted Delilah ... he'd been *that* insistent on putting distance between himself and Mikhail.

And me.

"What crawled inside him and died?" Mikhail murmured, seeming more amused by the wolfhound's coldness than anything else. Then again, very little didn't amuse Mikhail.

I let out a long breath then held out an arm. "Give him to me." I said. "I'm taking him inside."

Mikhail shifted Klaus, but paused. "Ah ... but you—"

"*Luther*! Don't you dare!" Delilah padded over to us, and gathered up my son before I could take him from the fox.

"Why—" I began.

"You're *soaked*!" She huffed. "And *you're* the one worried about him catching a chill? Honestly." She tucked the babe against her shoulder and I tipped my ears back, mortified.

Lucius strode past us atop his own horse, giving me an amused expression as he pulled out his travel flask, finishing off the last of it before he undoubtedly hit his brandy reserves back at the manor.

"How do you like bein' henpecked, son? Is it everything you'd ever dreamed it'd be?" He chuckled.

"And *you* shouldn't be drinking while you're riding!" Delilah turned an admonishing look on the old man, and he shut his muzzle. "You can barely dismount as it is, with your leg. If you fall off your horse and ruin your good one, I'll hear no moaning and groaning when you're bedridden!"

Lucius cleared his throat, and spurred his horse into a trot, fleeing down the road to catch up with Johannes. Delilah turned her gaze back on me and I straightened like I was staring down a sergeant, at attention. But she only gave a soft sigh, and rocked Klaus.

" ... I'm very glad you're all home and safe, Luther. You'll have to tell me how it went."

Specter nudged me with her nose and I reached a hand back to stroke her. She wanted to go back to the barn, get dry, get some food and rest ... and I felt much the same.

"Well, I met Finnegan." I said, beginning to walk down the roadway, leading my mare. "For one..."

Now it was her turn to look a little embarrassed, and I arched an eyebrow at her. "Yes ... he's a nice fellow." She said, carefully.

"It's alright, Delilah ... I know." I said. "And I'm hardly upset by it. It makes sense that you needed to have another man on hand. In case I was a raving lunatic, and all."

"You *are* a lunatic, Luther." She smiled softly, reaching her free hand up to stroke the soaked shoulder of my greatcoat. "But that's alright. Only a lunatic would have dealt with this family ... or married me."

"Delilah." I spoke softly, "Please. Tell me at least one thing. Were you at any point hoping it would be him?"

We reached the barn and she turned, holding Klaus close as the wind whipped up. "Honestly, Luther..." she glanced down at the little boy, " ... in the beginning ... I was a little afraid of you. Finnegan seemed far less ... intimidating."

I swallowed.

"So ... was there ever a point? Yes." She murmured, and stepped up to me until she was almost resting against my chest. She lowered her muzzle into the loose scruff of fur along my neck, where my collar was open. "But ask me again now. I'll tell you I love my husband ... and that I wouldn't rather be married to any other man." She smiled up at me. "And that he is much more handsome when he isn't so full of self-doubt."

I sighed and wrapped an arm around her, holding her there for a time. "It's just hard to meet a man like that and know he might have been the husband to you that ... I can never be."

"Luther," she said, "you're the only one who feels that way. And I don't know why. It's a mystery to me why you continuously find yourself lacking when it comes to me ... but can be such an arrogant ass at everything else."

I began to say something, but she just smiled, and I gave up on whatever protests I'd been forming. Instead, I kissed her again.

Mikhail had dutifully remained silent as we walked, doing his professional courtesy and turning his ears to the wind, taking no part in our private conversation. He'd even put some distance between us, while we spoke. I knew of course that he could hear everything we were saying, but all that mattered was that he made it no business of his. After the last few months spent getting to know the fox and the intricacies of this whole 'courtesan' arrangement better, I was actually fairly certain he wouldn't. Mikhail wasn't nearly as devious as I'd thought he was, upon first meeting him. He was just young, curious, and ... a fox. He had a taste for mischief, but in all of our family's private dealings, he'd been careful to fade into the background and keep his muzzle shut. And he'd had ample opportunities since his stay here to dispense our secrets ... not to mention, he'd acquired a few more secrets than he came here with.

My tongue got a little loose when I was bedding someone ... I'll admit that. I'd expected I might get overly-personal with Mikhail from time to time, and I had. Mostly just talk of my past, though. A lot of talk about my childhood. A lot of talk about Klaus...

What I hadn't expected was the strange kinship Delilah had forged with the boy and all the odd ... entanglements that had caused. Suffice to say, my petite, gentle wife now had secrets she kept even from her own father. And *God* forbid Cuthbert ever knew.

I wasn't sure exactly what was happening between the three of us, but I knew it was getting more and more complicated day by day, and probably not for the best. It wasn't that I didn't trust Mikhail around my wife. In fact, if I'd thought there was any kind of *physical* attraction there, I would have encouraged it to the utmost, but that wasn't the case. And he'd assured me he preferred to avoid being shared amongst family members like that. Apparently similar situations had ended poorly too many times for other people in his profession. I could definitely understand that.

I loved my wife. But I was becoming more and more fond of Mikhail as time went on, despite my best attempts to keep him at arms-length. I was an emotional man. I had been through this several times in the past, and I knew the twists and turns it took and where it inevitably ended. I couldn't get this close to someone without eventually coming to feel something towards them. And unlike my wife, Mikhail was ... compatible with me in *all* ways. I'd been doing my best to try and focus mostly on the physical end ... keep my association with him firmly situated in the carnal part of my brain. For a time, it had even been working.

But this sudden fondness Delilah had taken in him and her increasing attempts to actually *involve* the fox in my family life, was making it more and more difficult to treat him like an outsider. I wasn't sure she even knew what she was doing to me. I wasn't sure Mikhail even knew that I was beginning to see him as more than just a whore. Perhaps if he knew, he'd laugh at me.

I'd been thinking about it the whole time I was gone, and the incident in Cheron had brought other, more distant memories of the same sensations I was having now to the forefront. I'd been through this cycle before. The desire not to get *too* close, the daily, constant need to convince myself that all I wanted was a partner to rut with ... that that was all I *needed*. This is exactly what it had been like in the first few months I'd been sleeping with Klaus.

I hated to equate the connection to sex ... but that's earnestly what seemed to set these feelings aflame inside me. It annoyed me to think that I was such a shallow man, but maybe that wasn't it. Maybe I was just so damned emotional, I *couldn't* be involved sexually with another man without coming to feel something for them.

Passion made me ... passionate. And sleeping with another man for any length of time inevitably made me fond of them. Sharing my family time, my house, even my children, with that same man ... God knew where that would lead. Even if he *was* a whore. Even if everyone but the 'holy knight' approved of his being here.

I think Delilah mistakenly believed we could all just be fond of one another and get on like good friends. But I knew myself better. And ever since Klaus, I knew how deep my feelings for another man could go. I didn't want those feelings to compete with my feelings for Delilah. She was my wife, and whether or not I was equipped to be a proper husband to her physically, I wanted to be there for her, emotionally. As I had been thus far. I wanted to be there for my children, and for this family ... and I just wasn't sure how Mikhail fit into all of that.

I was getting ahead of myself, though ... and I knew when I was being paranoid. Being tired only made me more so. I stroked my wife's ears once more, a gesture of affection I'd come to know by now comforted her greatly. She smiled up at me.

"I'll get Klaus inside. He and Brook need to eat, anyway. And then I should probably change..." she laughed, looking down at where her petticoat was stained with rain water, a bit of mud, and a few discolored stains on her white linen dress, where she'd hugged me. I looked down at myself, quirking a jowl.

"Apologies..." I muttered.

"I'm the one who ran into *you*." She giggled. "Don't apologize. Besides..." she nibbled her lower lip, "you look very handsome when you're all ... tousled." I smoothed a hand over my fur again, self-consciously, and she only laughed again. "I'll see you at dinner, Luther." She called back while heading towards the house, that smile still on her face.

" ... for a woman so disinterested in bodily pleasures, she certainly compliments my appearance quite often. Even when I'm at my worst." I muttered, glancing down at myself, and shaking my coat out.

"You *are* handsome when you're tousled." Mikhail stated from behind me. "And she's not disinterested in bodily pleasures. I think you and I both know that fairly well by now."

I glanced over my shoulder at him, knowing that smirk was there. And it was. "Please don't bring that up." I said, as I shoved open the barn door and began to lead Specter inside. "I ... don't even want to think about that, at the moment ... I have enough on my mind."

"I can't help it. I find it highly amusing." His smirk widened and he headed inside and leaned against the support beam, while I started removing Specter's tack.

"I know you do." I said irritably. "And I said I didn't want to talk about it. It was a mistake."

"Why?" he countered. "I don't see how it did any harm. I would think you'd want your wife more involved in *all* the aspects of your life, if she wishes to be. I doubt she'll speak a word of it."

"I'm sure she won't." I said, as I hung my mare's bridle in the infamous supply closet Mikhail and I had once shared, upon our first meeting. And ... several since. "That's not my concern. I just think..." I paused, my hand stilling on the saddle rack. " ... I feel like ... if my wife has any kinds of desires ... in that regard ... it isn't the most healthy way for her to exercise them. She's my wife. She shouldn't be playing audience to her own marriage bed."

"She seemed to enjoy it." He smirked. "But honestly Luther, if you're that concerned you aren't fulfilling your marriage duties, take her to bed once or twice, yourself. I'm sure she wouldn't reject you, or judge you."

The saddle in my hands slammed down on the rack, startling Mikhail, and he went silent. I didn't respond, just hefted a bucket of grain and began heading over towards Specter's stall. By the time I was pouring the grain in, I felt his presence behind me and his hands hesitantly moving over my shoulders. I let out a long breath, but I didn't rebuff him. His fingers kneaded into my shoulders, and I set the bucket down, leaning against the bars of the stall for a few moments as he worked some of the tension from the long ride away.

" ... bad trip?" He asked quietly, after a few moments.

" ... no." I said at length. "Just long. I'm tired."

"Would you like me to go?" He asked, and I shook my head. He didn't know how much I wanted him to stay.

"I smell like the road." I muttered, snuffing out a breath as I got a whiff of my own scent.

"I figured I'd be polite and not say anything." He spoke over my shoulder, sliding a paw down my back slowly. I felt his muzzle press into the scruff of my neck, where my fur jutted out from beneath my collar in a ragged mess. I could feel him smile against the nape of my neck, and release a long, warm breath. "Lucky for you, I don't mind dirty dogs."

I closed my eyes, feeling the always-gentle touch of the fox's paws, slipping under the hem of my coat, to my thick leather utility belt. My hips instinctively craned into his touch, but with a concentrated effort, I slid my palm down to grip his, and moved it away.

"Not here." I forced myself to say, with some effort.

"Hasn't seemed to bother you in the past." He nipped at my ear.

"It still doesn't." I assured him. "But right now, I need a bath ... and I need to visit a chamber pot. As soon as possible."

He actually chuckled. "You couldn't have just stopped somewhere along the roadside?"

"Apparently," I grunted, latching the stall closed, and heading back towards the barn doors. "According to ornery old spaniels ... 'Pedigrees don't piss in bushes like wild animals'."

"Yet another painful part of Pedigree society, eh?" He smirked, as I hurried past.

"You have no idea."

The bath had been ... amazing. And that was putting it lightly. I hadn't enjoyed warm water in over a week and while a year ago I would have laughed at the idea of a heated bath, after a year's worth of pampering I was growing accustomed to them.

The fox I'd shared it with had, of course, contributed greatly to my enjoyment. Both for carnal and humorous reasons. While water had little to no effect on my coat, Mikhail looked completely pathetic soaked. He shrunk to about half his size and insisted on having almost no part of his body above the water except his nose and eyes, or he began shivering as helplessly as a jackal in the northern seas. The fox wasn't exactly at his most majestic in a bath tub.

He still looked pretty good bent over one, though.

I let out a long breath I hadn't known I'd been holding so long as I made my way down the east wing hallway, buttoning my vest as I went. My fur was still just a bit damp and sticking to my undershirt, but I felt clean, relieved, and physically refreshed. It's amazing how much of a difference it made for my mood.

That turned dismal all but immediately, when I saw the man stalking up the staircase in my direction. The wolfhound had changed, too ... I couldn't tell if he'd bathed, but he was out of his road wear and back to his military clothing. And the look he got on his face when he saw me from down the hallway made my fur stand on end.

"Luther," He growled, crossing the space between us in five large strides, "you're late for dinner."

I balked. "I ... what?"

"Your family is *waiting* for you downstairs. They served the meal twenty minutes ago."

"They ... could have started without me." I said, narrowing my eyes at his accusatory tone, and gesturing out the window. "The sun's not even down yet. I wasn't aware I was so tardy, but I'm sorry. I'm making my way down there now."

"You haven't seen your wife and children for a month." He spoke harshly. "They want to spend *time* with you. You're heading off to sea in a few weeks' time, I would think you would prioritize what little time you have left with them, before you go."

"I'm ... a *bit* late for dinner." My hackles rose, and I barely kept myself from snarling at the man. Where the hell had this come from?! "It's hardly the end of the world, and I don't like your tone right now. I needed to wash up before the meal, we've been on the road for weeks ... I hardly think it warrants such a reprimand!"

"Washing up? Is that all?" He retorted, and I tipped my ears back, glancing back at the doorway. Mikhail had not emerged from the washroom, yet ... I suspect he could hear our argument from the other side of the door. Cuthbert held my gaze for a long while, until I looked away, betraying my guilt. His expression only grew angrier at that ... but just when I thought things were about to grow more heated he only turned, and began walking away.

"You're expected downstairs, Luther. I won't delay you from your family a moment longer."

I watched him, feeling something rise in my chest ... the crushed-down weight of all of my objections and outrage at his cold, dismissive behavior over the last month. It began to bubble over, and I couldn't fight back the feeling any longer. He was robbing me of this argument by leaving.

No. Enough. I was tired of it all this pedigree nonsense, keeping civil and repressing every damned thing for the sake of ...

pleasantry. This man was pissing me off, and I needed to have it out.

"*Johannes*!" I shouted, loud enough that it echoed down the entire east wing. He stopped in his tracks, and slowly turned to face me. This time I crossed the space between us and got in his face, unwilling to let the height difference intimidate me. "*Enough* of this! I'm fed up with this cold shoulder *horse* shit! What the hell is your problem?! Two months ago, you and I were sparring together, shooting together, and spending time in each other's company like we were comrades! I thought we had respect for one another ... I thought we were going to go into the service as *friends*. I thought hell ... we have our differences, but he's my fellow, we've been through a hell of a lot together, and he's not the kind of man who'll judge me the same way every other damned jackass has!"

Cuthbert stared down at me evenly, and waited a few moments, for me to fall silent. Finally, he responded, "Are you done, sir?"

"No!" I growled. "I am not going to be *done* with this until I get an answer! I *deserve* an answer from you!"

"I am bound to this family, sir ... and by that oath, I am bound to you now." He said. "I am your servant, in this house. I say little about my ... disagreements ... with your lifestyle, because it is not my place to."

"Hang that!" I knew by now Mikhail, and likely half the house could hear me, but I just didn't care. "I don't give a damn about any of this master servant shite, or class boundaries, or even *rank* right now! You're going to be my Commanding Officer in a few weeks' time ... we need to settle this *now*! Talk to me, damn it! Man to man!"

He closed his eyes for a few moments, and then slowly opened them, his grey gaze meeting mine, unflinching. I stared right back.

"Your lover has no place in this house, Luther." He spoke firmly, and with the kind of conviction I'd heard in the voices of priests, for many, many years. "Your aberrant behavior has no place in this house. I have long accepted you have these personal issues, and that you have no desire to put a stop to them ... but I cannot turn a blind eye when you invite it within these walls. I am warden of this family, and you are endangering it."

"You never *accepted* anything about it!" I shouted back, "You never even tried! I thought at least you'd gotten *over* it, but clearly that isn't the case, either! How the hell can you still be judging me based on this?! It is *one* aspect of who I am, and it doesn't define me as a person! What's more, I don't think it's a *negative* aspect of myself, at all! It's just not what *you* believe in!"

"That is your opinion ... and your perspective." He replied, his voice still maddeningly calm.

"And God's opinion is more important than conceiving one of your own?!" I demanded. "You've never even considered *my* perspective ... all that matters to you is what's written in some damned book, scribbled down by men thousands of years ago, when we all still crawled around in the mud!"

"Do you want to talk about not respecting others' perspectives, Luther?!" He raised his voice moderately, reminding me for a moment just how loud the man *could* be, with that deep, rich brogue of his. "When, at *any* point in the entire time that you have taken up residence at this house, have you given credence to *anyone's* opinion other than your own?! When have you *ever* respected my faith? When have you ever considered my feelings, or the feelings of others around you, when you flout the creed we try so difficultly to live our lives by?"

I tried to form a response, but he continued before I could find the right words. "*We* have bent around the very fabric of our morals for you, I most especially." He continued. "It isn't only this issue with this ... whore. You have no respect for God, for the rules that govern the society you have so fortunately become a part of. You hardly have respect for your father-in-law, and you *certainly* have never shown any mutual respect towards the difficulties I face, serving and standing beside you, when you are such an ever present source of hardship to me to follow my oaths.

"I understand you've had disagreements and struggles with the

Church, but many of those were by your *own* obstinate behavior, by poor decision-making on your part. You *murdered* a man. You fled a work camp, lied innumerable times on official military transcripts to continue your naval career and you respond to every person who judges you with aggression, and often *violence.* We are all judged throughout our lifetime, Luther ... fairly or unfairly. You refuse to accept that many of your problems were by your own making. You put *every* bit of blame on religion, and society."

He took a long breath, visibly steadying himself and dropping his voice somewhat. "My faith ... is based on ideals. Ideals are upheld by *men*, and a man can choose to interpret things as he sees fit. I'm certain many use my faith as an excuse for horrendous deeds, but for every wrong done in the name of God, lives have been saved by the same convictions and aspirations. Young children with no hope, with no chances ... facing a desperate future, with none to pull them from the fire..." he said meaningfully, " have been taken in, and raised, and brought up by the very same men you curse, mock, and dismiss as cruel zealots. I hear you insult these men, my mentors, my *faith* ... day in, and day out. And I have kept my silence. Because I understand that there were some ... not those who raised me, but those wearing the same robes ... who hurt you, and made you bitter towards us."

He gave me a chance to say something at that point, but ... I was struggling to come up with the right words. He raised his ears, waiting a further few moments, but when I still came up short, he continued.

"Luther ... I have *not* judged you based on whom you take as your lovers. Despite everything I was raised to believe. If I gave *that* much credence to the tenets, knowing that alone would have been enough that I wouldn't have let you anywhere near this family. I do *not* follow my tenets to the word ... most holy men don't. I gave you every chance in the world to prove yourself, beyond the few sins I knew of. Every man commits sins, and they are *his* to contend with, when he meets his maker. I do not believe in casting judgment ...

that is God's place, not mine. You must come to terms with who you are, and whether or not *you* feel you are right or wrong ... your soul is *yours*. The only person whose soul I am fit to judge is my own."

"But you *are* judging me." I finally bit out, frustrated and angry. "You're judging me *right* now. You say all this self-righteous, holier-than-thou shit, but you don't *act* on any of it! You've been treating me like a stranger since Mikhail came to stay here, and that is the *only* thing that's changed! You've admitted outright that he's the reason you're angry at me! So what the hell is that, if not judging?! Could you only deal with it when you weren't seeing evidence of it?! Is it easier for you just to deny it, and pretend I'm just a normal man, like the rest of you?! I mean for God's sake," I thrust a finger down the hallway, towards the staircase and the dining room beyond, "Lucius is the reason Mikhail is even here! I was doing my damned duty as Delilah's husband, I was trying to be chaste, before Lucius brought him here! I *tried*, alright?! What more do you want from me! Lucius brought Mikhail here, and he assured me keeping a courtesan here was all *acceptable* by your damned social etiquette!"

"Lucius isn't always *right*!" Cuthbert raised his voice, growling out the last word. "The man has made countless mistakes throughout his lifetime, and he will continue to make them! Don't you think I've spoken to him about this, as well?!"

"You'd barely speak to me about it, until I pushed you to!" I replied.

"Lucius *is* my friend!" Cuthbert shouted back, the words shoving into me like a battering ram. The air fell still between us for some time, and I waited for him to amend his statement ... but he didn't.

"And I'm not." I finally said, quietly.

"I have known you barely a year, Luther," he said, his voice dropping somewhat, "and yes ... until recent events ... I had thought it possible. Despite our *many* differences, conflicts of interest, and the total lack of respect I've received from you ... despite, even, our religious differences. I would have put that all aside ... if I thought I could trust you."

"And Lucius—"

"Lucius *earned* my trust." He stated, stonily. "Over the course of many years, while we fought together on the Dark Continent. You do not *know* Hell. You think your life is difficult here? You do not know what we have seen, what we have had to do to survive. You do not understand hardship. You're a young, arrogant, fool." He punctuated the words, mercilessly. "My bond with Lucius and with Captain Shaw was forged in the deepest, most primal recesses of the most terrible land in God's creation ... and you cannot understand that bond, let alone aspire to claim it with me. You press me at every turn, Luther, but I have dealt with it. But this ... this, I cannot tolerate. You're endangering this family. The family I am sworn to protect."

"By letting Mikhail stay here?!" I demanded, some of the nerve rising back in my voice. "I fail to see how he poses *any* threat to Delilah, or my children! Let alone to Lucius!"

"The threat isn't in him." Cuthbert replied. "It is in his presence. And what repercussions it could have on your family."

"Lucius has assured me the staff are discreet." I insisted. "He's kept courtesans over the years, and I doubt you *hated* him for it!"

"The prostitutes he brought here were women." He stated, matter-of-factly.

"And that's the only thing that matters, isn't it?!" I exclaimed. "That's the whole damned heart of the matter! That's all that *ever* matters to you people!"

"For someone who rails so much against being lumped in with other 'deviants', despite being an individual with other qualities," Cuthbert said, "you are very quick to associate all men of God into one group, and hold us all accountable for the sins of the few you've had personal quarrel with."

"It's the *religion* that's the problem!" I growled.

I noticed that his shoulders fell slightly at that, and he turned his gaze out to look out the window into the dark yard beyond. " ... you have not heard a single word I've said." He stated quietly.

"Because everything you've said is the same damned blind hatred I've gotten my whole life!"

He turned his eyes back on me, took a moment to compose himself, then spoke again. "Alright, Luther. Disregarding your continued lack of respect for my faith ... let's suppose you're right. Let's suppose every man of God will react to your secrets with hatred and blind, righteous indignation ... that they all desire to harm those who violate the tenets."

"They've shackled me in cells, lashed me with a damned cane ... put me in the stocks!" I responded, angrily. "What else would you call that?!"

"I'm sorry for that. It must have been terrible." He said calmly, and with real pity ... which only made me angrier.

"Don't act like these things are meaningless!" I belted out. "I almost *died* in prison because of this!"

"I'm not dismissing your pain, Luther. I know it was great." He said, quietly. "But I want you to think back on every single thing that's happened to you, because of this prejudice. Think of every pain you've endured because of this one, seemingly insignificant facet of who you are."

"I do. Every damned day." I snarled.

He nodded, his eyes locking on mine.

"Now imagine all of that happening to your son."

My breath caught in my throat, images coming unbidden. The world stopped. Seconds froze in the air, and my body went cold. Every lash, every moment of humiliation, every injury ... whether it was my father, a crewmate, or a priest inflicting it ... all of it rushed back to me, in one singular, terrifying moment.

"Or your daughter." Johannes continued, quietly. "Or your wife. These things don't only happen to heretics ... they affect all who are within reach of them. There are many, many very overzealous men of God, superstitious, ignorant people ... in every walk of society ... who fear and hate what they can't understand. And when they find you, they will be violent. They will not ask questions. And they will be merciless. In the past, it has only been you that suffered their wrath. But your life has changed. You have a family. And you need to start putting their needs above yours."

"I don't..." I trailed off.

"Everything you do has consequences, Luther. And now, those consequences affect the people closest to you." He gestured down the hallway, towards the wash room. "Every day that man is here runs the risk of who you are, your past, your secrets ... coming to light. Your children are young now, but what happens when they are old enough to start forming memories, and understanding the world around them? How will you excuse his presence? How will you explain all of this to them? How will your wife? Will you even care by then?"

I swallowed, knowing precisely what he was about to say ... because I'd been pushing down my own, very similar concerns, for weeks now.

"You cannot be prioritizing that man over your family ... and that is *exactly* what you're doing now." He gestured towards the stairs. "I couldn't give less of a damn whom you bed when you aren't here, at home ... if you must know, I find it morally reprehensible for *any* man to be intimate outside his marriage ... never mind that *I am the man* who spoke your oaths before God, and actually *married* you. I knew the marriage was a sham when I performed it, and it took a sizable amount of moral questioning for me to make peace with it, but I *did*. Because I was convinced at that time that you truly cared for her, even if the marriage wouldn't be the traditional sort."

"I *do* care about Delilah." I insisted.

"If you did, you wouldn't be putting her and your children in danger like this, just to appease your own base desires." He replied in a hard tone.

"You don't understand." I explained, helplessly. "Men like you can't *possibly* understand. You have it *so* damned easy. You can have everything you want out of life, and it's *acceptable*. You have your beautiful wife, your family, your conventional family—"

“Whom I never *see*.” He interrupted me, in a raised voice.

“I assumed that was a personal choice.” I muttered. “Lucius would release you from your duties as often as you wanted.”

“It isn’t about *duty*, Luther.” He replied. “It’s about how much of my job I take home with me ... it’s about sparing them *my* problems.”

“What ... you’re the most ... well-put-together man I know, Johannes.” I said, with an arched eyebrow.

“Do you think I *want* to spend my time away from my wife and children?” He questioned, and I heard something rare from him ... a tremble in his voice. Cuthbert was not a man prone to showing signs of weakness, either physical or emotional and that had sounded like both. “Luther ... if I had known what kind of man I was going to become, after so many years seeing and living through the ... atrocities, I have witnessed ... I never would have subjected a wife to any of it.”

I blinked, going quiet. Cuthbert’s voice was unusually emotional, at the moment ... more so than I think I’d ever heard from him.

“I don’t sleep like a normal man anymore.” He said through his teeth. “I wake almost every hour, and feel compelled to check my powder, or test the trigger on my crossbow. Often, I cannot fall asleep again until I have. If *anyone* comes upon me when I am distracted, let alone sleeping, I run the risk of harming them. I can’t be around my youngest children, or the screaming of the babes makes me relive watching countless mens’ amputations. I have to recheck every article of clothing before I dress, because I am earnestly afraid I will find poisonous insects hiding in the folds.”

“Johannes...” I murmured.

“I keep to my quarters here to *spare* my family.” He said. “It is a sacrifice I determined necessary when my fifth child, Anne, came upon me in my study one day, intent on ambushing me. She was seven years old at the time ... she didn’t understand how many men I’d lost to the Cathazra’s guerilla soldiers ... to *real* ambushes. I almost broke her arm.

“We aren’t children, Luther. Children concern themselves only with what they 'want'. If you think men like me have a better chance at marital bliss ... you're probably right. But we are soldiers. After war, nothing in life is easy again. I have given up on many of the things I wanted, because it was what was *best* for my family."

He turned, and straightened out his cuffs. And for the first time, I noticed something about the gesture I had never seen, in the whole year I'd known him. He shook out his sleeve when he straightened the fabric...

... as if to shake something loose, from inside.

"You need to consider what truly matters to you, before you consider your wants, Luther. The world may not be a fair place for a man like you, but it *is* the world we live in and your actions affect more than just your own life now. I can't tell you what to do, it is not my place. But until you can make the choices that are right for your family, and not just right for you I cannot respect the way you live your life. I love this family. I cannot trust anyone who endangers them."

I watched him head for the staircase, and this time I didn't stop him. Silence descended on the hallway, trapping me with my thoughts. Mikhail had still not emerged. I could no longer hear the sounds of my family at the table downstairs ... they *must* have heard the argument. Everyone had moved off to their rooms for the night.

A large, ancient mirror hung in the hallway, framed on all sides by ornate, old silver. From the opposing wall, it caught my reflection perfectly, and he turned to regard me as I noticed him.

I'd very rarely seen myself, throughout my lifetime except in the distorting ripples of water. The perfect representation before me was a hard-edged, angry, spiteful dog, getting old before his time. The longer I looked at him, the angrier I became, and the more inadequate I felt.

I saw myself moving across the hallway, and before I knew it, I'd put my fist square down the center of the reflection, the glass shattering out like a spider web, the frame toppling off its nail to crash on the hardwood floor.

CHAPTER 12
CONSUMMATION OF VOWS

Sometimes, things have a way of colliding all at once, and misfortune often rears its head at the precise moment you were warned it would.

I'd fallen into a bottle for the rest of the night following the argument I'd had with Cuthbert ... I'd even turned my wife away from my doorway. They'd broken the lock the following morning, when I wasn't downstairs by the time lunch was served ... and immediately called a physician. I'd been too drunk to realize the lacerations on my fists from the broken mirror were bleeding so heavily, and I'd passed out. The physician blamed the alcohol. Lucius blamed me.

And Delilah had blamed ... Johannes.

Everyone in the house had heard the argument the night before. Perhaps not in detail, but they knew what the issue was over. Delilah was disgusted with her 'knight' and convinced he'd worked me into a depression, no matter how much I denied it. Mikhail himself had stopped by only once, expressing sorrow that he was the cause of the fighting and asking if he should return home. I was half tempted at this point to tell him yes, but I'd been too light-headed all day to think properly, and I didn't want to make a decision now I'd regret later.

Johannes *had* left. He'd apparently gone home in the morning after Lucius had 'requested' he take some time off. Which was probably for the best, because if he'd seen how much Delilah had been crying all day, he might have left forever.

Lucius had only had brief words for me. I think the whole affair was just too much drama for the old man ... he preferred his problems 'simple, and stabbable', as he'd said himself on many occasions. This whole mess was outside *both* our areas of expertise unfortunately. He'd only told me he felt Johannes was making an enormous fuss over nothing, and that no one else in the house took offense to Mikhail's presence. Delilah couldn't have been in more agreement with that statement.

My family was telling me to ignore the wolfhound's words ... to carry on as though this was all just some religious tantrum of his, and to feel no shame over what he'd said to me. They likely assumed Johannes had been more unkind than he had.

The fact of the matter was, the wolfhound was right in perhaps the most important regard. I'd known since I came here that my past could, at any point, come back to haunt this family. They'd known that when they took me in, and nothing could be done about it ... but Mikhail, or *any* man I became close to, who became involved with my family ... were like an anchor poised at any moment to plunge us all down into the same hell I'd crawled my way out of.

All it would take was one servant who knew my 'sins', and could prove them. One acquaintance of Mikhail's, or Mikhail himself to hold our entire family hostage, with the truth. My very own children could betray it at some point in the future, speaking innocently on the goings-on of our house, in some public place, never knowing what they were revealing. Even if we did keep it from them, that would mean a lifelong lie to my son and daughter.

God ... what if one of my children chose to follow in my footsteps? They couldn't have inherited it through birth, but ... if we made it seem so acceptable...

Just because I didn't think the way I lived was wrong didn't mean I wished it on anyone else. The mere thought of my children being subjected to the same prejudice, humiliation and pain I'd faced throughout my lifetime sent a chill down my spine.

Johannes was right. Maybe for the wrong reasons. Or maybe he honestly *was* only concerned about the family. I just wasn't certain any more. It was hard to believe a man *raised* by the Church would be open-minded enough to ever accept me, but it really felt like he *had* been coming close, up until two months ago...

In the depths of my heart, I knew that this was all ... wrong. So damned wrong. I'd known it was wrong, my entire life. I had failings. I had faults. I'd done many things throughout my life that I wasn't proud of.

But loving men was not a sin. I couldn't ever believe it was. Before, it had been more a matter of pride. The inability to accept that the way I'd been since I was a child meant I was an evil person. I just hadn't wanted to be wrong.

But it was more than that, at this point. Losing Klaus, and feeling the hole he'd left inside me collapse over time ... it was a pain I had *never* felt before, and it was worse than any lashing. Worse than any humiliation. All of the anger inside me had finally snuffed out over the last year and I'd slowly come to terms with why it hurt so damned bad. I'd earnestly loved the man. And I could accept now ... that he had loved me, as well. He used the last moments of breath he'd had left inside him to tell me so.

Agreeing to everything Johannes had told me last night ... accepting the fact that I was *wrong* for feeling this way ... would be a disservice to the man I'd loved. It would be like saying everything we'd had was a lie. That his feelings, and mine, were an aberration and nothing more.

And I could never believe that.

It would probably be a point Johannes and I would always

disagree on. But he was right about his fears for my family. Regardless of how right or wrong the tenets of the Church were ... they *were* out there, governing nearly every facet of Amuresca. They had hurt me. They would do so again, if my secret was ever discovered.

And this time, my family would be involved. My wife. My children.

Asking Mikhail to leave was the most obvious answer. He was preparing to go home in a few weeks anyway, after I left for sea. But Delilah had already been asking when he'd next return. I think she believed so long as I was home, during the winter months in between my trips with the fleet, the fox would be taking up a residence with us.

I'll admit, I'd been hoping the same.

I leaned down in bed, putting my head between my knees. My tea had gone cold, and I hadn't the stomach for any of the bread they'd left me on the night stand. I was in misery. I was guilt-ridden, sick, and considering asking one of the few pleasures in my life to leave, return me to the state of agitation that had prompted my father-in-law to bring him here in the first place, and fixate instead on the unfulfilling lie of a marriage to a woman who deserved better than me...

And despite all of that, Johannes would still be bitter towards me when he returned. The Fleet Captains I was going to be serving under for the next few years all loathed me, save the one fellow who would be a constant reminder of whom should *actually* be fulfilling the role I was failing so miserably at.

For the first time in my life, I was beginning to understand how a Pedigree could have everything in the world, and still be miserable. This was all so damned complicated, it was making me long for prison. All of my anger had been certain and righteous then ... the world had made sense.

A pounding at my door snapped me from my thoughts like a bowstring falling back. My ears rang with the noise and I closed my eyes, putting my fingers to my brow. The blood loss had been giving me terrible headaches all day and even though by now I was certain I was through the worst of it, the headaches weren't subsiding.

"Come in." I said loud enough to be heard through the door. I didn't recognize the knock, so it was likely a servant. I'd know if it were Mikhail or Delilah.

The sound of a cane and heavy footfalls surprised me, and I turned to see Lucius entering, shutting the heavy mahogany behind him. I hadn't bothered to rest under the covers, so I merely slipped to the side of the bed, making to get up. He waved a paw at me, shaking his head.

"No, no ... please. Remain seated. I know you're still recovering."

"You didn't have to come all the way to this wing, sir." I said, running a hand over the tousled fur along the crown of my head. "If you needed to have a word with me, I would have come to your study."

"Are you kidding me?" The old man chuckled, dryly. "For once, I'm not the most infirm man in the house. Let me enjoy this rare moment. Besides ... I need to be getting a bit more exercise, at my age. This damned leg keeps me so immobile, I'm getting too broad around the middle for even an old man."

I gave a weak smile at the barrel-chested man. "I'm sure the brandy has more to do with that than your limp."

"Used to be I kept up a strict exercise regime." He sighed. "I could carry two full water pales on a broomstick over my shoulders on my laps about the grounds. I did five miles, every morning. Threw logs, wielded a saber with the best of them. You should've seen me as a young man." He winked, chuckling, "Drove the ladies mad."

"It's probably best I didn't know you then." I smirked. "I'm sure you were quite the heart-breaker."

"Now, now ... I was always a gentleman. I never made false promises." He pulled a cigar out from his pocket, as well as a match and his flint. "And not a one of them left disappointed."

"Come here just to boast about your youthful prowess?"

He lit his cigar up. "Someday Luther, you'll be an old man ... and reminiscing about your younger years will be as close as you get to splendor, again."

"I'll be dead before then."

"Only the good die young, son ... and I don't think you're that selfless."

I chuckled. "Alright so ... you couldn't have honestly come up all those stairs just to tell me I'm going to be old someday."

He was silent for a time following that, looking pensively down his cigar. He was rarely silent so long ... and it was even rarer he had trouble making eye contact with me.

"What's wrong?" I asked quietly.

" ... I'll start off with ... something simple." He sighed. "I've made a decision on which assignment the fleet shall be taking, this year."

My ears perked, and I sat up straighter. "That seemed to be giving you some trouble." I said, sympathetically.

He took a long drag of his cigar and turned to look out the window, at the setting sun. The room was cast in a dim orange hue, the smoke sifting out from his nostrils catching in the beams of light.

" ... Serwich is under attack." He said, the words heavy on his tongue.

"Serwich," I lowered my brow, "I saw that on several of the scrolls you were reading over in Cheron. The ones stamped in the royal seal..."

"Those were Calls for Aid." He said in a low, worried tone. "The Crown receives countless requests every season, from all corners of our Empire. Unfortunately, our fleets are stretched so thin, we can only answer the most pressing. Our great motherland has spread her people so far, in our hunger to consume the world ... we can no longer protect many of our holdings. The Colonies on the Dark Continent are the most egregious example. It's turning into another Carvecia, but *far* more deadly. We have no place there. Nothing those lands can give us is worth the cost in lives."

"Serwich is one of the colonies on the Dark Continent?"

"It's more than just one of them. It's the one I captured for the throne." He said, darkly. "The ... crowning achievement of my naval career. The victory that put the *Cerberus* fleet in the high standing it has now." His tone was bitter, and his eyes fell to the hardwood floor at that. "And the single greatest mistake of my life."

This was the place Johannes spoke of with such fear, and pain. The 'hell' he had alluded to. I'd heard the very same primal terror in Lucius's voice, when he'd told me of it nearly a year ago. I recalled the skull in his study, and the torn, foreign banner ... the exotic symbol burnt on scaled hide. It was where Lucius had been crippled. Where Cuthbert had been so deeply scarred he could no longer live beside his own family. Whatever had happened there, it had been sufficient enough to frighten two of the most fearless men I'd ever known, and bound them for life. And it had won a poor wolfhound from the Islands the respect of Captain Shaw, a seasoned Pedigree navy man with a clear disdain for the lower class.

And whatever had happened there, Lucius had chosen not to return, or to send his fleet back, for nearly a decade.

"Your colony is under attack?" I asked quietly.

"They have been under attack near-constantly since the place was founded." Lucius replied, tapping his cigar out on the ash tray near the dresser. I never used it, but Lucius kept them in nearly every room. "The natives ... the Cathazra, they call themselves ... are demons. They have been haunting those forests since the moment the very first Amurescan set foot in them. Every attempt at negotiation failed. It took us years to find a translator who could even communicate with them ... and even once they began picking up pieces of *our* tongue, nothing we could get out of them was remotely civil. They don't think like we do. They're animals. Like the ancients but worse. They don't even have respect for their own kind. The whole reason the tribe that dwells within the same area as Serwich has taken such offense to the Colony is because they don't want to move a mere few miles downriver ... because a larger, more powerful tribe of Cathazra dwells further south, and the beasts fight amongst themselves as often as they come after us."

"Couldn't we just pay them for the land?" I offered.

"We tried. Nothing we have is of value to them." He sighed. "They worship pagan gods, and they have their own ... barbaric ... culture. They are aggressively self-sufficient hunters, and isolationists in the extreme. They don't believe in trading food or alcohol, they barely wear clothing at all, and they seem to have no concept of the value of gold ... which is unfortunate, because their land is rich with it. The Crown wants their lumber, and they want to dig up every river bed on that damned continent."

My mind went back to Cheron at that ... one of the few places left in Amuresca untouched by forest stripping, hunting, and civilization in general. I remembered how the wild beauty of the place had made me feel ... and how much I'd appreciated it. The only reason Cheron had remained the way it was is because the land had nothing of value to the throne.

"Maybe it's best if we just pull our people off those shores ... give up the colonies." I suggested. "Before things get worse. It sounds as though they're too dangerous for us to civilize, anyway."

"I have been saying that for over a decade, now." Lucius spoke in a low tone, with an undercurrent of frustration. "I have *testified* to it, in royal court. But the Crown doesn't wish to hear it. The Dark Continent is the only land left in the known world with such fortunes. The King hasn't seen a man die of dysentery, or watched a wound caused by one of those beasts' guerilla soldiers become infected with maggots. All they see is a solution to the national debt. Lumber ... spice ... gold. Never mind the poor, desperate souls who went and won it for them ... or the struggling, fearful people who dare to live there now."

He put his cigar down in the ash tray, seeming to have lost his taste for it. " ... I settled most of those people there, Luther. They braved the sea on *my* ships to journey to that accursed place. Most of them were innocent, poor laborers who were so desperate to feed their families and own a plot of land, they took the greatest risk imaginable ... and left their home. These are *good* people. They've been there for over a decade, now ... there are whole generations being raised in Serwich. It isn't just laborers ... there are women and children there. All of them in constant fear from the natives."

He looked up at me at that, his eyes haunted with memories I couldn't see. "They don't just kill us, Luther. They *hunt* us, like game. And then they devour us, and sacrifice their prisoners to their ... heathen gods. They do not care who they kill. I have seen their winged beasts pluck children from the streets, like a hawk snatching a fish."

" ... children?" I wondered, quietly. Even the Huudari had held back from slaughtering children in times of war against our country, and they were a nation of slavers.

"The ones that lead them ... those that walk as we do." He said, "The locals have taken to calling them 'Dragons', because their hides are crimson ... they seem to have more honor and intelligence than the rest, but even they are not afraid to employ the worst tactics, to win. They always strike from ambush. The beasts that fly drop mixtures of sulfur and burning pitch from the sky and set structures and boats aflame. We've yet to find a truly effective way to shoot them down ... cannon-fire generally won't reach, and it's too hard to aim the culverins at something moving so fast.

"The ones that dwell in the water putrefy their meat before they eat it," he said with visible disgust. "Their bites almost always lead to infection and they dip their arrowheads in a combination of this ... bile ... and poisons from the creatures in their forests. Most times when you are shot you never even see them, but any wound from them can be deadly. I lost far more men to disease, failed amputations and infection than anything else."

"Sir?" I questioned, partially interrupting him. He glanced up. "I don't mean to halt you, but ... are you telling me all of this because you're sending the fleet back to Serwich?"

He hesitated long enough that I knew the decision weighed on him, but then he only shook his head. "No." He said at length. "I have no desire to send my men, my friends, and my son-in-law to such a hellish place. Not so long as it can be prevented. I firmly feel that nothing we could do there would be of any good, to anyone. The only solution to that place is to abandon it."

"But the people there—"

"Yes, until the Crown sees what I have been trying to show them for over a decade now ... the people there must be protected." He gave a long sigh. "That is why, for many years now, I have watched the Calls for Aid come through court, ensuring that there was always a fleet to answer their call. The coin to be made there is great. There is almost always an Admiral willing to take the task of protecting the colony on. None of them stay longer than a year.

"Admiral Nelson has answered the call this year," he said with some obvious disdain in his voice. "His fleet isn't ... insufficient ... but under his leadership ... well, I was concerned. Shaw wanted us to take the contract. He is the only Captain under my command who survived our conquest of Serwich, so many years ago ... he feels strongly that it is our duty to protect the place. He isn't wrong."

"That's what you were arguing over." I murmured, in understanding.

"It's an argument we have been having for a decade now." He admitted with a long breath. "Every year, when the contract inevitably comes up for renewal, Shaw tries to push me to answer the call. But it is *my* fleet. They are my men. I earnestly feel, in the very depths of my heart, that the *Cerberus* and her sisters were *never* meant to return to that place again. We were lucky to escape those waters once. I fear if we return ... she'll never come home."

He went silent for some time after that, his expression tense and pained. "But ... she is also *my* Colony. My responsibility. If I could go, myself..."

"You don't want to send the fleet because you can't go with them." I supplied, knowing where his heart lay. I would have felt the same way.

"Serwich is this family's responsibility, when all is said and done. One of these years ... we will have to answer the call." He said grimly.

"The natives have been in a lull as far as out-and-out war goes for some time now, but there is always trouble. Eventually, I expect things will get worse. It is all but inevitable. And then we will *have* to return.

"But ... not this year," he finally said with a long sigh. "Admiral Nelson can have at it this year. My fleet is not prepared, you'll be serving your first year, Johannes is in no shape to return to that dark place ... the time is not right. No," he took up his cigar again, and took a long draw, blowing it out slowly, "I'm sending the fleet to assist Admiral Cross, dealing with the South Sea Privateers. His fleet's the only one with the mettle to take on those blaggards, and they are *badly* outgunned. I'm sure he'll be grateful for the help."

"Sounds like a good time." I couldn't help the slight, roguish smirk that worked its way over my muzzle. Admiral Cross and his Black Flag Fleet were legendary throughout the navy. The man had sunk more Carvecians than any dog alive, he had one of the nastiest groups of bastards amongst his crew roster, most of them ex-prisoners, and he was infamous for getting into a dispute turned fist-fight with the King himself ... in *court* ... and somehow avoiding execution, or lifelong imprisonment. Likely because no one else was crazy enough to take on the South Sea Privateers, and the Crown knew they couldn't do without him.

I was looking forward to meeting him.

"It seems a good fit for my fleet." Lucius agreed. "And a good fit ... for you. You'd better show Heinrich Cross what you're made of, because I'm sending him a letter tomorrow telling him I expect great things of you. He's docked in the Capital right now."

"Well now the pressure's on." I muttered.

"I brought you into this family to bestow honor upon my fleet, Luther." He pointed his cigar at me. "You had best not disappoint me."

"I'll do my best, sir."

He chewed on the edge of his cigar and leaned back in his chair, his gaze moving back towards the darkening window. There was that silence again. The conversation had run its course, and it had returned. There was something that was immensely troubling him. I could see it in the discomfort in his features, in the way he sat, in the way his tail twitched where it hung behind the chair.

"Lucius..." I caught his attention with his name, but all he did was flick his eyes towards me, then avert them again.

This couldn't be good.

"What did you actually come here to talk about?" I pressed.

He opened and shut his muzzle a few times, as if he wasn't certain how to begin, or even approach what he was trying to say. At last, he shifted and reached into the vest pocket hidden partially by his overcoat, gingerly pulling out a slightly rumpled letter, with the wax seal broken.

" ... I have been warring over whether or not to show this to you all day. Especially considering your state, and your argument with Johannes, last night."

I narrowed my eyes at that.

"I eventually decided that it was too pressing to keep from you." He slowly lifted the letter, and offered it across the few feet separating us. "I warn you ... it is not pleasant. I'm very sorry, son." The way his words fell at the end of his statement, I felt my heart drop. Whatever this was, Lucius was concerned.

No, not just concerned, he was pitying me.

I took the letter, slowly ... and unfolded it. The parchment felt heavier in my hand the moment I saw the seal emblazoned at the top.

The symbol of the Holy Order, the Church of Amuresca.

I swallowed, suddenly wishing I'd drunk my tea. My throat was dry, and my head was spinning more than it had been this morning when I'd woken bleeding out onto my comforter. The letter was addressed to Lucius, not to me. It was formally written in elegant cursive, but the beauty of the script masked its hideous content.

I got one paragraph in before I felt sick. My heart fell into the pit of my stomach, and a creeping, cold fear prickled at my entire body.

" ... an Inquisitor?" I whispered, numb. "They're sending an Inquisitor? How ... why..."

Lucius's head was down and he'd left his still-burning cigar in the ash tray. He knitted his hands, slowly, before looking back up at me. "I don't know, Luther. I ... don't know."

My hands fell into my lap, the letter with them. I hadn't even the nerve to keep reading.

"They must have a reason." Lucius said, almost under his breath. "The letter only states that they have reason to suspect our family of lineage fraud, which is a very great offense, when you're talking about Pedigree titles."

My body began to shake, and I pushed back at the fear with raw nerve.

It was happening again. In this place I'd thought I was safe. They were *never* going to leave me be. It didn't matter where I went. They would *always* find me.

"I can't say why this is happening now, as opposed to when we first filed your marriage documents ... or when we first had papers made for the twins. Who knows how the Church handles their damned witch hunts? They might have honestly just been sitting on this for a while." Lucius sighed, and then looked at me. "But Luther ... I have to ask you."

I raised my gaze to his, holding the edge of my bed, so as to not betray the shaking in my hands.

"Is there any possibility ... any chance at all," he said, "that you may have seen someone recently, someone who knew you ... who may have told the Church about your past?"

I was silent.

"Information travels fast in the Church. It could have even been someone you saw months ago, perhaps at a formal event. Can you think of anyone you might have recognized? Or who might have recognized you?"

Several more seconds passed silently between us.

"I ... don't know." I admitted, at length. "I can't, it's possible ... but I can't ... remember clearly..."

He sighed, leaning back in his chair. "Well, let us hope, if you were betrayed, that that is in fact the case because the only other alternative is much closer to home."

My ears snapped up at that. "It *wasn't* Johannes. How could you possibly—"

"I suspected some time ago that your relationship had soured." He said. "I witnessed it degrade the moment I brought the courtesan in. I had hoped he'd swallow his pride and handle the damned fox, but apparently I overestimated his tolerance level. He's never made such a fuss over *my* dalliances."

"Johannes is too loyal to *you* to do something like this..." I insisted. "This affects the entire family."

"Do *you* think he puts his faith in God *beneath* his devotion to this family?" Lucius questioned. "Because I have never been sure."

I had no answer for him. And now the maelstrom inside my mind was spinning with this other, terrible possibility. It was too much. It was all too much.

Would Johannes have betrayed us, betrayed this family he'd served for almost two decades, all because of Mikhail?

... because of me?

"I'd prefer to think, for the moment, that we were betrayed by some outside source." The old spaniel said sourly. "But regardless of how it happened ... it happened. And the Inquisitor will be here in a few days' time."

"I'll leave now." I said, hoarsely. "If you'll just allow me some of my possessions and coin, I'll take Specter, and –"

"Calm down, boy." Lucius put a hand out. "I'll have no more talk of fleeing, now ... you hear? We're going to figure this out."

"You don't know what an Inquisition is like!" I raised my voice, my tone breaking on the last word. "Have you ever ... have you even *seen*—"

"It isn't going to be like that." He said, putting a hand on his knee and giving me a firm shake of his head. "You're in a different world now, Luther. A world where the Church treads *far* more lightly than they do in the lower rungs."

"But—"

"The law, even Church law, is different for the Pedigree class. And right now, that's to your advantage ... so just listen to me." His voice was authoritative, and strangely calming. The way I'd always imagined a father should have sounded. Commanding silence, but not harshly. Assuring me.

I fell silent and did as he asked. I listened.

"I've never been through one of these myself, but I've known others at court who have. Lord Ranquest had to deal with an Inquisitor a decade or so back over a lineage issue. His family got through it, and everyone *knows* his grandson is a bastard."

He pushed himself up onto his feet, and despite his condition ... began to pace. "They're going to ask us a lot of very difficult questions, but I've already started running my daughter through what she needs to say—"

"Delilah knows?" I interjected.

"Of course she does." He replied. "I spoke to her before I came to you. This concerns her as much as it does you. For all I know, it concerns her *more* than it concerns you. Delilah's children *are* bastards. There were issues with lineage in this family *far* before you ever showed up, so stop martyring yourself."

"I'm not—"

"I can see it in your eyes," he growled. "Stop it. This is everyone's problem. You aren't the cause of every misfortune to strike this family. In fact, you've been the solution to many. So stop looking so sullen, man up, and pull yourself together."

I straightened my shoulders, swallowing. "I..."

He glared at me.

" ... yes, sir." I said, obediently.

"There now." He put his hands out on the handle of his cane. "That's the young lad I know."

I realized in that moment that my hands had stopped shaking. I earnestly felt ... better. Somehow. The effect Lucius had on me was stunning ... and I wasn't sure when he'd gotten such power over me.

But unlike every other man who'd wielded power over me in my lifetime, I felt like I needed Lucius. He *was* the father I'd never had. I couldn't understand God's will in bringing me to this man so late in my life, but ... if meeting Lucius and his family *was* some plan mandated by a greater power ... it was the first in my lifetime that I was thankful for.

"Delilah has actually been prepared for this for quite some time." Lucius said. "We knew no matter whom she married, she might have to defend her children's' legitimacy at some point in her future. We have had a script prepared since the fourth month of her pregnancy. She wasn't even particularly startled when I told her about this. She would be ready now, were the man to knock at our door. I would be ready. What matters now is readying *you*."

He pulled another folded document from his coat pocket. This time, it was considerably thicker than a letter. He placed the folded papers down on my dresser.

"That is your script. Memorize it. Expect they will ask you questions that are not there ... I'm certain we couldn't have thought of everything. Be nonspecific if you go off-script. The entirety of how you met Delilah, had your dalliance, and came to reside in this manor afterwards ... are all there. Your wedding was private and I served as witness, so we do not need to bring Johannes here ... or even admit that he was the man who married you. We do not need an excuse as to why the wedding was private. The timing makes it obvious Delilah was pregnant at the time and that is the only excuse we need. Do not obfuscate the fact that you impregnated her before marriage. That alone is disgraceful, but no threat to us, legally. And it will go a long way to disprove any inklings they might have of your true ... preferences."

"Do you think they know?" I questioned, quietly.

"It's possible they suspect." He said, confirming my fears. "But the bottom line is, and you *cannot* forget this ... they have *no* proof. Eyewitness accounts are not even enough to de-legitimize a Pedigree line. They would need written proof. Some kind of letter or a correspondence between yourself and one of your lovers ... *during* the time Delilah's children were conceived."

"I never wrote to Klaus. We were on the same ship." I shook my head. "And before that, I couldn't even write."

"Then there is *nothing* they can do." He said firmly. "Except for intimidate you. They haven't even cause to lay a hand on you. There will be no whips and chains in my house. If they begin to threaten you physically ... you are within your rights to fight back. Understand?"

"Are you certain?" I asked, seriously.

"Dead certain," he replied coldly. "If any of these men touch you ... respond to force with force in kind. Try not to kill them ... but do *not* let them push you into a confession. All they can do is attempt to frighten you."

"I understand." I said, solemnly.

"There is one further thing." His confidence waned a bit on those words, and some of the worry began to creep back into me. But the way he looked at that moment ... it seemed almost more ... embarrassed, or uncomfortable, than concerned.

Before I could ask, he cleared his throat. "In cases of lineage fraud, the Church's primary concern is to prevent a divorce."

"I have no intention of divorcing Delilah." I shrugged. "Aren't divorces all but unheard of amongst the Pedigree class, anyway?"

"The process to divorce a Pedigree woman is arduous, and only undertaken in the most extreme incidents." Lucius agreed. "But ... annulling a marriage ... is far easier. Especially if there is a lineage issue. There must be a justification given, though. And the most common is ... for a husband to claim the marriage was never consummated."

"None of this matters." I said quickly, almost cutting off the last word. "I'm not *going* to divorce Delilah, or try to nullify the marriage, so it isn't even an issue."

"They have no reason to believe you. Or I, for that matter." Lucius said. "I could have married you to her simply to legitimize the pups ... only for you or I to file for a nullification, afterwards. We could claim the marriage was never consummated."

"She had *pups*." I said, exasperated. "This is *nonsense*."

"Actually, it's *true*." The old spaniel stated pointedly, narrowing his eyes at me. "I *did* marry you to my daughter almost strictly to legitimize her children. They aren't your children. I *could* make the claim that the marriage was never consummated, and cite your history as proof. *You* could make the very same claim, and leave this marriage scott-free."

"Why would I ever do that?!"

"Because I pulled you out of prison!" Lucius declared. "Because this whole thing ... your marriage to my daughter, the legitimization of your 'family', could just be an agreement between you and I, a ruse that benefited the both of us. I falsified your naval documents, but all they need do is *dig* deep enough, and they'll know who you are. And the reality of it is ... they'd be *right*."

"But I'm not going to divorce her!" I said, standing up. "So what the hell does it matter?!"

"It matters because it's one more claim they have against us. And I don't like your tone." He snapped. "I don't know why you're getting so riled up about this. It's easily settled."

I slowly sat back down on the bed. It took me a few moments, but I finally summoned the willpower to speak, without yelling. "How?"

"I've ... spoken to my daughter on this subject, as well." He said, very clearly trying to keep the conversation formal, despite his discomfort. "She says ... your marriage has not, in fact, been consummated."

"I imagined you *knew* that." I said, trying to keep the sarcasm from my voice.

"Earnestly?" He arched an eyebrow. "I thought you'd taken my daughter to bed at least once ... if not more so. I have ears within the servants. I know you've shared your marriage bed. Often, if what I hear is correct."

"All we do is sleep." I muttered.

"You could do that in your own rooms."

"I'm *fond* of your daughter." I spread my arms. "I enjoy her company. It doesn't follow that just because we're sleeping together, we're fu—"

He put out a hand to stop me. "None of that crass gutter talk in my house, please. Especially not where my daughter is concerned." He pinched the bridge of his nose for a few moments, before continuing. "I understand this isn't the most pleasant situation for you, Luther ... but you married my daughter. There are a few basic duties entailed."

"You swore this *wasn't* going to be part of this arrangement!" I objected.

"Oh for *God's* sake, man!" He whuffed out a breath, glaring at me. "Once or twice won't kill you! I don't feel I'm asking much, and this is *extremely* awkward to even be speaking on—"

"Awkward for *you*?!" I cried out. "What about me?! What about your daughter?!"

"My *daughter* is in *love* with you, man!" He replied, bluntly. "I swear to you, she will not *mind*. Despite the unfortunate incident with Irving, my girl is a strong woman, and she cares for you very deeply. She understands these are the duties associated with marriage. It is what's expected of a Pedigree woman, and most endure it far more frequently, for the rest of their lives. She'll manage."

"Why the hell does it even matter?!" I insisted. "We're already lying to them about *everything* else. Delilah and I can claim the marriage was consummated ... every night for the last year! They have no way of proving otherwise!"

"Delilah was heavily pregnant when the two of you were officially married." He said with a long sigh. "We never went about the ceremony in the traditional fashion. It hardly seemed to matter at the time, but ... we never insisted upon a witnessed breeding."

I tipped my ears back. " ... excuse me?"

He ran a hand over his muzzle, closing his eyes for a moment. "Tradition for Pedigree women ... is to have their first breeding, their first night with their husband ... witnessed."

"That's *vile*!"

"It's the only way to legitimize the bloodline." He grated out. "It's tradition, Luther. A very important tradition, which we overlooked because Delilah was already pregnant. If I'd known then that the Church was going to perform an Inquisition on our bloodline, I would have insisted upon it *then*. I'd been hoping we could avoid it."

"You cannot *possibly* be considering subjecting Delilah to that!" I pounded my fist against the bedside table. "After what she's been through?! She doesn't need any more *humiliation* associated with sex!"

"Delilah understands her duty!" He shouted. "She understood this tradition's importance from childhood! Every Pedigree woman does! I endured it with my wife, my father and my mother endured it ... proving bloodline and breeding is *part* of being a Pedigree. A marriage must be documented, or children born of it can never be legitimized. I'd hoped we might avoid it ... but this Inquisition will bring our secrets to light if we don't go about things in an orthodox fashion."

"I won't do this." I said between grit teeth.

"I am not *asking*, Luther." He stamped his cane on the hardwood floor. "When you were brought here, I told you this life you were inheriting came with sacrifice, and responsibilities. This is *one* small task, however unpleasant for you, that will go a *long* way to convincing that blasted holy man your marriage to my daughter is on the level, and potentially avoid what could be a lengthy, difficult Inquisition. Please..." his tone dropped slightly at that, to become more sympathetic, " ... I am asking for my daughter's sake. This will go a lot harder on us if you don't cooperate."

I bit the inside of my mouth, just to keep from yelling again. I couldn't reply to the man at all, even though I knew he deserved a response. But I knew the second I opened my mouth, I was going to explode, and all the frustration and anger coiling inside me would be unleashed. And none of it was meant for him.

" ... if it comforts you any," he said, "it won't be overseen by a priest. They always send one of the Neutren as a witness. It's considered less ... improper ... for the woman. They're hardly men anymore, after all."

I fisted my hands in the sheets, staying silent. Lucius looked on me, concerned.

"Luther..."

"You're not giving me an option," I bit out, "so I don't know what else you want from me. Please ... I just ... want to be alone, right now."

"Luther, I understand—"

"No." I said immediately, my voice acidic. "No. You don't. None of you understand. So stop claiming you do. I don't want to talk about this anymore. So please, just ... go."

He went quiet at that, and reached over to snuff out his cigar. And then without another word, he straightened his jacket, averted his now somber gaze from me, and headed out. I heard the door shut behind him.

When Mikhail came by later that evening, I knew one of my family had sent him. He'd been making himself scarce all day, and he seemed almost frightened, ears back, tail tucked, when I answered the door.

I leaned in the door-frame, shoulders slumped. "Who sent you?" I immediately demanded. "My wife, or the old man?"

"Lucius thought you shouldn't be alone." The fox said, quietly.

"May I come in, or ... shall I return to my quarters?"

I honestly considered sending him away for a few moments. I'd gone through a quarter a bottle of bourbon at this point ... not near enough to get me anywhere close to drunk, thanks to a lifetime of tolerance-building naval drinking ... and I probably would've been further along, but I hadn't wanted to leave my room and risk facing my family. Not a one of them.

" ... come in." I said at length, slipping back inside. The fox followed me, his delicate paws padding softly behind me. He shut the door, equally quietly. Everything he did was always so graceful, somehow the antithesis of my pounding and shouting my way through life.

I headed back over to the bed, sitting down heavily, and reaching over to finish off the last of my cold tea. I had stubbornly refused all of the servants that had tried to come in and bring me dinner, afraid somehow that they knew the goings-on of my family. Lucius had said, after all, that they knew how often I slept in Delilah's room, and I'd thought I'd been keeping that fairly secretive.

They might have even known she'd shared a bed with Mikhail and I, that one night...

I could only hide behind the mahogany doors of my room for so long, and I knew it. But I felt like here, until I pitched myself back out into the world again, here at least ... my pride was still intact. Nothing this personal was anyone's *damn* business except my own, and *maybe* my wife's. And my wife and I were content with things the way they were. Lucius had no right to demand what he was asking, and the Church *certainly* didn't.

This was a nightmare.

The bed dipped a bit, and Mikhail sat beside me. For now, he abstained from physical contact, perhaps sensing the aura around me. It wouldn't have taken a particularly perceptive man to know the state I was in. I'd never been very good at concealing my emotions. Most of the time, I didn't even try.

"Please don't tell me Lucius told you *everything*." I said, morosely.

"No..." he began, and I felt the but coming, " ... but ... Delilah did. I'm sorry. I really would have been content staying in my quarters ... none of this is my business—"

"It's fine." I muttered. "Hell, let's just tell the whole damned world. In a few days' time, some monk gets to watch me fuck my wife, like we're some bloody carnival."

Mikhail knitted his fingers together, his gold eyes looking down into his lap. " ... yes, but ... it's not so bad, is it?"

"I beg to differ." I growled.

He bristled a bit at the growl, a general vulpine reaction to canine warnings, I'd noticed. But he bravely moved a bit closer to me, venturing even to try and take my hand. "I only mean that ... it could be worse, Luther. From what Delilah's told me, once this ... thing ... is over ... they have practically no case. The marriage, the pups, everything's legitimized. And it's just the one time." He reasoned, in a soft-spoken tone. "I know it's not a place you wanted to go with your wife ... let alone under watch, but—"

"Everyone seems to think it's *so* damned easy, don't you?" I turned on him, and he almost immediately shrunk back at my tone. "It's so bloody *simple* to all of you. *So* minor a 'sacrifice' for me to make. Man up. Get through it. It's just the once, after all! How *bloody* bad could it be?!"

"Luther..." He leaned away from me, and the slight twinge of fear in his features hurt me, but I was too overwhelmed with something else at that moment to care. Some nameless emotion I'd fought against throughout my entire life, *every* time this came up.

"How can *no one* in the world understand me?!" I demanded. "Even the people in this family, who *know* how I am! Even *you*! Has it ever occurred to you all that *just* maybe ... I *can't* do this?!"

Mikhail went completely silent at that, his wide, golden eyes regarding mine for a long time. I felt my breath escaping in pants, my heart racing.

In the end it was I that turned around first ... unable to look at the fox, whose expression was beginning to shift from one of fear to one of sympathy, and understanding. I stalked away from the bed, my hands going to my dresser, knocking papers, a brandy sifter, and whatever else sat on the crowded surface aside. I *must* have had another bottle of alcohol somewhere in the room...

"Luther," the fox murmured from across the room, "are you—"

"*Don't say it!*" I roared, backhanding the last glass sifter on the countertop across the room, where it shattered against the wall. Mikhail flinched only once, but to the fox's credit, he didn't bolt. At least not yet. In fact, he braved another few words.

"This isn't something you need to be ashamed of." The vulpine insisted quietly. "Not all men are meant for women."

"No, just *every* other *bloody* man in the world!" I let my back fall against the wall, closing my eyes and facing my muzzle towards the ceiling. "I *know* you've worked for female clients. Every other lover I've ever had ... they have all been ... *capable* with the opposite sex. Even Klaus!" I pounded my fist back against the wall. "That bastard muddled his way through two mistresses, just to keep up appearances! We used to talk..."

My words ran off like water through a leaking hull and I put my palm to my brow, running it down over my eyes, so that I couldn't see the fox's sympathetic expression any more.

" ... I don't mean to offend you, Luther." Mikhail said carefully, in that same tentative tone. "But ... have you ever tried?"

"*Yes*, I've tried!" I exclaimed desperately, still unable to look him in the eyes. "Do you honestly think I've gone my entire life without *trying* to live the way that *doesn't* get me beaten and jailed?! Yes, I bloody tried! I tried when I was younger, with the girl my father intended me for ... and if the ... humiliation of *failing* wasn't bad enough, she went and told her damned *brothers* afterwards. Do you know how long those bastards mocked me?! My *father* found out!"

"What did you do?" Mikhail asked.

"I beat the ever-loving *hell* out of them!"

"No, Luther..." he sighed, "I mean ... what did you *do*? With her?"

"I know *how* to fuck a woman, damn it." I growled, finally dropping my hand and snarling at the fox. "I just..."

I couldn't continue after that. My chest felt like someone was eating away at it. Everything about that day was flooding back to me. The fear, the humiliation, the anger...

You aren't a man. A man could do this. Every man can do this. Even the men you've slept with. It's so damned simple.

What the hell was wrong with me?

I slammed my fist back against the wall, until I heard the wood crunch. Mikhail abruptly got to his feet, and hurried to my side. And in perhaps the bravest moment I'd ever seen from the young fox, he ignored my rage and took hold of my arm, corded steel in small, soft paws ... and pressed himself up against me.

"Nothing is wrong with you." The fox spoke softly, one of his paws slipping up over my cheek, running over the jagged fur along the back of my neck. I tipped my muzzle down, leaning my forehead down into his, and closed my eyes.

"I love her." I said quietly. "I honestly ... truly do. I just..."

"You aren't the only one, Luther." Mikhail's paw gently lifted my chin, until he was facing me. "It's just that ... we have to hide. There are many ... many men ... who just ... aren't meant for women. It's just how we're made."

"But you—" I began.

"There are other ways to please a woman, Luther." Mikhail gave the slightest of smiles. "But ... I still primarily only play escort for female clients. I've never had any interest in women in ... that regard. And I grew up in a brothel, helping the girls dress. So I believe I'm fairly certain by now."

I sighed, dropping my head down against his shoulder again. He stroked his paws up over my ears. "I'm sorry." He said.

"You haven't done anything wrong."

"I'm sorry for assuming ... like everyone else had." He ran his palm over the scruff of my neck slowly, knowing by now how much it calmed me. "It was a presumption based on ... well ... you're very ... masculine. I suppose that's a very poor way to judge."

“Why not?” I rumbled, derisively. “Every other man seems to judge masculinity based on how well you drink, fight, and make a woman scream.”

“You are most *certainly* a man, Luther.” Mikhail said with a soft laugh, running his paws over the musculature along my shoulders. “I can attest to that personally. In fact if you must know, you’d be the fantasy of many a male courtesan ... most of the sorts who hire us are soft, lazy, impotent noblemen.”

“Please don’t use that word.” I begged.

“I’m sorry.” He said with a light kiss along my brow. “But you aren’t. I have to ask, though ... are you absolutely certain you can’t do this? Maybe ... you were just young...”

“I’ve tried it twice since.” I said with a sigh. “It’s hard to avoid womanizing, in the Navy. The first was a disaster ... but luckily, I was alone with the woman. The second, I tried drunk ... thinking it would help. It didn’t, but it *did* provide me a legitimate excuse for failure.”

“There are ways to get it done.” The fox said with a pensive look. “If ... you absolutely must. But honestly Luther, I think if you just told Lucius—”

“*No*!” I declared fiercely, then tampered down a bit on my tone, trying not to terrify the poor man again. He’d endured enough of my rage tonight already. “No...” I said again, my ears falling. “I can’t ... I can’t...”

“It’s alright.” Mikhail soothed, “I understand. You don’t need to explain it.”

We stood there for a long time, and I slowly slipped my arms around him, holding him close to me, wondering why the hell it could be so easy, with him ... and so impossible, with my wife. And realizing that it was *always* going to be this way ... a sense of helplessness sunk over me.

“If you aren’t going to give in,” Mikhail said, the seriousness of his tone catching my attention. I stared down into a pair of very intense, golden eyes. “Then I can help you. We’ll con these bastards once ... and they’ll never be able to come after you again. Try to look at it that way." He said softly. "Try not to focus on the lie. Try to think about the life you'll be able to lead, when this is all over..."

"I ... how?" I asked, honestly not sure what the fox had in mind.

"Well ... there are a few basic tricks you can use ... most of which you may have already tried." Mikhail conceded. "But I'll tell you what I know, all the same. In my trade, you learn how to make your body respond ... even if you don't want to."

"Have you—" I began.

He gave a mischievous smile. "You'd never know. But ... no. I've never had to. Not with you."

" ... alright." I said after only a few more moments of consideration. I took a long breath, and swallowed my pride. "I'm willing to hear you out."

"Well," he began, "for one..."

When Delilah answered her door, she was in her sleeping clothes. The shift was about the most undressed I'd ever seen my wife, and thin though it was, she wore her undergarments beneath. All the same, the night air was cold in the hallway, and it brought certain ... assets ... into more stark contrast, forcing me to stare down the reality of what I was here for all but immediately.

"Luther?" She looked up at me, bleary-eyed, and I realized guiltily that I'd woken her. It hadn't even occurred to me how late it was. She rubbed some of the sleep from her eyes, and blinked up at me. "Is ... everything alright?"

"Yes." I stated quickly, then sighed. " ... no. But you know that, already. Delilah ... can I please just come in?" I didn't mean it to come out sounding as hurried as it had.

"Y ... of course." She stammered, then opened the door entirely for me, and let me inside. It wasn't often I entered my wife's personal room anymore. Not since she'd been off bed rest. It was almost as I'd remembered it, except for two small standing frames on her dresser, little painted renditions of her two children. I remembered when

Lucius had had them commissioned for her, after she'd been so upset the children weren't going to be sleeping in her bedroom anymore.

A small candle was lit on her dresser, the room flickering with the meager light, but little else. My wife looked to me from across the room, her arms crossed over her chest, eyes sparkling in the candlelight. She looked confused, but not frightened ... which was a start. I know I'd been a wreck the last few days. Apparently by now, she'd learned to deal with my tantrums.

"Luther ... I know father came and spoke to you." She said softly. "But we could have spoken in the morning. You look exhausted. You need your rest."

"Delilah." I said, wetting my suddenly dry tongue. "I need you to tell me something, and please, be completely, unapologetically honest with me."

" ... alright." She promised.

"You've told me many times ... that you don't require we be physically intimate." I said, and I knew immediately by the slight widening of her eyes that I'd caught her off-guard. "Is that because you don't wish to?"

"Luther, I—"

"Please. You cannot *possibly* hurt my feelings in this matter." I promised her. "Please ... tell me what's in the depths of your heart."

She studied me silently for a short while, as though trying to discern what had compelled me to come here, and ask her this, in the middle of the night. Really, I couldn't blame her.

"Luther," she said softly, at length, "I love you. I think I've loved you since ... almost the first week I knew you." She admitted. "You aren't anything like Irving ... and to be earnest with you ... I have put all of that in my past. I am a resilient woman."

"I know you are." I agreed.

"I told you I didn't require you as a partner ... because I don't need those pleasantries to be happy with you." She said, going almost doe-eyed as she said it. "But ... that doesn't mean I don't want you."

I'd almost wished to hear otherwise from her. It would have made this so easy.

"I love you." She repeated, quietly. "I would be very happy to be with you ... as a wife lays down with her husband. But I will never require that from you to secure my happiness. I am already happy. We have two wonderful children. I am immensely blessed. I need nothing else."

She sat down gingerly on the edge of the bed, adjusting the hem of her nightgown around her legs, as she did. "Is this because of what father said? We ... we can find a way around it. I'm certain—"

"It's the easiest solution, Delilah." I murmured, and slowly moved over towards her, sitting down beside her. Her bed was so much softer than mine. "You haven't ever dealt with an Inquisitor before ... have you?"

She only shook her head.

"Even if they can't hurt you," I said, "they'll tear you apart. It's what they do. They dig, and twist, and lower you, until you can bear no more. They do it all with a civil tongue, with guilt, by finding your secrets and using them against you ... using those you care about against you..."

I saw her eyes flit to the two small paintings of her children, and I only nodded.

"Yes, even them. They'll threaten everything we are and they'll hold no quarter. They'll discover the truth of what happened with Irving. They'll use it against you, like a wedge ... prying into every other facet of who you are, and turning all of our lives inside out. They'll destroy this family."

"And," I said slowly, " ... I can prevent it. We both can."

"I have no issue undertaking this if you don't, Luther." She said, slipping her hand over mine. "I will endure it."

" ... when is your next heat?" I asked, watching her stiffen the second the words left my mouth.

"I-I-"

"I know it's an inappropriate question." I sighed, softly. "And I'm sorry ... I don't mean to embarrass you. But ... it's important."

She was silent, and for a moment I was afraid I'd frightened her off already, but she only replied after a further few seconds, and I realized she'd just been counting dates. " ... two weeks." She said. "Or ... thereabouts."

"Lucius can probably put them off for two weeks, if need be ... with some kind of excuse." I mused, almost to myself.

"Why must we do this during my heat?" She questioned. "I ... are you hoping for children?"

"No." I sighed. "I'm very content with the twins."

"Then why—"

"Because it's a factor ... that may improve our chances." I answered, trying to keep my voice steady. "I'm ... not immune ... to the same effects it has on other men. It will help."

Praise be, she didn't question me any further past that. She only nodded.

"I may conceive." She said.

"I know ... but the chances are slim, from just the once. Aren't they?" I queried.

" ... it has happened before." She murmured.

"Delilah, we have to do things this way because of a failing on my part." I said, biting back on my pride for the woman I cared for. "But, I am not insensitive to the dangers you face in another pregnancy. My hope is that ... nothing will come of it. But I swear to you, if it does ... I won't go to sea, this year. I'll stay at your side."

She looked up at me, at that. "I couldn't ask you to—"

"I swear." I repeated, and reached over to stroke her cheek, gently. She looked up at me, the light brown orbs of her eyes still flickering with the candlelight cast from the now nearly-melted stick floundering on her dresser.

After a few more moments, she nodded, and nuzzled into my palm. I stroked her muzzle and cheeks, and up along her soft ears for some time as I had many nights when we slept beside one another.

It made what I was about to ask all the harder.

"Delilah," I began, my throat parched with trepidation, " ... I need to attempt this at least once before that night."

Her eyes widened at that, and she looked up at me, in realization. " ... now?"

"I..." I paused. How to say this without sounding ... awkward ... "I'm ... prepared, now."

"Oh." She replied, but she still sounded confused.

I sighed. " ... Mikhail and I were talking about this, and ... he's ... helping..."

"Oh!" She said, in realization. Or at least I think so. I never knew exactly how 'educated' my wife was about these things. "A-alright." She said, and stood all but immediately ... which was not exactly the reaction I'd been expecting. She slipped her hands down to the hem of her nightgown, then paused. "Should I ... should I disrobe?" she asked, shyly.

"That's generally how it's done." I replied. "Your figure above won't dissuade me, if that's your concern. I intend to turn you on your stomach."

She flushed in her ears, and I instantly felt like a jackass. This was a Pedigree woman. I couldn't be talking to her like she was some wharf whore.

"I'm sorry." I said. "I just ... it's just one of the other ... things that might ... help."

"No, no." She assured me. "I-I don't mind. I'm not embarrassed. I just ... if it would be easier for you, if I was clothed..."

"Husbands generally undress their wives, even in Pedigree society, don't they?" I asked, honestly curious. It made little difference to me, honestly, though I didn't want to admit it to her. What mattered rested between her legs, and there'd be no avoiding that.

She was silent a moment, tugging at the hem of her night gown, eyes downcast. "Irving didn't..." she said, quietly.

I narrowed my eyes. "Irving wasn't your husband." I stated. "I am. Undress."

She flushed ... more ... but began to do as I bid her. It was an odd experience for me, I'll admit. Almost surreal. I'd been married to this woman for months, now ... and I had never seen her nude. I didn't find the female figure displeasing. It just didn't elicit the ... spark ... that got me riled.

Delilah was petite, but not thin. Her fur was soft, well-groomed, and as I was soon to learn ... dotted in liver-colored patches, like splashes across snowy white, down her torso, legs and arms. She was shy about undressing, but I didn't look away. I wanted my wife to know I wasn't afraid to look on her.

I smiled slightly when she was done, and offered her a hand. She took it gingerly, and padded towards me, barely taller than me standing, while I was sitting.

"You're beautiful, Delilah." I murmured. "No less so clothed, in my opinion ... but I'm honored to enjoy such a rare sight."

"You're the only man I'd ever come before like this." She said softly.

That hit me with a pang in the heart, reminding me how seriously my wife took her vows to me, but I pushed aside the guilt for the moment. It wouldn't do me any good right now.

"Lie down for me." I said, releasing her hand, and standing. I began to unbutton my vest. As I was halfway done with my shirt, I heard her shifting in bed, and felt her eyes on me. I turned to regard her as I dropped my shirt over a nearby chair, unable to ignore the slightly girlish smile she had at the moment. I quirked an eyebrow at her. "What?" I asked.

" ... I get to see you naked now." She answered shyly, lying slightly curled-up on her side amidst the tousled comforter.

"You've *seen* me nude, already." I pointed out, "With Mikhail."

"You hid under the covers the whole time!" She complained, wriggling a bit. "I could barely see a thing."

I rolled my eyes. "I'm sorry ... I'm not accustomed to performing for a crowd." I removed my thick belt, letting it drop to the floor, and shucked out of my britches fairly easily. The smallclothes were last ...

and something inside me agreed, at the very least, with how enrapt she was as I removed the last vestiges of modesty.

If pride worked, so be it. I'd accept that.

I moved over her fairly swiftly after that, and she shrunk back some into the bed, which only made me more concerned for what was coming. I leaned over her, and ran a palm down her cheek.

"Delilah, are you certain—"

"Yes." She said, quickly. "I didn't mean to shy away. I'm just a little nervous. But I still ... want ... to."

I sighed. "I'm ... I'm very ... very sorry ... if I'm too rough with you. It's just ... how I am. If I try to go slow—"

"Luther." She leaned up, and gave me a soft kiss. "I'm not afraid of you. And I am not delicate ... I swear. I have given birth ... twice. This can't possibly compare."

"Touché." I murmured.

I felt the gentle, explorative touch of her paw, slipping down my chest ... and it occurred to me that I had only ever touched my wife's face, and hands ... and vice versa. She paused when she saw me watching her, and made to pull away.

"Should I not—"

"No, that ... might honestly help." I said, encouragingly. "That and ... patience..."

"You have me for the rest of my life, Luther." She said softly.

I let out a long breath. She looked up at me, silently. There was no judgment in her eyes. No expectations. Some of the pressure left me, as I looked down at her. Some...

I leaned down and kissed her, deeply. Kissing a woman had never felt wrong ... especially not Delilah. It had also never felt ... sensual. But in this moment, I tried to will it to be what it had never been. I tried to do as Mikhail had told me.

Don't focus on what she is, physically. Focus on how you feel for her. Focus on how much you care about her. Close your eyes ... do nothing but feel.

It was so hard to ignore the reality of it all ... but I tried. I tried so damned hard. There were certain things I couldn't overcome ... things that had fought my success with this my entire life. The scent of her arousal sent off pinpricks of caution, through my body ... the feel of a breast beneath my paw, as I tried to reciprocate her actions ... the last thing I wanted to do was recoil from this woman. I wasn't repulsed by females ... I just...

... everything about it felt wrong. That was the only way I could describe it. Like some piece just wasn't fitting in place in my mind. The familiar sensations I'd always had with my male lovers, the fires that grew inside me when I felt their bodies under mine, when I kissed them, and their musk hit my nostrils...

I closed my eyes. I'd told myself that was not a place I was willing to go. I wouldn't imagine another lover while I was with Delilah. It hadn't worked for me in the past, and it was a disservice to her. I had my pride, and fantasizing about another while I was with my wife was a line I wasn't willing to cross.

I was doing this for her. That was it. I'd overcome many things throughout my lifetime. I would overcome *this*.

I slipped my larger paw over hers, and lead it to where it needed to be. I was burgeoning ... it never took *much* to get me that far, it was almost a perpetual state of being, for me. But despite the relatively minor state of arousal, she still gasped a bit into my muzzle, when she took hold of me.

" ... are you alright?" I asked, pulling back only slightly. I didn't want to break this momentum.

" ... y-yes. I just didn't expect—"

"I'm ... barely unsheathed."

"O-oh ... " she said, slipping a glance down between the two of us. " ... really?"

"Nnh-yes ... and keep doing that. Your hands are soft." I rumbled.

She seemed encouraged by that, and I closed my eyes, focusing on the sensation. This part was the same no matter whom your partner was, honestly ... and the fact that my body was responding was gratifying in and of itself.

But then, I'd gotten this far before. It was the next part that was difficult.

"It ... keeps getting..."

"If you're about to compliment my size, please don't hold back." I gave an almost amused whuff. "Ego-stroking does almost as much for me as..." I trailed off, as I felt my knot thicken, and realized in that moment that I might honestly have a chance at this. "Delilah," I said, taking a hold of her hand, and gently removing it. "Turn over. Please. Now."

She looked up at me wide-eyed, but then did as I'd ordered, and slipped onto her belly beneath me.

I took a long breath, steadying myself behind her. My paws slipped over her rear, and I ran her tail through one palm ... a habit I'd gotten into over the years. Maybe if I went through the same motions...

The problem came, as it always did ... the moment I started pushing into her. For one, the girl was actually a tight fit ... which was no benefit to me in this situation. The hard push made entering her difficult, it even hurt a bit ... and it probably hurt her, too. I heard her muffle herself against the sheets, and a pang of guilt added to my already mounting doubts. I tried to push past them, as I'd so far been doing successfully.

This was where it always fell apart. The second I began to wane, it was a vicious cycle of the negative responses from my body, and crippling self-doubt.

I felt for my wife, but there was only one way I was going to get through this. I started immediately ... I started hard, and I didn't stop. I held myself over her so I wasn't pushing any of my weight into her, but I knew I must have been hurting her, anyway. She was holding tight to the sheets, muzzle pressed down into a pillow. I couldn't see her face, but that was probably a good thing.

I thought perhaps, for the first minute or so, that I might be making progress, but I was rowing upstream. *Everything* about this was just *too* different. I loved my wife. I truly did. But it felt just as wrong as it ever had and almost more so this time, because I gave a damn about the woman I was with, and I knew I was hurting her.

I knew after the second minute that I was fighting a losing battle. I could probably keep this up ... but I couldn't round the bend. Delilah had gone strangely silent, and tense around me ... in every possible way. I stilled, and leaned on one arm, catching my breath. I felt her shift slowly beneath me, and with a staggered, defeated sigh, I met her eyes.

"I'm sorry, Delilah." I murmured. "I'm ... little more than a weapon, at this point."

"You ... you don't want to keep trying?" She questioned, her voice oddly hoarse, and trembling.

"I can't..." I averted my eyes from hers, " ... it won't do any good. And I'd rather not ... hurt you for no reason."

" ... you aren't hurting me." She said quietly.

"You don't need to—"

"Luther." She whispered, shyly. "I don't know ... *what* you're doing to me ... but it does not hurt."

I took a moment to take in her meaning, before she continued, in a pleading voice, " ... will you please continue? At least ... try?"

I leaned down, and nuzzled into her soft nose. I stayed there for a time, before I shifted back up, and took a long breath.

"We'll keep trying." I promised. "As long as you wish."

By the morning, we were exhausted. I was tense in nearly every muscle of my body, frustrated and battling the overwhelming feeling of failure I'd felt so many times before. The only difference was, this time I'd come close. Closer than I ever had before. I wasn't certain if that attested to my wife's tenacity and patience, or the tips Mikhail had given me.

The resignation was settling in, but I was trying to scavenge some confidence out of the whole mess. I *had* come close. Maybe, while she was in heat...

Delilah leaned against my back, running her paws gently over my sore, tense muscles. I felt her hand slip around my thigh, to take hold of mine, her fingers threading through my thicker, calloused ones.

If there was one comfort I could take from the evening, it's that I was fairly certain that somewhere amidst my personal struggle ... I'd shown Delilah that lovemaking could be more than pain, and humiliation. I had never before pleased a woman, and it unfortunately hadn't been, nor might it ever be, a mutually pleasurable experience...

... but it had still been worth doing.

CHAPTER 13

INQUISITION

"Excuse me, sir?"

I ignored the servant for the moment, as I headed hurriedly down the staircase. I didn't mean to be rude, but the Inquisitor was set to arrive very shortly and my time was growing slim. Lucius waited for me in the lobby, nervously gripping his cane. I saw him dismiss another manservant from his post in the sitting room. He seemed just as distracted in his thoughts as I was, because the spaniel hardly noticed me as I came upon him.

"Where is Delilah?" He asked offhandedly, as I came to stand beside him.

"Upstairs, readying herself. I gather you saw the carriage from the road, as well?" I muttered.

"I've been watching the windows all bloody day." He sighed. "I don't know why I bothered ... these men are like the tides. Inevitable and always irritatingly on-time." He turned to address me on another subject, I can only assume, but paused as he looked over my shoulder. And then he smirked.

"Excuse me, sir?" The servant from the staircase had apparently followed me and this time, she tugged on my sleeve.

"I don't mean to be rude," I sighed, glancing at her, "but I am exceedingly busy at the—"

The fox smiled at me, and I nearly fell off my feet.

"What in the *hell* is this about?!" I demanded, gape-jawed. I heard Lucius chuckling from behind me.

"You don't like it?" Mikhail smirked at me, stooping to give an elegant curtsy. The damned fox was dressed like one of the house servants. One of the *female* house servants, long white apron and all.

I turned to glare at Lucius, who wasn't bothering to keep the expression of mirth from his features. "You said you were going to ensure he was out of sight during all of this!"

"Oh, but he is." He chuckled. "Hidden in plain sight. You didn't notice him at all. It's fairly remarkable how well he pulls it off, isn't it?"

"I ... that..." I gave an exasperated snuff. "That isn't the point!"

"And here I was hoping you'd like it." Mikhail put on his best feminine voice. It wasn't much of a stretch for the tiny fox.

"Aye, we both thought you'd get a kick out of it, honestly." Lucius said around a cigar, as he fished for a light in one of his pockets. "We tried the manservants' garb first, and he just didn't look right in it. Boys that work the grounds here don't look like ... that. He fits in better with the girls."

"First off," I growled, "I like *men*, men who dress like men. The fact that he ... is convincing, at this ... only makes it *more* disturbing."

"But I'm so pretty." Mikhail insisted, with a tail bob.

"It's uncanny." Lucius agreed, taking a long drag of his cigar. "Young lad could almost pass for his mother, in her prime."

"Oh, Lord Lucius," Mikhail said in a light, sultry purr that sounded every bit the vixen he was playing at the moment, "it's been ages since we've seen one another ... but I'll bet you're every bit the man I once knew ... where it counts."

Lucius slowly arched an eyebrow, glanced aside and gave an unsettled cough, which I'm certain wasn't caused by his cigar. "Let's ... move this conversation along." The old man muttered. "It's beginning to make me feel ... confused and uncomfortable."

"Imagine how I feel!" I said, exasperated.

"Look, son," Lucius looked back towards Mikhail, although I noticed he was now pointedly avoiding eye contact, "we needed to hide the boy somewhere, until this is all over ... and sending him off to one of my residents, or one of the local inns would only have caused more scandal. This is a small county. A courtesan stands out, and there's only one manor about that he might be working for—"

"Fine, fine." I waved a hand, both at the old spaniel and the fox. "But ... please ... try and stay out of sight. I don't want to get caught staring at one of the 'servants' and attract more attention to you than you already will by yourself. I hope the damned Inquisitor isn't a bloodhound."

"I'm wearing a vixen scent." Mikhail smiled.

"I noticed." Both I and Lucius said in unison. Then we both glanced away, awkwardly.

A sudden rap at the front doors jarred us all from the moment. Mikhail headed off, swiftly. I straightened my sleeves, self-consciously. Lucius cleared his throat and headed for the doorway. I heard Delilah padding up behind me. I reached a paw out for hers and soon felt her fingers wrapping gently around mine as she came to stand beside me.

"I'm frightened." She admitted quietly.

"Everything's going to be fine." I promised her, even though I wasn't certain, myself. Lucius had managed to put the Inquisitor off for a few weeks with some statement about handling issues for his fleet and being unable to be at home. Delilah and I had used the time to prepare, as well as we could ... and to wait for her heat.

It was perhaps the best tip Mikhail had given me and I was again grateful the fox was here with us. Ironically despite what Cuthbert had forewarned me about, having the courtesan present might save my marriage to Delilah in the end. He'd been enormously supportive already, playing a neutral party for my wife and I to speak to on our concerns and troubles ... both physical and non. I don't think I could have spoken to any other man about the ... issues ... I had with women. Certainly not Lucius, and he was the only other man who knew my situation. Mikhail was nonthreatening and as I'd come to discover, had a lot of personal experience with my lifelong struggle. I'd not even been able to speak on even terms with Klaus about how I felt with women. Mikhail had, at last, helped ease some small part of the shame I'd always associated with it.

The only unfortunate part of it was ... it had exponentially increased my fondness for him, in all the ways I'd been concerned about.

Now wasn't the time to worry about that, though. Right now, one of the servants was opening the doors to the Denholme manor and three men were entering, two in robes, and one in priest's vestments. The priest would be the Inquisitor, but I would have known that regardless of his regalia. The canine was a tall, aged weimaraner with a pair of spectacles perched high along the bridge of his nose. He held himself straight-backed and walked with purpose, his eyes scanning the domicile like a hawk. The two men with him were obviously Neutren. You could always see it in the more hunched, defeated posture, the way they slunk around like every step was tiring. They both seemed to be mixed breeds, they were both overweight and simply-groomed and the light had gone out of their eyes long ago. Their gaze was dull and glassy, like they'd gone feral.

I slipped my paw from Delilah's as the man fixed his gaze on us. The ironic thing was, I honestly wanted physical contact with my wife at the moment, but to an outsider, it would look like we were just trying too hard, or putting on a show. Instead, I straightened my posture, and watched the priest greet Lucius curtly, before he headed in our direction.

The man could not have made it any more obvious he didn't feel like wasting his time with the old Lord. It was actually incredibly rude. This was *his* house. He deserved more than a nod and a half-muffled greeting.

But the Inquisitor's attention was solely focused on me the moment he'd laid eyes upon me. Which didn't bode well. It suggested he knew me by sight, somehow. Or perhaps he just knew I was the husband, being as I was the only younger, non-spaniel in the room. I wasn't sure. Either way, his stare was making me uncomfortable.

It didn't get any better when he closed the distance between us. And unlike Lucius, he did not even offer me a handshake.

"You would be Luther, I take it?" The man asked crisply.

"Yes." I nodded, offering my hand. "Luther Denholme."

He looked at the offered hand for a few moments, before narrowing his already slim eyes, but taking my palm in his all the same. His grip was tight. "We shall see about that." He responded, his tone impassable. His grey eyes fell on Delilah at that and she visibly bristled, but I put a hand to her back, where I hoped he couldn't see me, trying to assure her. "And you must be the young lady. Where are your children?"

I felt a tremor pass through her at that. "You ... want to see my children? So soon, Father?"

"I wish to ascertain their bloodline." The priest said. "Visual inspection is key to this. Only to ensure they have some resemblance to their legal sire."

Again, I felt her shuddering. All I could do was rub her back in slow circles and hope she remembered everything we'd gone over, so many times. The greatest key here was not to *show* this man how afraid of his rulings we were. She was already terrified, and I could tell. I hoped he couldn't.

"After you've taken me to the children's' room and I've completed my visual inspection, we'll move on to your belated witnessing ceremony." The priest said as he reached into the simple leather satchel he carried over his shoulder, pulling out a scroll, and a quill and ink case. He gestured to one of the Neutren, who moved up to him and took the items. "Robert here will be your witness." He stated as the boxer mix stepped back. "You should tell your servants to ready whatever room you intend to use now. I won't be long with the children."

"So soon?" Delilah asked, shocked. "We ... I ... it's barely noon. I assumed we would at least wait until nightfall, when it is natural—"

"Let me make this very clear to both of you, and your entire family." The priest said firmly, and loud enough to ensure Lucius could hear him, it seemed. "I am an ordained Inquisitor, here to confirm that your family is not committing fraud against Amurescan law, the Church, and God himself. This is not a social visit. There will be no pleasantries exchanged. I expect my visit here will be brief. I anticipate to have my answer by the end of this night. I am very good at my job, and I guarantee you ... it shall not take any longer than that, unless you are all extremely uncooperative. And that will only make my job easier, because I will then *know* you have something to hide."

He looked around the room at all of us. Even Lucius was dead silent. "If you've nothing to hide, you've no cause for fear. But if you are lying to me, I *will* find you out. Make no mistake."

I felt Delilah's hand reaching for mine, and I couldn't deny her, regardless of how it looked. Thankfully, the priest didn't seem to notice.

"Now," he began again, "take me to see the children. We will commence with the witnessing ceremony immediately following. A man must have no issue taking his own wife to bed, at any time ... and a woman must be willing at any time. The ceremony is a legality at this point, anyway, considering you've already children. I'd imagine we'd all like to get it over with."

"Yes, Father." Delilah said quietly.

"Sir ... Father." I corrected myself, and his eyes snapped to me. "We ... haven't even gotten your name yet."

He was silent for a few moments, before responding, "Father will be fine. My name is of no importance in this matter. The children?"

"Upstairs." Delilah murmured, and began to head towards the

staircase. The priest and I followed. I caught his eyes drifting over my hand as it quickly separated from Delilah's, but he said nothing.

Watching the Inquisitor critically inspecting my children had to be one of the most insufferable experiences I'd ever endured. And I'd endured quite a lot, throughout my lifetime. There was just something so much more violating about watching a man judge the two slumbering babes I'd come to regard as *my* responsibility, my flesh and blood ... whether or not they were. Unknowingly or not, I'd committed myself to playing the role of protector to the two little creatures, so innocent and incapable of defending themselves to this cold, inscrutable man.

I wanted him to get on with this quickly ... get back to judging *me*. I was accustomed to being judged. I had a firmer constitution, and if the damned priest got tough with me, I could deck him across the jaw. Brook and Klaus weren't even *aware* they were being looked on like two cuts of meat on a block, being weighed and measured in what might possibly be the most important moment in deciding their future lives ... their station in society, the Church, the main determiner of how they would be permitted to live in the world from this point on.

The irony of it all was, if the Church knew Klaus and Brook's actual, shameful lineage ... they would be better off. I'd already decided that if this whole thing were to go south, I'd simply tell the truth and let come what may. The only person it could end poorly for was me. Delilah would be in no worse a position, save in social circles, and better that than in a Church cell. I would tell them the conspiracy had been mine from the start. They'd spare an old man and a woman with two legitimately Pedigree children.

It was the best-case in a worst-case scenario. The hope was that we'd pull this all off without a hitch. But if we didn't ...

It was an odd thing for me, to be considering the things I was. Not because I was marveling at my own selflessness, but because I was reflecting on how selfish every *other* decision I'd made in my past had been. This was perhaps the first time in my life I couldn't comprehend putting my own interests above those of the people around me. And that realization was throwing the whole of my past into stark contrast.

Johannes may have been right about some of the things he'd said about me. Even fighting Irving had been a selfish desire for me. I'd cared for Delilah then, yes, but ... killing him had done her absolutely no good. It had done this family no good, only caused them more strife and worry. It had accomplished nothing but assuaging my own overgrown need for justice. I'd been angry. I'd wanted to hurt him. Kill him. And I had. It had been for me.

I was starting to understand why Johannes stayed away from his family so often. Sometimes the best way to protect the people you cared about was through inaction. We were violent men. We'd lived in violence, seen violence all our lives ... Johannes and Lucius more so than I. And somehow, Lucius had managed to find a balance, maintaining a stable state-of-being and living up to his family responsibilities without his wartime experiences coloring it all. But with Johannes, I'd seen that not all succeeded in that task.

I was young yet, and I'd already made many mistakes. I shuddered to think what further ones I would make that would impact my family.

This wasn't going to be one of them though. If anyone was going down for this, it was me. And I'd go down fighting, as soon as I was a considerable distance from my family.

My gaze shifted back to the weimeraner, his frigid grey eyes sweeping over the two unwary pups, clutching each other in their crib. I was grateful at least that they were sleeping at this time of day. Generally they were wide awake and fussing, but they'd eaten only an hour before. They were only babes of course ... they'd hardly have memories of this, but some nonsensical part of my brain was still relieved they weren't awake and conscious of the inspection.

"And they were born between the 30th and the 31st?" The man

questioned as he pulled a ledger, a quill and ink from his bag, and began making notes. I couldn't read what he was writing from where I stood. I fought the urge to push my way over there, just to know what he was writing about my children.

"Between the two days, yes." Delilah said patiently. But I knew my wife and I could hear the same trepidation I was feeling in her voice. "There were some complications with the birth."

"So I've read, in the physician's report." The priest murmured, before finishing whatever he was scrawling. "I don't suppose, lady ... or you sir," he said as his eyes rose to fall on mine, "that you might have any idea at the date of conception?"

I swallowed back the lump of ice in my throat. "No. I'm sorry." Delilah only shook her head.

The way the man's features shifted ever slightly at that unnerved me. The priest wasn't an expressive man, but any subtle change surely meant *something*. It was frustrating, because I was generally good at reading people. This priest was a blank.

"Mnh, very well." He murmured as he began to repack his bag. I waited. I felt Delilah shifting uncomfortably beside me. But no more words came. The priest simply packed his bag, and shouldered past me out of the room. I lowered my brow, letting out a breath. Delilah looked up at me, uncertainly.

I found the man reconvening with the two Neutren outside the children's' room, conversing quietly. I didn't mean for my tone to come out sounding as irate as it did, but I was becoming nervous.

"Is that it, then?" I questioned.

He turned to regard me, raising an eyebrow. "I have completed my visual inspection. I cannot question babes."

"I just mean," I sighed, " ... I-I mean ... what happens now? That was very quick. I'm not even certain what you were looking for—"

"What happens now is, we perform your witnessing ceremony." The priest said as he handed his ledger to one of the Neutren. "My man here has confirmed for me that you've a room available. As a complete male, it would be inappropriate for me to attend, so you'll be in Brother Robert's hands from this point on. Afterwards, you will both be questioned. And then I will conclude my notes and return to the Monastery, where your case will be reviewed."

"Now hold on—" I began, but Delilah put her hand on mine, casting a pleading glance my way before turning her attention back on the priest.

"What my husband is concerned about is just that ... this seems to be happening so fast." She said in a far calmer tone than I could have ever mustered. "We want to be certain you have everything you need. We have nothing to hide."

"I have been conducting these investigations for over twenty years, miss." The weimeraner said. "Believe me when I say ... you will hide nothing from me. Just do as I ask."

Delilah and I both fell silent. The priest gestured to one of the two Neutren. "Now then. Brother Robert will be accompanying you. Personally, I find the witnessing ceremony an inessential and baseless affair for a lineage issue, but it is tradition for any marriage. Why you chose to put it off so long is beyond me. Be done with it, then return to me. And we will speak further."

"Yes, Father." Delilah said. I returned the statement in kind, in more of a murmur than anything else. The priest began to descend the staircase, the second Neutren following in step behind him. I wasn't sure why the second man was even here. Presumably as a baggage handler for the priest. Who the hell knows.

We began to follow the Neutren towards the room where Delilah and I would inevitably be playing our role in this horrid performance. I deliberately fell back in step, Delilah noticing and doing the same as we walked. When we'd put about ten paces between us and the Neutren, I lowered my voice and spoke. There was a chance he might still hear us, so I kept what I said vague.

"If you aren't prepared to do this—"

"I'll be fine." She said firmly. Then her eyes softened and she looked up at me. "Will you?"

I nodded, though doubt still lingered heavily in my mind. "Thank you for ... agreeing to time things as we have. I think it will help."

"This is important to all of us." Delilah said softly.

"I won't fail you. I swear it." I promised, in a lower whisper still.

"You won't." She confirmed softly, with a hand on mine. I gave her an odd look at that ... she sounded very certain. She blanched a bit in her ears and fixed her gaze on the floor. "I ... decided to speak to Mikhail, as well." She admitted. "About what I might do to ... he was very ... educational. There is no limitation on how we go about this. And I have learned a thing or two."

I made an uncertain noise in the back of my throat. My wife had spoken to Mikhail? I can't imagine what the fox must have told her. I was glad I hadn't been around for that, though.

Honestly, it was best I didn't think on any of this any further. It was starting to hurt my head.

I kept my mind focused on the task at hand. As we reached the room, I took Delilah's paw in mine again. Regardless of what happened today, I was glad for once in my life not to be alone in it.

Lucius had worn a track in the floor of his study by the time I rejoined him. The second I pushed open the large mahogany door, I saw his entire body go rigid, his ears perking, tail pointing. He immediately began to cross the room towards me, his limp seeming more pronounced, today. Likely due to stress.

"Good God boy ... you're shaking." He reached out and put a hand on my shoulder to steady me. His eyes were full of concern, possibly even fear. "Tell me everything went—"

"It's done." I confirmed, seeing his entire posture go lax the moment the words left my mouth. "Delilah's ... well. Everything is fine."

"Good lad." Lucius blew out a breath, patting my shoulder. "What then with these nerves? I know well how uncomfortable the experience can be, but it's done. You look as though you're headed for the noose."

"I might very well be." I muttered. "The Inquisitor wants to speak to me, first."

"Yes, well ... we knew there would be questioning." Lucius said. "Still boy, it's alright. Just stick to our story."

"I don't think that's going to be possible." I uttered.

Lucius' expression immediately went from concern, to surprise, then became very serious. "Explain." He said.

"I saw the Inquisitor in the hallway, as I left the room Delilah and I shared." I said. "He was ... holding a stack of letters and papers, leafing through them for something. I ... I caught sight of one of them, because..." I closed my eyes, my head dropping, " ... it had the Coat of Arms for Klaus's fleet engraved at the top."

Lucius' eyes widened. "Are you absolutely certain?"

I nodded, running a hand over my ears. " ... the fig tree, with the dove in the branches. I'll never forget it."

Lucius fell silent. After a moment or two, he stiffly wandered back over to his chair and sat down heavily.

"It has to be my military transcript." I said quietly. "My real ... military transcript."

"I thought we had them all destroyed." Lucius said irritably, his tone gone far darker than a few moments hence. "Damned. I put a lot of money out into the wind to wash your record clean. I'd hoped at least your time aboard the Winnipeg was erased from the books. That was key."

"I know what I saw." I said. "Lucius ... I'm going to do whatever I have to. I thought you deserved the courtesy of knowing. He's questioning me in less than ten minutes. I'm going to tell him all of this was my plan. Take the blame."

"The *hell* you are!" Lucius growled. "I am not letting you *hang* yourself for me! I'm an old man, I can take whatever those bastards are going to dish out. You need to be here to take care of my daughter!"

"They aren't going to *let* me do that!" I replied, my voice fierce, but not yelling. I'd become paranoid of this man ... God knew, he could be listening right now. "Don't you see that? If they know the truth and we put it on the Denholme family, everyone in this family suffers! Delilah, the pups ... and they'll *never* let me remain here, let alone allow me to inherit anything. The Church can *destroy* this family. Your name. Your holdings. Your *fleet*."

"*Think* for a moment, boy!" Lucius bit out. "Use your mind! God gave you a brilliant head on your shoulders and you're so quick to disregard it for gut instinct!" He glanced briefly at the thick, closed doors of his study before dropping his tone. "Who else could have perpetrated this scheme but me? How in God's name could you have plotted something like this? From prison? How would you have known our family was in need of a suitor?"

"I ... could claim I heard it through the Navy." I stammered. "Irving was commissioned—"

"Jeremiah was commissioned on *land*!" Lucius gestured skyward with the one hand not gripping his cane. "That boy never even *saw* the sea! His family *lost* their fleet many years ago and even if they hadn't, his position would have been due to title only! He went to the Academy at Birkenhurst. His family *owns* the Academy! If that boy had 'contacts' in the Navy, they were prisscoats like him, not men who'd seen time on the Winnipeg, or any of Klaus's ships! That dog may have been daft, but he saw combat every season. None of Jeremiah Irving's' friends would *dare* set foot on those boats."

I went mute, struck by how very little I'd known about the man I'd killed. No. Not killed. Murdered. Legally-sanctioned or not, that's what it had been.

Lucius gripped my shoulder again, his expression looking almost pleading, at this point. "I know you want to do the right thing for my girl here, son ... but this isn't it. A poor lie will only infuriate the Inquisitor. He is going to ask you questions I know in my heart you haven't answers for!"

I slumped, my mind lost again. And just seconds ago, I'd had such conviction. Fear that things would go poorly, certainly, but also conviction that I knew the course that I need take. God, I missed the days when my decisions had always seemed so much easier. The more and more I'd gotten pulled into this world of Pedigrees, Officers and the Denholme family, the less black and white the world had become. It's like someone had turned me on my head and asked me to navigate skyward.

"What do I do, then?" I asked the old man. It would have ground against me to ask any other man for a command so all-important.

"You go to speak with this man." Lucius said, sternly. "You stick by our story, for however long it seems he accepts it. If it becomes obvious that he knows the truth, you shut your muzzle. You tell him to speak to me and you say *nothing* else. You go to see my daughter, if you're allowed ... because if they take you from here in shackles, it will be a long while before you see her again. Tell her you love her and hold your children. I'll have word sent to Johannes to return to the manor, so Delilah is not left alone while we sort this mess out."

"You'll be here for her—" I started.

"If that man knows who you are, he knows I set you free." Lucius stated pointedly. "He knows no other man would have had the power, resources and interest to arrange this charade. They will take us *both* away."

"Lucius..." I swallowed, my ears tipped back.

"Buck up, boy!" He gave my shoulder a shove which actually sent me back a pace. The depth of confidence in his voice was so convincing, it sent a shudder through me that had nothing to do with the force of his hand. "Be the man I know you are! You're a soldier! You're a damned navy man! And you aren't going into this fight alone. These bastards aren't contending with some limp-wristed, delicate Pedigree fops! You and I have taken our blows, killed men and bested far more menacing enemies than these holy men. And what we can't do, I'll hire every smart fellow who'll take my coin to manage. Hell, I'll sell the *Cerberus* and her sisters to buy those bastards off, if we have to. You're a part of this family, Luther. If we sink, we all sink together. I don't consider losing you to be a viable option."

Something burned in my chest, seeping through me like rains on parched soil. I felt my throat constrict, my limbs heavy and yearning for something I can honestly claim I'd never longed for before, in the entirety of my life. The feeling was overwhelming and alien. I didn't know where to fit it into my world view.

" ... thank you, sir." I said at last, swallowing something back. "I-I've never..." how to say what was in my mind, I didn't know, " ... no man ... who has ... not been my lover..." I stumbled over the words awkwardly. "You just ... mean more to me than you can ever know, Lucius. I've never had so much respect for—"

"Enough of that, son." Lucius sighed. "You're not very good at expressing yourself in this regard. Come." He extended an arm to me.

How he'd known exactly what it was I'd needed, I didn't know. But I immediately crossed the space between us and embraced him. The old man clapped his arm over my back, and masculinity, dignity and pride be-damned, we just held each other.

"If my father had ever done this for me," I murmured against his collar, "I might be a better man than the one I am today."

I heard Lucius give a rough exhalation of breath, before he released me and looked me in the eyes. "My father was a bastard too, Luther. You cannot let it color who you are. And if you truly have as much respect for me as you say, you must have respect for yourself as well. I wouldn't have trusted my daughter to a lesser man."

He looked down for a moment. I felt the need to do the same. The room fell silent.

"I suppose this sort of thing doesn't come natural to men like us in general." Lucius said at length, clearing his throat. "What I mean to say is ... give them hell. And know you won't be going into this alone. Delilah and I both care for you. You're family now. And that's a bond greater than any. Even God can't sever it, regardless of what the men of the cloth who claim to represent him have to say about it."

"Yes, sir." I replied, feeling the strength return to my voice.

The room the Inquisitor chose to question me in was one of the servants' dining quarters, and thus extremely small and confining. There was one window in bad need of washing, the light it let in minimal and yellow. I didn't take my seat until the 'Father' himself had.

"Let's begin at the beginning." The priest spoke as he pulled his stack of letters from his bag, as well as the ledger he kept with him.

"Alright." I responded, leaning back in my chair. "Would you like me to start with my own obviously lower-class lineage, or just start off right when I first met Delilah? I'd imagine it's obvious upon first inspection that I'm no Pedigree. We were very clear about that when we filed the pups' documents—"

"Actually," the weimeraner adjusted his spectacles, "I'd rather you started with your commission upon the *Winnipeg*, and your sordid relationship with the recently-passed Klaus Richter."

And just like that, it was over. I'd barely gotten into our fabricated story. In a way, it was almost liberating. At least I didn't have to feed him a lie for an hour, only to be told he knew otherwise at the end. Spared us some time.

"What's the point?" I sighed, leaning an arm over the back of my chair and no longer bothering to keep a decent posture. "You probably have everything about it in that stack of papers there."

"Everything but your perspective on this whole shameful affair." The priest responded without skipping a beat.

"At this point, I have to send you to Lucius to talk this out." I growled. "But honestly, I think I deserve to know at least one thing. Why would you come in, demanding all the things you have ... going about all of this like it was a legitimate Inquisition, when you already knew the answers? Do you just like putting people through the ringer? Twisting them to watch them cringe? Forcing my wife and I to undergo that *humiliating* ceremony, just so you could get your jollies? I might be a shit, but my wife is a *damn* decent woman, and *she* didn't deserve all of this."

"Do not misunderstand me, young sir." The Inquisitor looked across the table at me with that unswerving, maddeningly calm expression. "I take neither joy or dislike in my work. It is simply the work that God requires I complete while in this lifetime, so that I might aspire to a better place in the next. I conduct myself as I do to maintain some decency in what are otherwise thoroughly indecent matters, as God would prefer his servants be civil. I went about things with your family as I have with every other, to deduce the truth of the matter in the way I have always done so before."

"But you knew the truth!" I spat. "You had it right there in your bag, the entire time!"

"Truth is personal." The man said. "I do not simply want the truth on paper. I want your truth. I want this family's truth. I cannot get that from third-hand accounts or documents."

"Third-hand accounts." I repeated. "Someone *did* speak to the Church about us. Who the hell was it?"

"That is not within my purview to speak on."

"Hang that!" I slammed my fist against the table, the silverware gathered on the opposite end clattering. The hell with this man. I had no reason to hold back at this point. "No one at the Church said a *damned* thing about this marriage months ago, and now suddenly you've all taken an interest in the goings-on of our house? If it's someone close to me, I deserve to know!"

"I can say only that concerns over your family's lineage were brought to our attention by someone whose words we had great reason to listen to." The priest said, unfettered by my outburst. "Someone who holds quite a bit of sway in the Church. And it seems they were correct."

I growled, but again he didn't seem unnerved in the least. "It hardly matters who brought this to our attention. Your father-in-law made an attempt to cover up your records, which honestly only made the trail easier to follow. We know everything we need know about your past, I hardly need you to elaborate on much of that."

I clenched my hand in a fist. ... Lucius would be angry at himself for this, now. I know the man had thought he'd had this handled. Nothing compared to the resources of the Church, though.

"If you don't wish to speak on your relationship with Admiral Richter, it's hardly necessary for me to know every detail. I have the report of the priest who first questioned you here." He pulled out a few pages clearly ripped from another of their ledgers, scanning them quickly with his eyes. "Mnh. I see why they wanted this covered up. The Richter family would have been shamed for generations...."

"Why?" I demanded. "Because he said he loved another man? Klaus Richter loved all his men. He gave his life to defend them. I can't think of what else that could be, other than love."

That got an almost annoyed expression from the man. "The issues regard his *physical* attachment to another man, not the bonds you speak of."

"Why in the hell does it matter?!" I slapped both my palms down on the table. "Whom we *bed* has nothing to do with a man's character. If that were truly the case, every man involved in a loveless marriage would be just as much a sinner!"

"Those that choose to seek physical relationships outside the sacred bonds *are*." The priest defined. "They are just far harder to prosecute, being as their sins are so ... widespread. Believe me when I say, had I all the time in the world ... We can only do what we can. And I will not argue the merits of God's will with a Heretic. It is not for men like you to understand. When you face your maker, you will be enlightened of your wrongdoing. I am not a preacher. It is not my job to convince. But if men like you, your Admiral and your father-in-law—"

"Leave Lucius out of this!"

" ... were permitted to do entirely as they wished without reprimand," he continued, "the lineage of our people would devolve back into feral barbarism. God has a plan for us and deviant behavior like yours is an obstruction to that plan. You affect more with your actions in this lifetime than just yourself. You affect generations to come."

"Our family is *happy*." I insisted. "You're the ones destroying us!"

He was silent for a few moments. "I can see that I will get no further with you." He said at last, shutting his ledger and standing. "Send in your wife. I'll get the rest out of her."

"Like *hell* you will!" I stood as well, pounding my finger into the man's chest. "You deal with *me* for your bloody questions, and you will leave my wife *alone* from this point on! She's done nothing wrong, and I won't let you tear her apart! You said yourself you have everything you want, except our perspective. You want my perspective? You're getting it! I have been waiting my *entire life* to have these words with one of you, so *sit* and *listen*!"

Much to my surprise, after a few seconds, the man did just that. He knitted his fingers together, leaned back and looked at me, expectantly. I was caught so much off-guard, I almost stumbled over my next words. Almost.

"I don't care what your scholars say that their scholars said God said." I talked down to the man, unable to sit when the words were erupting from me like waves crashing into a cliff face. "The Church and I have *never* seen eye to eye and that's *no* fault of mine! I was never given a bloody chance. God made me the man I am. It's *men* who reject me! And I will not apologize for it! I have denied it only to survive and for the sake of those around me. It's cruel that I must do that at all, but I do it, because I love these people more than I love my pride."

"But you are living in sin." The priest said, stone-faced. "God does not wish this ... farce ... for you or these people. And the Church does not permit it. The punishments for such egregious lies will be great, in this life and the next."

I curled my lips back into a snarl. "I will *not* watch you hurt my family. And Lucius and I will *not* go down without a fight. But if someone is to hang for this, it should be *me*. All the Denholmes did through this arrangement was avoid dishonor and disgrace. They live their life by your laws, but they were put in an impossible situation. I have done legitimate wrongs ... wrongs I know you have in those papers. But all Delilah and Lucius wanted was a family. A family without the *monster* who actually sired those pups."

I felt my mouth go dry and summoned my strength to continue on. "I am honored ... to be part of these peoples' lives. They brought me here with promises of a fleet at my command, but I've not so much as spent a day at sea yet, and I don't care if I never do. You can take everything away from us, but you will *never* take away the fact that I love these people, or shame me for feeling it. It doesn't matter what kind of a man I am. They've accepted me. I love my wife, I love my father-in-law and I love my children. And they love me. I don't need God's love. And I don't need the Church's permission. All I need is here." I affixed a fist over my chest. "You can take me away from them, but we will *always* be a family."

The weimaraner leveled his gaze across the table at me for what felt like an eternity, saying nothing. I could hear the grandfather clock in the main room just beyond, ticking away the seconds. I wondered where my family was ... if they were out there, listening. If they'd heard anything that had been said in this room. Lucius would probably have my head for not coming to him immediately.

But it felt so damned good to say it all, finally. Regardless of what happened from this point on, I felt as though I'd crossed a threshold in my life. Every time I'd ever had to face one of these men in the past, I'd accepted what they'd told me to accept. Recited the passages they'd told me to recite. Most of the time, I'd even renounced my actions.

No more. Love was not a sin. No matter whom you chose to love.

The priest pushed himself up to a standing position, hands splayed on the table. And then he reached down and set his bag on the old, worn wooden surface, shifting through it.

"Very well." He spoke in an even tone. "I am satisfied, then."

I narrowed my eyes at him. "What?"

He tore a page out of his ledger, took out his quill and ink and began readying the pen. "I am absolving you of your sins, young man. From this point on, you've a fresh start. I suggest you make the most of it."

I blinked, bumping into my chair as I stepped back. "What—why? I don't..."

His gaze rose to meet mine and I was again taken aback. His entire expression, his demeanor ... everything about it was changed. There was a softness there now, almost peaceful, but profoundly tired. "Because ... you have truly repented. It's so very rare, in these times. A fragile thing, which is better nurtured than further punished. The world has punished you enough, child. Live from this point on as a good man and God will forgive you for the sins of your past."

"I don't ... this..." I stammered, "What the hell is going on here?!"

As he had been the whole time, the man was calm. But there was something wholly different about his bearing, now. He began writing again. "Our country, even the Church, is floundering in debt, young man."

"What the hell has that got to do with any of this?" I asked, lost and beginning to become frustrated.

"The Church can no longer afford to fight Pedigree families over lineage issues. Especially not in cases this unimportant. Were your father-in-law a politician or in any way related to the royal line ... perhaps..."

"So you put us through this for nothing?!"

"Not for nothing, lad." The priest said quietly. "Your families' sins may not be major ... and I suspected upon speaking to my source that they might have arisen from wrongs done against them, which made me sympathetic to their plight no matter the case ... but yours are quite substantial. You are extremely fortunate to have fallen in with these people, or you *would* have perished in prison. Your relationship to Admiral Richter notwithstanding, your history of violence and repeated lies on military documentation to continue a commission which *long* ago should have ended—"

"Alright." I snarled. "You've made your point. What does any of this have to do with my family?"

"I discovered your documentation when I performed my actual investigation into you. You seemed a man prone to fraud and violence. I was concerned for your family, specifically your wife."

I clenched the edge of the table, but he continued before I could get a word in. "Peace." He spoke in a calming tone. "You must agree there was reason for concern. A man with a long history of favoring men as lovers enters into a false arrangement with a noble family, in possession of a great many riches, but to attain them, you had to accept your responsibilities in a Pedigree world and become husband to a young woman and father to two children who weren't even of your bloodline. I like to expect the best in people, but I've seen too many years to be so optimistic. You have shown at many points in the past your ... inability ... to follow orders, or change your behavior. If I did nothing to inquire into what kind of man these people had welcomed into their life and then something happened ... I would be remiss in my duties. Inquisitors judge. It is what we do. But I've always preferred..."

He paused at that, a certain sadness shifting over him. "I have always preferred to see it as a responsibility towards preventing harm ... not causing it. Some people in this world are monstrous. It is our task to find them and stop them, before innocents are destroyed by their actions."

"Tell that to the men who lashed me, when I was fourteen." I dug my claws into the table. "Or the Inquisitor who put me into that work camp. Sixteen hour days! Barely enough water and food to live on—I was skin and bones when I escaped!"

" ... some of our own order are monstrous." The priest murmured, cinching his eyes shut for a moment. "The most painful Inquisitions are those amongst our own brethren. I am sorry if you've suffered at our hands. I'm sure it has done you no good. Take what I offer now as your salvation. And make the most of it, I beg of you. Our souls may be eternal, but our lives are unique and fleeting, and we've only one chance to live as the men and women we are. Don't let the trials of your past dictate your future. You said yourself that you've made selfish mistakes in the past. From this point on, live for those around you. I believe a man was not meant to lie with another man, but regardless of your choices in that regard ... there are far greater sins in this world. And even greater good we can do. One sin does not undo all other acts. Live as a good man ... and God will look past your sins and accept you. I believe you have a chance. In the end, the love which you have for your family is what matters most. God will see that."

I felt myself settling back into my chair, slowly. Heavily. All of this, every word leaving this man's mouth, was counter in sentiment to every word I'd had from a holy man in the past. Yet much of what he was saying was the same. Why did it feel so different?

Accusation. Blame. Guilt. None of it was present in what he said. All the religious doctrine was there, embedded in every word. This was a man of God. A man who had devoted his life in service to the Church. He'd come here to judge me, just as every Inquisitor judged a Heretic. But it felt like, above all, he'd come here to understand. And no one had ever tried to do that for me, before.

"You believe me when I say I love them?" I asked, my voice sounding childish in my ears.

He gave a tired smile, the first I'd seen from him yet. "I suspected the moment I came into the manor and saw you attempting to hide the way you held your wife's hand. Your continued desire to be physically close to your wife without making a show of it was a tipping point. A man who hides his affection for those around him is a man with nothing to prove. Your love for your wife is real. Robert's report was also very enlightening."

"He did a report on how we behaved in bed?!" I said, exasperated.

"How a man behaves with a lover is indicative of a man at his most vulnerable." The priest revealed without missing a beat. "And most men don't show so much care with a woman they have no feelings for."

I ground my teeth. I wasn't sure what was happening here, but whether or not all of this was good news for me and the family, it was unnerving how well this old, thin man had seen through me. I hadn't even realized what he'd been looking for the whole while.

I watched him finish penning something on the piece of paper he'd torn from his ledger, as he finished speaking. "You still seem to have tendencies towards a brash temper and little control over your words. Your fierce defense of your family was proof enough of that. But I am glad," he said as he topped his ink bottle with a cork again, "that it is now directed towards protecting the people you love. I hope over time they will bring more warmth into your heart, and calm the fires inside you. From this point on, young man ... whatever ills befall you shall be of your own making. You have a chance in the world. A family who cares for you, a path in life, and a clean record."

"But—"

"As far as I am concerned, you have repented." The priest said. "Whether or not you realized you were doing so. You have humbled yourself by accepting that others come before you. You suffered greatly during your many earlier punishments ... and that is sacrifice enough for your previous crimes, as far as I'm concerned. You have become a better man than the man in these record books. Becoming a husband and father can have that effect on men. And in the strictly physical sense," he sighed, " ... you have married a woman, and taken her to bed. I would say you're quite turned-around."

"But I—"

He held up a hand. "Please say no more on that, I beg you. I know you're fond of asserting your intentions ... loudly ... but in this case it would be of far greater benefit to you to not declare your future intents on ... that score. As far as I and my report are concerned, you are a husband and father with a healthy relationship with your wife. I won't ask you to renounce your previous lovers, but please spare me from declaring whether or not you intend to take future ones ... outside your marriage. My report pertains only to the situation at present and in any case, it's really not my business ... now is it?"

It took me a few moments of stunned silence before I could respond. " ... no." I responded. "It's not anyone's damned business but mine and this family's."

"And as of this moment, our business is concluded." The man shut his ledger, placing it back into his bag. My gaze fell again to the small letter he'd penned. As he was putting away his ink, he noticed my attention drawn to it and picked it up, handing it to me. "That is for your father-in-law." He explained. "To address his own minor ... fumbles with the law, in forging documents."

"All that's here is a passage from the Holy book and a number." I muttered, confused.

"It's an indulgence." The priest gave a wry smile. "Lord Denholme's crimes were minor, but his dues must be paid. And he can certainly afford them."

"This is a bribe." I said with an arched eyebrow.

"It's a fee the Church requires, to excuse minor crimes and grant forgiveness in the eyes of God."

"Whatever you tell yourselves so you can sleep at night..."

"I sleep in rag robes, on a straw mattress." The man sighed. "That is what the High priests tell themselves so they can sleep at night. Please do not confuse the two."

"What will happen with Delilah's pups? With ... my pups?" I asked as the man stood. I began following him, though he stopped at the door to finish our conversation.

"I see no reason to punish two young souls for the err of another." The man said after a moment of thought. "And once the indulgence is paid, the Church will investigate no further. This Inquisition will disappear into an archive. I find it highly unlikely anything about the pups will ever be uncovered. As far as anyone need know," he put a hand on my shoulder, "they are yours."

That sealed the very last concern I had. My chest rose and fell in one long, exhilarating sigh. I saw the priest reaching for the door knob, and determined I had to say one more thing.

"If I might say something..." I spoke, and waited until he turned around to address me. "Father," I began, and I believed in this case that the man deserved the honorific, "you are very good at your job."

He gave me a long look, his grey eyes falling to the ground for a few moments. "Thank you." He said, his voice in earnest. "Truly. I've pardoned many men who never believed themselves guilty of any crime to begin with. And so few have ever understood how difficult this can be. It's good to know my life's work has been appreciated by some."

He began to reach for the door, and then paused again. "Oh, and one more thing," he cleared his throat. "You might want to tell the young vulpine who is wearing a servant's dress that if he wished to be beneath notice, snooping around every corridor was a poor plan."

I balked, running my palm over my muzzle for a moment, trying not to look like I was hiding my face. Even though that was precisely what I wanted to do. "I didn't even notice at first ... how the hell did you know?"

"As you said, young man," he finally turned the knob, with a wry smile, "I am very good at my job."

It was seven weeks before Lucius finally recalled Cuthbert. We'd held the fleet in port over a month longer than we'd planned for and I could tell by the tenseness in Lucius' jaw every time he read a letter from Shaw that the Captains were becoming restless and demanding answers. But after everything that had taken place with the Inquisition and the following weeks, Lucius couldn't risk sending Cuthbert or I away. There'd been a follow-up or two from the Church after Lucius had sent the indulgence they required, but most of it seemed like paperwork and little else. That wasn't the main reason for our concerns, or for delaying the ships, though.

We'd never heard from the Inquisitor again. I hadn't even known his name.

Cuthbert had apparently also been in correspondence with Lucius, but of what they'd been speaking over, I knew little. I knew at least that Lucius had told him about the events that had unfolded after he'd left and about the Inquisition. I hadn't asked how he'd responded to hearing about it all. The Inquisitor may have only reinforced many of the things Johannes had said, but I hadn't liked the way he'd said them and I had doubt about the man that ran much deeper than they ever had before. I think Lucius did, too.

The Inquisitor had told us whomever had reported our family was someone in high standing, who was greatly respected by the Church. It was hard to think they weren't referring to Cuthbert. Neither I nor Lucius could think of anyone else who knew our secrets who fit that description.

So as I saw the man's silhouette on horseback approaching the house, I steeled myself and put aside all of my other mounting concerns. I'd had a lot of respect for this man, but if he was a threat to my family, he couldn't be a part of it any longer. Lucius was in agreement with me. We both stood to meet the wolfhound as he cantered into view. He slowed as he approached the main circle near the front doors, his black horse coming to a stop and tossing its mane as he began to dismount.

When he saw us both awaiting him, he pulled off his riding gloves and looked beyond us, to the door. "Where is Delilah?" He asked. No doubt he'd expected her to come meet him at the door, as well. But even she was aware of what we suspected at this point, and in any case she wasn't in any state.

"Inside." I replied, my voice steady for the moment.

"It's good to have you back, Johannes." Lucius began.

"It's good to be back, sir." Cuthbert nodded, stopping before us and looking between the two of us for a few moments, clearly at a loss as to why we weren't all heading inside. The servants took his horse and Lucius, like a gentleman, waited until they were out of earshot. "We need to discuss a few things, Johannes. Just you, Luther and I."

"Please." Johannes nodded, likely expecting it was something pertaining to the fleet.

"I am trusting in a lifelong relationship to have the truth from you, Johannes." Lucius said, his tone stern and commanding.

"You will have nothing but." The wolfhound assured him, raising an eyebrow. "Pray. Speak."

"Did you reveal this family's secrets to the Church?" I demanded. "In *any* fashion. I don't care if it was in a confessional. Someone told the Inquisitors about my past, and about the pups' true heritage. Was that you?"

The man's eyes widened and he hurriedly answered, "God no! I would never ... I am this family's protector! I am sworn to you all—sir ... sir, you cannot possibly..."

Lucius was only silent. I watched Cuthbert's expression fall. "You think I would do such a thing, sir?" He asked, sadness in every word.

" ... I'm just not certain anymore, Johannes." Lucius said with a long sigh. "You're one of my closest comrades-in-arms. You're like a brother to me. But I do have trouble at times imagining you putting our friendship over your faith."

"My faith is what founded our friendship!" Cuthbert insisted, trying to keep his tone level. Of all the time I had known the man, I had never seen him so desperate to defend himself. It hurt just to watch. "Knights live in service to their Lords. You are more than just a friend to me, sir ... you are my foundation. I am devoted to you! To your family!"

"More devoted than you are to the Church?" Lucius queried.

"You cannot ask me to answer that!"

"I can and I am. But what you've said is answer enough."

"You would have to commit a *great* sin, an unspeakable sin, before I ever considered betraying you." The wolfhound said hoarsely. "What's more, I would have been betraying your daughter as well! How can you believe I'm capable of that? That I'd be so petty? You know me, sir. You know I wouldn't do this. Please..."

Lucius seemed to be weighing his words for a time. I remained silent. This was, above all else, an argument between two friends. I may have played a role in the conflict, but it wasn't my place to judge the wolfhound now. This was Lucius' decision.

He sounded as though he was being honest to me. And Johannes had never been a man prone to lying. But if not him, then whom?

"Alright, Johannes." Lucius finally said with a sigh. "I am going to take your word on this. It's the least I can do, after all the years you've devoted to my family. And to me. I never wanted to believe any of this to begin with."

"I would never have put you or this family through so much grief and worry." Cuthbert said, looking to both Lucius and I at that. "My personal issues with your son-in-law aside, sir ... I know what an Inquisition can do to a man. To a family. I wouldn't have wished it, or its after-effects, on any one of you."

"Good." I spoke up at last, feeling here that I needed to say something. "Because it's caused a problem for all of us. One this family will need to contend with, together."

"What's wrong?" Cuthbert's expression went from defensive to worried, in the blink of an eye.

I turned, looking up into the windows of the east wing.

"Delilah is pregnant." I replied.

CHAPTER 14

FATHER

"How in God's name did this happen?" Cuthbert's voice rang out through the empty hallway as he and I headed down the east wing. I stopped short of turning the corner at the tower end, knowing the closer we came to Delilah's room, the more likely it would be she'd hear us.

"The same way most of your children were conceived, I'd imagine." I lifted my hand to my brow, willing back a headache that had been threatening to rear its ugly head all day. I'd hit the rum a little hard last night, after our talk with the physician.

"Obviously." Cuthbert replied. "But I'd always thought we needn't worry—"

"The Inquisitor who came here insisted upon us performing a witnessing ceremony." I stated. "I did my duty as her husband ... as your faith requires. This is what happens when a man and a woman live the way God intends, isn't it? This is what's *supposed* to happen."

Cuthbert seemed not to have a response for that. He only opened and shut his mouth a few times, dryly.

I turned, continuing down the hall. Cuthbert followed me after a few steps. I continued speaking, as well. "I wish in his infinite wisdom, God hadn't seen fit to afflict my wife's lineage with mental and physical illness surrounding childbirth, if that was indeed his plan for her. But I suppose even the big man overlooks things from time to time. Can't be helped, right?"

"That isn't fair, Luther." Cuthbert began.

I turned sharply on my heel, snarling at the man. "No, Johannes! It isn't. Delilah is petrified! Of something completely outside her control, and mine! And this time, I did it to her. This time it's my fault."

"A child you sired ... could be a blessing, for this family—"

"Not if it kills my wife!" I snapped back. "It's a miracle she survived Klaus and Brook's birth. Half the children I knew growing up lost their mothers to childbirth, and most of them had pups many times before, with no such issues! How much better do you think Delilah's odds will be?"

The wolfhound's ears and tail fell, and he seemed to be out of comforting assertions.

"I don't like playing roulette with my wife's life." I growled. "But the Church didn't give me a choice. We went about everything the way we did because we *had* to, not because this was something Delilah or I wanted. There's no helping any of it now. If for whatever reason it all ends well, I'll be eternally grateful. But I don't like our luck this year."

"Luther..."

"Just come see her." I sighed. "She's missed you. And she needs all of our support, right now."

"She's ill already?" He asked, worried.

"She's fine." I said. "But the physician's insisted that this time, she needs to remain in her quarters for the entire pregnancy, to prevent any outside afflictions. She isn't fond of the idea of being caged. She's very unhappy."

"I can imagine." He muttered.

"Luther, I can't *do* this! I won't!" Delilah insisted, sitting cross-legged on her tousled bed. I saw discarded sewing needles and what looked like a small stuffed canine toy sitting on the bedside table, as well as four or five books.

I sat down on the edge of the bed with a sigh, extending an arm to her. She pressed herself into my jacket and buried herself there, moving a small arm around me tightly.

"The physician knows what's best, love." I tried to assure her. "I know it seems like a long time—"

"I'm not even sick!" She looked up at me, pleadingly. "I'm not even getting ill in the mornings. I don't want to stay in here for eight months! Please!"

I stroked my palm over the crown of her head and rubbed at her ears, gently. She leaned her forehead against my shoulder, curling her body against my side. We'd been having this conversation for over a day now and I honestly didn't know what else to say to her. The physician insisted she needed to be kept indoors, preferably in her room, for the entire duration of her pregnancy this time. He seemed to think preventing her from outside sources of illness would ensure she'd deliver far more safely, and might even help with the aftereffects.

It ... sounded right, to me. Maybe. What the hell did I know?

Still, if it had been me, I'd be railing against it even more than she was. It seemed a cruel thing to imprison the woman in one room—even if it were a comfortable one—for three quarters of a year. Even if it was to protect her. It was like we were keeping her as livestock. I couldn't imagine how it must have felt from her perspective.

Not to mention, Delilah's primary issue after she'd given birth last time was her lethargy of spirit and depression. And this was certainly doing nothing to improve her spirits. How miserable would she be by the time she actually gave birth?

"Listen..." I shifted my hands to Delilah's shoulders, holding her at arms-length, so I could speak to her face-to-face. "I know this is hard. But we have to trust the physician. We don't understand the body or the mind like he does. All we can do is respect his opinion. The only medicine I know involves alcohol and dressing field wounds. I'm outside my element here. We all are."

Cuthbert came alongside us and spoke in his deep brogue, bringing Delilah's attention on him. "The young woman I know does what's necessary for those she loves. Please have pity on us, Delilah. Lucius, your husband and I would suffer greatly if we were to lose you. Do this for us, and for this child. Imagine how beautiful a little pup born of you and your husband will be."

Delilah looked down, murmuring, "I have two beautiful children. It doesn't matter where they came from. Luther *is* their father."

"Look at it as being their guardian." Johannes spoke from beside me. "You're protecting your family, Delilah. A life only you can bring into the world. As your father, Luther and I shed blood to protect this country, your sacrifice will be your freedom ... and only for a short time."

Delilah still looked crestfallen. I wrapped my arms around her again and pulled her in close.

"I love you." I whispered. "We'll get through this together."

"You're leaving." She said in a voice muffled by my coat.

"I'm not going anywhere." I promised her. "Remember? I swore it to you." Delilah's eyes widened as I spoke. "I intend to keep my word. I'm not going out to sea this year."

"Luther—" Cuthbert began.

"I'm decided on the subject, so don't bother." I said to the wolfhound over my shoulder. Oddly, I got no further objections from him. He just looked indecisive and saddened.

"I don't want to keep you from the sea any longer." Delilah insisted.

"It's not up for discussion." I stated frankly. "I'm not abandoning you to this. We're having this child together. Just as we did the twins."

"Then I shall remain as well." Johannes said from behind us, causing both Delilah and I to turn and regard him in shock.

"No..." Delilah shook her head, "Johannes, the fleet needs you."

"Shaw is a very capable man." He replied. "Certainly capable of handling a few privateers. I am far more needed here. Besides, my own wife gave birth to our two youngest daughters only months ago. It will afford me more time to visit my home, and be with my own family."

I gave him a silent, thankful look. He and I may have had disagreements, but I knew how much he meant to Delilah. He'd quite literally been her Knight since she was a child. I knew his presence would give her comfort. I didn't doubt that he intended to spend time with his family, but I knew he'd only mentioned the last part to ease Delilah's conscience for keeping him from the fleet.

Delilah surprised me in that moment by lowering her brow, and looking as threatening as a small woman in a night gown could manage. "Alright. But if you're both to be staying home, I'll not have any more of this childish squabbling and fighting."

I glanced away. Cuthbert only gestured, helplessly for a moment, struggling for words. Eventually he managed a, "Delilah—" before he was cut off.

"I don't want justifications!" She said, firmly. "I know you two disagree on a lot of things, but you're the ones telling *me* to focus on what matters. Why can't you do the same?"

"The things we disagree on are things that matter, Delilah." Cuthbert insisted.

"We ran the gauntlet with the Church, Johannes." Delilah said in a moment of utter clarity. I saw the words settle heavily over Johannes. "Whatever concerns you had for the family, we have faced the worst and gotten through it. I don't know what your personal issues with my husband are," she glanced at me, "and I'm sure you behaved very immaturely, Luther ... but all I hear when you two fight are two young children carrying on, not two grown men talking things out with civility. Whatever your argument is, you're only making it worse conversing the way you do. If you have disagreements from this point on, I don't want to hear them from the other wing of the house! Behave like gentlemen, for God's sake. We're supposed to all care about one another. That means hearing each other out, and you can't hear anyone over your own yelling, now can you?"

If I'd not been sitting on it, I'd have tucked my tail between my legs. I saw a similar guilt straining Cuthbert's features. Neither of us had the nerve to say anything in response. My wife was right.

"Good." She said at length. "Now make amends. Or so help me, I will shed my petticoat, run out the house naked and gallop through the snow, until I've every cold, flu and affliction this county has to offer!"

Johannes and I looked to one another. He gave a sigh after a few moments and offered a hand. I lifted my eyes to his, not willing to accept the olive branch unless I thought it was genuine. As always, he was hard to read. But whether or not he was actually considering the words we'd shared and my perspective on the matter, his desire to assure Delilah was certainly earnest.

I decided that was what mattered most at the moment. I took his hand and shook it firmly.

By the time I made it to my room that night, I was utterly exhausted. The day had been trying, both emotionally and physically. I'd taken out a lot of my fears and frustrations on a long ride. I'd pushed the both of us to the breaking point, taking the grounds no less than twenty times, cutting through even the wooded areas at a canter. Specter had been up for it, but I was finding as I limped my way up the stairs that night that I might have been less-so. It had helped to clear my head, though. So much so that my mind was nearly a blank by the time I'd downed a quarter a bottle of rum and crawled my way back up to my room.

Being too drunk and too tired to feel much else was precisely how I intended to end the night, in fact ... but as my eyes adjusted to the dim candlelight in my room and I vaguely wondered if it had been one of the servants who'd lit the single candlestick burning atop my dresser, I saw something gold shift like embers, strewn atop the deep red blankets covering my bed.

The fox flicked his tail, giving me a sliver of a smile in the dim light. I stood there and stared at the nude, slim young vulpine for a moment or so, placing the rum bottle I'd intended to finish atop my dresser as I tugged loose my cravat.

It was the perfect spark, lighting a wick inside me. This was precisely what I needed right now ... even more than more alcohol, or sleep. It was everything I required at that very moment. How the fox had known to be here, right now, when I most needed the relief he offered, I didn't know. I suppose when it's your craft, you get the timing down.

I stripped to my britches without much further hesitation, not a single word passing between us. I moved over the boy, locking his hips down with mine and catching his muzzle in a hungry, invasive kiss, which he did absolutely nothing to resist. His lean, soft body strained up against mine, fur pressing into fur, and our sheaths both hardening against one another.

Before long, I was panting and rutting against him. I could feel his paw desperately trying to stroke me, or himself ... I could hardly tell anymore. At one point he gripped the both of us and stroked us in unison. The feel of his warm, slick length against mine was more than I could stand. That's when I turned him over.

I found my release the first time around far before he did, but I was still hard even after I'd spilled inside him. After another few moments of thrusting up beneath his tail, I knew when I heard him crying out in that certain way only foxes did that he'd ruined my sheets. My paw crept around to stroke his spasming length as he moaned hoarsely and leaked the last remnants of his climax into my palm.

There was fire in my blood that night. I took him twice more over the course of several hours, the two of us sharing the bottle of rum

I'd brought up in between. By the third go, I knew I was completely finished. My body felt like lead and it was all I could do to put half my weight on my arm as I collapsed atop him, not wanting to crush the small fox beneath my body weight.

I knew it would be some time before my knot went down enough that I could comfortably withdraw, so I just lay there, catching my breath for a while. He did the same.

It was a full moon that night. The pale, grayish-blue light streamed in through the intricate black iron crossbars over my window, the air growing chill as the already floundering embers in my fireplace went out. I hadn't the energy to get up and rekindle it. My lover was warm, and even more so once we'd pulled the comforter over ourselves.

I closed my eyes a moment, imagining the swimming sensation of the alcohol's buzz was the gentle rocking of the sea, and the warmth in my body everywhere that Mikhail's lay in contact with mine was the heat of the Huudari summers.

I'd been ripped away from it all for so long now ... but despite that, in this moment, I was at peace. There were so few things in the world that quieted my soul like the sea. It was becoming impossible to ignore that Mikhail was one of them.

I opened my eyes slowly, the fox beside me taking a long breath. At some point we'd shifted so that he was lying beside me and somewhat curled up against me, my head resting across the soft, downy fur along his chest. I could hear his heartbeat, slowing steadily as his body crept closer and closer towards sleep. It would have been a perfect, comforting end to what had been an otherwise difficult day. Why I didn't just leave it at that, I don't know to this day. But it hardly matters. What I said next I would have had to say at some point in the future, and I'm sure his answer would have always been the same.

"Mikhail," I began, my voice heavy with my body's desire to finally sleep, "I'm at a loss ... as to how I see you anymore."

He was silent a moment, but stroked my ears with his palm. "What do you mean?" He asked softly.

"I care for you." I murmured. I felt his chest rise and fall at that, though his heart remained calm. I lifted my head, so that I could look him in the eyes. "I'm beginning to care for you ... deeply. More and more with every passing day, in fact. Everything you've done and continue to do, for me and my family, only endears you more to me."

Mikhail was silent, his expression hard to read. I wish I could have gleaned more from it. What little I saw there seemed torn between indecision and something akin to sadness.

My throat felt parched, but I continued despite it. "I ... don't know what to do." I admitted. "It's not only I. My wife is fond of you, too. In a wholly different way, but ... your good relationship with her only reinforces the part of me that thinks ... we could—"

"Luther." Mikhail murmured, stroking his palm slowly down my cheek scruff, then giving a long sigh, his eyes slipping closed. "I'd ... been hoping, with you ... this wouldn't happen."

"What?" I felt my chest start to go tense, all that peace slipping away.

"I..." he gave another long breath, " ... Luther ... I'm ... a courtesan. By our very nature, we become involved in the families we serve. Being empathetic, caring about the people you work for, being there for them and helping them through their personal difficulties ... it's ... something I pride myself in, greatly. I do honestly and truly care about you and your family. I care about and ... understand ... your struggles, in many ways. Many personal ways, in some cases..."

I looked down at him, helplessly. I wish I could have looked him in the eyes, but he seemed unable to hold my gaze at the moment.

" ... perhaps if we hadn't met in this way." He said softly. "If you weren't a client."

"What does it matter?" I insisted, reaching a paw up to stroke the soft, pale fur along his cheek. "If you feel for me and I feel for you—"

"Because that contract will always be there, Luther." He said, finally looking up at me. "The nature of our relationship will always be what it is. You can't un-ring that bell."

"You could stay with our family." I pressed. "Delilah is fond of you, Lucius doesn't mind you being in the manor, and we'd find an excuse in time to explain your presence to the children. We'd support you just as we do now, you'd be part of the family. You'd be my lover instead of my—"

"Whore." He finished. I felt my ears fall and I went mute. "The nobles can dress it up with a lot of pretty words, Luther ... but that's what I am."

"You're so much more than that to me." I said, swallowing.

Mikhail gave a weak laugh. "A man from Thervon once told me the same, when I was younger and far more naïve."

"I'm not *like* them." I said, alarmed at the growing desperation in my voice. "You've been at my side for months. Surely by now—"

"I know you're not, Luther." He whispered, leaning in to brush his nose over mine. "I believe you. I know you're a good man."

"Then why—"

"Because of who we are." He said. "Nothing more and nothing less than that. No matter what, you can't change how our meeting one another happened, and what founded all of this. And it will always color who we are to each other. Always."

He sighed, letting his head fall back into the pillows gathered in a loose, strewn pile at the top of the bed, staring up at the ceiling. "One of the first things my mother told me, when she finally accepted that I wanted to follow in her footsteps and take up this life ... and it was a hard thing for her to come to terms with ... but she told me, above all else, that love is not found through a transaction. Courtesans and clients have tested the boundaries of professional and personal relations since the day the practice came into being, and it always ... always ... ends in tragedy, sadness, and regret. I've heard so many stories..."

"We would be different." I strained, knowing I sounded desperate now, but no longer caring.

For a moment, he honestly seemed to be wavering. But it was only for a moment.

"It's always tempting to think that." He murmured. "That somehow, you might be the exception ... but the truth is, I can't afford to take risks like that with my life. And neither can you." He lifted his head at that, locking his gaze with mine. "We're both relatively young, Luther. We have too much to lose. Too much time left..." His eyes softened. "You have a family. Seeing a courtesan every now and again is one thing, but ... a lover ... someone would discover us, eventually. Or someone could discover what my trade truly is and put the pieces together. I'm a prostitute, Luther. You can't make a man like me a part of your big, important life. It would destroy us both."

"It would *complete* my life." I said, my voice straining. I could feel a lump like a stone in my throat. "I love my family. They are a piece of my completion ... something I've never had. But they are only one piece. I've had the other ... imperfect as it was ... I loved him, and was loved in return. If I could feel that way again ... and have this family ... at once ... I would finally be a whole man."

Mikhail only smiled. "You want so much."

"Why is it so much to want something every other man can have so easily?" I asked, although I wasn't certain who I was asking at that moment. "Men like Johannes can have a family and be with the person they love. Why can't I?"

I'd come so close. It had honestly all seemed, for a moment, like I could have the impossible.

"Because we aren't like them, Luther." Mikhail whispered, stroking his fingertips up over the curve of one of my ears. "It will just ... never be easy, for us. It may not even be possible."

I dropped my head to his shoulder, crestfallen. But he continued speaking.

" ... but I like to think it is. I prefer to think if we are patient, if we make the right decisions and perhaps if luck is on our side ... in time, even we can love, and be permitted to love. It is possible. Just ... rare."

"If it's so rare, perhaps we've only one shot at it," I murmured, "If that's the case, my other half died on the deck of the *Winnipeg*."

"You seem a man prone to second chances, Luther." Mikhail ran his hand down my shoulders, gently. "Or you wouldn't be here."

"You've the most kindly way of breaking a man's heart." I lamented.

"I wasn't looking to cause you any pain." He said softly. "But it's better this way. I hope you'll forgive me."

"I never would have blamed you." I responded. "I know I'm a difficult man. And everything surrounding me seems to turn to ... insanity. You're right to get your distance."

His ears tipped to the side and he looked on me sadly. "I meant it when I said I cared about you. If we'd met any other way—"

I held up a hand, sitting up slowly and reaching for the nearly-empty bottle on the bedside table. I finished it off in one long swig, not caring when it hit my parched throat like burning oil. I wasn't drinking to relax anymore.

"You have to leave." I said, pushing myself up out of bed, unsteadily.

Mikhail shifted his thin figure out from beneath the comforter, reaching for the clothing he'd discarded on a chair nearby, his entire posture somewhat limp, like an animal retreating from a predator. "Certainly," he murmured, "I'll ... be off—"

"From the manor ... not just my room." I half-placed, half-dropped the glass rum jug on my dresser, the sound it made ringing out louder than I'd even meant for. "Take whatever time you need to gather your things tomorrow. I'll see to it that you're compensated before you leave."

"Luther—"

"Mikhail, I'm sorry!" I said, turning around swiftly and using the dresser to balance myself. "I don't mean to be cruel, but ... I-I can't do this. I understand why you feel the way you do and it's ... fine. You're probably right, even. About everything." I conceded, but my heart wasn't in the statement. At this point I was just rushing through words to get them out of me, just so that I could clear him out of the damned room and hate myself without watching him give me that sympathetic look.

"I just can't ... I can't continue on with things the way they were, alright?" I let my head fall, both from exhaustion and because the floor was a more welcome sight, right now. "I'm an emotional man. I can't sweep how I feel under the rug as easily as ... you seem able to—"

"Luther, that isn't fair." He insisted.

"Maybe not," I conceded, tiredly. "But ... regardless of how civil you've been about all of this, I see no reason for me to torture myself. If this is just a job to you, then fine. I understand why you need to see it that way. But I ... can't anymore. So..." I waved a hand at him, still not looking up, " ... job over. I'm sure you can find another benefactor soon. I'll ask Lucius to double your pay for the last two months. You've earned it, helping my wife and me."

"Luther, I *am* fond of you." He sighed, trying to approach me. "We can still see one another—"

For perhaps the first time since the very first day I'd known the fox, I shoved him away. He was so shocked by the slight push that he had to put a hand back to catch himself on the chair nearby, looking at me wide-eyed.

"Please stop making this so damned hard!" I begged loudly. "I don't want to treat you like a whore! I *never* wanted a whore! I wanted a lover!"

He shook at that, the words sounding cruel to me even as I said them. But I couldn't stop myself. "I can't feel like this," I said, pursing my fingers and daggering them towards my heart, "and go about things like we were before. It would just make me ... yearn for something I can't have, all the more. Your presence would cause me nothing but pain."

"I just..." Mikhail seemed at a loss. "You ... don't wish to see me again? Not ever again?"

"It's all or nothing for me, Mikhail." I said, my tone dropping, finally. "I can't compromise. Not on this."

The fox seemed to want to say more, but whatever it was, he clearly thought better of it after a few silent moments. The pain in his eyes was palpable, but the tears never came. Nor did mine. I couldn't remember the last time I'd cried in my adult life, except in pain. Even when I'd thought it appropriate.

Mikhail was a small, delicate young man. I'd expected he'd cry. Fortitude of will comes in many forms, I suppose.

He'd donned the rest of his clothing and his fur-lined cloak before I'd even lifted my gaze. And without so much as a backwards glance, I watched him leave the room.

Some say that when it rains, it pours. For a sailor, a storm is a loathsome thing. My life has never been a steady progression of ups and down, separated by evenly-paced twists of fate, like so many others seem blessed with. It seems that the tragedies of my life come all at once in droves, like the massive waves that build upon themselves in a maelstrom, until they crash over your deck and send you down to the depths in splinters.

The last year of my life had been the hardest I had ever faced. Starting with the death of the man I loved, my imprisonment, my difficult transition into a world of Pedigrees and responsibilities I was wholly unprepared for, of learning how to love and accept strangers into my life, and allowing myself to be laid bare and vulnerable before them. I'd had to come to terms with the fundamental foundations of everything I'd once called my world perspective ... that a man like me had to fight his way through life. I was good at fighting. But what I'd learned above all else over the last year was that fighting the forces that obstructed my happiness was not always the best answer. That violence and aggression, whether justified or not, often had consequences. And that for every perceived wrong I'd suffered, those who I hurt to avenge myself had their own life perspective.

It was something many wiser men in my life had tried to tell me over the years, but I'd never listened. Even now, I find it difficult to accept. It's so hard to fight the fires inside me that compel me to retaliate against what seems an unjust world. So easy to convince myself I have no other choice. Sometimes, there really isn't any other option. When your back's pressed to a wall, a saber is the only course of action.

But I'd done much throughout my lifetime that could have been prevented. Retaliated against men who posed no immediate threat to me, simply because I felt they needed to die. Lucius himself had told me many times how grave the consequences for living my life this way could be. As with so many others before him ... I'd ignored him.

I wish now that I'd listened.

The days coming would prove to be the culmination of many wrongs done by men, colliding at once. And I had been a contributor to the cycle of pain and grief, playing my role recklessly and without heed, despite the protestations of the people I loved, so many months ago.

Mikhail was preparing to leave most of the day, but I'd shut myself away almost strictly to avoid seeing him. I'd ruined what had been a perfectly amicable relationship between a man who comforted me and got on well with my family because I'd pushed for more. For too much, it seems. I couldn't just be content with things the way they were. He'd even given me the chance to go back to things as they'd been before that night, and I'd denied him. Because I had to have things entirely my way, or not at all.

My wife was shut in her room, unable to even see her own children lest they afflict her with something. She was facing an uncertain future that had been of my making. In a few months' time, I could lose her.

Cuthbert and I were in no real better state than we'd been before, despite our show for Delilah. And the fact that his feelings towards me might improve upon learning I was sending Mikhail away only made me more bitter towards the man, and his Church.

I was leaning on the window sill in the parlor, nursing a concoction the maids had put together for me, mixed with tea, to fight the hangover that had been nipping at my head since this morning. I had a very heavy tolerance for alcohol, but depression weakened my ability to handle it some, sending my energy into a tailspin.

I heard Lucius approaching and knew it was him, strictly because of the familiar, heavy sound of his cane striking the hardwood floor. The man moved to my side, gazing out the same window I was at the dead garden beyond.

" ... I've given Mikhail the amount you requested." He spoke.

"I hope it wasn't a bother."

He only shook his head. "Hardly. Our estate spends more on tea, each month." He glanced over at me. "I would ask why, but honestly, it is not my place. I'm certain you have your reasons, and I'll respect your privacy."

"Thank you." I murmured, most of the affect gone from my voice by this point.

He stood there with me for a time. It was still early morning and the clear, sun-stained skyline just visible above the trees was promising a beautiful day ahead, the weather not matching my mood. The chill crept past the glass window panes, but I could feel it was already beginning to warm. Today would be fairer than it had been all week.

I kept my arms crossed over my chest, looking nowhere. I was fighting the urge to think ... had been all night. I didn't want to worry about Delilah's life, about my failing relationship with the wolfhound, or the fleet that would be leaving port soon without me ... going to sea, leaving me landlocked for another year. But a man could only drink for so long. I couldn't spend the next year in a stupor. Only a weak man crawled into a bottle to escape his problems, and I refused to be a weak man.

"There is always another chapter, Luther." Lucius' deep voice broke the silence, and I looked over at him tiredly.

"Sir?" I queried.

"I know things have seemed rather grim and difficult over the last year. God knows I've felt it, too." He replied.

"You always seem to face it all ... stalwartly." I sighed. "Even doing things to push me up, when I've needed it most."

He put a hand on my shoulder. "What else is a father for?"

"I'm a father, now." I said, worriedly. "I still can't help but feel weighed down by it all. I have trouble handling my own problems. I don't know if I'll ever be able to take care of my children, too. I thought I was a strong man, but..." I glanced down at the window sill. "I can't keep up the ... fortitude of spirit you seem to. What am I lacking? Experience? Time?"

"That's part of it, I'm certain." He gave a thoughtful expression, scratching his chin. "But it's not all about age, or even experiencing yourself with the world, Luther. A lot of what you're speaking of is just ... going through life with certainty and conviction. That is what inspires and supports those around you. That is how a leader is made. And most of that confidence is just ... faith."

"I don't have much of that."

"I don't mean faith in God, boy." He smiled wryly at me. "I mean faith in the world. In people. In your own life."

"I don't have much of that, either." I stated bitterly.

"Well now, that's a problem." He reflected. "A man without faith in himself is of no use to anyone. Not those around him ... certainly not himself."

"How can I have faith in myself when I make so many damned mistakes?" I asked, looking to him. "When the things I do, even if I *knew* they were right at the time, are meaningless or the cause of even *more* problems? How can I have faith in people when they make just as many, or more mistakes than I do? You can't have faith in something so unreliable ... somebody that can just ... die, or disappear, or abandon you..."

"Men like Cuthbert feel that way, Luther. Many in this country do." Lucius said. "They can't believe in people, not even themselves, because they see too much fault with the world. That's why they worship something untouchable, unknowable and all-powerful. Because it makes them feel better to put their trust in a concept of all that is righteous and good ... in a being that cannot be wrong, cannot be questioned. That's how they get through their lives. And that's why they so stubbornly cling to that belief. Because it is always there for them when people are not. But some men..."

He looked to me at that, " ... men like you and I ... are made differently. It is neither a better or a worse way to live, but it *is* who you are. We question. We do not accept being commanded, of putting another moral authority above our own. You could call it arrogance ... in a way, I suppose it is. But regardless, it is why we stubbornly forge forward of our own recourse, with our own code. It is what makes us leaders, but also what makes us brash, stubborn, and prone to acting on instinct.

"If you were a different man, you would have accepted the way the Church asked you to live long ago. You would have blended in, an unhappy man amongst a sea of unhappy men. But you would have not had so much hardship. You would be safe in the flock ... not attempting to shepherd it.

"All you lack right now, Luther ... is conviction." He stated, resolutely. "You are still young. You are still uncertain of yourself. You've rejected the kind of faith men like Cuthbert have. You have to find that faith within yourself. You'll have to put faith in those around you as well. In your fellows. In your family."

"I had faith in a man once." I murmured. "He died in my arms. No 'next chapter' there."

"We don't know that." Lucius said, pointedly. "Death is a chapter of life. It's just one we cannot read ahead into. Wherever Klaus is now, he had to move on without you."

" ... why?" I asked, my voice gone hoarse.

Lucius only put his paw back on my shoulder. "Because we needed you here."

The weight of his paw on my shoulder remained for a moment longer, before I heard him turn. I pivoted to see him walking back towards the dining room table, his limp more pronounced today, likely due to the shift in the weather.

"I was going to wait some years before I gave this to you." He said as he stopped at the edge of the table, near what looked like a small, flat leather footlocker. It was a bit worse for the wear, like it had seen travel. He began unlatching it and I moved closer, peering down curiously at the case. "You've no lawful right to wear it now ... but it's in great need of repair and re-tailoring, in any case ... and I thought you might want to see to that personally. Besides," he clicked open the brass hinge, slowly opening the lid, "I wanted you to know that *I* have faith in you. And that I know in my heart that someday, you *will* be donning this. There isn't any doubt in my mind."

I reached down slowly, hesitantly into the footlocker, gently pushing aside the canvas which wrapped the folded garment ... the drab grey peeling back to reveal unmistakable crimson, inlaid with a torn golden trim. My breath hitched when I saw the anchor patterns so meticulously carved into the gold buttons, unique alterations he'd made, replacing the brass on every other Officer's coat.

I ran a thumb lightly over the surface of one, the distinct ridges I'd felt so many other times beneath my hands. My mind became awash with memories I'd been fighting for over a year now, flickering moments through time, each of them stabbing down through my breast bone ... made all the worse by the fact that his scent lingered in the sturdy fabric.

"The lapel is torn from where he was run through." Lucius spoke, stoically. Unlike me, he was maintaining his composure, but I could see him leaning more heavily on his cane. "Other than that, there is no major damage. You'll need to have it re-tailored for yourself. Klaus was a large man."

"How did you get this?" I asked, breathlessly.

"His family refused to have him buried in it. The garment itself is ... valuable, strictly due to the amount of gold on it." I could hear the ire in Lucius' voice as he spoke. "I attended his funeral while you were in prison. I knew the regimentals they buried him in were not his own. He was always a bit of a peacock ... took a lot more pride in his regalia."

I had to laugh, although it came out half-hearted and bitter. "He did." I agreed.

" ... I knew what kind of a woman his mother was. His father was no better, but he passed years ago." Lucius said. "I approached her at the wake and accused her of holding onto the garment. She denied it at first, but when I offered to purchase it from her at thrice what it was worth..."

"Madame Richter ... loathed her son." I murmured. "I watched them interact only once or twice. I've rarely seen such disrespect between family members, except in my own upbringing. It made me understand why he cast aside his riches for the open sea, even in the worst of months. He could have lived out his ... winters, at least ... at his manor, rather than chasing northern ghosts through frozen seas."

"Klaus Richter's love for the open sea was born of a desire to escape his family." Lucius said, looking to me. "The sea is the one place we are all free. When you return there, I want you to know he is with you. He didn't abandon you, Luther." His brown eyes settled on mine, his next words forever embedding themselves in my memory. "We are all on the same voyage. We take many different routes, and some are shorter than others. But we all have the same destination. Do not rush to yours. No matter when you arrive, he'll be waiting for you there. Live your life with conviction. Enjoy the few fleeting moments of happiness and triumph, but do not focus on your victories if you wish to have confidence in yourself. A man isn't truly judged by his accomplishments. Our strength comes from enduring our failures, and our losses. That is when we are most tested. That is when a man's character is truly shown."

I held the coat in my hands, feeling the fabric slip through my fingers as I unfolded it. The more the garment revealed itself, the more of him I felt through it. I knew in that moment that Lucius was right. Perhaps it was a shallow thing to cling to, but someday, I knew I'd need the assurance it afforded ... the reminder it would grant me, of his voice booming in my ears on the deck of the Winnipeg, the very first battle we shared ... when we'd been little more than midshipman to an Admiral. The way his hearty laughter would fill the Captain's cabin those many night hours we spent together, the rum passed between us. The scent of his fur, when I lay beside him at night, wondering what we'd ever come to.

Klaus was gone, but he'd lead me here to this point in my life, to Delilah and Cuthbert. To Lucius...

It was hard to say I came away from it all feeling better. I was poised on the edge of a knife, and at that time, I didn't even realize it. But what transpired between Lucius and I that afternoon has proven to be one of the most resounding moments in my life.

I will never forget it.

"You know that your coming to visit me so often rather ruins this whole concept of protecting me from disease, does it not?" Delilah smiled warmly, leaning back into my arms.

"Oh?" I quirked half a smile down at her. "Why is that?"

"You might infect me with your filthy, filthy mind." She giggled, girlishly.

"Filthy mind?" I responded, mock-offended. I snatched her by the waist, careful of her now three-month-along belly, but creeping my fingers around her hipline to tickle at where I knew she was most vulnerable. She cried out and batted at me playfully, trying to escape.

"Look who's talking." I growled. "I have *seen* some of the novels you read."

"Those a-are—" her words came between bouts of uncontrollable laughter, "—roman ... tic!"

"Oh, quite." I smirked. "You mean ... the kind of 'romance' that —" I struggled to get a better grip on the wriggling woman, "—runs down your ... thigh."

"You are *so* crass!" she beat at my chest, laughing.

"It's just as dirty even if the author calls them 'feminine petals', Delilah." I asserted. "Or ... what was it? 'Unsheathing his saber'?"

"Stop reading my books!"

Something cracked and rang out distantly, sharp and loud enough to jar us both from our reverie. My body went rigid, fur standing on end ... and I could feel Delilah's pulse quicken in shock. We went still, my hands slipping from my wife as I shifted off the bed and went immediately for my boot knife, stalking towards the window.

I heard Delilah from behind me, sighing. " ... Johannes needs to warn us before he goes out shooting. It always frightens me."

I didn't turn, looking out what little of the yard I could see from the window, which from the east wing wasn't much. The trees obstructed most of the vision from here. "Johannes is in the library this time of day." I murmured. "Like clockwork. He always reads for two hours before supper, from his holy book."

"Father's out shooting?" Delilah wondered aloud. "That's odd. This isn't a good time of year for sport..."

"He might be on the range." I muttered, sheathing my knife again.

"Then he finished his walk early." She said as she adjusted the hem of her gown, where I'd jostled it around.

My ears perked. "He was already out?"

She nodded, running her fingers through some of the loose curls along the edge of one of her ears. "He came by half an hour ago, before you did. He said his leg was bothering him. He likes to walk it for a while when it's gone stiff. Usually he walks for at least an hour, though ... it must be particularly paining him, today ... Luther? Where are you going?"

I tugged my coat on hurriedly, jogging for the door. "Just stay here, Delilah. Don't leave your room."

"Luther!" I heard her shout, as I dashed down the hallway, my feet pounding against the old, hardwood floors.

I'd always had a sense my father had once likened to a 'feral instinct'. I could feel when a storm was approaching, when danger prickled at the back of my neck, creeping along my spine in shudders the way it felt at this very moment ... howling inside me that something was wrong.

Something was terribly wrong.

I took the steps in bounds, leaping to ground level over the rail once I was halfway down, startling a passing maid, sending the tray she was carrying clattering to the ground. I cut through the great room, the distant light from the windows in the thick, old doors at the front of the manor beckoning to me to speed my pace.

I burst out onto the grounds at an only marginally slowed pace, knowing the moment the wind hit my nose that, to my horror, my instincts had been dead on. I could smell blood in the air ... distant, but unmistakable. Blood, and ... gun powder...

I tore across the patchy, wet field, kicking up mud beneath my paw pads as I leapt the brook, pushing through brush and cutting between trees as my lungs strained, propelling me faster and faster, towards the scent, defining itself by the second. My gut twisted into a tense knot, my mind rebelling against the reality as the crumpled figure grasping at the base of an oak tree came into view.

"*Lucius*!" I cried out desperately, skidding through the rotten, cold leaves at the edge of the river bank, losing traction as I neared him and slamming down onto my knees at his side, immediately reaching for the man's shoulders and trying to help the struggling old spaniel up from the ground.

The breath wheezed from his muzzle, signs that he'd already

retched up blood evident on the white fur along his lower jaw. He was shaking almost uncontrollably, and as I moved my hands down to part his vest, I realized I was as well.

The wound was low in his abdomen and his shirt was so saturated with blood, I could hardly tell where the bullet had entered, but I knew the moment I saw it that it had to be agonizing. Gut wounds were some of the most terrifying and often mortal injuries I'd seen in my years in the navy, because depending on where you were punctured, the body could poison itself and there wasn't anything a physician could do.

"Luther..." the spaniel's voice was thick with rising blood and rough as a bear's.

"Don't talk." I insisted, forcing my eyes away from his injury and trying to focus on what I had to do, now. "We need to get you back to the manor," I said, trying to work an arm under his, "the physician tending to Delilah can—"

The old dog shoved me with what had to be fading strength, rebuking my attempts to lift him, and giving a rasping, pained groan. I stared at him, trembling, not knowing what he wanted.

He reached for me with a bloodstained palm, gripping my shirt and looking me dead in the eyes. Even if his were hazed with agony, they had not lost their intensity.

"He's still ... here-ngch!" He clutched at his stomach wound with his hand, gripping me tighter with the other. "On ... the grounds. He'll go ... for the ... manor."

"Then we're going together!"

"De ... lilah." He growled, commandingly. "Please ... save ... my daughter."

"Lucius—" I shifted to my feet, looking down on the man helplessly.

"*Go!*" He roared at me, in the single most authoritative order I had ever had from the man.

Nothing in the world could have stopped me from fulfilling the old spaniel's command.

I didn't even turn to look back once as I fled back through the forest, lest it slow my pace a single step. The farther I ran from Lucius, the more I felt him slipping away from me. My heart sunk, imagining that the words we'd just shared might be our last. But all I could do was what he'd demanded. I forced myself to focus on reaching Delilah as swiftly as possible.

Lucius had said 'he'. I knew at the very least that a man had done this.

Who? Why?!

I knew too that he was armed. As I pounded through the front doors, my lungs screaming, rushing for the staircase again ... I realized belatedly that all I had on my person was my boot knife, which was barely adequate to de-scale a fish. But none of that would matter unless...

My vision narrowed, the world paling before me, my heart sinking through the floor as I stopped in the hallway. The servants' entrance door was open. Remnants of mud-caked paw prints led towards the stairs.

"*Delilah!*" I screamed, taking the staircase in threes and fours, using the rail to pull myself along faster.

God, whoever this was, they couldn't possibly know the layout of the manor, could they? There were so many rooms ... it would take them an eternity to find her—

I heard my wife scream, followed half a second later by another cracking shot, this time inside the house. My veins turned to ice.

She'd left her room...

Much to my shock, when I turned the corner, I saw Delilah standing, her white petticoat spattered with blood, but none of it her own. Johannes stood before her, saber pulled, Delilah clutched behind his back. His left thigh was bleeding heavily and he wasn't putting any weight on his leg, but almost more pressingly, he had a gash across his muzzle, one of his eyes cinched closed in pain.

A tailless feline stood before the both of them, his clothing tattered and stained. I could smell his reek from here and saw signs of mange across his neck and what little I could make out of his hands. A gun was discarded on the ground at his feet, but more importantly, he had an old, rusted cavalry saber trained on my family, the first few inches of it already stained in blood.

Johannes was a trained soldier, but his skill with a blade had never been his strong suit and I knew he stood even less of a chance with a useless leg. I made to pull my boot knife as I ran, but realized as I drew closer that it simply wouldn't be enough, even as a parrying weapon, with the miniscule guard the utility knife had.

The cat was fast, darting into Cuthbert's blind side, which also happened to be the side his leg was injured on. The wolfhound grunted, trying to put weight on his foot as he moved to block the feline's blow, but I saw his knee buckling.

Making a split-second decision, I barreled between the two of them, clapping my palms over his blade as he swung down and praying the weapon was as dull as it looked.

It could have been worse. The steel sliced through my palms, but my thick, calloused palm-pads and a firm, desperate grip stopped it from cutting too deeply. The cat snarled in alarm, and I twisted the weapon, forcing his arm to follow. To his credit, the madman held fast even as I yanked him in close and heard his shoulder dislocate.

He spat at me, his saber clattering to the ground. I cracked my skull into his, my world going white and spinning for a few moments, but I'd wagered well ... he crumpled to the ground, stunned entirely. In the few seconds I had, I stumbled backwards and fell to my knees, sweeping my hand at the vague location his blade had fallen, giving a satisfied growl as my hand found the hilt.

The mad feline was already springing to his feet, despite being unarmed. I leapt to stand before my family, saber raised to meet him.

"Peterson!" Cuthbert called from behind me, pushing Delilah behind him with their backs to the wall, as he recovered from his near fall. "Good God man ... you don't have to do this! Please!"

The feline bared its yellowed fangs, hissing out a curse but little else. And then he charged claws out, like a mad animal. I had no choice.

I took one step to the side, and with little more than a momentary twist of the wrist, I ran the blade up cleanly below his ribcage. He'd left himself open in every conceivable way ... it hardly required any effort.

The cat stiffened on my blade, his yellowed, sickly eyes gone wide for just a moment. I knew I'd gone clean through a lung, possibly even through to his heart. His entire weight suddenly fell on my sword, and that's when I knew he'd died. I let him fall to the side, pulling the old, worn blade out and shoving him off the last of it with my knee. He fell to the ground, lifeless.

I turned in time to see Cuthbert stumble against the wall, his breath coming out harsh and ragged as he held himself up, palm flat against the wallpaper. Delilah stood behind him still, paralyzed in fear, her eyes now trained on the dead stranger in our hallway.

"Luther," Cuthbert rasped, "you ... have my most sincere gratitude ... I-I don't know what compelled this madman to ... or how he—"

I barely heard him. I stooped to pick up the man's gun, in case the creature somehow came back to life. "Johannes," I spoke over my shoulder, "Lock her in her room. Stay with her. In case there are others."

"I don't—" he stammered, "Luther, where are you going?!"

"Lucius is hurt." I said, hoping they'd attribute the weakness in my tone to shortness of breath, not the overwhelming fear I was earnestly feeling at the concept of what I'd find in the woods.

"*Luther!*" Johannes called after me as I took off running again.

"Get the physician!" I commanded. "Bring him to the brook, near the gnarled oak!"

He was gone before even I was able to make it there.

I shakily put a palm to the soaked, cold bark of the old oak tree. Now to become a memorial to the father I'd never had. I swayed where I stood, dragging breath in through my lungs, fighting back the crashing and conflicting waves of grief and rage that were building inside me.

Slowly, knowing I was losing the battle to hold up my shuddering form, I sunk to my knees into the cold earth beside him. My mind went blank, my body forgetting to breathe, everything disappearing in that all-consuming moment.

A terrible, familiar warmth crept into the fabric along my knees where they rested against the ground. I was kneeling in his blood. I could feel it sinking into my fur. That fading warmth was his life ... extinguished forever in the cold evening air.

This couldn't be happening again. This couldn't ... *possibly* be happening again. It couldn't be real.

I felt a vicious, wrathful roar rising inside me. I let it ring out through the clearing, howling skyward.

I don't know how long I screamed. I beat my bloodied hands into the ground, ceaselessly, consumed by anger I didn't know how to constrain. It was only when two strong hands gripped me from the shoulders and forced me to my feet that I considered stopping. I whirled a fist into my attacker, only to find Johannes, still favoring his right leg, but fighting me all the same. He held my wrists apart, using the height he had on me as leverage to subdue my struggling.

In one moment it was white hot ... and then all at once, the strength drained from my body and I collapsed against the wolfhound's chest, catching my breath, my thoughts gone numb. Dimly, I saw the physician rushing into the clearing, bag slung over his shoulder. He rushed past us towards Lucius, but I knew there was nothing he could do.

" ... his name was ... Peterson." Johannes murmured, his voice sounding monotone and strange, like he was in shock. " ... he once ... served aboard the *Cerberus*. Lucius had him court-martialed and jailed. Many, many years ago. But ... why ... how..." His words faded off, lost.

My head down as I stood against the wolfhound, my mind lost in the haze of anger, confusion and disbelief ... it was sheer happenstance that I caught sight of the gun I'd discarded when I made it here. Stumbling away from Johannes, I leaned down to pick it up, my fingers running shakily over the long, ornate barrel and the carefully carved handle.

"Johannes..." I murmured, disbelievingly, " ... this is Irving's gun."

CHAPTER 15

THE RIGHT COURSE TAKEN

It rained for days. The sky just opened up, drenching all of Circenshire and the Denholme grounds. It was like God himself was crying for my father-in-law.

My father. Or the closest I'd ever had.

I couldn't sleep. I couldn't eat. I could barely keep steady my breathing. Every gasp of air I brought rasping from my lungs was a reminder of how I was alive, and he wasn't. Every intelligible voice I heard sounded like his, uttering the last words he'd spoken to me. I was deaf to the world. All I could do was relive the last moments I'd had with him, again ... and again ... and again...

And my pain was barely a sliver of what Delilah was feeling. My young, tortured wife was beyond my help now. I'd seen her through a lot of turmoil this year, but there was no consoling her now. I had never seen a living thing so destroyed. My ghostly presence did nothing, even when I mustered the willpower to somehow, for her sake, act like a man. All she did was cry. All I could do was sit in silence, watching her unravel.

My every waking moment was consumed by an anger so fierce, so bloodthirsty ... it frightened me. I walked the halls of the manor like a vengeful spirit with no victims on which to unleash my rage. The assassin was dead. Johannes had left the manor, to track down the man's trail, to discover how he'd travelled, how he'd come to be on our estate. Where he'd come from, and who'd sent him.

But we knew. How he'd come to be here hardly mattered. We knew who'd sent him. They'd made their point, via the very gun I'd slain their treasured son with.

Which made all of this ... the horror that had befallen my family, that had stripped away one of the best men who'd ever walked the earth from his beloved daughter ... my doing. My arrogance. My fault.

It felt selfish to even reflect upon my own pain. Ever since I'd lost Klaus, Lucius had come to be the stabilizing force in my life. The most important man in the world to me. But I didn't even deserve to count myself amongst his mourners. I had been a stranger to this family barely a year ago, they'd only just taken me in and embraced me as one of their own, and as I'd done with almost every other good thing that had come my way throughout my life ... I had destroyed it all.

I'd had to handle the estate in Cuthbert's absence ... and my father's absence. I don't know how, but I'd muddled my way through the preparations for the funeral. We'd laid him to rest only a night ago, in a private ceremony only the servants, myself and my wife had attended.

Everything felt unreal. Every hour since he'd died was hollowing out my insides. And the space left was pooling with something black and insidious. A sort of need. One I'd never imagined myself capable of feeling before. I'd lived with a lot of anger and outrage, my whole life. But this was different. This was indiscriminate.

I wanted to kill someone. And I was beginning not to care who anymore. Someone had to die for this. Someone other than the deranged, feral assassin was behind this. And some part of me knew ... just *knew* ... that they would escape justice. I could feel it in Cuthbert's hesitation, when he'd taken to the road. When he'd pleaded with me to stay home with my wife and allow him to track the man, despite his injuries.

Well he could hang. I'd caused this. I would avenge it.

The desire for blood had been rising inside me since Lucius had died, but it had peaked to a fevered pitch over the course of the last few hours. My veins were on fire. I could hear my heart pounding in my ears, like I had one foot on the rail, ready to leap aboard an enemy vessel. I'd felt this way before, when I'd been on the verge of throwing my life on the line on the battlefield. Except this time, it wouldn't leave me. All it did was escalate inside me, folding in upon itself ... roiling.

As of three hours ago, the Irvings' plot had stolen more than one life.

I knew when I heard the front doors creak open, the sound of pounding rain echoing down the hall, that it was Cuthbert returning. No one else had left the house since we'd laid Lucius to rest last night.

I remained where I was in the parlor, sitting in one of the old wooden dining room chairs, outside the small room the physician had moved Delilah to. The physician had finally sedated her an hour ago ... the only mercy he could bestow on her at this point. I hoped only that her dreams were somehow better than the nightmare she'd endured the last few days. But somehow, I doubted they were.

I heard Cuthbert's unstable footsteps, his claws sounding against the checkered tile floor. He was walking with a cane now ... although unlike Lucius, the physician assured us it would only be temporary. I raised my eyes slowly, to meet his approaching figure. The wolfhound was soaked through, his rain coat doing little for him but weighting him down. He looked more worn and weary than I had ever seen him, his eyes bloodshot and no expression of hope in his features. Only grim knowledge, which I knew he'd soon impart upon me.

I tensed my jaw. I was inches from snapping. I'd honestly hoped he would come with *some* news that might prevent the last of my control from slipping.

"Luther." He spoke quietly, stopping some feet from me, his eyes falling away from mine.

"Tell me what you know, Johannes." I demanded, my voice barely above a whisper.

He hesitated, looking to the doorway behind me. I knew in that moment that he sensed the tragedy had continued in his absence. I saw his grey eyes tighten to slivers, his hand gripping his cane to keep from wavering on his feet.

All the same, he answered me. I'm sure he sensed how very badly I needed those answers, right now.

" ... I traced him as far as Levyn, by following carriage routes." He said, morosely. "Until I found the man who brought him here. It took some coin and a bit of ... creative information retrieval techniques ... but I found the actual carriage driver himself. He admitted to me the whole affair once I had him alone."

I looked on him, numbly. He seemed nervous at my lack of reaction, but continued a few moments later.

" ... they used servants, it sounds like. The man who paid the carriage driver was a stoat ... whom I've no doubt was working for the Irvings. But I've no inclination of who he was, other than that he was a stoat. And I doubt we ever shall. The carriage driver has only a slim recollection of him. The trail dies with him. But thanks to what I was able to learn from him, I can guess at what transpired."

"Tell me." I uttered, lowly.

"Charles Peterson was one of Lucius..." Cuthbert trailed off as he spoke his late Lord's name, his voice breaking ever-so-slightly at the tail end. He gathered his strength again, before continuing, "He served ... with us, on the expedition to the Dark Continent, when we founded Serwich. He was a midshipman. Later, a scout. I never knew the man terribly well until the incident that got him court-martialed. He was one of many men that became afflicted with an illness we came to call the 'Seer's Fever'. It starts with pox. Roughly one-third of the men that are afflicted die from the pox alone, but should they survive that, we thought ... wrongly ... that the disease passed."

He swallowed. "It does not. It somehow sinks into a man's mind. Unseen. And it destroys them. Drives them mad. We didn't start seeing signs of it amongst the men until our third year there. Peterson was one of the first. On a field mission ... scouting along the river, something happened to overturn their boat. We're still not certain what ... whether or not it was an attack by the natives, or Peterson himself ... but only he returned to us. His story was fractured and made little sense, but we accepted it ... until we found the bodies of the men in his unit washed downstream, with flintlock wounds. The Cathazra do not use guns.

"The Seer's Fever causes hallucinations. It's not the man's fault he was made a lunatic. We didn't have him put to death. We thought, foolishly, the physicians back home might be able to help him. But by the time we got him home, the man was spouting nonsense, claiming Lucius was a demon sent to torment him. Why he fixated on the Admiral, I don't know. Likely simply because he was his Commanding Officer."

His eyes fell to the floor. "We all pressed to have the man executed. Lucius wouldn't hear it. He wouldn't kill one of his own men, simply because he was afflicted with a disease. But there is no cure for Seer's Fever. All of the men we've brought home have either died from it, or been locked away for life. Peterson was one of the latter. And there he should have remained."

"The Irvings released him." I murmured.

He nodded, gravely. "All the carriage driver was able to tell me was that he was paid to retrieve a recently-paroled man from the Ravly Institution, and to bring him to Circenshire. Peterson had a map on his person, marked with the Denholme manor's location. I suspect that was also a gift from the Irvings ... along with the gun. His effects were his own otherwise."

"They set him loose in the world, pointed him at Lucius, and armed him." I said, slowly standing. "What now? Who do we go to with this?"

Cuthbert was silent a long while, his brow twitching once, the exhaustion I saw in his eyes layered now with frustration and helplessness. At length, he answered me.

"No one." He said between his teeth. "We cannot do anything."

"Why." I growled, not even deigning to utter it as a question.

"The same reasons we couldn't the last time we were wronged by them. Because the Irvings have, and continue to be, a far more wealthy and influential family." Cuthbert answered, solemnly. "Because we could never afford to fight them in court and win."

"It's still worth the fight." I curled a lip. "They killed him. It doesn't matter that they did it vicariously."

"Yes, Luther ... it does." He insisted, the strain in his voice evident. "It makes all the difference. That's why they did it this way. There was nothing illegal about what the Irvings did. Even if we *could* trace it to them ... which I must be honest, I do not know how to do ... all they did was take a man out of the care of an Institution into their own. They could make a thousand arguments as to why. Rich military families have been studying diseases from the Dark Continent, and providing care for those who suffer them, for over a decade now. The fact that they provided him with transit, coin and a weapon is suspicious, but—"

"*Suspicious*?!" I snarled. "It's *murder*! You and I both know it! Anyone with half a mind would see what they intended! They delivered a dangerous *lunatic* with an insane grudge against his Commanding Officer *to* his doorstep ... *armed*!"

"It doesn't matter, Luther!" Johannes responded, raising his voice to meet mine. "Don't you see?! The world isn't a *just* place! The strong abuse the weak! Those with money, power and influence rule! The courts will obey *them*!"

"*Lucius was not weak*!" I roared.

Johannes leaned heavily on his cane at that, his eyes dropping away. " ... no. He was not." He said, after a tense moment of silence.

"That man was the strongest, bravest, most admirable man I have ever known."

"And you'd dishonor his memory by letting these people get away with *murdering* him?!"

"If you want to honor his memory, Luther, protect this family!" Johannes shouted. "Have you any inkling of how much pain I am in?! I swore to protect this family over fifteen years ago, and I *failed.* Years, and *years* of service ... only to let one diseased, mad soldier slip past my guard! He would have killed Delilah if you hadn't come to us! I have failed in *every* possible regard!"

He looked me in the eyes, reaching forward tentatively to take hold of my shoulder. I recoiled, and he pressed on, desperately. "Please let me do what little I can now, and let me lend you my wisdom! I have lived a longer life than you. I have lived in this society, I *know* these people far better than you do. I see how this will all end, if we do not stop it *here.* Lady Irving has too much over this family as it is. Her reach extends too far for us to stand against her, in any meaningful way—"

"Lady Irving?" I snarled. "The one who planned this was a woman?"

"Jeremiah's mother," Cuthbert said, resolutely. "It could be no other. She is a spiteful, power-hungry creature. And she fears nothing. She even inferred that she knew of her son's trespasses upon Delilah, the one time we attempted to reach out to them." I could hear the venom in his words as he recalled it. "She is without mercy, Luther. If we pursue this any further, she will tear this family *apart.* It is what she wants. We cannot give in to this cycle. We cannot win. And it will never end, unless we stop it here. For God's sake ... the woman has contacts in the Church! There are two Ordained High Priests amongst her family. They could begin the Inquisition upon us anew—"

"She knows what her son did to Delilah?" I bristled, the fur on my neck standing up past my collar, my canines bared. "And she has contacts in the Church?!"

"Yes, that's what I'm..." he faded off, silence crashing between the two of us. I gave him just long enough for the words to settle that he could come to the same, inevitable conclusion I had.

I knew he had, when he uttered, "Oh, God..."

"That woman is the one who called the Inquisitor down on us!" I spat. "She knew! She knew, because she knew *her* son sired Delilah's pups!"

"Luther—" Cuthbert put his hands out, desperately.

"How can you say you're defending this family and let all of this stand?!" I demanded, shoving his hands out of the way. He stumbled back, catching himself on his cane. I didn't even care when I saw the hurt in his eyes. "You're right, Johannes." I said, venomously. "You *have* failed. But I am *not* going to shirk *my* duty to Lucius, or to Delilah. These people need to pay. They need to pay with their *lives*!"

Johannes looked on me a long moment, before straightening himself up and mustering the strength back into his voice. ", Luther ... you already *took* one of their lives! And look where it's gotten us! Look at what has happened!"

I bit back my words, swallowing a stone. Damn this man for saying exactly what had been eating away at my mind for days now. The words struck me so deeply, precisely because I'd been torturing myself with the very same ones.

I felt my anger slipping towards self-loathing. I clung on. I needed this rage, right now. I needed it.

"Hate only begets more hate!" The wolfhound said, his voice growing hoarse. "Pain only begets further pain! If we aren't the ones to raise our heads above this mire, they are going to drag us under *with* them! No matter what that man did, Jeremiah had a family, and your actions hurt them as they are hurting us now! All we're doing is trading blows. This will only stop when one of us is obliterated!"

"Then let it be them." I bore my fangs, as I spoke the words.

"Think of your family!" The wolfhound begged. "Don't you think it's hard for me not to act upon what we know?! We have to think of the family, of what further harm might come their way! Lucius may be gone, but Delilah, your children—"

"Lucius isn't the only life the Irvings took!" I cried out, my voice breaking. "Johannes, they killed my *child*!"

Cuthbert went still and silent. The parlor echoed with the remnants of our words. I fell back against the wall, my right fist pounding down on a nearby table with a hollow bang. In my left, I was clutching a pistol. I'd been holding fast to the weapon for hours now. I don't think Cuthbert had even seen it.

"Delilah ... lost the child." I said, my throat as dry as my eyes. I was certain by now I'd lost the ability to cry. If the last several days couldn't bring the tears forth, they'd never come.

Johannes had no words. He only stood there in continued silence, more forlorn than angry.

I was angry enough for both of us.

"I would have had a son, Johannes." I rasped. "A *son*! They are the reason for *all* of this! They stole away one of the few decent men left in the world, and they *killed my child*!"

"We knew..." Johannes spoke, weakly, " ... Delilah might have ... trouble..."

"She lost the child because she lost *her father*!" I shouted back. I saw him wince, but he didn't argue the point with me. We both knew the truth in this. He was just refusing to see things as I did. He could wrap himself in denial all he wanted. I was done. I was done with all of this.

"That woman dies." I stated, my voice rough as gravel. "She dies, and anyone who gets in my way ... dies."

"Luther, that's murder—"

I raised the pistol in my hand. I knew then that he hadn't seen it, because his eyes widened and he stepped back, looking earnestly surprised.

"That includes you, Johannes."

The wolfhound looked between the barrel of the raised weapon and I. The helplessness I'd seen in his eyes moments earlier was there now in triplicate. He reached one hand out, trying once more to make contact with me somehow. But when I pulled back the safety ... he stopped.

"Luther ... please." He pleaded softly. "Don't do this. This family needs you. Delilah needs you."

I stared down the barrel of the gun at him, narrowing my eyes.

"You have never felt that way." I said.

He raised his eyes to mine, over the barrel, before murmuring, " ... Lucius did."

For a fraction of a moment, I felt his words penetrating my skull. The very same illusions which had been tormenting me for days now ... which had made every voice I'd heard sound like Lucius, like the old man ... giving me one of his lectures...

If he was here, would he be saying what Johannes was saying? Would I have listened to him, as I always did? Was I ignoring what Cuthbert was saying, simply because of our previous disagreements?

The fact is, I couldn't know. I had forever lost the counsel of the old Admiral, whose wisdom and guidance I'd hoped to have in my life for decades to come. This is precisely the sort of thing I would have consulted Lucius about. And he would have said something incredible, something undeniable. Something I could not help but obey.

But he wasn't here. They had taken him away. They had taken *so* much away.

"When I kill that woman," I began, and I instantly saw Cuthbert's expression fall, "I will do it as the nameless piece of gutter trash I was before this family took me in. It *will* end with me ... because I won't be a part of this family from this point on. They'll have nothing on the Denholme name."

"You would leave Delilah, and your children?" He asked, sadly.

"I'm not doing them any good. I'm only going to hurt this family more, the longer I remain a part of it."

"You're wrong." He said quietly. "About everything."

I dropped the pistol onto the table with a clatter and strode over towards the wall, where I lifted my coat from the rack and shouldered it. I pulled off my cravat, unbuttoned my vest and looked to the far wall, where the Denholme coat of arms, sewn into an old tabard, stood over two wall-mounted, sheathed naval sabers. I strode over to one and lifted it from the wall mount, pushing it through my belt.

"You don't even know where the Irving family lives." Johannes insisted from where he stood, hobbling a few feet towards me, until I turned and cut him off with a long stare.

"Pedigree families are easy to find. Especially the richest ones," I said with barely a thought.

"Luther..."

"Please tell Delilah I love her," I murmured.

"Do you?" He retorted, eyes narrowed.

"You know I do. She knows it. I just want her to know it once more." I replied, pushing the door open.

"If you did, you wouldn't do this to her!" His parting words stuck in my ears moments before I let the large mahogany door slam behind me, and stepped out into the rain.

Treneval, like so many other Amurescan cities, was clogged by vendors, carriages and beasts of burden. The continuing rain pounded down onto the sparsely-cobbled roads, populace milling about through the refuse-laden streets. The cacophony of overcrowding was ever-present, voices clashing in different dialects, even the occasional foreign tongue sounding through the din. The city was primarily canine, as most of our cities were, but at any given time a dozen different species milled within my field of vision.

Specter remained calm despite the ox-drivers boxing us in, or the mud-stained soldiers marching wearily past. She'd been loyal to a fault this whole hellish month ... a silent, but welcome companion. She was the only thing save the clothes on my back, my blade, and the few coins I'd had on my person that I'd taken with me when I'd left the estate. I worried somewhat for what might happen to her when my task came to its inevitable conclusion, but I'd trained her well. She was too fine an animal to be sold for labor or slaughter. I had hopes she would find a good home.

I wish I'd had more foresight in other regards. The lack of coin had become a problem over the last two weeks. Going hungry and without accommodation was, of course, something I'd grown used to over the course of my life, especially when I was in between fleets or running from the Church. But as much as I loathed to admit it, I'd grown accustomed to the Pedigree lifestyle over the last year. Living poor was harder now than it had been in the past. I'd finally put on some weight, and now I was growing skinny again. Sleeping in fields was harder than I remembered, my stomach was rejecting spoiled meat, and I was beginning to notice the fleas. I'd never known the joy of living without them until I'd lived at the Denholme estate, with access to baths whenever I wanted one.

But the pains my body was experiencing were petty, compared to the deprivation I felt without my family. I missed my wife. I missed my children. I wanted to sleep beside her, to wake and eat a meal with her and feed the two small babes porridge. I wanted to hold Klaus again, and feel him nosing the scruff of my neck.

The pain of being without them was fostering a bitterness inside me, feeding into the anger that still simmered since the assassination. The Irvings were responsible for all of this. They'd taken away Lucius and destroyed our family.

I was trying to hold onto those feelings, at least...

But all the hatred I had for this family, whom I'd never even met ... who had hurt us so gravely, without even having the nerve to do it in person ... all of it was equaled by a sense of self-loathing and a growing feeling of doubt. Cuthbert's words echoed in the back of my skull, feeding into my already heavy guilt.

I'd come so far over the last month. I'd tracked this family down, finally, but I'd had to dig around in more seedy establishments and outposts than I'd expected I would. The Irvings had a prominent residence in the Capital, which I'd found quickly ... but it wasn't their primary residence and it wasn't where the family matron, Elizabeth Irving, lived.

I'd had to go as far as the Institution where this Peterson man had come from, to dig any deeper. What was left of my coin had gone to the guards there, to discover when and where the Headmaster took his leave at night. I'd beaten the rest out of him.

The Irving woman must either have found it necessary, or taken great pleasure in locating Peterson at the Institution and requesting he be released ... because she'd done it herself. Unless some other elderly spaniel woman was gallivanting about, freeing convicted murderers. There'd been a sizable amount of coin involved, of course. The Headmaster hadn't come cheap. And getting the truth out of him hadn't been easy. He was missing several teeth and entirely declawed, by the time I'd gotten through with him ... but he'd live. If you called that living.

Honestly, I didn't care about the collateral damage, at this point. And in any case, it's not as though civilized cats needed their claws, anyway.

I'd briefly considered taking what I knew at that point to the authorities, but dismissed it after nary a few hours of consideration. The amount Lady Irving had paid the Headmaster *alone* gave me a far better idea what the wealth gap between her family and the Denholmes must have been, and I was beginning to have a better understanding as to why Lucius and Cuthbert had found the idea of fighting them in Court impossible. This family wasn't just wealthy. They were *extravagantly* wealthy.

I'd thought the Denholme manor and the lifestyle they lead was posh. They were destitute poor as far as nobility went. Lucius truly had put all of his family's wealth into his fleet.

Having an eye-witness account of what had happened wouldn't matter. Hell, if we had a confession in writing, it probably wouldn't matter. Cuthbert was right. People this rich couldn't be fought.

Not legally.

So here I was. The Irvings kept a city home in Treneval. A manor, in the upper end of town. Once I'd gotten to the city, it had been as simple as heading to the wealthiest districts and spending time at the bars the servants frequented. Tongues got loose when alcohol was involved. And apparently, the Irvings were horrendously abusive patrons, because it had taken barely a day before I heard one of their house workers complaining ... about the matron in particular. It hadn't taken much to pry further information from her, even when I hadn't been particularly subtle about it. I got the feeling she suspected I had ill intent, but didn't care.

I had everything laid before me now. I'd been watching the residence for the last few days, tracking the family's movements. Unless there were residents that remained permanently indoors, I was fairly certain I'd seen the entire family, by now. There was a spaniel man my age, whose speckled fur was too much unlike Jeremiah's to be related. A woman I could only suspect was his wife, who resembled Jeremiah, if younger. Perhaps a sister? And then there was Elizabeth.

The matron of the family was younger than Lucius had been, but still older than Cuthbert and I. She was every bit a Pedigree, from the pinched-waistline dress she wore to the derisive way she regarded every other living thing. Unlike her son, she was thin and delicate, as was the style for feminine Pedigree beauty these days. She walked like a heron, carefully picking her steps, as though even the ground offended her. I'd seen her only from a distance, but I swear I knew everything about the damned woman, just from a glance.

I could see her in my mind, getting the news about her son's death. Flying into a broiling rage, taking it out on her serving staff. Entirely neglecting the disgusting, horrible crimes Jeremiah had committed against Delilah, dismissing anyone's grief but her own. Swearing vengeance.

I could see her, sobbing over a story peppered with falsehoods, colored from her perspective ... about how her dear son had been swayed in by a harpy of a woman, hungry for his family's riches, had sullied himself so far as to father children with her, only to be rejected with his offer of marriage. I could see her telling this story to her family members, those with rank in the Church, who immediately launched the inquiry upon our family's lineage. The Inquisition which put Delilah and I through such discomfort and personal pain.

She might have even believed it. Jeremiah may well have told her the whole tale from his perspective, and despite knowing his character, she may have pushed back her intuition and simply believed her cherished boy. What mother wouldn't?

All of that didn't excuse the next bit though. She must have gone through *great* pains, dug about through military transcripts and rumors, or more likely, had a hired man do it for her, in order to find someone skilled in the business of death, who also had a grudge against Lucius. Not many men could fit that bill, he seemed beloved even amongst his most difficult Captains.

She'd found Peterson. She'd gone to the Institution he was kept at, *personally*, to pay for his release out of her own pocket. She'd hired the carriage-man to pick him up, to equip the mad feline with the very gun I'd beat her son to death with. She'd delivered him to our doorstep ... knowing full well what he would do.

Of course, she couldn't have known precisely what would happen, at that point. Which meant she didn't care who in our family paid ... only that we suffered. That day, Lucius may not have been walking the grounds. The feline may have crept into our house unseen, slain innocent servants, Delilah ... our children...

Her grandchildren!

All of these things, this woman must have considered. And still, she did this. There were so many points at which she could have rethought her actions. Realized the insanity of it all. Stopped.

Lucius would still be alive. Our lives wouldn't be torn to ribbons.

This is what I saw, replaying itself in my mind every night, again and again. All the imagined scenes came together into one terrible mosaic, which I'd come to find as undeniable truth. This was how this had all happened. There was no question. That woman was the architect of it all.

She had to die. She *had* to die.

That was the mantra that played through my thoughts, this day, repeating in some kind of odd rhythm, with the rain. The sounds of the city around me joined in, like an orchestra was coming together towards some great finale, some terrible crescendo. And at the end, I would die too. Whether by her house guards, or by a noose in a few days, once I declined any desire for a trial. Once that woman was dead, I wanted it all to be over. I wanted the world to be rid of me. I wanted to be rid of the world.

A year ago, I'd been nothing. Then I'd had everything. In such a short time, I'd been reduced to nothing again. I could blame no one but myself, I knew.

But I would do *one* good thing with my life as I took my final bow, and I was convinced this was it. I would take this woman to the grave with me, purge her from this world. And destroy any remaining threat to the family that had welcomed me so warmly into their fold. I would secure Delilah's peace of mind, and the children's' safety. I would be gone, but they would never need fear these monsters again. It would be the only real contribution I'd ever made in the world. But I'd die knowing I'd done something. Something worth doing, for once in my miserable life.

It was liberating and terrifying all at once. I'd found myself thinking of God and what lay beyond, these past few weeks, more than I ever had before in my life. I'd been a soldier half my life, faced death innumerable times. But this was different. This was like the duel, except there was only one conclusion, and regardless of how everything else went, that conclusion left me dead.

Some part of me hoped it really *was* just a blank void, that I'd rot in the ground and disappear. Because if the Church had been right all this time, I was certainly a sinner. A Heretic. And wherever I passed on to, whether it was to some horrible, hellish place, or to a 'lesser life', what was in store for me was not going to be pleasurable.

Although, one of the greatest punishments, they said, was to be reborn a vulpine. A shadow of a canine too low to even breed back into our lineage, forever trapped in lesser lives for all time, haunting the earth again and again as wretched, deceitful creatures.

Personally, I'd never had any issue with vulpines. In fact, some of the best men I'd known at sea had been foxes, and I had to admit, the 'freedom' Mikhail had often spoken of for those outside the Amurescan Church sounded appealing. Too low to be of notice, perhaps even too lowly for them to waste their time tormenting.

If that was what lay ahead, I welcomed it with open arms. I'd probably make a damned dapper fox. Maybe I'd meet Mikhail again...

But I couldn't really say I believed in any of it. The closer I got to death, the more fanciful it all felt. Like a story men had long ago concocted, so they could face the reaper with hope, rather than despair. That's all religion really was. False faith for those who feared death. And an excuse to impose one's personal beliefs on the world around them by declaring some higher power felt as they did.

My ears flicked back as I heard the sound I'd been waiting for. The sharp, punctuated stamps of many well-shoed hooves on pavement. The clattering of an audaciously-expensive carriage, going far too swiftly for these crowded roads. A badger woman with a babe slung over her back nearly dropped a loaf of bread I'm very certain she paid her last few pence for, trying to get out of the way in time. The carriage driver, a sharply-dressed whippet, shouted angrily at her as the carriage sped past. I held my horse's reins taut, more holding myself back than the well-behaved animal. And I watched the familiar carriage pass.

She was late. She was almost always home by five sharp, tonight she was ten minutes late. And probably rushing to get back home to a guest, or some other nonsense. I fixed my gaze on the carriage windows as it passed. And I saw her.

Sitting needle-straight in her seat, protected from the rain by metal and glass, shielded from the filth and poverty in the streets she so carelessly ordered her man along. That younger woman was with her, and they were talking. She looked displeased as ever ... likely over whatever had made her tardy.

And then, in a moment I hadn't expected, she turned and looked my way ... as though sensing my eyes were upon her. Or maybe the dying sun had caught my eyes, flashing reflective in the dim throng of the crowd. And the expression of mild annoyance dropped from her features, replaced by something else.

I liked to think it was fear.

But then she was gone, and I pulled Specter back into the crowd, knowing she'd never be able to double that monstrous carriage back. Surely right now, she was questioning. She'd never met me, but I was certain she knew of me. She knew a Heeler had married Delilah, had wed into the Denholme name. Knew I hadn't died. Knew I might hold a grudge.

I had been hoping to catch her by surprise, but this was hardly a setback. I still would. I still knew the servants' entrance, and she had no way of knowing that. I still knew how to steal my way through their city manor. I didn't need to get out, only in. Up one flight of stairs, to her bedroom. I would let her wake before I sunk my blade into her. I wanted her to know it happened. I wanted her to go to the next life with regret. With fear in her eyes.

Lucius had died with dignity. Even in his last breaths, he thought only of his family. I'd seen no fear for himself in his eyes ... only fear for his daughter.

This woman would die a coward. And I wanted to see it. I needed that satisfaction, before I met my end. I don't know why, but I did. It was a dark part of myself, I knew, but I'd sunk so far into the depths by now, I was only waiting to hit the bottom.

By the time I'd made it to the manor, the carriage was inside the grounds, pulled up alongside their stables. I could see it inside the gates, several of the servants tending to the horses nearby. The woman and her daughter were already inside. The lanterns were being lit for the night. I pulled Specter into a nearby alleyway and tethered her. And for a few moments I ran my paws down her flank, then her long neck ... and finally, down her nose. I leaned my forehead against her brow, closing my eyes.

"I'm sorry." I said quietly. "I don't wish to abandon you ... this is just where my life has lead. When they come for you, be a good girl. You'll have a better life if you behave for them."

She snuffled, stomping her front hooves, pawing at the muddy ground. I stroked my fingers through her ghostly mane, sighing.

"Please forgive me." I said softly once more, then tethered her reins to a laundry hook on the nearby building wall. She tried to follow me, as I left the alley. I heard her whinnying for me, even as I made my way out into the street.

Movement from an opposite alleyway suddenly caught my eye. I leveled a long look across the road, not certain if my mind was playing tricks on me, or if there was...

A tall, canine drunkard stumbled out of the dark, fetid alley, a bottle held clumsily in one hand, a cane in the other. He ambled down the road, wearing his wide-brimmed hat askew, a coat two sizes two big and soaked as thoroughly as my own, if far more ragged. He gave a nasty, rattling cough even as he went for another drink from whatever piss-beer he'd been imbibing.

I blew out a long breath, trying to set my nerves to rest. I needed certainty, tonight. I couldn't afford to be startled by every passerby.

I waited in the very alleyway the drunkard had come from for hours. I sat on an overturned crate under an awning, head down. In my current condition I blended in well with most of the city's other homeless underclass so the few guardsmen that went by gave me little more than a sneer, or barked at me to relocate from the upper district. None went so far as to enforce the second.

My sword was hidden in my coat, tucked under one arm. When at last I knew the Irvings would be turning in for the night, I stood, shoving it up my sleeve and holding it by the hilt. I'd wrapped the brass so it wouldn't shine in lantern-light, and though the current position forced my arm to remain rigid straight, it was better than lashing it over my back, where it would be more difficult to go for should I need to dispatch a guard.

I hoped very much that I wouldn't have to. I honestly wasn't certain I could strike to injure. It was not something I was well-practiced in, and I didn't want to kill an innocent man, just because he had the misfortune of standing between me and that woman.

But I would if I had to. Rock bottom.

The guard the Irvings kept here was minimal, but the fact that they kept a guard at all suggested that perhaps I wasn't the only man with a grudge out for them. They must have played politics fairly hard. I wondered how many other lives they'd destroyed.

That and so many other reassuring thoughts surged through me, feeding my bloodlust, as I approached the wrought iron gates along the side wall. There were two men permanently stationed out front, but the gates here were higher and I expected they didn't think them climbable.

Clearly, they had never considered an intruder accustomed to climbing rigging.

I had to remove my sword from its hiding place for this and push it through my sash ... or rather, the tattered remnants of one I'd saved, from long ago. I don't know why I'd brought it ... I just felt I needed to have Klaus close, even now. The sashes of the Amurescan Navy were identical, no matter what rank wore them. They'd never be able to tie the red waist-wrap to my deceased lover, but it filled me with conviction and security to have some remnant of him beside me when I died.

I'd hoped someday to wear his coat. Another dream I'd left behind. This would have to do. I honestly don't know how he would have felt, seeing me right now. Klaus had been at once a very simple and very complicated man. I was certain he believed in justice ... but vengeance? I don't know.

Regardless, this was my life, not his. I had never checked my behavior with him when he was alive, and I wasn't going to start now. I didn't care if he would have disapproved of this. I held his memory tight because I needed to, not because I felt he was guiding me. The man had never guided me. I had guided *him*.

And if I saw him in the next life, he'd accept what I'd done. He'd accept it, because it had been my choice, and he'd always valued free will above all else. He'd understand.

The fence was no obstacle to me. The wrought iron beams were tall, requiring cross-beams every few feet, which made them almost laughably easy to climb. The top was a tad trickier to navigate, ribbed as it was with long, forked spines. But those too were avoided easily enough by straddling them between the gaps and swinging a leg over. For a moment, I was glad for the weight loss.

I negotiated my way down even faster, footpads thudding into what I regretfully learned the moment I touched down was an expansive puddle. The splash sounded ludicrously loud to my ears, and I found myself darting for the nearest bit of green ... which ended up being a low shrub ... in hopes of dodging the eyes of the front gate guardsmen.

I waited an eternity, but nothing came. No shout, no footfalls ... nothing. Perhaps they hadn't even heard me over the rain.

I slipped from the bush, keeping low as I crept my way through the rock garden, so heinously out-of-place in this poverty-stricken, cramped, fetid city. Whereas some families crammed eight bodies into one-room apartments, these people flaunted their wealth by wasting space, then walling it off from the upsetting world beyond.

Yes. Hold on to that anger. Ever closer now. The house loomed before me.

I pressed my back to one of the brick walls, sliding around a corner swiftly and remaining there, frozen. Still, I heard nothing from the front guards. They either hadn't seen me, or they were around the very corner I'd come from to inspect the noise. I braced myself, thinking my luck poor and my discovery inevitable.

Still, no one came. I let out a long breath and collected myself. I was against the left wall now ... out of view of most of the guardsmen. There were two more that walked a route, but I'd see them coming a ways off, and they rarely came to the left side of the house. The manor was squeezed tightly up against the fence near the wash room and the gap was hard to trespass. They rarely came here.

I was nearly in the clear already. The servants' entrance was fifty feet off, in a nook beside the cellar door. No one guarded it. The servant had told me they left it unlocked most nights, to ease late-night trips to the outhouse for the staff. They were supposed to lock it, but they never did.

I prayed my information was correct, or I'd have to find a guardsman with a key, and use the front doors. And that wouldn't be particularly subtle.

I began walking through the dark yard, sticking close to the wall and looking for the cellar. I saw well in the dark, but on a night with so little moonlight, my vision was dim. Once inside, I'd have to travel through the kitchens, I'd take the servants' hallways as far as I could, so I didn't need to use the main staircase. There were guards inside, too, and they were just as well-armed as the exterior—

I froze, hoping my eyes deceived me. But as the moon pushed aside one of the rainclouds in the sky just a sliver, enough to expose my eyes to what meager light it offered, the lawn came into focus. And I knew what I saw was no shadow.

A tall, scarecrow-like man stood just beyond me ... thirty feet in front of me. He was facing me, features darkened, but discernibly imposing. The man was clearly canine, of that I was certain merely by smell, but other than that I knew little. The rain obscured his scent a bit even, so I wasn't certain if he were commoner, guardsman, or Pedigree.

But I recognized the coat. And the discarded, wide-brimmed hat hung over the staircase banister leading up to the servants' entrance. The doorway I needed to trespass. The doorway he was standing before. I also recognized the spindly cane he clutched in one hand.

It was the drunkard. The man I'd dismissed, as he came stumbling from the alleyway I was to use as my waiting point. And he was armed now. A hand crossbow was slung over his back. Why he didn't have it out and loaded, I wasn't sure.

I narrowed my eyes, my mind flying over what I should do. Certainly not call him out ... the guards might hear. No, words had no place here. I couldn't afford to satiate my curiosity. He must have been another hired man for the Irvings. An assassin, or a specialist of some sort. Whatever the case, he was in my way. And he'd seen me.

I reached with my opposing hand to my sleeve, pulling the sword from its sheathe and letting the leather case fall to the sodden ground, discarding it. I readied myself for a charge, assessing the man even as I did. I was certain he had a melee weapon on him somewhere ... or he was a fool. But he couldn't be terribly good with it. He leaned on the cane not for show, but for support. It was not part of his costume. That was a real limp. I could see it in the way he stood. I'd seen it in Lucius so many times.

My claws dug into the soil, and I pitched myself forward, thudding across the grass towards him. And then he spoke.

"Luther..."

I dug trenches in the lawn in my sudden, frantic skid, nearly toppling forward in shock. My body shuddered with the revelation, my heart freezing in my chest.

" ... Johannes?" I murmured, disbelievingly.

Now that I was closer, even past the grime of the city streets he'd so liberally applied, and the dark soak of rainwater into his grey fur, I could see it was him. He was barely in better shape than I ... haggard, tired, no better in appearance than the street trash he was impersonating.

That cough, I was soon to discover, was real too. It leapt from him with a rattling, chalky sound and I winced for more reasons than concern for my old would-be friend.

"The guards—" I whispered, fiercely.

"They will not bother us." He said, when he'd cleared his throat with some difficulty. "None are in the waking world at present."

"Good God, Johannes, what did you do?" I declared, glancing

back towards the gate. Through the rain and darkness, I could not see it.

"Made use of toxins we took from the Cathazra 'wyrms' on the Dark Continent, at last." He replied, coolly. "Have no fear. This variety induces only sleep. One of them fell somewhat poorly. He'll have a nasty bump, but little else."

"How—"

"Their ale. The watch here has it delivered from the tavern next door, where I've kept residence. The woman who delivers it leaves the glasses unattended for approximately fifteen seconds while she goes to prop open the door on her way out." He responded. "It's amazing how fast-acting it is, even diluted. And lucky that the ale here is of poor quality, because the poison isn't tasteless."

I looked back on the man, cowed suddenly by how easily he'd expressed that. Like it hadn't been much of a challenge. I'd found no good solution for the guards, save avoiding them, and resorting to killing them if I had to.

"I suppose that explains how you negotiated the gate with that leg, as well." I muttered. "Filched the keys, did you?"

"Hours ago."

"I didn't know you had a talent for pick-pocketing, let alone handling poison." I said.

"Begging your pardon, sir, but there are many things about me you do not know." He replied. "Especially those which pertain to my combat expertise ... which are many and varied, but have never concerned you, because they are far less flashy than my negligible skill with a blade. I have always preferred the subtler route. Something you oft overlook."

"Why are you here, Johannes?" I demanded, coldly. I didn't lower my blade.

"To stop you." He said simply.

"We've had this conversation." I waved my sword at him. "Now move. You didn't talk me down then, you aren't going to now, when I'm on the precipice of concluding all of this."

His breath came out in a long, ragged sigh. " ... I knew you would be stubborn, sir ... but ... I came prepared for that."

I readied myself. Perhaps he had more poison on him. Even so, he had no readily available method I could see of administering it. An arrow, he would have to load and fire. I saw no signs of a bamboo dart-gun, or anything else so exotic. So how would he come ... ?

He did nothing. And that's all he did. He stood there before me, unmoving. He pulled no weapon, said nothing further. He did ... nothing.

"What the bloody hell are you waiting for, then?" I raised my voice somewhat. If the guards truly were unconscious, I wanted to know. If they weren't, the confusion that came when they arrived might give me a chance to slip past the wolfhound.

But no one came. Johannes just stood there in the rain, facing me. My breath came out in pants, my heart thudding in my ears. The doorway stood just feet before me, yet it seemed now more unreachable than it had a month ago when I'd first left Circenshire.

"I cannot let you do this, Luther." He spoke, his face carved in stone, rain falling down the hollows beneath his cheek bones. "If you wish to pass ... you'll have to carve your way through me, first."

"Why?!" I cried out hoarsely, in frustration and anger. My hand shook as it gripped my sword, my whole body thirsting for blood.

God, I didn't want this. I'd thought myself willing to cut my way through anyone, but not this. I was so close to the verge, I might even be able to do it. But that thought alone made my stomach churn, displaying for my conscience, in full view, how far this anger had pushed me. Johannes and I had disagreements, but ... cutting him down did not feel like an action that belonged to me. It belonged to someone else. A monstrous man, who'd cast aside his civility for bloodlust, no matter what stood in the way ... friend or foe.

That's what you've become, my mind chided.

I shook my head, battering back that voice yet again. It was the same voice that had given me such doubt, all this time ... had tormented me with guilt and grief. It was the voice screaming for me to stop all of this. And I'd engaged in a screaming match with it every night in my dreams, since the day I'd given in to this desire for revenge. I'd waged war against it.

Johannes was only giving physical voice to it, now. Just as he had, a month ago.

"Why do you have to make this so hard?!" I yelled, no longer caring about the guards, conscious or no. I was aware how simple-minded the question sounded, but at the moment I just didn't give a damn. "Damn you, man!" I whipped the saber through the air, ferocity in my every word. "Damn you to *hell*! Leave me *be*! My mind is set to this ... it is *all* I have, anymore!"

"You have a family." He said, his brogue tinged with some of the strength I'd seen in him over the last year, but beneath it was a very real physical weariness. He wasn't well. He'd pushed himself very hard to be here, to the point that I had very real fear for his well-being. He was putting little to no weight on his leg, which means he'd been pushing it, because it should have been far more healed by now. And he might not recover from whatever affliction had a hold of him ... it sounded serious. He might have even been dying. I couldn't know.

I wasn't even sure how long he'd been following me on my mad chase. He knew where this residence was, so perhaps he'd come here and waited for my inevitable arrival. Or perhaps he'd set out from Circenshire a mere week ago, only just arriving here in time to stand before me right now.

Regardless of how, or when, he'd gone through hell. Only to now stand in my way, asking that I cut him down.

"*Move*!" I bellowed.

He shook his head, coughing again. " ... I cannot, sir. Cut me down if you wish to follow through with this. I will not move."

"*Move Johannes*!"

"I cannot, sir." He repeated, jaw set, gaze remaining on mine. He wanted me to look him in the eyes when I did this.

I bit my lip until I tasted blood, and gave an outraged howl, answering the burning desire in my veins, reigned in just barely since I'd set foot on these grounds. I charged forward, every ounce of anger, retribution and the ever-present hunger for blood I'd had since Lucius had issued those last, dying words to me ... flooding through me into my arms, pooling in them a strength I knew would hew through the maddening, self-righteous, stubborn wolfhound, cutting him in twain before me.

It was the memory of Lucius, and not his final words, but the most treasured memory I held of him, that stuck in my heart, froze my blood and stilled my blade. Inches from the wolfhound's neck.

Him standing beside me in the parlor. The scent of cigar-smoke and brandy, of the subtle cologne he wore ... the thin rays of the sun throwing his liver-spotted fur into fiery contrast with the finer white along his muzzle and cheeks. Klaus's coat in my hands, and the old spaniel resting his paw on my shoulder, settling comfort into my bones, like my father never had. Making me feel safe, like I was a pup again. Explaining the world to me, with such certainty ... wizened by the years he had on me.

"We are all on the same voyage. We take many different routes, and some are shorter than others. But we all have the same destination. Do not rush to yours. No matter when you arrive, he'll be waiting for you there. Live your life with conviction. Enjoy the few fleeting moments of happiness and triumph, but do not focus on your victories if you wish to have confidence in yourself. A man isn't truly judged by his accomplishments. Our strength comes from enduring our failures, and our losses. That is when we are most tested. That is when a man's character is truly shown."

Johannes never moved. I gave a baleful, anguished cry, my sword falling from my hand weakly, onto the ground with a damp and useless thud. I fell back from him, legs weak from travel, starvation and what was now becoming an all-consuming ... emptiness ... causing me to buckle into the grass on my knees.

Everything that had propelled me for the last month was falling away, losing its fire, crumbling inside me, and leaving in its wake ... nothing. Which, I realized, was all it had ever been. I was shelled-out, emptied, and hollow without it. And if it could be lost like this, it wasn't conviction. It wasn't justice. It wasn't anything so substantial.

Anger. That's all it had ever been. And anger wasn't enough for me to cut my comrade down. I wasn't the cold man I'd thought myself. I hadn't the nerve. I just *wasn't* that kind of man. I could never be that kind of man.

"Why ... ?" I begged Johannes, weakly, looking up through the rain at the implacable wolfhound. "Why won't you just ... let me go? I could have ... it would all have been..." My hands fell to my knees, my head falling with it. Rain slid down my cheeks.

That's all it was. Wasn't it?

"Because I took an oath, sir." Johannes spoke, an edge of emotional frailty in his voice, like a man recalling his own past with an old friend. I wondered very much ... what he thought of, when his mind went to Lucius. He'd known him so much longer than I. I had thought of Delilah, but never the pain the wolfhound must have been in. And especially so, since— "I failed to protect the man whom I was sworn to," he said, still with that tremble in his tone. "But my oath was not only to him. It was to his family. To the Denholme name. I am a Knight. I protect my Lord's family. It is what I am sworn to, until the day I die."

"Then go protect them!" I flung an arm in the direction of the gate. "Protect your family!"

"*You* are a Denholme, Luther!" His voice rose, at last. And behind it was that certainty, that conviction which I'd heard in Lucius, so many times. The commanding air, the steel behind his words ... that of a man decided and unwavering.

That quality I had always lacked ... which Lucius had wielded with such ease. These were men. These were men who'd seen the world, come to terms with their demons, faced the very worst in themselves, and triumphed. Not because they'd overcome every obstacle before them, not because they'd won every battle, but because they'd never *given in*. They'd never surrendered to the worst instincts inside them ... never let the winds batter down their sails. They'd only forged onwards, through every storm, regardless of the damage it did to them. They had scars. Some were as visible as a limp, some lingering in their mind, invisible to all but those closest to them. But they'd never given their families up either. Their families loved them, and they had never abandoned them. Perhaps *because* they had never abandoned them.

This was the precipice of no return. Every loss in my life paled in comparison to what I'd endured this past year. Every slight against me, every injustice I'd weathered and survived ... not a single triumph in my lifetime would matter if I crossed that threshold, and became a murderer. I would be everything they'd always told me I was. It was beyond being a sinner, or a Heretic. It was about right and wrong. I could argue every other case of violence in my life, but this was cold-blooded murder, and nothing less.

Perhaps Cuthbert saw the realization dawning in my eyes, because his softened. And he strode forward, even putting weight on his bad leg ... until he was a foot from me.

"You are part of my family, sir ... Luther." He spoke, quietly. "Just as Delilah is. Just as Lucius ... was." He swallowed. "If I let you do this, you will die. And I will have neglected my duty. Again. Please..." He slowly moved his good hand down, offering it, palm-outstretched.

I looked up at him, and the offering.

"Please," he repeated, his tone pleading, "I can't ... fail ... again. Allow me to fulfill my duty. Let me return you to your family. To our family. Delilah needs you. Your children need you. The fleet waits for you. For a leader. For an Admiral who is fit to step into the gap Lucius left."

"I'm one-tenth the man he was." I said, my voice that of a ghost, almost drowned out by the rain. "And I've done nothing for Delilah but ... bring her pain..."

Johannes was silent for a long while, before continuing.

"Luther..." he said, " ... I have never seen her so happy, as when she is with you."

I looked up at him at that. I wanted to know what he said was genuine, and not some empty compliment meant to change my mind. Johannes was a poor liar, and right now I saw nothing but truth in his features.

"It frustrated me." He admitted, almost ruefully. "It was ... one ... of the reasons I took issue with you, although it pains me to admit it. I have known her so very long. But I cannot ... even Lucius could not ... reach her as you did. I do not pretend to understand why. But you've a sensitivity about you that most men lack. You are emotional in ways that ... perhaps Lucius and I never allowed ourselves to be, in the presence of a woman. You express yourself, unafraid. Unashamed."

"It is easier," I said, "to be laid vulnerable before a woman, when you aren't trying to impress her."

"I wouldn't be surprised if it's as simple as that." The wolfhound replied, quietly. "Male pride is a hard obstacle to overcome."

I had pride, I wanted to say. I just didn't need to bandy it about in front of a small woman. And maybe it really was that simple.

"I don't understand it." He said, again with that edge of frustration, but a sort of acceptance, now. "But you are for her what no other can be. And it is your strength that has seen her through her ordeals. She needs you now more than ever. She will continue to need you. And your children will need you."

"The fleet—"

"Needs a real leader." He said. "I am not fit to lead men as someone like Lucius was. I am just not that sort of man."

I recalled what Lucius had said to me, about leaders and followers. About Johannes, in particular. And it struck me that the wolfhound must have made peace with that long ago, because there was no sense of disappointment in his eyes when he spoke of it. No desire or longing. He didn't want this task.

"Shaw—"

"Has no empathy for the lower-class, which make up over half of our fleet," he said. "With Lucius dead, I have inherited command of his fleet, as he promised. I will never abdicate the position to Shaw. Or Singhe. I think you understand why."

He held his hand where it was. It wavered only due to the weakness in his arm, in his entire body. I left him waiting no longer. I took it, took hold of my sword, and stood.

He shifted his palm to my shoulder, leaning forward. "Please do not leave me to care for your family alone, sir," he said weakly. "You are Master of the house now. You must fill the gap Lucius left, or the family will never recover. Delilah will waste away without you. The children will grow up without a father."

Like I had. Like Johannes had. The words were unspoken, but I could see them there. Perhaps Lucius had been father to us both.

"I cannot be the sort of man Lucius was." I said, my voice hoarse again. Choked.

"No." Johannes agreed. I looked to him at that, and his eyes met mine. "You will be your own sort of man. That is what he would have wanted for you. Not to obey him for all time, or emulate him ... but to come into your own. To become the sort of man you are meant to be." He looked past me for a moment, to the door, then down to the saber I held in my hands. Then back to my eyes. " ... and this is not him." He finished.

I looked at him for a long while, my mind churning like choppy seas. So much of what he said was at odds with what he'd previously professed about me. How could he trust me now, after all the misgivings we'd had in the past?

"You haven't always liked the sort of man I am." I said, challengingly.

His hand squeezed my shoulder, and I saw him brace himself for what he was to say next.

" ... I was wrong then." He said, letting out strained breath. "I have lived my life according to a certain Creed ... to a certain faith. But, the foundations of that faith were not issued direct by God. They were written by men's quills, put to words by their interpretations. Long have I know this. And that is why I have tailored some of my beliefs over the years, so that I might wear them through many occasions. Through many struggles. So that I might hold fast to them, even when the world and, I daresay, my own common sense, force me to question them. It is a continuing process ... not a task which shall ever be completed. I shall have to tailor and adjust these beliefs until the day I die."

I tipped one ear to the side, giving him a sidelong look. " ... is there room in those beliefs for a man like me now?"

"That depends greatly upon what you do here, tonight." He said very seriously. "I am willing to believe that..." he steeled himself, it seemed, " ... that the choices a man makes, concerning his lovers ... do not determine what kind of a man he is to be. But ... you must be the example. I have nothing else in this world to base this opinion upon ... but you, sir."

He stepped back, at that. His grey eyes settled on mine, knuckles gripping his cane, tightly.

"Show me what kind of a man you are, sir."

I watched the rain fall between us. It had thinned somewhat, the night air seeming less oppressive, the air flowing into my lungs far more easily. It was as though a weight had lifted from my chest, and I could breathe again. I took in a great, long breath, the sensation flushing through me, sending my head abuzz, my blood flowing with a different sort of strength.

" ... Johannes..." I said, fighting back the twitch in my features, the remnants of what was still substantial anger and bitterness nipping at my heels, " ... you're ill. We need to get you home. You sound terrible, you fool."

I saw his shoulders fall and he began leaning far more heavily on his cane. After a long moment, his moustache turned up in a tired smile.

"Indeed, sir."

I turned my chin upwards to follow the slope of the manor beside us, towards the window far above I knew to be Elizabeth Irving's bedroom. For a long moment I stared at it.

" It seems so wrong that we should just let them ... triumph." I growled. "That woman should not be content and comfortable in her bed, while we suffer as we do."

"That woman lost her son." Johannes said, gravely. "She shall never have comfort again, so long as she lives. And she will live forever looking over her shoulder, terrified of what might come."

"I doubt it." I snuffed. "She doesn't seem the sort to fear ghosts and phantoms."

"Ghosts and phantoms aren't what she'll fear." Cuthbert said with a certainty that made me arch an eyebrow, and give him a long look.

"You mean the guards?" I queried. "Even if she wakes after they do ... all she'll know is they all caught some bad ale. Not that her family came so close to the same fate she wrought upon ours."

He shook his head. "She'll know by morning. Take my word."

"How?"

"I returned something to her bedchamber."

My eyes widened, and again, I found myself taken aback by the wolfhound. "You..." I began, " ... you were inside?"

"I entered the grounds a full hour before you, sir. You waited quite a while in that alleyway. I had ample time." He winced as he began to walk, boldly across the lawn, clearly very certain that the guardsmen would not see him. He must have honestly poisoned them all.

And he'd already gone inside, all the way to her bedroom, and out again, to wait for me? With a limp?

There was a *lot* I didn't know about Johannes Cuthbert.

"What did you leave?" I asked, jogging to keep up. "Johannes? What did you leave in her room?"

He gave a bitter smirk, the first I'd seen on him in a long while.

"Her son's loaded pistol on the bed beside her."

I stared at him, mouth agape.

"I'd say that will send a fairly strong message ... wouldn't you, sir?"

Johannes had pneumonia. I'd insisted he visit a physician as soon as we'd made it a county away from Circenshire. He hadn't seemed well enough to make it home. And it turned out I'd made the right call, because the physician we saw admonished us both quite strictly for not seeing to his illness sooner, and told Johannes he would most certainly die.

A week later, he was on the rebound, and yelling at me night and day to take Specter and head home. He insisted he'd be fine where he was, until he was well enough to take to the road again ... but that Delilah would not survive another day without me. I was certain he was exaggerating, but by day's end he had quite literally knocked me off my feet several times, and I was growing tired of the abuse. I left cursing him and nursing a swollen cheek.

At least he'd be well. Apparently it would take more than an oft-fatal illness to purge the world of Johannes Cuthbert. I had a suspicion I'd never be rid of him.

And for that, I was grateful.

I was glad at least I'd had a few days with a physician to purge me of the filth from my time on the road before I returned home. The more lasting effects were still there, but ... at least I'd not be bringing fleas into the house.

I was riding the dirt road through outlying Circenshire when a wave of nostalgia hit me, nearly knocking me out of my saddle. The weather, the trees, the world ... it was all exactly as it had been, almost two years ago now, when I'd first come here. I'd been skinny and freshly-washed and clothed then, too ... a peasant in rich man's clothing. Unsure what waited ahead of me. A bit frightened, more than a bit wary.

The difference was, this time I knew I wouldn't be running away. No matter what came, from this point on, this was my home. I would go to sea, I would fight for my country, I would travel far and wide ... but this is where I would always return. This was where my family waited for me. And no matter what befell us in the future, whether I lived another thirty years, or another day, there would be people here who loved me. Regardless of what future lives, if any, lay beyond this one ... I would exist here forever. Like Lucius. I would live on, in the hearts of the people who cared for me, in their children, and their children's children. It didn't matter if we weren't bound by blood. Family requires no breeding, no blood ... only love.

I was bursting through the front doors into the parlor before I'd so much as tethered Specter outside, startling a serving girl with a tray of tea, whose face all but instantly lit-up, when she saw me.

"Master Luther—"

"My wife, Betty." I implored the young girl. She only nodded, put the tray down and hurriedly headed to the small room on the first floor, where Delilah had been treated by the physician when she'd lost our child. It chilled my heart to know she remained there still, but I set my jaw and opened the door.

Sunlight spilled through the yawning doorway as I slowly, silently stepped inside. I saw her there, thinning as much as I had ... sitting weakly upright in bed, staring out the one small window in the room. The soft curls of fur along her ears were matted and tangled, her fur unkempt over what little of it wasn't covered by her nightgown.

I swallowed back the hurt I felt at seeing her in such a terrible state ... and knowing that I had been almost entirely to blame. But I put it aside for now. The last thing she would need from me was doubt and guilt. I was here to do as I should have done, months ago ... to give her strength.

"I'm not hungry, Betty." She said disinterestedly, her voice nearly emotionless. I steadied myself, then spoke.

"I'm home, Delilah." I said softly.

She spun to face me, brown eyes widening and taking in the sun, her pupils nearly disappearing in a sea of light chocolate brown. I saw her tremble, from quivering lip to a full-bodied shudder, and then the tears welled in her eyes, and she was struggling at her sheets.

I crossed the room in a few long strides, taking her fiercely in my arms and holding fast to her, my eyes squeezing shut as I buried my nose against her neck. I could hear her crying, could feel her small arms seeking any purchase on me they could find. I sat there with her, saying nothing, only giving her everything I could. Even when her sobbing rose to frustrated hiccups and she beat her fists weakly against my chest, I didn't move. I let her have it out.

"How could you have left us?!"

"I'm sorry, Delilah." I whispered, rocking her body against mine. "I was ... more than a fool. I was acting like a child."

"I love you!" She cried. "The children love you! I thought you loved me!"

"I do." I said, quietly. "I do love you. I didn't behave like it. And I'm sorry. I don't know how I'll ever make it up to you..."

She pulled back from me, her eyes red and angry. "You don't *ever* do that to us again! Do you understand me?!"

I looked down on her helplessly for a few moments. There would be many times I'd leave her, in the future. I knew it. She knew it.

But I'd never leave her like this again. That I could promise.

"I'll never act so selfishly again, Delilah." I swore. "On your father. I swear it. I can't promise that I won't endanger myself ... I am a soldier..." I leaned down, nuzzling my forehead into hers, locking our eyes together. "But I will never abandon you or this family, in my heart. Just as your father never did."

She sniffed once more, then clung to me again. And I held her. Battered, starved and broken. We were still alive. We'd weathered the storm. I didn't know how long the voyage ahead would be, but ... I knew everyone I'd loved and everyone I still loved would be waiting for us, or would join us some day, at our destination.

And I would never be alone again.

CHAPTER 16

EXCERPTS FROM THE JOURNAL OF LUTHER DENHOLME

Spring, 30th of the month, in Our Father's Year 956

I haven't ever been one for keeping a journal, or holding onto my memories. But I'm convinced that's because I've never believed there's been anything in my past so worth hanging onto. After the events that transpired these past years, I feel differently. So, here I am ... making an attempt to jot all of this down. What souls will care to read it at some point in history, I do not know. More likely, it will disappear into the archives of time, like every other fabrication we leave behind. But I feel I need to try, because at some point my children or my children's children might wish to understand what kind of a man I truly was, or how I came to be a part of our family. They deserve to know the truth.

Klaus Richter's family, as well as the whole of the Amurescan Navy, took great pains to keep secretive and hush up the man he truly was. They have painted the pages of history with lies. They did this because they felt it was less disgraceful to his name. But I feel differently. No matter what has happened throughout my life, no matter what is to come, I want my family, my comrades, the future generations to know who I truly was, and who the people in my life truly were.

I submit that the above chronicles the true events of these few years of my life, as honestly as I could portray them. These years were a turning point for me. They made me the man I am today, they instilled in me the values I hold tight to now, and solidified for me what matters in my life. I declare not that what I found is right for every man, only that it seemed the best course for me, and I am glad that I took it.

The sense of self-assurance and certainty I had been seeking, the point at which I was able to grasp the same strength and wisdom I'd envied so much in Lucius, I know I will not find right away. I'm not certain I'll ever be as firm in my convictions as he. I hope only that I'm closer now to being the 'sort of man' Lucius believed I was meant to be.

But in writing all of this down, I've seen how much I've changed in these few, short years. And I am certain, at least, that these changes needed to be made. The hardships have been many, but for the first time in my life, I have purpose. I am no longer listing aimlessly through the shallows. I am on course.

However my descendants or the historians may judge me, this is the sort of man I am. I may not be able to live honestly, in this age ... but I will have the truth known, once I am gone from the world. Perhaps future souls, struggling with the discrimination I've endured, will find answers in their time. Perhaps even acceptance. Love.

I want them to know how difficult this was. How painful. How many struggles my family and I faced. And I want them to know that despite it all, I was never ashamed. I have done many wrongs, taken many actions which I now regret, apologized for many things throughout my life, but never for who I am. This is the one truth they can't deny you, the one freedom they can never strip away. You are who you were meant to be. Do what you must to survive, but never question that.

On that at least, I have great conviction of will.

I suspect that even now, shrouded in the comforts of my family and the Pedigree life, I may never be able to live as I wish. The few brief years I shared with Klaus may well have been as close as I will ever come to a lover, in that sense. But I am not without love. I have my family, my wife and children, my comrades-in-arms and the memories of those passed to warm my heart when the cold nips at my heels. To ask for more seems selfish.

I would be lying if I said there wasn't still a void there. But earnestly, I'm grateful for all I have. And who's to say what the future holds. I am a man of many passions, and I am not so naive now as to believe I'm past being ruled by them. I've little doubt the fires inside me will burn again, and when they do, well...

I have Johannes now to check my swing, whenever I'm a footfall from pitching myself overboard. He's precisely the sort of man I need beside me. Perhaps he can save me from being run away by poor choices.

I'm sure he'd like to think he can, anyway.

But, I digress. The reason I dated this journal entry is because of what transpired only a day ago, at the Officers Ball in the Capital. An event so resplendent, I immediately knew it needed to be committed to paper, so that I might relive it again and again and remind myself there is hope in the world, even for those of us who hide who we are. A memory of intense courage, from a woman whose suffering has equaled, if not surpassed my own.

My wife.

The Officers Ball is arguably the largest social event the Amurescan Navy holds. The three-day-long ball takes place in the Capital building itself, where the King keeps Court. I had of course never attended in my days as a midshipman, and for the past several years, only Lucius had gone. But this year, I had no choice but to attend.

We could have ducked out, I suppose, but it had been nearly half a year since Delilah had lost our son and the whole incident with the Irvings had played out. We were approaching the spring, and that meant the *Cerberus* fleet would be shoving off soon on another contract. And this year, I would be shipping out with them, as Cuthbert's subordinate. Just as Lucius had decreed in his will.

All four Captains of the fleet would be in attendance at the ball, and it just didn't make sense not to hold our talks of contracts any other weekend. It was too convenient for all. So, I'd swallowed my arguments, and agreed at once when Cuthbert requested I go. It would be a horrible show of disloyalty if I didn't.

What had surprised us both was when Delilah had asked to go. She was well enough by then, both physically and mentally, or at least I hoped so ... but she hadn't left the manor since her father's death and I knew it still hung heavily in her mind. It was a quiet sort of mourning now ... I would occasionally find her walking the hallways near his study, or sitting on the hill that overlooked his grave. On those days, I would join her. Sit with her in the sun, or the parlor. And we would talk about him. Fondly. She would tell me things from her youth, from his youth ... facets to him I had never known.

Rarely, she would cry. But she never looked worse for the wear afterwards. I hoped what little I was able to offer was helping, and Cuthbert assured me it was.

It was like watching a wound heal. It would just take time.

I hadn't thought her ready for this, though. Traveling to the Capital was no small trip, we'd be on the road for nearly two weeks, we'd have to leave the children behind, the ball was enormous and she'd be inundated by the Pedigree society we'd been dodging for so long. Even Johannes disliked the idea of her coming.

But she'd told us, with strength in her voice, that she was the wife of the Master of the house now, and that she intended to live up to her responsibilities. I didn't understand it and the 'responsibilities' associated with women of a Pedigree line had never sat well with me, but they mattered to Delilah, and I wasn't going to demean her by questioning them.

We relented, at length. Neither of us could ever have denied her, and I'm sure she knew that. Without Lucius around, she was more Master to this house than either Johannes or I. And I trusted that she knew what was right.

The trip, at least, had been pleasant. I won't get into detail, but over the last few months, Johannes had finally opened up a bit, as I'd long ago wished he might. And he'd begun sharing the stories of his youth, especially those years he'd spent serving in the *Cerberus* fleet under Lucius. And so it was, most days we travelled were spent listening to him tell his tales in that rich brogue, Delilah and I transfixed. I suspect he was trying to be more open with Delilah, in the way that I was. And it was working. It warmed my heart to see the two of them growing closer.

And one night, while we were staying at an inn in the Capital, he thanked me for the 'example' I had put forth. I still don't understand why it is straight men have so much trouble speaking to women ... but I only told him he need not thank me and to think nothing of it.

We prepared for the Ball. I was able to dress in uniform again, which suited me now better than it had when I'd been a skinny lout. Johannes wore his Admiral's colors sharply, cutting quite the figure in his military sash, with medals marking the many difficult conflicts he'd been a part of. Over his heart, he wore a square of red cloth, pinned with a small silver sword through it. It was cut from Lucius's sash, from his days in the navy ... to represent that Johannes had served under an Admiral who had lost his life in battle.

I wore the same, from the remnants of Klaus's sash.

Delilah wore a beautiful gown, and even I had to admire her. I don't suppose I appreciate feminine beauty the way most men do, but I challenge any man to show me a woman more beautiful than my wife. Popular perspective be-damned. I was proud to have her on my arm.

In all the preparations, one thought had never occurred to me, nor to Johannes. And if it had struck Delilah, she'd never spoken of it.

That is, whether or not the Irvings would be present.

We'd heard nothing of them since the incident at their manor in Treneval. To be fair, we hadn't tried. Although Johannes assured me he always kept his ear to the ground, and would be doing so far more astutely from now on, lest they try something else against us.

But nothing had happened. To pardon the expression, I think Johannes had put the fear of God into them.

I knew only that they were apparently beginning construction on a new fleet, to replace the one they'd lost. Why, I couldn't understand. I suppose because they'd always been a naval family and wished to maintain their pride in that arena. But no member of their family was *in* the Navy any longer, and though I'm sure they'd push their future generations towards it, the tradition had clearly died off within their ranks.

More likely, they'd hire a Captain from outside the family name and profit off his ventures. I cared not.

All that concerned me was that perhaps now they were too occupied to be of threat to us. That was Cuthbert's hope, as well. And we went on with our lives.

That is, until the first night of the ball.

The affair was every bit as pompous and stuffy as I assumed it would be, and I was every bit as out-of-place as I'd known I would be. But at least soon we'd be meeting with the Captains. And listening to Johannes argue with Shaw about sea contracts, hell, even perhaps taking part myself, would be entertaining and far more centered in my area of expertise. I just had to stick it out until then.

My wife similarly seemed not to be finding it easy to fit in. She hadn't been to court in years, after all, and it showed. She spoke to a woman or two she seemed to know, was even greeted by another, older military man ... likely a friend of her father's. She introduced me to several men like him, but I got the overwhelming feeling I was being judged by each and every one of them.

By the time we'd passed the first two hours, I was fairly certain bringing her had been a mistake. And judging by the look on her face, she suspected the same.

"Give it time, love." I murmured, my arm slipping around her waist. I watched a woman nearby crinkle her nose in disgust at the blatant public display of physical affection. I sighed, and withdrew my arm.

" ... you don't need to do that." Delilah said softly, in a sad tone that made my heart sink. "Propriety hardly matters ... when your name is already blacklisted."

"You're exaggerating." I assured her. But then I gave a long sigh, muzzle twitching. "Perhaps I should leave you be. It's my presence they're reacting to ... not yours. They wouldn't give you such a wide berth if I wasn't here."

"You're my husband, Luther." She said, clearly gathering strength in her voice, although it sounded brittle. "I will be not be ashamed to be seen with you. And, in any case..." her eyes swept the room, "It's not my choice in husband they're so discomforted by. It's the man I rejected. And the circumstances surrounding it."

I ground my teeth. As frustrating as it was, I knew she spoke the truth. The horrible part was, many of these people likely suspected what had transpired between the Denholme and the Irving families. They might not have known the gory specifics, but Delilah's children were full spaniel, and that would only become more obvious with time. What's more, men like Jeremiah Irving often had reputations. Surely some here suspected what had come to pass. The duel only confirmed our outrage. Even Lucius's death was probably the stuff of gossip, here.

Our entire family was probably the subject of many of these twittering, shallow peoples' conversations right now. And that would have been upsetting enough, but what really stung ... and what must have been eating away at Delilah ... was the fact that if any of these people suspected, or even knew what had happened ... they would still do nothing. Nothing except bask in the scandal, speak their suspicions about who was at fault like it was entertainment. All the while, Delilah's plight was forgotten. The horrible truth of what had happened was shushed in favor of pleasant conversation, and to maintain 'civility'.

Living a lie as I was, I knew her pain. But what had happened to Delilah was an injustice on every possible level. And it enraged me more than my own struggles ever had.

Somehow, I stayed silent that night. My wife and I stood together, near one of the massive pillars lining the Royal Ballroom. We kept to ourselves, awaiting the arrival of the Captains. We weren't alone, at the very least, and that's probably what saved us. We'd be standing together like this, part of these peoples' society, but not, for as long as we came to court. We were outsiders in our own Class.

I didn't realize then how much we would embrace that, in the future.

There we would have stayed, apart from it all, silently basking in only each other's company ... if not for the arrival of a family, fated long ago to change our lives. Tonight they would again clash with us. But this time, the battle was not mine.

I felt Delilah's entire body stiffen the moment they entered the room. My eyes followed hers, but somehow knew, before I spotted them. My fur bristled beneath my collar, my body tense, poised on my toes. My hand ghosted over the hilt of my saber, my instincts roaring inside me.

The Irvings.

Elizabeth Irving led the procession, on her arm some dim-eyed suitor half her age, who looked as though he wasn't entirely certain where he was. Her daughter and her husband followed, along with a bevy of wait staff helping them through the door, taking their coats and brushing off the pollen from the men's shoulders and collars. The clothing and jewelry their group wore cost about what it would have to feed a family for a lifetime.

Elizabeth's dark, piercing eyes swept the room. Despite the loud, noisy, massive ball room, it took her only a few seconds to spot us. She froze similarly in place when she did.

We held each other's gaze for a long while. I wasn't sure what I hoped to accomplish, but it was impossible to take my eyes off of them ... my intended targets, not so long ago, but yet a lifetime ago. Tonight they were safe from me. But that doesn't mean I wanted them to feel so.

As they sifted into the crowd the matron constantly looked over her shoulder, even as she had to greet the plethora of guests here who knew and valued her acquaintance. I let my gaze leave her at last, content that I'd made my stand.

But Delilah ... Delilah was still frozen in place. I saw her eyes following the family, unwavering. I looked down at my diminutive wife, wondering what torment she must have been in, watching them go about their lives. I reached down and took her hand, wrapping my fingers through hers and squeezing softly, wanting to offer any kind of comfort I could. She must have felt so helpless. She must have been so frightened.

I couldn't have been more wrong.

I don't know what passed through Delilah's mind in those moments. I'll never know what *her* inner thoughts were, and I wish I did, so that I could recount them. But in the following minute, this small, fragile, grief-stricken woman would show me what strengths she still held, despite what the world had taken from her.

"Luther," she spoke quietly, and my attention could not have been more fixed on her. I held my breath, waiting on my wife's next words. They were not what I expected

She slipped her hand from mine, looking over the white-furred, delicate paw. And then she held it before me, and I saw in those endless brown eyes an intensity I'd only ever seen before in her father.

"Show me how to make a proper fist." She demanded, softly.

I looked into my wife's eyes for only a moment of hesitation, then reached down gingerly with my far larger, calloused hands ...

and folded hers into an effective fist, her knuckles forward, thumb folded along her pointer finger.

"Like you're holding a pitcher you mean to pour." I said, evenly. "Knuckles-first."

She only nodded, then stepped away from me and into the crowd. I didn't even call after her.

It felt wrong to intrude on this. As much as my mind screamed at me to follow ... I knew this moment belonged to her, and that any decisions she made from this point on were her own.

And whatever they were, I'd support her.

I lost her amidst the crowd ... but I caught sight of her again as she stepped into the small clearing near the serving tables where the wine was kept. She kept her pace even then, striding forward with purpose towards the thin spaniel woman standing beside her daughter, wine glass held delicately in one spindly paw.

I saw Elizabeth turn just in time to see Delilah when she was but a few feet from her. I could see the shock in her expression from where I stood, but it was *nothing* compared to what was to come.

Delilah wound back an arm, strode forward in her beautiful white gown, and connected with the Irving woman's jaw in a blow that echoed across the ball room.

And I swear, I had never been so proud of any person in my life.

Elizabeth Irving stumbled backwards into the serving table, a sense of déjà vu sweeping over me and sending me into a barking laugh, as the scene played itself out startling close to what had befallen the woman's son in the Denholme manor, over a year ago. She clung to the table edge, nearly pulling a punch bowl down with her, several of the wine bottles tumbling and clattering to the floor, emptying their ruby-red contents onto the expensive white marble tiles. Most of the people surrounding me cast disapproving looks my way at my reaction to the sudden scene ... but I couldn't keep the smile from my features if I'd wanted to.

As if to further my mirth, Elizabeth's foppish companion fled from her side barely a second later, her daughter and her overweight husband doing little more to help their mother. The daughter, at least, called out. But she made no motion to defend the matron.

Delilah stood over the shocked spaniel woman for a few moments, and though I couldn't see her expression, I liked to imagine the condemnation behind those eyes. The torchlight burning there, lit at last by years of suffering in silence.

Elizabeth shakily got to her feet, nursing her jaw, hatred burning behind her gaze. If she was smart, she would say nothing. That seemed to be the course Delilah was taking. The silence between them remained, until Delilah finally turned, and began to retreat. The whole of the ball room joined in that silence, all eyes on the nearly unbelievable scene.

And then Elizabeth made her mistake. She spoke.

"You think you can accost me like this, in *full* public view, and retreat as though naught happened, you *harlot*?!" She gave a *very* unladylike snarl on the last word.

I saw Delilah stop at that, saw the seriousness in her eyes, and the resignation. But besides that, there was a sort of peace there. Like something was at last falling away from her. She turned to face Lady Irving, still silent.

"You and your entire *disgraceful* family!" The spaniel shrieked. "You soil this regal place with your mere presence! Your peasant husband has *no* place in the halls of Pedigree families, we're likely all to catch his fleas! You sully yourself by sharing his bed!" She spat, then sneered. "But I suppose you sullied yourself long ago, you destitute little whore. What does further disgrace mean to a family like yours, after all? God has exiled you from his flock. Even the worms reject the rotting corpse of that arrogant *cur* of a father of y—"

"You will *never* address my father in such a way, ever again!" Delilah finally responded, her voice powerful, despite her frame. It carried through the entire chamber, to every waiting ear. And right now, that was everyone.

"And I will *not* be lectured on my own disgrace, when it was not of my making!" Delilah continued, my chest swelling as I heard not a hint of fear in her voice. "The disgrace that has befallen me belongs to your family, Lady Irving ... by the hands of your son, Jeremiah!"

My breath stilled in my chest. I felt the whole of the air in the room shifting, and all eyes fell to Elizabeth Irving. She seemed a mixture of frightened and mortified, and was staring death into Delilah's gaze, warning her that she still held our secrets over us.

But it was an empty threat now, and we all knew it.

"I have accepted what you call my 'disgrace', Elizabeth." Delilah spoke, finitely. "I have embraced it, in fact. I have lived with what your son did to me and I have not just endured ... I have flourished. And so has my family." She steadied her breathing a moment. "I am not afraid of you. You hold no power over me any longer."

"My son was *lured* by this greedy little creature!" Elizabeth snarled again, an edge of desperation in her voice. It was obvious she was not speaking to Delilah, but to the crowd. Whether what she said fell on deaf ears or no, I couldn't know. Surely some here would believe Delilah. More might believe the Irvings, strictly because social standing forced them to.

What she said next was her second mistake.

"These paupers wanted our riches, nothing more! And now they bring these claims against us?!" She cried out.

"Your case is somewhat flawed by the fact that I rejected your son's proposal, isn't it, Lady Irving?" Delilah replied, evenly.

Grasping at, I suppose pity, Elizabeth sobbed, declaring, "My son is dead and buried, by *that* mongrel's hands!" She thrust her finger across the room in my direction. The few patrons still near me inched away, trying not to appear frightened. I didn't bother looking apologetic. In fact, I rested a hand on my sword hilt, rather preferring the space I was suddenly afforded.

"Your son tried to cheat my husband, and still lost his life. In a legal duel." Delilah said.

"My son wasn't just killed!" Elizabeth's voice broke. "He was *mutilated*! There was nothing left of my boy's face, when they returned him to me! I could barely recognize my own child! That man is a beast in gentleman's clothes! He took my son from me!"

For the first time since I'd known this family, I felt a real pang of guilt for the wrongs we'd done them. I could hear sincere grief in the woman's voice when she spoke of losing her son. Regardless of what sort of man he'd been, I felt pity for his mother. And I was suddenly very glad that I hadn't killed her, months ago. This cycle needed to stop. All we'd done was create more and more victims. Both of us.

Delilah's voice lowered. "I'm sorry for your loss, Lady Irving. Truly."

"You're *filth*!" The spaniel was screaming again, throwing her arm in an arc before her, still gripping the table behind her. "All of you! You're hedonistic, violent heathens! Not a one of you is fit to walk these halls, or have *any* place in society! You belong in a gutter, and that's where your family will end its lineage, mark my words! You're already inviting the lower-class into your blood," she gave a disgusted, enraged noise, "and already, it is corrupting you! Whatever wrongs you claim *my* family has wrought upon you, all here know they are lies!" She raised her voice at that, but across the crowd, I saw many doubting faces.

"The wrongs wrought upon my family by yours were terrible," Delilah said, voice steady, "but not a one of them compares to the pain I've lived with ... by staying silent."

Elizabeth's words fell off her tongue, at that. Whatever she'd planned to say next, she seemed deflated by Delilah's conviction.

My young wife shook her head slowly. "Let me make this profoundly clear to you, Lady Irving." She spoke clearly, but without shouting. "Whatever condemnation, gossip, or social exile my family must from this point on endure, it is not worth this denial. I do not care what you, your acquaintances, or anyone in this Court," her eyes swept the ballroom, at that, "thinks of me. I know what transpired ... and I suspect many here do, as well. And I am tired of suppressing the truth for the sake of civility and pleasantry. Too many women have done that before I..." she spoke, sadly,

"… and that is why it continues, unacknowledged … and unpunished. In my case at least, I will no longer stand for it." She held her head high.

I swallowed heavily, wanting so much in that moment to step forward and embrace my wife. I knew how astoundingly difficult all of this had to be for her. And I wanted to tell her, right then, how honored I was to be her husband.

How many women in this room had suffered the same as Delilah? How many more would?

I was not the only one dealing with discrimination in this world. It humbled me to have it laid so bare before me. To watch someone else stand up for who they were, to declare that they had suffered unduly. To challenge our world, our insular little world, this society Amuresca had concocted … with the wrongs it had committed, was still committing, against her.

By doing so, she was exposing herself to the worst kind of ridicule, laying herself bare before all of Pedigree society. It wasn't a lash, it wasn't imprisonment … but the ramifications would be felt far longer. Our family would fall out of favor with nearly everyone Delilah had ever known following this. Those who didn't side with the Irvings would still find her conduct here unbecoming … lowbrow. Uncivil. They would take pains to distance themselves from us as much as possible from this point on.

A Pedigree family cut from the Pedigree world grew poor, quickly. Circenshire was barely a hamlet, we couldn't eke a living from it. Not the sort of living we had now.

I guess it was time to start sinking pirates.

My silent words were echoed a moment later by a long sigh, and a voice that had manifested beside me.

"I hope the South Seas are rich with plundered goods this year." Cuthbert muttered. "Because our trade contacts are all about to cut ties."

"This is what happens when you marry commoners into your line, Johannes." Another, deeper voice joined in. I turned to see Shaw, arching an eyebrow at him, but all I got in response was an impassive look. He clearly didn't care that he'd just insulted me to my face.

"If the young woman I've taken into my care finding the willpower to do something this brave is a direct result of her marriage to Luther," Cuthbert replied, "then I believe peasant marriages should be mandated, from this point on. It would do the Courts a lot of good." He glanced around the room, arching an eyebrow, " ... possibly the health of the children born from such marriages as well."

Shaw scoffed. "I forgot ... I'm talking to *two* peasants." He shook his head, his jowls curving downwards in disapproval, but I sensed it was more ribbing than actual disgust. "Well, you mongrels enjoy the rest of your little woman's show. I'll be upstairs in the smoking room. Let's discuss how it is we plan to rebuild your family's holdings following this fiasco, shall we? You have a fleet to maintain. I've no desire to relocate my command at my age. If you can't afford your own ships, we've all got a problem."

He strode off, and I saw Cuthbert's moustache turn up in a slight smile, as he watched his old comrade go.

"... he grows on you." He assured me.

"Aye, like a mold." I grumbled, my eyes sweeping back over the crowd. My wife had retreated from the clash with Lady Irving, at last, leaving the spaniel woman dumbstruck and as obstinate as ever. I could already see her talking to her approaching acquaintances and family as Delilah left.

"I apologize," I said offhandedly to Johannes, who turned to regard me, "I know at least some of this *was* my influence. I didn't mean to muddy up your family with ... uh ... 'peasant manners'."

"I'm glad you did." The wolfhound said, almost serenely. "Sometimes Pedigree civility is horribly un-civil."

"Sometimes you just need a good fistfight to settle matters?"

I swear, he almost smirked.

"Sometimes." He said.

"I think she settled on the one right conclusion to all of this." I murmured. "It's the secrets, the lies, that hold the power over us, not the Irvings themselves."

He looked to me at that, his eyes sympathetic. I saw the understanding there, and shook my head.

"Don't," I said, quietly. "We both know I can't take the same risks she did. The consequences are far more deadly. I'll handle my life as things are. If the moment comes, it comes. This isn't my fight, right now ... it's hers."

"This battle, from the very beginning, has been hers." Cuthbert replied, softly. "We were merely her soldiers."

I nodded at that. It was easier to see Delilah as she headed back through the crowd, this time. They were parting around her, and not in reverence.

I couldn't stand it anymore. I strode forward, meeting her a few feet from where I'd been standing, embracing her. She did so without shame, this time, caring little for the spectacle we made.

As I stood there with her in the crowded ballroom, the guests in a wide halo around us, I told her everything I had wanted to say, the whole while I'd been watching her. How much I loved her. How proud of her I was.

How proud of her Lucius would have been.

CHAPTER 17
HOME

E*arly Winter, 5th of the month, in Our Father's Year 961*

The ground crunched underfoot this morning as I strode out the Inn we'd spent the night in, and mounted Specter to finish our ride towards Circenshire. Towards the manor.

Towards home.

So much has happened these last five years, it's hard to recount it all. I've kept a separate journal whenever I'm aboard the *Cerberus,* which I shall try to bring home by the time it is full, but for now it sits in my Captain's quarters, awaiting what tales will span the remaining pages.

Johannes likes to call me vain for wearing my Admiral's coat when we travel the roads, but it's not pride at my newly-appointed position that has me donning it each morning ... it's the lingering memories it affords me, keeping me warm as we travel the roads.

Distant memories, now. Dark, smiling eyes. A regal white-furred

Admiral from long ago, the man whose death propelled me both into the role I fill now, and the grief that came with earning such responsibility.

Pain fades with time. No matter how much you believe you'll cling to it forever ... in time, it becomes hard to remember why it was it once hurt so badly. My losses linger, but I carry on.

Klaus. Lucius. My unborn son.

I have two wonderful, healthy children, who even now await me at the manor. Likely outside, the little rogues ... driving their mother mad as they disappear each day onto the grounds. Klaus at least always returns promptly for meals, a trait which I'm fairly certain will be with him for life. He's going to be a big boy, and a bigger man.

Luckily, his personality seems almost entirely that of his mother's. Quiet, reserved, often shy. I say luckily because I expect he'll be hard to handle once he grows older were he not so docile. The unfortunate bit is, he'll probably also be ill-suited for the Navy.

But then, I don't require my children follow in my footsteps. In fact, considering what I've seen at sea throughout my lifetime, I'd almost rather they not. Klaus has a head for math, oddly. I hope he does something distinctly boring with his life. I hope he never lifts a blade.

Brook, I worry for. Both because she is already a strikingly-handsome little girl who, I've no doubt, will be a heartbreaker someday ... a possibility which unsettles *many* fathers, I'd imagine ... and because of the sort of personality she is already displaying. I see so much of Lucius in her.

With Cuthbert and I gone half of every year, my six and a half-year-old daughter is becoming the 'man' of the house. Her behavior is beginning to undo even her mother's endless patience, and I don't know what to do about it myself, except ... hide how much it amuses me.

Brook has made a habit of stealing into her brother's room to don his clothing, and gallivant about the grounds, convincing all our staff she is Klaus ... thus dodging her tutoring and her duties, and getting her brother in trouble all at once. Delilah's letters from home while I was away this season were particularly frazzled, when she discovered Klaus had in fact not attended a one of his fencing lessons this year ... that Brook had been trading her desserts to him to take his place with the tutor.

Their spotting is somewhat different, but it seems only Delilah and I can tell them apart. That farce will fall out soon enough if Klaus keeps fattening himself up on Brook's desserts, but at the moment it's causing no end of havoc at the manor.

I'm a poor disciplinarian. I'm more prone to stealing the children off to play on the grounds like a fellow miscreant than doing my fatherly duties and setting them to rights. Unfortunately, by now they've gathered this, so any attempts I make to impose structure upon them are meeting with blank stares. They seem to have found me out for the rogue I am.

Which of course doesn't make Delilah particularly happy.

I find the best thing I can do when I'm home is to be as loving as possible with my poor wife, and distract the children, so she has *some* time to herself. I'm also capable of seeing through Brook's disguises, which makes it more difficult for her to maraud about when I'm home.

When you really get right down to it, though, I can't argue that the little girl has a point. Her frocks and gowns are horridly uncomfortable, she can't ride her pony well side-saddle, and she can't climb trees at *all* in them.

Who could argue with that logic?

In all seriousness, I worry for my daughter. She has a fiery spirit which, in a young boy, would be celebrated. We would all anticipate the great challenges he'd meet in his life ... the great pursuits that lay ahead of him, boundless in possibility. He would almost certainly follow in my footsteps. Go to an Academy. Train for the Military, or the Navy. He might even someday inherit my fleet, my command.

But for Brook, her only great pursuit would be marriage. She couldn't even pursue a career ... she was a Pedigree woman. At some point down the road, the charm of her youthful pranks would dissolve into cold reality. A girl could not wear britches. A girl could not wield a blade.

She could never even sail on one of her family's own ships. Superstition turned law saw to that. Women were prohibited from setting foot on any of His Majesty's warships. She could travel aboard a vessel if it were demilitarized, but that was it.

Somehow, despite the fact that I had never even bred into this family, despite the fact that I had kept my secrets unknown to my children thus far, my daughter was already set to repeat the same troubles I'd faced throughout my life. Albeit for entirely different reasons.

I wanted my little girl to be who she was. But I also wanted her to be happy. And as I'd found out myself, sometimes the two cannot be one and the same. I'd found many compromises over the years, to survive in this world as a different sort of man than what was acceptable.

What compromises would Brook need to make? Would she be happy?

I'd found my place in the world. It had taken over thirty years, and though I'd never say I was completely happy, I'd come to accept the fact that few men were. What I wanted for emotionally in life was met by my family, by my comrades, and by my memories. What I wanted for physically ... well, I was well-off now, and things that had once consumed my life growing up, like food, a secure home and health, were no longer concerns. And as for more carnal needs ... I dealt with them when they arose. It was, it turned out, far easier to meet those needs now that I had ample coin. And men you paid kept your confidence, did what you asked without argument and slipped from your life whenever you needed them gone. I had companions in several ports now, none of which I'd allowed myself to grow close to.

I'd learned my lesson in that regard.

I'd found that employing them for the most basic services kept us at a reasonable distance, while still meeting my needs. Making love was off-limits, and would likely always remain so. It stirred feelings inside me, and the last thing I wanted was to fall for a whore again.

My Naval career was shaping up well, to put it lightly. The season I enlisted, we met with Admiral Cross and his Black Flag fleet. The man was salty and bitter as I'd been led to believe, and hadn't the warmest welcome for us when we joined him that year. Apparently, Shaw had led the fleet the year before, assisting Cross in the South Seas, and it had been an unsuccessful year. Cross was just the sort of man to claim a year bereft of bloodshed was unsuccessful anyway. They'd done little but scare a few privateer vessels off the trading lines, without sinking a single boat. Cross had been pursuing privateers in the South Sea for over a decade. He wanted blood. He had it out for at least a dozen different Captains, and their respective outfits.

I was as motivated to be proactive as he, though ... I had a family to support and a lot of pent-up frustration and anger to unleash on these blaggards.

We waged a bloody campaign in those waters, which had stretched these five years, in the seasons that were fit to sail, anyway. Cuthbert and I were in our element, doing what we were meant to do, and our success reflected that. By the end of the first year, we'd sunk a dozen vessels, retaken cargo for the crown and for ourselves, and sent a bloody message to the privateer fleets.

By the second year, our sails were feared, and I at last had a friend in Admiral Cross. The old dog was hard to win over, but if you reap enough death in his waters, he notices.

The third and fourth year were spent primarily ensuring Cross could handle the patrols himself from then on. I didn't want to steal the old man's thunder, it was very clear he wanted to live out his life and die in those waters. The South Seas were his, I was just along for the ride.

By the fifth year, not a single Captain of our fleet could deny I'd risen to the task. Singh still opposed my appointment as Admiral, but I think he did so out of sheer stubbornness. Having Shaw's vote meant a lot. The other Captains tended to decide as he did. It was hard to say when or how I'd impressed the Mastiff ... or if I even had. Maybe he just saw that I fell into a command role more naturally than Cuthbert. Maybe he wanted to at last free his comrade of the responsibility he clearly didn't want. Maybe I honestly just impressed him.

Shaw rarely spoke his innermost thoughts. But I was glad for his confidence in me, all the same.

My first year at the head of my fleet had now come and gone, and I was exhilarated by it. We'd taken on several commissions this year, more than I can recount, but we'd met with success in all. We'd even gone to join Cross for a month or so, to aid him in tracking down a fleet that had been giving him some trouble.

What awaited us next season, I couldn't say. But I was ready for it.

Johannes and I rode down the drive, my eyes going to the manor ahead, wondering where my children would jump me from. They'd gotten good at ambushing me each year as I came home. Well ... good for children their age, anyway.

"Our possible contracts have come already." Johannes said, as we pulled our horses to a stop beside the stables. I dismounted, the tall wolfhound doing the same. For some reason I couldn't care to remember at the moment, I felt a wistful pang of nostalgia when I saw one of the ground keepers emerge from the supply closet just inside the stable building.

"So soon?" I queried, running a paw down Specter's muzzle, and fishing in my pocket for the wax-wrapped apple slices I'd been eating, holding out the rest of them for her.

Johannes nodded. "Along with a complete list of contract appointments already claimed this year."

I arched an eyebrow at him curiously when he said that. There'd been something in his tone ... something nervous.

"*Daddy*!" I heard Brook's voice from the edge of the woods, and turned to see my two little ones dashing out from the trees. So no ambush this year. They'd probably not known exactly when I'd be getting home.

All the same, Brook flung herself into my chest, forcing me to give a muffled 'Nnnfh!', her outstretched arms wrapping fiercely around my shoulder, her legs kicking in the air. Klaus came at my knees, panting from the sprint, eyes wide and happy as he clutched my leg.

I smiled down at the boy, ruffled a paw over his ears and readjusted my daughter so she was better situated over my shoulders, against my back. I hefted her up some until she could hold on herself, then smiled down at my boy, and held out my hands.

He smiled excitedly and extended his arms, so that I could take hold of them. And I swung the two children about a few times, smiling broadly as they shrieked happily at their favorite game.

I had to stop before long though, panting. "You two are getting a bit too big for this. Your dad's got a bum shoulder." I let Klaus down, stretching said shoulder.

Brook dropped down, wearing a dress for once ... probably at her mother's insistence. Her tail wagged frantically, and she piped up, "Mom said you wouldn't be home for another ... half of an hour."

"You can say 'half-hour', honey." I smiled. "We made better time than we thought we would ... Klaus, stay away from her hooves." I said over my shoulder. The boy was playing with Specter's tail. It was a miracle she hadn't kicked him already. The last thing Klaus needed was a head injury. He didn't need to take after his namesake *that* much.

"Mom's inside!" Brook said with a smile, pointing. "There's lunch!"

Klaus's ears perked at that. I chuckled, then leaned down, nuzzling the top of each of their heads, and nosing Klaus.

"Go on, then. I'll meet you in the house. Tell your mother I'll be right there."

"Alright, daddy." He said, quietly. Then with one final smile, he and his sister took off.

I stood, watching them go. As they did, I looked out over the grounds, my eyes tracing the path the stream took, towards a distant oak. From here, I couldn't see the grave. But I knew he saw us.

"What's wrong, Johannes?" I asked now, my tone serious. I wanted to know what the pause in the wolfhound's voice had been, before we entered the house. Once I was inside, my time belonged to my family ... not to fleet concerns.

He remained silent just long enough to really worry me. I turned to regard him, arching an eyebrow.

"Tell me. Please."

His gaze drifted over the yard as well. Perhaps so that he didn't have to look me in the eyes. Or perhaps he was looking to Lucius, just as I was. I was soon to discover why.

"Serwich has issued a Call for Aid this past year, while we were at sea." He said, gravely. " ... and none answered it."

My eyes widened.

"The natives have declared war. They are uniting under one leader. The casualties are already in the hundreds." He said it quietly, barely a whisper. " ... and no fleets are answering the call."

CHAPTER 18
TIDES

Early Fall, 21st of the month, in Our Father's Year 962

It is now a certainty. Serwich is in dire straits, and no fleet is coming to their aid. They survived one year without the protection of a fleet. They will not survive another.

Our nation's fleets are exhausted, over-extended across our vast, unstable empire. The Carvecian War took its toll, depleting our navy long ago, and we have struggled to replace what we lost over this last century. Ironically, the need for lumber to rebuild our navy is what propelled the expansion onto the Dark Continent, the same need that prompted our nation had to once again colonize a foreign land. But it is that very expansion that has now stretched our resources even farther, and is even now costing our country's coffers more than it was ever worth. It's as though our nation gambled away all we had on a risky hand, and now we're so far in, folding would mean we lost it all for nothing.

Stubbornness is a time-honored Amurescan tradition though, and our King will not give up his hold on that accursed land. There *are* riches to be had there, no one disputes that fact. But every week, we learn the death toll has grown. Men aren't only being lost to native aggression, but to disease, to transit, to infighting and piracy. We have enough trouble protecting the trade routes between Amuresca and Carvecia ... committing any fleets to protect the ships that sail to and from the Dark Continent is impossible. Warring with these native 'Cathazra' aside, even the route there is considered a fool's errand. One-third of the ships that take the trip never return. It is a three-month-long voyage, even in the best weather, and Privateers have been quick to capitalize on the vessels, hulls bursting with valuable goods, who *are* brave enough to trespass the unprotected seas.

At this point, losses aren't being measured in just men, any more. They are measured in ships, and then in fleets. Every day we receive news on what's now being called 'The Dark War', I wince internally, as though my old wounds are acting up. And I remember the haunted look in Lucius's eyes, as he spoke of the horrors of that place. The creatures that dwell there...

I don't have to look far from home to have some understanding of it all. That place left an indelible mark on Johannes which he will have to bear for the rest of his life. It left Lucius physically crippled, and I've come to believe he had deeper, mental scars he simply didn't speak of. The skull of one of these 'Cathazra' creatures still hangs in his study, undisturbed. I haven't had the nerve to touch it, let alone take it down. Every time I venture into that room, which I have left almost precisely as it was when Lucius was alive, I find myself drawn towards the ghastly, ivory eye sockets. I cannot deny there is something pulling me towards it ... like some distant drum, pounding in time with my heart, beckoning me to this strange, unknown place.

It is perhaps the last terrifying frontier in our world. And the desire to escape Amuresca, to see the world, to experience those frontiers where man dare not tread, is what drew me to the Navy to begin with.

Do I want this? I'm honestly not certain. I feel both a thrill and freezing sensation in my heart, when I think about it. I have absolutely no interest in the Crown's pursuit of this land, no interest in the riches to be had there. My family does well enough hunting privateers, and I'm good at it. My fleet is good at it. We rarely take casualties doing so, and it has secured for us a future and a fearsome reputation. I like where we have settled in 'society' ... and by that I mean we are barely a part of it, at all. The Denholme name continues to exist both inside, and outside of the Pedigree class. We are, in essence, simply a Naval family who happens to be moderately wealthy. The other Pedigree families who deign to keep company with us are sparse these days, but those that are we know to be true friends and comrades.

In general, we seem to ... make society uncomfortable. Few are fond of us, but none would dare threaten us. Our relationship with the Crown is closer now than it was before, being as active as we are in protecting trade routes, and having the sort of combat record we do. The Denholme coat of arms is feared across the South Seas and we're beginning to make our mark on Carvecian Privateers as well. The King values any man who increases his wealth, so we're welcome at Court. Not that we attend.

I think we frighten society, as a whole. And that suits me fine.

It seems to suit Delilah just as well. She keeps a small group of friends, whom we know for certain make no pretenses around us, or they wouldn't have kept our acquaintance. It's a far more honest way to live and socialize. Delilah's focus is mostly on our children anyway, so staying out of Court seems to agree with her. I don't think she ever enjoyed any of it to begin with. She's always been a shy girl, and a bit of a homebody. She's come into her own as a mother, and I see no issue with that. Not every person wants to take the world by the horns. Some prefer a simple, family life. As long as she's happy, I'm happy.

It seems like our life has finally settled down, and honestly, were it not for this situation with Serwich, I would be happy to live forever like this. I would be content and fulfilled to hunt pirates for the rest of my days. Or at least until I'm inevitably killed, or injured so badly, as Lucius was, that I must retire.

But the more Johannes and I have scanned the weekly contracts and calls for aid as the months have drawn closer and closer to the spring, the more inevitable our destination has seemed. I see the fear in the wolfhound's eyes when we've spoken on the possibility. I know it is the last thing he wants in the world. To be honest, it's the last thing I want for my fleet. My own feelings on traveling there aside, I am only in my second year as Admiral and though most of my fleet is quite fond of their 'peasant Admiral', as so many have taken to calling me behind my back, my position of leadership seems like it's not quite on firm enough footing for something as serious as open warfare. Men's loyalties are tested most when facing losses, when facing death ... and if we go to this 'Dark Continent', there will be plenty of both. That much is a certainty.

I am frightened to know how I will cope with losing men as well. Will it weaken my resolve? How will I endure under pressure? How well will my instincts and my mind obey me, when I must make decisions in which the lives of my crew, the armed forces in Serwich, and a population of over three-thousand are concerned?

This in particular is often a subject of conversation between Johannes and I. He reminds me, time and again, that if we take up the military outpost in Serwich, I will be commanding more than just the men of my fleet. I will be Commander-in-Chief of an entire settlement, with all of the responsibilities that come with that. My decisions will affect every life in that colony.

He worries I may be swayed by emotion, rather than obeying logic. Leaders are oft called to make decisions, terrible decisions, he says ... which we must divorce ourselves from, for the greater good. Lucius made many such decisions when he founded Serwich. Cuthbert became his man for enacting such decisions, for seeing them through.

Essentially, although these were not the words he used, he handled the dirty work. Sniffing out mutinous men, the night raids into the forests to find enemy guerillas, scouting the land to find the lizard like creatures' settlements for future targets ... and working with physicians on critically ill and dying patients, trying to find cures to some of the terrible illnesses that afflicted our people.

It was these tasks, Johannes tells me in a haunted tone ... these tasks, not the open combat or the deaths of his soldiers, which torture him to this day. The horrors of the Dark Continent, the terrifying creatures that live there and the challenges of the terrain and climate may have been the most obvious difficulties ... but the tasks that morally challenged him, made him question his notions of right and wrong, are the stuff of nightmares.

"You can be the most righteous man who walks the earth." He tells me one morning, as we sit over tea and transcripts. "Rock-solid in your beliefs and convictions and then one day, you're presented a choice ... where your options are piss, no matter which way you look at them. And then it becomes a question of which is the greater evil. And how far you feel you can lower yourself, to accept the lesser of the two."

"So you find a third." I'd replied, finishing my tea. "There is always another way."

He looked slowly towards me, and then only shook his head, destitute. "No, Luther." He said. "Sometimes ... there isn't."

We are three weeks from deployment now, though ... and a decision must be reached. We had one last conversation on the matter this morning. And this time, we involved Delilah. I know she's sensed these past months that something has been weighing heavily on my mind. She has been good enough not to press, only to comfort me at night and lend what support she can. But she needed to know what we decided.

It went over about as well as I expected. I hate seeing my wife cry, but she knew as well as anyone in the country now knows what it means to be stationed on the Dark Continent. She grew up watching it affect her father and Johannes. I hate to put her through it again.

But we haven't any choice.

She begged, even pleaded with me. She urged me to think of our children ... which of course, had already been weighing heavily on my mind. I know the chances that I, Johannes, or our entire fleet will not return home are high. She knows this as well as I.

But over three thousand lives depend upon us. And Lucius himself said that Serwich was this family's responsibility. I think he'd intended to return to duty, should the need ever come ... his injuries be-damned. If he'd died in combat on those bloody lands, I'm sure he would have died with bravery, and a sense of closure.

I am the extension of his responsibility to that land now. I am Master of the Denholme name, and I intend to fulfill my duty, regardless of how I feel, personally, about the whole matter.

I don't give a damn about this war, one way or the other. I feel, as Lucius did, that it's a waste of time and lives. In some ways, although I know little about them, I even understand why the savages there fight our incursion. Uncivilized or no, it's their homeland. If they feel the need to resist our offers of trade and decline any desire to live as we do, that's their prerogative. They may be no better than animals, if everything I've heard is true ... but they're intelligent enough to speak, to worship their own ways and have their own society of sorts. What right do we have to intrude, really? Even if it were for their own good?

I've had a lot of people tell me that changing my ways would be for my own good. I respectfully disagree.

But they can't be allowed to butcher our people. There are families there, women, children, and non-combatants. Innocents.

We're committed to doing our duty, nothing more, and nothing less. Because that's what soldiers do. We aren't politicians ... we aren't rulers. This isn't our war. But those are *our* people.

Delilah cries almost every night now. I hold her, trying to assure her all will be well. I might be lying to her. I don't know.

Tomorrow, Johannes tells me I need to be inoculated. I'd never heard of this process before, but he insisted upon it. One of the accomplishments he and the physicians at Serwich finally pioneered during his time there was a way to protect oneself against the worst illness in the land ... this dreaded 'Seer's Fever', the very same illness that afflicted Peterson, and drove him mad.

The inoculation process sounds horrifying, but he's told me it's the only way. Tomorrow, they'll make minor lacerations along my legs and arms, and spread over the open wounds a paste made of herbs and the infected puss from the boils of others who've been afflicted with the disease. He has warned me the next week following the administration will be disorienting and hellish, both physically and mentally ... but that very few actually succumb to the disease and die, if the inoculation is applied correctly. And after I survive it once, I'll be immune to it for the rest of my life.

Or at least, that's the theory.

He and Lucius both underwent the process, after they discovered it. He has told me very little of exactly what to expect, which leads me to believe it's going to be worse than he's implied. But if it's the only way to avoid losing my mind and possibly my life to this contagion in the future, I see no other option.

I begin the treatment tomorrow. I know at least to expect the pox, joint pain, flu-like symptoms and eventually, the infamous 'visions', the hallucinations that give the Seer's Fever its name. I don't know how severe it will all affect me. I'm in excellent shape, so I've hope I'll pass through it only a little worse for the wear.

I'll have little to do while I'm on bed rest. I'll keep this journal close and perhaps write a thing or two more.

CHAPTER 19
SEER'S FEVER

E*arly Fall, 22nd of the month, in Our Father's Year 962*

I've passed the first day in abject misery. It took barely three hours before the symptoms began setting in, since my treatment this morning. My body is wracked with chills and nausea, I was warned not to eat for the entirety of yesterday, but it's made little difference. It doesn't stop my stomach from heaving. The physician insists I drink water as often as I am able, even if most of it won't remain inside me.

I am still able to keep a steady enough hand to write, but I'm beginning to grow weak. I can feel the pain settling into my bones, and I know this is only the start.

Other than the physician, who keeps his visits short, I have been joined by Johannes as often as I have need of him, and sometimes when I haven't. He is immune to my condition, but unfortunately, no others in the house are. So for this week, I must be without my wife and children. I've spoken to Delilah through the door, but only briefly. I don't want her to know what I am going through. She's worried enough of late.

Johannes and I lied to her and told her the inoculation was entirely survivable. The physician assures me only those with already weakened bodies generally succumb, but the chance is still there. And I certainly *feel* like I'm dying.

Johannes tells me the first two days are the easiest part.

I quake to think what follows this.

Early Fall, 23rd of the month, in Our Father's Year 962

I will write sparingly today. My body feels as though it's falling apart, fiber by fiber. The nausea is less of a concern, but only because the pain is so great it overshadows it. Even as I write this, I am shaking. But I felt I needed to chronicle this.

Something has begun happening to my vision. Or perhaps it's my mind? I ... cannot tell.

Ghostly flashes of color, like fireflies, or perhaps like candlelight, dance out of the corner of my eyes. I turn, but they flee from my gaze. I can only see them when I do not try.

Every now and then, when I am waking or falling into fitful slumber, they bravely flit before my eyes, startling me into the conscious world again. When I sleep, they dance before me in full view, the colors warm and inviting, like shifting figures, out-of-focus and far away. Sometimes I imagine I smell things ... exotic scents ... perhaps from my travels?

I fell asleep before writing this with the scent of fragrant flowers on damp ocean winds, sandalwood and incense. Somehow, it soothed the pain in my body to some degree ... enough that I was able to sleep, at the very least.

Red blossomed all around me, dancing shapelessly in my

dreams. I have never seen anything so beautiful in the waking world as what I saw, when that vague firefly took form, at last.

I wish I could remember what I saw.

24th *of the month*

I cannot stay awake for long periods of time any more. I'm so very tired.

Delilah said she loves me, says she is going to help me through this. I told her I loved her, but to stay away.

Other men come, with voices like Cuthbert, or the doctor. But their faces twist, smear like paint. I tell them that someone is erasing them. They tell me to sleep. They are the ones in danger, but I cannot help them. So hard to move.

One of them is trying to drown me. I fight as hard as I can, but still they pour the water down my throat.

Something is burning, and I don't know where. I see the fire, sometimes ... all around me. It will consume me.

My firefly comes to me in my sleep every night. He looks on me with gold, burning eyes. I reach for him, and sometimes he reaches back. His presence is always a comfort. He speaks to me in words I cannot understand, and covers my body in earth when I burn ... protecting me from the flames.

He is the one who should bury himself in the ground. Sometimes, I see flashes of emerald in his gaze. Verdant, like a forest. A green bulb grows there, in his right eye. Does he know?

25*th*

The bulb bloomed, today. It was red

Flowers, burning

My firefly burns

I am screaming in pain ... but the skull is screaming, too

I want to be home. I want my firefly back.

I see the docks in the distance. They are all waiting for me there.

I see his eyes there. I am getting closer...

Early Fall, 27th of the month, in Our Father's Year 962

It has now been two days since I've begun my recovery. This morning was the first in which I had a real, lucid moment. I'd been in what felt like one long nightmare, before that, waking only to receive care from the physician, or to thrash against my bed in convulsions. At some points, I must have mustered the strength to jot what I was seeing down in my journal, because there are a few nonsensical scrawls in the previous pages. I wish I could remember precisely what I was trying to say then. Johannes says that many of the things he saw when he experienced the worst of the Seer's Fever have had more meaning as his life went on.

One thing, at least, I now understand.

The 'firefly' that came to visit me in my sleep and saw me through the worst of my hours awake was no hallucination.

It was Mikhail.

I'd seen him far more clearly yesterday, but we hadn't really been able to converse. I was at least certain by now it was him, tending to me, swathing me in blankets through the worst of the chills and changing out the wet cloth on my forehead, when I was burning up. I'd had it confirmed by Johannes this morning, who thankfully, had kept his tone neutral on the matter.

I had absolutely no idea why the fox from my past had suddenly re-entered my life, and why now of all times. When I'd asked

Johannes, he'd said only "Delilah", as if that was answer enough. I hadn't the strength to question him further.

Today, he entered my room following another visit by the physician. Or at least, I assume he did. I'd fallen asleep after the physician had left, and when I'd woken, he was just ... there. Sitting on a stool by my side, precisely as I remembered him from five years ago.

Well, there was something in his features that I suppose looked older. Experience, perhaps. He'd been very young when I'd known him ... he was in his mid-twenties now. Closer to the age I'd been when I'd joined the Denholme household.

Still beautiful.

"...Luther." He gave a slow smile as I came-to, my bloodshot eyes falling over him.

"I thought you were a dream." I murmured, amazed how weak my voice sounded.

He produced that sly, fox grin. "There are some who might say I am."

"I'd count myself among them."

He reached up and undid the clasp of his fur cloak, slipping it from his shoulders and shifting his seat from the stool to the edge of my bed. And as I struggled to push myself up some, he draped the garment over my shoulders, protecting me, I suppose, from the chill in the room.

I *was* incredibly cold, for some reason.

I tried to reject the gesture, though, shaking my head. "You shouldn't ... you shouldn't even be here." I insisted. "This is ... contagious."

"I was inoculated for Seer's Fever when I was sixteen, Luther." He said, gently pulling the warm garment closed over my upper body. "Once the sailors started coming back with it, all of us at the brothel house were. In my trade, you have to be careful."

I gave a soft sigh, leaning back against the backboard of my bed, and trying not to let everything from the past come rushing back as he leaned over me and I caught the scent of his fur.

It was hard.

"Why are you here?" I had to ask, although I did so without being accusatory, only plaintive.

He leaned back, looking on me with those soft gold eyes. "Delilah wrote to me." He said, quietly. "We've kept up a correspondence since I left the manor. She told me you'd be undergoing this ... and why." His voice dropped some, his ears dropping with it. "I wanted to see you again, at least once more, before you left."

I looked down into my lap, not certain how to respond. My wife had been writing to him for five years? I don't know why it surprised me as much as it did. They'd been very friendly when he was here. I don't know why I'd thought their acquaintance would end when I decided ours had to.

"And I thought ... you might need the companionship." He said, still timidly.

"That's over." I said resolutely.

He actually laughed. I'd forgotten how lyrical it was. Which made sense, I suppose. He'd always said he was a stage actor, or wanted to be one. He'd even sung for me on occasion, when he'd been here. He was no opera singer, but he had a very genuine quality about his voice I found endearing.

"I-I didn't actually mean *that*, Luther." He smirked. "Actually, I've ... gotten out of that life."

My eyes widened. "You have?" I said, and I couldn't hold back the hint of hope in my tone. It had been five years. What did I actually expect?

He only looked on me, sadly. "It doesn't change what we once were, Luther. I'm sorry."

I just nodded. I didn't have the right words for a response. I was too exhausted to really reflect on the what-ifs right now, anyway. I'd save that for another lonely night in the future, and a good bottle of whiskey.

"Actually, I'm ... with someone now." He admitted, after a few moments of silence.

As much as I'm loathe to admit my failings, the first thought that came to my mind was not happiness for the fox, but an overwhelming desire to say 'he'd better not be another customer'. I just didn't want to think he'd violated his rule for someone else, someone who was better than me, someone more deserving.

I realize now, of course, how selfish those feelings were. But I couldn't help how I felt.

"Lucky dog," was all I said, instead. I was having trouble looking at the fox now. Why was he here, torturing me with this?

"Bear, actually." he said with an awkward smile.

That one made me blink. "A bear...?" I had to actually wrap my head around that for a few moments. The images that came to mind were—

"He's a furrier, from the North Country." He said, with the sort of tone most men got when they spoke of their lovers, female or male. "I met him a year ago during a trip I took to visit my family. Our carriage became overturned in a snow storm, and the driver went for help, and never came back." He said somberly. "If he hadn't happened upon me, I'd likely have frozen to death. I didn't expect any of it to happen, but ... life takes us places we can't anticipate sometimes."

I turned to look out the window for a few moments, taking in the sun. It was open ... the weather was beginning to warm, despite the chill in my body. I tried not to think about whom this man might be, and what it was he possessed that I hadn't.

He hadn't been a customer. All of my failings aside, that was the main difference. They'd fallen for one another the way most people do. The way Klaus and I had. Despite all my envy, I hoped it ended better for them.

I'd long ago made peace with all of this. It hurt to have it stirred up, but not as much as it had initially, at least. Mikhail had his boundaries and I had to respect them. But God, it was hard.

I felt Mikhail's hand settle over mine, gently. The warmth of him ... the fact that we both sat in the same bed we'd shared five years ago … it all came together in a nostalgic mosaic, reminding me what I'd once had and would never have again.

I stayed strong. I was past the age for these flights of fancy, too old to humor such immaturity any more. Mikhail had never been anything but kind to me, and I had to be happy for him. I had to see this pain as nothing more than what it was … envy. And I had to wish him well, and mean it.

I really did want him to be happy.

Acceptance of what we want and what we are likely to get is part of getting older. Lucius had faced it, staring down the barrel of a defunct marriage to a mentally compromised woman. He'd done what a good man should and soldiered on, and though I'm sure he'd always felt a void in his life, he'd gone on with no less passion for life, love and family, never inflicting his pain on those around him.

Five years ago, I would not have been capable of equaling the old spaniel's resolve. But today … today, I could.

I turned to look to Mikhail, squeezing his hand, tightly. And I managed a genuine smile.

"I'm happy for you, Mikhail." I said, truthfully, even if my voice was hoarse and somewhat choked. "Truly, I am. I hope this man deserves you."

I saw the tears stinging at his eyes. And he slipped forward, into my arms, and embraced me.

"Thank you, Luther." He said, around a growing sob. "I couldn't … I couldn't let you go off to that … terrible place … without making peace with you. It would have haunted me, every day of my life."

I held him tightly to my aching, withered form. The illness still clung to me, but my strength was returning, slowly but surely. It had almost felt, in the darkest moments, that I might slip away. But he'd been there with me. He'd done me more of a service than he could ever know, just by his presence. He'd given me the sort of comfort he'd once given me, when we'd been lovers. Even if I'd not realized it was him. I'd felt loved, protected … in a way I hadn't in so long.

In a way, it was a fitting end to our relationship. Despite the fact that everything between us had ended, five years ago, I'd never felt any sense of real closure. Knowing he'd wanted that very same closure warmed my spirit. We may have met under the wrong circumstances, but he'd cared about me. And I'd cared about him.

"It can happen for any of us." He promised softly, his muzzle tucked into the hollow of my throat. His paw stroked through my matted, coarse fur. "Don't give up."

I wanted to believe him. But I was starting to feel age creeping up on me. I'd lived through too much for my years. I had lived and loved many times, and many times, I had come so close, only to have it all snatched away by fate, or the cold hands of death.

Every person alive has forged through similar pain, on their way towards ... what, we can never know. I am, as I have said so often, a man of many passions. It is all but inevitable that they will rise again. But no matter what happens, no matter what lies beyond the horizon for me, I no longer face it all alone. Even if my loved ones cannot be with me, I know I will always return to them.

Two weeks from now, I leave for the Dark Continent.

But that is another story.

BONUS ARTWORK

About the Author

Rukis lives on a farm in New York, where she spends most of her time working on artwork, caring for her animals, and hanging out doing tabletop gaming with my friends. She is a huge fan of old school D&D, White Wolf, and Warhammer, as well as studying and collecting exotic fish (Cichlids, mostly) and drinking a *lot* of Dr. Pepper. Her menagerie includes a rabbit, some fish, two wonderful dogs, and a whole *mess* of chickens.

She is the artist of the comics Cruelty, Unconditional, and the ongoing series Red Lantern, which continues the exploits of Luther Denholme.

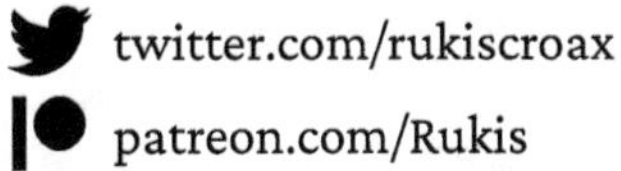

twitter.com/rukiscroax
patreon.com/Rukis

ABOUT THE PUBLISHER

FurPlanet is a small press publisher serving the niche market that is furry fiction. We sell furry-themed books and comics published by us and most major publishers in the community. If you can't get to a furry convention where we are selling in the dealers room, visit www.FurPlanet.com to shop online.

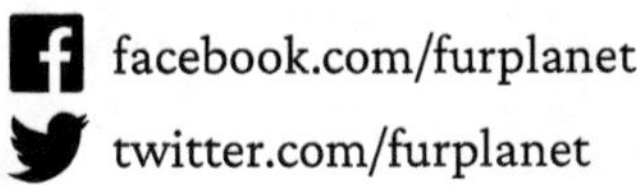

Printed in the USA
CPSIA information can be obtained
at www.ICGtesting.com
LVHW011739280124
769691LV00059B/77/J